RATS, BATS & VATS

DAVE FREER
ERIC FLINT

Rats, Bats and Vats

This is a work of fiction. All the characters and events portrayed in this book are fictional, and any resemblance to real people or incidents is purely coincidental.

A Baen Books Original

Baen Publishing Enterprises
P.O. Box 1403
Riverdale, NY 10471
www.baen.com

ISBN: 0-671-31828-4

Cover art by Bob Eggleton

First paperback printing, September 2001

Library of Congress Cataloging-in-Publication Number 00-040370

Distributed by Simon & Schuster
1230 Avenue of the Americas
New York, NY 10020

Typeset by Brilliant Press
Printed in the United States of America

ONLY FLUFF CAN SAVE US NOW . . .

A huge mass of Maggots was streaming up the hill from three sides, dark in the moonlight, except where the light flashed off snapping chelicerae.

"Okay, chilluns! All aboard the Maggotdom Midnight Express!" yelled Chip. "Grab your toys and let's go go GO!"

"Where is Fluff?" cried Virginia. "And where is the Professor?"

"Never fear! I am here!" The galago stood rampant in the moonlight on the trailer-top. Head back in a noble pose, he beat on his chest with tiny fists.

"Where is the Professor, Fluff?"

Chip would have shouted, "leave the stupid bastard," except he knew by now the others cherished the spiny alien. The rats and bats fanned out, searching and calling. Chip went to the cellar, with a piece of cargo netting. The Korozhet was behind the farthest vat.

"You must flee, human. The enemy approaches," said the Professor. "I will just delay you." The Korozhet retreated farther into the corner, rattling spines at him.

"We must look after you, Crochet. Come." He laid down the cargo netting he had brought. It was dim down here, and he'd noticed that the Crochet couldn't spot obstacles in the dark. It came out of its dark corner. When it was on top of the net, Chip flipped the other side over it. Virginia, and the rats Siobhan and Melene came running in as he caught the corners.

"Chip," Virginia yelled, "the bats have mined the place! It is going to blow sky-high in less than four minutes. We've got to find the professor and get out of here."

"Grab a couple of corners," said Chip. "I've just arranged transportation for your Pricklepuss."

The Korozhet seemed to be undergoing a sudden change of heart. "Indeed, Miss Virginia! Let us flee!"

BAEN BOOKS by ERIC FLINT & DAVE FREER

Rats, Bats and Vats

Pyramid Scheme (forthcoming)

Baen Books by Eric Flint

Mother of Demons

1632

The Philosophical Strangler

The Belisarius series, with David Drake:

An Oblique Approach

In the Heart of Darkness

Destiny's Shield

Fortune's Stroke

The Tide of Victory

The Federation of the Hub series,
by James H. Schmitz, edited by Eric Flint:

Telzey Amberdon

T'nT: Telzey & Trigger

Trigger & Friends

The Hub: Dangerous Territory

Agent of Vega & Other Stories (forthcoming)

Baen Books by Dave Freer

The Forlorn

To the world's grunts

Acknowledgments

This book owes a great deal to the advice of several people: Conrad Chu, for his tolerant explanations of technical aspects, our fellow author John Ringo for his input on military matters, and Aubrey Rautenbach for his patient advice on tractors and cropsprayers. I must also thank my longsuffering biologist/scientist peers, Drs. Ware, Wolber, Baker, Collins and Hawkes, for their help in solving the biological conundrums involved in building alien biosystems. Any errors are ours, not theirs. In addition to this, many of the great crowd at Baen's Bar (http://www.baen.com) helped with suggestions and snippets of information.

Two other people need especial thanks: my wife Barbara, and Kathy Holton, my proofreader. Between the two of them they turn my English into something readable, before I turn my pages over to Eric. Barbs also exercises enormous restraint and tolerance with a husband who lives in an alien world half the time.

Finally, I'd like to thank my friend and writing mentor, Eric (the Bear) Flint. Countless e-mail discussions, the chapters being passed to-and-fro, and not a few international calls, made this book—and also made it great fun to write. The constant sparking off each other produced a book I could never have written alone.

Dave Freer
Eshowe
KwaZulu-Natal
South Africa
November 11, 1999

Dramatis Personae

Hominidae
CHIP, *A Vat-grown conscript. A thing of rags and tatters.*
GINNY, *A damsel of high degree; and a secret.*
FITZHUGH, *The very model of a modern major.*

Rattae
FAL, *Great of appetite. Small of martial rigor.*
DOLL, *A rattess of negotiable virtue.*
PHYLLA, *A rattess. Though cattish of tongue.*
MELENE, *A rat-damsel of acumen, and a very attractive tail.*
PISTOL, *A rat-at-arms. One-eyed.*
NYM, *A giant among rats; and mechanically bent.*
"DOC," *A ratly philosopher and medic.*
ARIEL, *A rattess of fell repute. Fond of model majors.*

Battae
BRONSTEIN, *She-bat who must be obeyed.*
SIOBHAN, *A fussy mother-bat.*
O'NIEL, *A plump bat; but a true soul.*
BEHAN, *A loyal batty.*
EAMON, *A large and dangerous bat. And disgruntled.*

Et Alia
PROF, *Tutor to Ginny; remarkably like a sea urchin.*
FLUFF, *A galago, confused with Don Quixote.*

And a supporting cast of: one Jampad, various stalwarts, innumerable fools, and several million villainous Magh'.

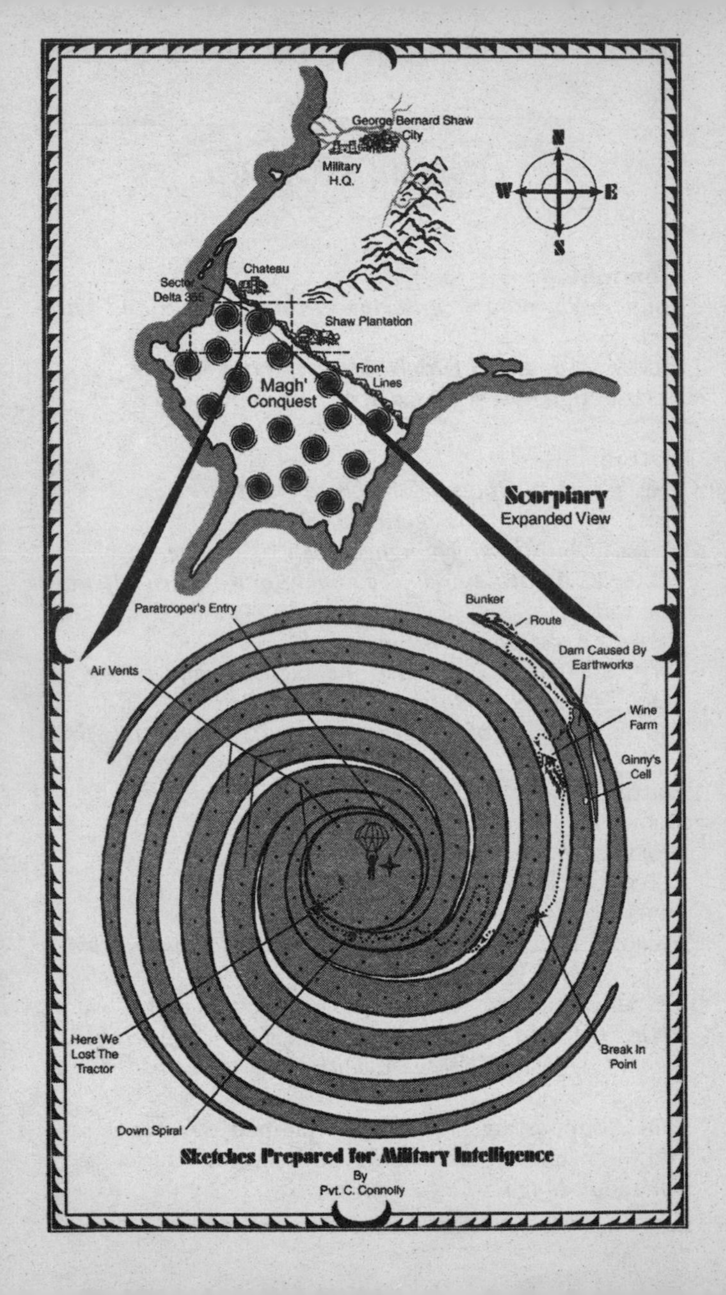
George Bernard Shaw City
Military H.Q.
N
W
E
S
Chateau
Sector Delta 355
Shaw Plantation
Front Lines
Magh' Conquest
Scorpiary
Expanded View
Bunker
Route
Paratrooper's Entry
Dam Caused By Earthworks
Air Vents
Wine Farm
Ginny's Cell
Here We Lost The Tractor
Break In Point
Down Spiral
Sketches Prepared for Military Intelligence
By
Pvt. C. Connolly

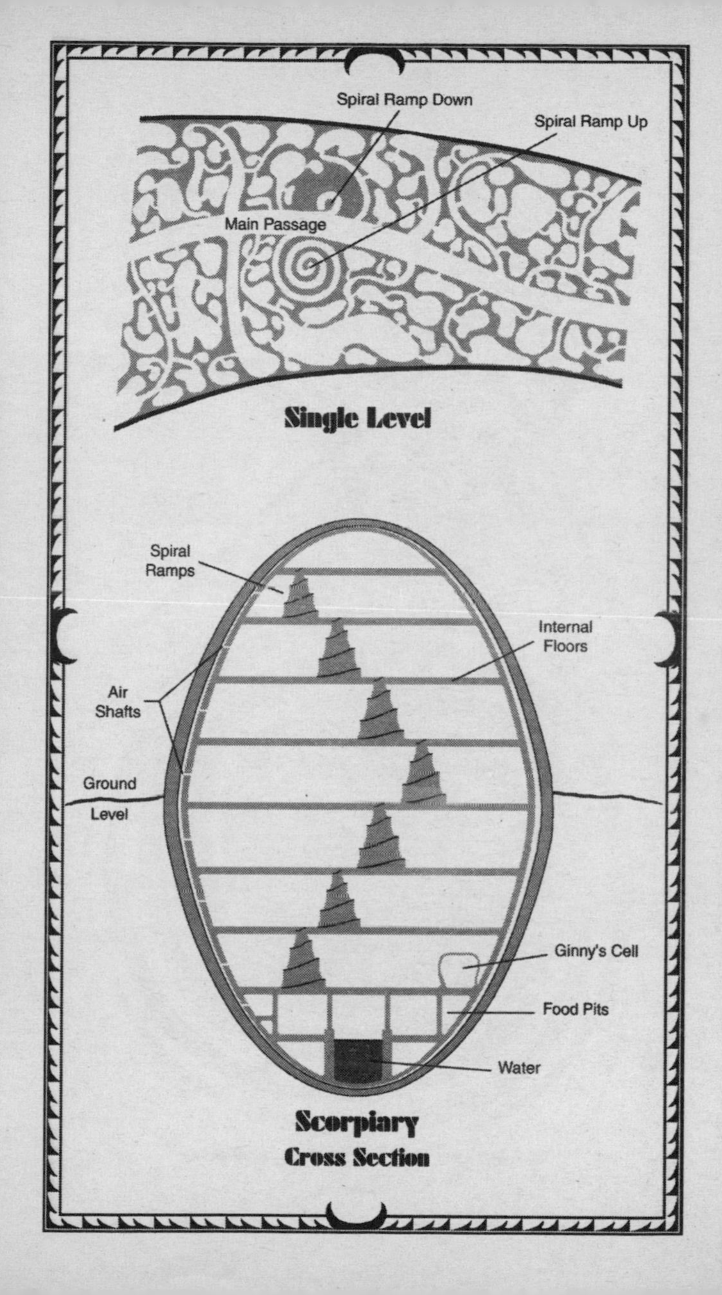
Spiral Ramp Down
Spiral Ramp Up
Main Passage
Single Level
Spiral
Ramps
Internal
Floors
Air
Shafts
Ground
Level
Ginny's Cell
Food Pits
Water
Scorpiary
Cross Section

Prologue:
A successful experiment.

The Expediter listened in silence. With difficulty, it managed to remain motionless. The Expediter was in the middle of its sex-interphase and the hormonal changes always made it irritable. That irritability interfered with its logical thought processes. The Expediter did not want to act out of simple aggravation.

Should it continue to prevaricate?

Lying was possible, of course, especially to such as these. Primitive creatures, really, the female as much as the male. But the Expediter thought that it would still be very difficult. Any explanation as to why the starship had left so hastily would seem contrived—even to the two stupid beings who were bombarding the Expediter with their clamor.

The Expediter pondered the matter for some time before coming to its conclusion.

No. Further prevarication would hardly be worth the effort. Besides, the Expediter thought that it was time to discover how well the protease haemato-toxin affected this species.

The dart-spines targeted, ocelli orientating them to center on the soft, bulging midriff-masses. The two beings in the room made no attempt to escape. They simply continued their babble. Apparently, they did not recognize the purpose of the spines. An interesting datum.

Razor-tipped, barbed harpoon-darts streaked out, each trailing their protoplasm hose. The skewering force of the darts cut into the gold head-filamented female in mid-shrill. Her bleat became a scream as the Expediter's internal myomeres pumped the massive dose of digestive-toxin into the soft-bodies.

The creatures threshed. The Expediter studied the ensuing process with interest.

Cell-lysis caused the circulatory fluids to pour out of the eating and scent-detection orifices. The soft, pallid epidermis ulcerated and erupted, spraying liquefied flesh. The bipedal beings were now twisting and writhing in bizarre contortions.

Another interesting datum. The Expediter had not realized that their vertebral columns could bend as far as that. Endoskeletons were strange biological adaptations. It made a note of that flexibility.

The Expediter watched as lysis continued. A full two minutes passed before the bodies finally lay still. Also worth noting. The digestive-toxin was not rapid, but it was effective. That, of course, was to be expected. The Overphyle had yet to discover a sentient species immune to it.

The Expediter disengaged the barbs of its harpoon darts, pulled them out and winched them back into itself. Then, after a moment's hesitation, decided not to feed. It was not particularly hungry, and there was always a slight risk with ingesting untested alien protein.

Multiple ocelli checked the room. Other than the two sprawled, bloody, ruined bodies there were no signs of the Expediter's passage.

Calmly, it left, locking the door behind it. In the silent and luxuriously appointed room, the only trace that remained of the murderer's identity was a faint camphor-naphthalene scent. That would dissipate within a few minutes. The Expediter itself was quite oblivious to the smell, but it hardly mattered. By the time the servants found the bodies, the odor would be indistinguishable from the general reek.

Chapter 1:
Under Enemy Attack.

Down in the bunker the music issuing from Chip Connolly's small portable radio stopped. "*We interrupt this broadcast of Forces-Favorite Radio with a newsflash. The bodies of the Chairman of the Board, Aloysius Shaw, and his wife, Gina, were found by household staff in an advanced state of decomposition. Despite this, servants claim that the Chief Executive Shareholder had been alive five hours previously. Foul play is suspected. Police are following definite leads and several suspects are being held for questioning.*"

Chip sat up. "I'll be damned," he muttered. There was no noticeable chagrin in his voice. "Somebody up and killed the rotten—"

He broke off, feeling the ground shake. A moment later, the bunker rumbled with thunder. Dust and dirt showered down from the roof. Chip sighed. Clearly, the lull in the bombardment was over.

Another shake and rumble, and dirt showered down on them again. Some sifted onto Chip's face. One of the other soldiers in the bunker sneezed in the darkness. They were being softened up for an advance. For the three hours prior to that brief lull, he hadn't heard anything much except for the endless pounding thunder of Magh' artillery.

Silence.

Shit! That meant—Chip flicked the infrared headlight on, just in time to see the whole wall behind Lieutenant Rosetski, Dermott and Mack cave in on top of them.

Out of the billowing dust stormed the stuff of nightmares: *Magh'.*

They were a variety of creatures designed to shred soft bodies. Their white pseudo-chitin armor gleamed and their chelicerae snapped angrily. Then the air was full of shouting and squeaking. In the wild, confused melee, headlight beams danced in the dusty air, as more and more of the invaders piled in.

The Maggot arrowscorp nearly got him. Chip rolled frantically, barely getting clear, thrusting his blade out sideways. The stupid scorp slid straight onto the Solingen steel. It wasn't standard issue, that knife. It was a real twenty-first-century chef's knife from Old Earth, which Chip had stolen from his employer's kitchen the day before he had reported to boot camp.

Good thing he had, too. The official crap the soldiers were issued wouldn't even have penetrated. The colony's steel plant would have been at home in 1870. With a standard-issue blade he'd have been dead already. Instead, Chip was able to enjoy the experience of having an arrowscorp slowly pressing down onto him, snapping its jaws eight inches from his face, about to kill him in, oh, maybe ten seconds or so.

The spine-tail streaked forward, barely missing his twisting shoulder with its venomous barb. Chip managed to grab it, just behind the stinger, and cling to the slippery, leathery pseudo-chitin. Corrosive venom dripped, inches from his arm. The Solingen steel slid slowly through some more Maggot, then stopped against a joint ridge-thickening. The Maggot's ichor dribbled off his wrist and into the dust as the creature pressed down onto him.

The back-edged jaws were only inches off his face now. The creature writhed, jaws snapping air just in front of him. Chip couldn't let go, and he couldn't win. In the clatter-clatter and effort-grunts of hand, claw and tooth combat, somebody screamed in a terrible, tearing agony. A scorp sting had obviously gone home.

"Help me!" another shrill voice shrieked above the tumult.

It sounded like a rat. Hell and buggery! He couldn't even help himself! Sweat was lubricating the hand that clung to the scorp's tail. Any moment now and he'd be screaming too . . .

Suddenly, his headlight silhouetted a batwing flutter, then highlighted a clash of inch-long white-white fangs in an evil, black squashed-pigsnout face.

The scorp went limp, its ganglion-ladder severed.

Chip shoved it away, gasping. "Thanks, Michaela!"

"Moronic, useless, be-damned *Primate*!" Michaela Bronstein fluttered off, dodging other reaching and snapping claws with ease.

"Get it offa me!" groaned a smothered voice from the dusty darkness. Chip's searching headlight showed a long tail protruding from under a St. Bernard-sized armored burrower. The stocky soldier heaved the dead

Maggot aside by the telson. A long-snouted plump rat-shape, as big as a small siamese cat, scrambled hastily out from under, with its red-tipped fangs exposed in a wicked, lean-jawed grin.

The rat leaped at Chip's throat, moving in a twisting maelstrom of teeth and raking claws. Sudden shreds flew . . . from the joint of the saw-edged pedipalp that had been about to take Chip's head off. The rat had disabled one claw, but the other claw would soon snap the rat. Chip's Solingen steel proved its quality again, slicing an exact "X" into the double ventral ganglion knot of the attacking Maggot. A quick, neat, precise job, like carving tomato roses.

"Shee . . . yit! That was nearly my head," panted Chip. He and the rat both scrambled clear of the falling Maggot.

Long insectivore teeth gleamed. "You owe me a beer, Connolly. Make it two. I've got a nice bit of tail I'd like to share it with."

"Bullshit! *You* owe *me*, Fal—"

The air boomed and fragments ricocheted off Chip's slowshield. Great! thought Chip, with relief. One of the bat-bombardiers must have blown the Maggot access tunnel. Now at least they only had to deal with what was already inside the bunker. Chip stumbled over something in the dust and darkness. Fell. Landed hard.

"*Get* your sorry whoreson ass *offa* my tail," chittered a feminine voice in the darkness. "You useless effing bread-chipper!" Chip scrambled to his feet. He'd rather fight Maggots than Phylla. That was one mean rat-girl!

Then, with a slow creaking groan, the main roofbeam fell in. Either the demolition charge or the Maggot tunnel must have undermined its support. Earth and roofing material descended in a tons-heavy avalanche. Chip grabbed the rat-girl and dived for the far wall.

In the creaking darkness a rat voice griped, "Malmsey-nosed whoremasters. My pack is somewhere under that lot."

The air was so full of dust, you could shovel the stuff. Chip coughed and felt about for his dislodged headlight. Rats and bats could manage in the total darkness. The bats had their sonar and the rats—built from a mix of elephant shrew, shrew and rat genes—could just about *read* by scent, and had keen hearing to boot. Humans still needed implanted infrared lenses and headlights. Maggots might have keen hearing, feelers and scent sensors, but were plainly blind to infrared. It was one small advantage.

"Anyone got a headlight there?" Chip asked softly. A Maggot could nail him *so* fast now. He still had his knife . . . but it was no use poking blindly at Maggots. He knew he had to cut precisely, and that he'd only have one chance. He wouldn't have said "no thanks" to his standard issue bangstick, an assegai with a cartridge set into the blade. It wasn't a great weapon, but it allowed some margin of error. It was a lot better than the rest of the issue crap: a stupid little ice axe thing and a trench knife you couldn't slice baloney with.

The slowship which had settled the planet of Harmony And Reason had taken the colonists out of the network of industries which twenty-second century technology needed to support its complexity. So, except for the clone units on the ship, the colonists were back at self-sustaining tech levels. From the manufacturing point of view, that meant nineteenth to early twentieth century. Which meant no monomolecular edged knives.

Chip had once tried to tell an officer—a Shareholder, naturally—why the thing was effing useless compared to his own. In typical officer fashion the jerk had told him to shut up, and demanded to know where his regulation trench knife was. After all, what could a veteran grunt know about fighting Maggots? Much less than some still-wet-behind-the-ears lieutenant, of course.

Still, the bangsticks worked. When you pushed them into the right bit of Maggot, that is. He really wouldn't have minded having his. It must be buried back there somewhere. . . .

He tried again. "Anyone got a light?"

Nobody replied from the darkness. But at least there were no Maggot scritch-scritch noises either.

"Who else is in here?" he asked, daring to speak slightly louder. He strained to hear one particular voice, hoping . . .

He'd seen the wall come down on Dermott. The slowshield would have protected her from the debris, but had she managed to get out before the roof came down?

"I' faith. I am, and so is someone who is lying on me."

"Sorry . . . Doll? Is that you?" It was the same rat voice which had been bemoaning its missing pack.

"Yes 'tis I, you fat swasher. I should have known by the familiar weight that it was you, Fal."

Chip cleared his throat, trying to clear away the constricting fear. "Let's have a roll call, guys."

"Piss off. Who do you think you are?" said another male-rat voice. Chip could tell, even in the dark. The male rats always had their vocal synthesizers adjusted to a low pitch, in the attempt to sound like real he-rats.

"I'm Connolly, rat. I'm a human, see. That means you take my orders."

"You've got more chance of falling pregnant, Connolly," groused the same voice. "You're not a whoreson officer, you're just a vatbrat."

Chip ground his teeth. There hadn't been a human reply yet. "Rat, I will pull your tail off, and then shove it down your throat until it comes out of your ass, if you give me any more lip. Now, who else is in here?"

There came a chorus of voices:

"BombardierBat Siobhan Illich-Hill."

"BombardierBat Longfang O'Niel."

"BombardierBat Cuchulain Behan."

As always, Chip thought the sound of an Irish accent coming out of their voice synthesizers was ludicrous, but the bats insisted on it.

"It is delusions of grandeur I think the human has," said another bat-Irish voice, leaden with resentment.

"Do you now, Eamon? Well, I think it is *you* who have the delusions. This is Senior BombardierBat Michaela Bronstein, Connolly."

Chip was relieved to hear Bronstein's voice. In some ways, he thought Michaela was even crazier than the other bats, but at least he'd always been able to get along with her.

"And, seeing as *you* want to know, I'm Melene, gorgeous." A rat-girl voice.

"Phylla. You flung me here." That rat-girl didn't sound too charmed about it. But Phylla was usually in a foul mood.

"Doll Tearsheet—at your service."

"Not *right* now, Doll." Fat Falstaff sounded more cheerful already.

"Shut up, Fal. I know you're here. Anybody else?" Chip hoped for a human voice . . .

"Nym."

"Pistol."

"Georg Wilhelm Friedrich Hegel."

Despite the name, that was a rat too. "Doc," as everybody else called him, was the platoon's medic.

Rats. Rats and bats. Chip felt for his torch again. Maybe he could see her. Then a bat voice said, "Try the other side of you, indade."

The bat-Irish idiom, as always, grated on Chip's nerves. "Why can't you just say 'indeed,' dammit?" he muttered, as he began feeling around. "Stupid friggin' affectation . . ."

The voice, still as heavily accented as ever, clarified the location: "About a foot from your knee."

He felt there. Encountered the hard roundness of his torch. Felt for the switch. On. There was no light, but he'd done enough globe changes in total darkness to manage to fix that, a lot faster than soldiers had once been able to fieldstrip their rifles. The light stabbed out through the hanging dust.

No Maggots. In the narrow uncaved-in section of what had been their bunker, a handful of rats and a cluster of bats pressed against the sandbag-wall. There were no other human survivors with them. Already one plump rat was scrabbling aside pieces of debris.

"Gotta find my pack. It's got my grog in it!" hissed fat Fal, digging frantically. "Damn near a full bottle too."

Two of the other rats hastily got up to join him.

"Oh, aye, that's right," said a bat sarcastically. O'Niel, that was. "Bring the rest of the roof down on all of us in your mad search for the daemon drink."

Fal, the paunchy rat, simply grubbed harder. "It's dig or die sober," he said with grim humor. "Besides, I might find someone. Maybe a grateful bit of tail."

"Yep. Only one thing worse than dying sober. That

would be to die a virgin," said his villainous one-eyed companion, Pistol, nimbly jumping clear of a cascade of earth.

"Ha, Pistol, as if *your* puissant pike ever found a rat maiden that had despaired of winning a rat's affection . . ."

"What we observe here is the moral quandary inherent in the empiricist approach to—"

"Oh, put a sock in it, Doc," Pistol said.

A flash of Chip's headlight showed him a rat with a daft pince-nez made of scrap wire perched on his long nose, also digging. That was the weird Georg Wilhelm Friedrich Hegel. That rat proved sanity was not necessary for survival.

Georg Wilhelm Friedrich was a soft-cyber experiment who had been drafted in when things got dire. Somebody had told Chip that Doc had been the product of load-tolerance tests on the vocabulary unit ROM of the alien-built cybernetic enhancement chips. Georg Wilhelm Friedrich had gotten a download of the whole of Hegel's *Phenomenology of Spirit* and *Science of Logic* into his ratty brain, along with a mass of other philosophical claptrap.

The result: the loony medic seemed to think he was a rat reincarnation of Georg W. F. Hegel. A reincarnation, mind you, in the body of a genetically engineered creature the size of a small cat, built on the genetic blueprint of an elephant shrew, with add-ons from real shrews and rats. Yes. Crazy. Chip thought it came of having alien hardware in their heads.

At least the rest of the rats in his unit had just gotten downloaded with Shakespeare plays, Gilbert and Sullivan and, for no reason Chip could imagine, a reading of Steinbeck's *Sweet Thursday*. Of course, ratty nature saw to it that they identified with the lowlifes and not the heroes, even in blasted Shakespeare. No Hamlets and King Lears here! But plenty of rogues and merry wives. As Fal said: they had been at a great feast of languages and stolen the scraps.

Fortunately the language units only picked out words from the material for the speech synthesizers. But the occasional phrases popped up, too. Usually, the rats being what they were, insults.

Chip shook his head. Musing about rat-language at a time like this? He knew, deep inside, it was because he didn't want to think about something else. Still, there was a chance, a desperately small chance. . . . He got up, and started pulling fallen material aside himself. He worked as fast as he could. There *might* still be survivors. Their personal slowshields would stop sudden impact, but couldn't resist the slow, steady pressure.

But, for all the haste with which they worked, and the badinage, Chip and his companions were alert. There was always a chance they'd dig up a live Maggot too.

"What about sober *and* a virgin?" said Chip to the tail end of the burrowing Fal, as he lifted a beam to allow Nym to get in to the next section. The only human they'd seen so far—the lieutenant—hadn't been alive. But Chip hadn't been looking for him anyway.

"You're as bad as these other useless rowdy, lecherous drunks," said Melene, one of the three surviving rat-girls. She was also digging. It sounded as if she approved of lecherous drunks.

Chip managed a decent grin. He wasn't really in the mood for this, but he'd learned how to get along with the rats. "Just a lot more expensive to get drunk so that you can have your wicked way with me, Mel."

This provoked a snort—of amusement from the rats and disgust from the bats. "I' faith, when it comes to drinking, Fat Fal will give you a run for your money," said Doll, reputed to be the baddest rat-girl in the army. She *would* know.

"Fal?" demanded Chip. "*Run* for my money? *Run!* Fal! Come on! Be reasonable. He gets exhausted picking his teeth."

"Listen . . ." snapped one of the bats. "They're coming. Quiet!"

There was silence. Chip's less-than-cybershrew- or batborg-keen ears could hear nothing. Yet obviously, the others could. After a few seconds it came, at first a faint whisper, then growing and growing. Arthropod clicking. The sound of myriad upon myriad Maggot clawfeet, passing right above them. If they made any noise now, the Maggot-diggers would come through the roof. All they could do was wait, knowing that their comrades might possibly still be alive under the debris. Knowing too that, with each passing moment, the chances for any buried friends diminished.

Chapter 2:
Really under enemy attack.

The tramp-scritch-tramp went on and on for hours. They were plainly right underneath a big Magh' push.

Trapped.

Chip could do nothing but sit in the darkness, conserving his torch power pack. He thought of sun and light and air. He couldn't help but think of the dead. Friends. Comrades-in-arms. And . . .

Dermott. *Damn!*

Here he was, as far as he knew the last surviving human in this hole. If he had to be honest with himself, Chip knew that they had no chance of getting out of here. It was a thought you pushed aside or you cracked up. He'd had to push aside the memory of death and the hope of survival so many times. After all, he'd been a conscript for seven months now. It felt like seven years. In this war he was a combat veteran. A conscript's lifespan in the front lines was usually less than three weeks.

Buddies were close, and yet . . . you kept your distance. You didn't want to get too close. Still, this time . . . he'd like to see another live human face. Dermott's, especially, but any human would be better than none. If push came to shove, Chip would even settle for a goddamn officer. Even if the alien soft-cyber enhanced rats and bats, with all their goofy attitudes and ideas, were still more his kind of folk than those sons-of-Shareholders were, he'd still like to see a living human again. . . .

Hell, he might as well wish for one with an hourglass figure too. And a few beers. A steak as thick as both his thumbs . . . Huh. He was getting more like one of the damn rats by the day.

The air was hot and stale in this hole. But at least the noises from above had begun to change.

"They're building." The low bat-whisper was the first thing besides Maggot susurration and his own quiet breathing and heartbeat that Chip had heard for hours now. He recognized Bronstein's voice easily enough. Despite the generic similarity of all the voices produced by the synthesizers, each rat and bat still managed to maintain a distinctive tone.

Chip ground his teeth. Maggot tunnels above them! Maggot tunnels could be miles wide and five hundred yards high. "Look, we've got to get out of here. We're gonna run out of air and suffocate soon anyway."

"We'd be foine if it wasn't for the primate using two-thirds of the oxygen," grumbled a bat. That was Behan, surly as usual. "Still, we should be able to start diggin' out now. Those builder-digger Maggots are really stupid. When I was in that mole in Operation Zemlya, we popped out right next to them. All they did was stand around and get butchered."

"When *who* starts digging?" sneered Fal. "You damn flyboys can't dig." The rat heaved his corpulent form upright. "Who does all the work around here, and why do we, hey, flyboy glamour-puss?"

"*Work!* 'Tis ignorant of the concept you rats are!" snapped the big male bat. He called himself Eamon Jugash . . . something or other. Chip couldn't remember. Or see the point. Bats didn't really have decent jugs, after all.

But that was bats for you. Bats always chose mile-long pretentious names for themselves, to replace their official Society-issued numbers. What Chip principally remembered about this one was that Big Dermott had said that that particular bat was trouble. He would tell her—

The realization hit him like a sledgehammer. He wasn't going to be telling Dermott anything. She was dead for sure, by now.

He was a bit shocked at how hard that knowledge hit him. It wasn't as if Dermott had had a dazzling personality or been any kind of a beauty queen. Not too bright, really, with a broad Vat face on a big workhorse body. But a nice girl all the same. A very nice girl. A girl with a dream . . . One more indebted conscript the Company wouldn't be collecting from.

Still, he had to make sure. Maybe—

He got up and began digging into the rubble.

"You're not going to get out that way, Connolly," said Siobhan.

"I'm looking for someone," he replied stubbornly.

"Nobody would still be alive."

"I know. But I can't just leave her. There's a chance."

"Dermott's dead," said the bat quietly. "A scorp got her, in the middle of cave-in. I saw."

Chip swallowed. He supposed that it had been an

open secret. A private life in the trenches was a wild dream. "Are you sure?"

"Sure as breath. It was quick and painless, Connolly."

That was a lie. Scorp poison wasn't. But Siobhan had seen her die. That was plain enough. Poor kid. He thrust his hands deep into his pockets, and swore quietly to himself.

He sighed, and started to haul clods away behind the digging rats. Every single time you said, "Don't get involved, or, if you're gonna get involved, just keep it physical." But you always ended up exchanging dreams. Dermott had wanted a farm. Huh. A Vat-born indentured girl who wanted a farm! Fat chance. Farm laborer was the closest vatbrats could get. Well. The kid had bought one. And the Company wouldn't be screwing her any more, either. Yep, the only way out of the Shareholders' clutches . . . die. And then, rumor had it, they'd bill your clone for the burial charges.

"Responsible socialism," the New Fabian Society Shareholders called the system they'd set up on the colony planet of Harmony And Reason. HAR—or, as vatbrats called it, Har-de-har-har. When they weren't just calling it the Company Town.

Chip had been born here—*grown* here, rather—in one of the New Fabian Society's genetic production plants. Grown in a Company Vat, raised in a Company Nursery, and educated in a Company School. His "parents" were shreds of cryo-preserved tissue some long-dead dreamers had sent off on a slowship to this new "Utopia" among the stars.

Utopia—ha! Even the Shareholders, so far as Chip could tell, didn't believe that crap. At least, he'd heard them whine enough about Harmony And Reason in the haute cuisine restaurant where he'd worked before the war. Not that he'd had much opportunity to listen.

He'd been an apprentice sous-chef after finishing Company school, and he hadn't had a lot to do with the clientele.

Still, he'd noticed that the Shareholders seemed to be especially grumpy about the sunlight. To Chip, the sunlight was not too blue, nor too hot. But the older Shareholders weren't local Vat-born clone kids like him. No, they'd been wealthy adults back on Old Earth—*philanthropists*, they called themselves—and had come along in cryo-suspension. The windows of Chez Henri-Pierre had been specially tinted to yellow the sunlight for them. According to them Earth light had been sweeter and better . . .

A rude voice interrupted his musing.

"Pull your finger out and move the damn stuff out of the way, Connolly."

Chip shook himself. He'd been falling asleep, he realized. Air . . .

"Dig us an air hole, Pistol."

"So that we can breath Maggot pong? And they can smell us?"

"We need oxygen, you . . ."

"Better make us some human oxygen out of your own air hole, you muddy rascal! I feel tired and I've got a headache. I don't feel like digging."

"Intercranial pressure because of vasodilation in the brain from oxygen deprivation," said Doc. "The lethargy is caused by raised CO_2 levels."

For a moment, Chip was startled by the assurance in the bespectacled rat's voice. But then he reminded himself that Doc had proven, more than once, that he was an excellent medic. At least, when he wasn't droning on about epistemology and ontology and the whichness-of-what.

Chip unlimbered the Solingen. It seemed an effort. Like bothering with perfectly scalloping that last potato of the hundreds . . . Like that, this had to be done. "Dig straight up, Pistol, or I'll shove this up your ass and ruin your sex life." He noticed that his outstretched arm was trembling.

It wasn't a long dig. Moments later the rat broke through. The Maggot-tunnel air was cool, sweet and fresh by comparison to the stuff in their hole. The one eyed rat took long whiffling-nosed sniffs of it. "So okay, Connolly, you damned dunghill cur. My head already feels better. Maybe I won't piss in your next beer. Even Maggot-air smells good compared to the stuff in here. But don't *ever* threaten me with that poniard of yours again."

That was one villainous old rat. There were times to back off, and this was one of them. "You can empty your bladder into the next beer I buy, if you like. It'll be yours. I owe it to you, I reckon. Lack of air was making me silly."

The one-eyed rat was mollified. In a manner of speaking. "I'm a whiskey drinker, you skinny bluebottle rogue. And I like triples. And I never pee in my own drinks."

"Give a rat an inch . . ." Chip smiled.

"And he'll think you're shafting him," concluded Pistol, with a suitable gesture.

"Will you two be getting out of the way so that we can all have a breath of air?" Eamon grumbled.

Chapter 3:
Behind enemy lines.

Slowly, they continued to dig a narrow passage, under the hardpan of what was plainly an ever-growing Maggotway. The rats were fine excavators, but the main problem was where to put the uncompacted material they were digging out. And a rat hole was going to be too small for Chip, although the bats could manage it.

A quiet council was held. "You guys had better dig out. We'd better block that air hole, too. Maggots will smell us out, otherwise. I'll break out and take my chances when you've been gone a while." Chip was nobody's hero—by definition—since he was still a live grunt. Heroes got dead. And the first thing a grunt learned was "don't volunteer." But there didn't seem much point in getting them all killed. They had a tiny chance. He didn't.

"The Maggots up there are building faster than we can dig," grumbled Fal. "My old claws are nearly worn out."

He puffed out his chest. Well, his belly. "Anyway, we'd *never* leave a comrade in distress." The plump rat even managed to get the words out without choking.

"Never?" asked Bronstein, her voice dry. Rats might be natural Maggot-killers, but they weren't known for suicidal courage.

"Well, hardly ever!" chirped Melene.

"And *certainly* not one who owes us drinks," added Pistol.

"We've still got a load of satchel-charges between us," mused Bronstein. "We should all go up. We can move a damned sight faster through their tunnels than we can with a fat old rat like you grubbing. And if they try and stop us, we can blow down the very heavens on them."

"The human's right for once," hissed Eamon. "What cause do we have to die for this Company-lackey primate? His kind wanted this war. Leave him."

"Damn you, bat!" snarled Chip. "The effing Company grew me in a vat too. Just like you. I'm an indebted conscript. Also just like you. Get that straight, squashed pig-face. And nobody wants this war, not even the goddamn Company, but if we don't fight, we're *all* Maggot food. Call me a Company-lackey again and I'll dice you into bat tartare."

The big bat bared his long sharp fangs at Chip and then studiously ignored him.

"He'll be killed on his own, to be sure, Eamon," said Siobhan timidly. She was the smaller of the two female bats, and didn't have Bronstein's self-assurance.

"Indade." Again, Eamon flashed his teeth. "And so will we all be, waiting for him. Is it not fair that one of these humans that put us all in bondage repay us with a distraction? I say, bat-comrades-in-arms, that we put it to the vote!"

"To Lucifer's privy with you and your vote," grunted Nym. "I'm going up." Nym was a veritable giant among rats, fully sixteen inches high. He seldom spoke, but when he did the other rats paid attention. Even the bats—even the belligerent Eamon—were careful not to aggravate Nym.

The one exception was Doc. The pedant-rat eyed Nym beadily and said: "Dolt. You forget the overriding precedence of epistemology."

Nym stared back at him. For some odd reason, Doc never irritated Nym the way he did everyone else.

"Huh?" Chip looked at him, puzzled.

Doc sniffed. "In layman's terms—" He pointed at the roof with a stubby rat digit. "The enemy is coming."

There was instant silence. Then someone said: "Fighters, too, from the sound of 'em. Lots of Maggot-scorps. They must have smelled us . . ."

"Out of the way." Bronstein waddled forward, moving as clumsily as the bats always did on the ground. She carried one of the bombardier-bats' small satchel-charges in her wing-claws. "I'll blow the roof and we'll run."

"Give it," said Pistol. "I'll shove it up the air hole. I can move faster than you."

"Okay. I'll put the timer on seven seconds. When she blows, be ready to run. Chip, you take that bag over there. There's half a platoon's worth of spare bat-mines in it. We might need them."

The debris was still falling when the surviving platoon members—one human, five bats, and seven rats—scrambled out of the hole.

They found themselves inside a roofed-over but plainly incomplete Magh' tunnel. It was cathedral high and filled with a tracery of mud beams at angles that were . . . wrong to the human eye. Maggots didn't work in straight lines or precise angles. The material resembled adobe, but the Maggot version was a lot stronger.

" 'Ware Maggots!" In the pallid greenish light of Maggot lumifungus on the walls, Chip could see a column of the scorpion-digger Magh' skittering closer down the passage. The bats were already flapping upwards in the high tunnel. At least they'd have a chance, now that they had flying room.

" . . . *Off to Dublin in the green! Our bayonets a-gleamin' in the sun!*" shrieked Eamon, diving on the Maggot-scorp column. He wasn't going to run . . . or fly from the enemy. The big male bat might be dead set on treating humans like shit, but he *liked* to fight, especially against the odds.

Well, Chip knew bats were like that. Crazy. After brewing up the cyber-enhanced rats, the genetic engineers at the New Fabian Society's labs had tried for more heroic and idealistic helpers for mankind's war when the bats' soft-cyber units were downloaded. They had put Irish revolutionary songs and old "Wobbly" tunes into the bats' vocabulary memory units.

Truth to tell, the bats *were* more idealistic and courageous than the rats. A lot more. But, in Chip's opinion, they were even more off-the-wall. And they were prone to endless political theorizing and disputation.

The rats claimed it came from hanging upside down and getting too much blood to the head—not to mention abstaining from drink and having sex only once a year or so. Chip thought the problem might be simpler. The bats didn't know if their enemies were the humans or the Maggots. (Neither did the rats, he suspected—but, ratlike, they didn't worry much about anything beyond the next moment.)

As always, however, the Maggots solved the problem. Magh' had no doubt at all who their enemies were—everybody else. Chip and the rats ran . . . well, like rats. There had to be some way out of here, surely?

Eventually they bolted down a twisting side tunnel, and then rushed back out again, nearly falling over each other in their haste. One of the biggest Maggots that Chip had ever seen had been coming the other way. Chip'd seen a lot of varieties . . . he thought he'd seen them all, but this was a new one. He reckoned the grunts 'ud call this one "Maggot-mutha."

"This way!" called Bronstein, as they boiled out of the tunnel mouth. Fluttering ahead of them, she led them into another narrow opening off the main Maggot-way. This time there was no huge Maggot in it. An explosion behind them briefly hardened their slowshields.

"That was one smart bat-move, Bronstein," groused Chip, in the aftermath. The bat had dropped the archway of Magh' adobe behind them with a well-placed satchel-limpet mine. Chip looked around the tiny irregular-walled chamber that was left to them. "This is a goddamn dead end! We're trapped in here!"

The bat's huge leaf-ears twitched. She rumpled her gargoyle face at him, flashing white fangs. "If you were any more microcephalic we could use your head for a pin, Connolly. On the other side of that wall I can hear outside noises. Is it a lack of interest that you have in going there?"

For an answer the rats began digging. Digging like fury. Even the tubby Fal moved with the startling speed that made the rats such powerful, if reluctant, allies in this war.

"Be using your tiny heads," snapped one of the other bats. Behan, surly as always. "We need a shot pattern, not a rabbit warren."

On the other side of the fallen archway, Chip could hear the Maggots starting to dig too.

When they broke through and spilled into the sunlight, Chip practically whooped from sheer delight. Ha! Not even a whining Shareholder could moan about how wonderful the sun looked today. A beautiful blue pinpoint in the sky! Still, he was careful not to look at it directly.

There'd been a time, not ten minutes back, when Chip had thought he'd *never* see daylight again. The first Maggot claws had been pushing through the debris when the bats had pronounced the shot holes deep enough.

Now, they were out and running. Maggot-scorps and diggers were child's play to avoid out here in this rough and blasted terrain. Quickly, Chip examined the area.

Once this must have been prime farmland. The war had shattered and torn it. No blade of green life showed in the pockmarked and cratered landscape. The Maggots were steadily turning it into Maggot-tunnel land. Chip and his twelve companions had broken out between the walls of two of the massive red tunnel-mounds which the Maggots erected everywhere in conquered territory.

"Can't we take a breather?" panted fat Fal. "Methinks we've got to have at least half a mile's start on 'em."

"To be sure. Rest and die, you fat slacker," said Eamon. He wrinkled the folds of his ugly face in that inimitable bat manner of sneering. "You *do* know you're going the wrong way?"

"Hell's teeth, maltworm!" snarled Fal. "You flutter-fellows can try going the other way. Half the Maggots in Maggotdom are back there. Besides, look." The fat rat pointed. His stubby little "forefinger" was a blunt digit. Rats could manipulate things with their "hands," but despite the best efforts of the genetic engineers their forepaws were still much less adept than human hands.

The horizon, beyond the walls of the tunnel-mounds, flickered. "We're *inside* the Maggot force field," hissed Fal. "You know what happens when your slowshield intersects that."

Indeed, they did. You fried. It was the Magh's inviolate defense against human-allied attacks. Every time the Magh' pushed forward, they'd seal their gains like this. For minutes the screen would be down while the Magh' pushed forward. Then the Magh' would be safe again.

Humans and their genetically engineered allies had been forced into World-War-I-style trench warfare by this. Worse, it was just defensive warfare. And for all their efforts, they had never succeeded in doing more than slowing the pace of the Magh' advance.

Still, it could have been worse, Chip admitted. The alien Korozhet had brought the human colonists advance warning of the impending Magh' invasion. And they'd helped defend the capital city of George Bernard Shaw against the first Maggot probes. Even if their FTL ship could not help the humans further—due, according to the Korozhet, to malfunctioning engines—at least they'd brought warning to the colony.

More than that, actually. The Korozhet also had slowshields, and the wondrous soft-cyber implants which had uplifted the rats and bats. The genetic engineers of the colony had "built" the rats and latterly the bats, to flesh out the ranks of the pitifully small human army. Instant genetic uplift was beyond them—but the implants solved that. Yes, the Korozhet had been glad to provide that advanced technology to the colonists—for a price.

And the price was steep, too. The Korozhet had no interest in anything humans had—except a few rare minerals, specialized agricultural products and some small animals which they said were useful medicinal products. It had meant removing precious farmland from food production. Which, in turn, had meant a leaner and even less savory diet for the colony's Vats. Needless to say, in his remaining time as a sous-chef, before he was conscripted, Chip had not noticed any decline in the quality of the Shareholders' cuisine at Chez Henri-Pierre.

He thrust the sour memory aside. The reality of the moment was more than enough to sour anyone.

Chip stared into the distance. "The front lines are a good few miles back that way. We could try to hide back there and break out when the force field goes down for the next push."

One of the rat-girls chittered distress. "Agreed. Our obvious course now—is—to hide." Chip could hear the exhaustion in Melene's voice, and accepted the reality behind it. They *had* to rest, and soon. The rats had speed, not stamina.

"Why don't we hide out up there?" Chip pointed to a cluster of rocks at the head of a narrow gully, maybe a quarter of a mile away. "If you bats stop fluttering around like a smoke signal, they won't see where we're going."

"We're not good walkers, Connolly," pointed out Siobhan.

"Cling onto me, then. I'll give you a lift." Despite the wingspan the bats were light-boned. Even a big bat like Eamon wouldn't weigh much more than two pounds.

The bats fluttered about him doubtfully. Then Bronstein settled on Chip's shoulder. "I vant to trink your blud." She bared her long white fangs and licked her lips with with a long, thin, red, red tongue.

Chip hoped like hell that that was just bat-humor.

The others settled on him too. " 'Tis a damned affront to my dignity, this," said Eamon glumly, clinging to Chip's left breast pocket. The sharp bat-claws pricked Chip through his combat jacket. The big male was a solid weight of bat, hanging like that.

" 'Tis the blood o' a virgin princess you fancy, Eamon?" chirruped a more cheerful Siobhan.

"Well, you're out of luck with Connolly, then," grumbled Phylla, limping along beside them. "He's as common as vatmuck. Not even a good prince, nor less a princess."

"No virgin neither," piped Melene. "Oft did I espy him a-giving the horn of abundance to Dermott."

"Belike *she* was giving it to him," snickered Doll. "An abundance of horn going about, anyway. Why do you humans take so long?"

"More like how do they make it *last* so long . . ." Phylla looked wistful.

Now, Pistol started whining. "My aching paws!" He peered up at Chip with a solitary beady eye. "How about a lift, Connolly? You owe me a bottle of whiskey, so a ride would be in order."

"A *bottle?* It was a drink—not even a double!" Chip protested.

"Whoreson caterpillar! A debt dodger. Come on,

let's all ride Connolly, like a mare," said Fal, who plainly thought *anything* rather than walking was a brilliant idea.

Rats jumped aboard and scrambled for purchase, clinging to his head, shoulders, clothing, pack and pockets. Chip sighed and accepted the inevitable. At least even the rats were relatively light. It was no worse than an extra fifty-pound pack.

Like an ambulatory hat-and-umbrella stand festooned in clinging bats and rats, he struggled up the slope to the shelter of the rocks. Fortunately, there was a lot of strength in Chip's stocky form, and even more stamina. But it was still a brutally exhausting slog.

As he planted one foot in front of the other, Chip gasped out his warnings. "I have to . . . tell you, bats . . . I take garlic . . . pills. My blood . . . pure poison. And you . . . useless bunch of freeloading . . . Rat-hitch-hikers . . . I charge . . . Cost you all . . . in drinks. Or next time . . . you can carry me!"

The last phrase came out in a rush. He had reached the boulders. "Come on, all off! I want to sit down."

Rats and bats scrambled clear, and Chip flopped.

"Someone should have a quiet look to see if they're after us yet," said Eamon. "A rat or the human," he specified, folding up his wings.

"Let me just catch my breath first," said Chip. "I'm absolutely exhausted."

"The human condition does not approach the Absolute Notion." G. B. F. Hegel sniffed and adjusted his pince-nez. "Not even remotely. I'm beginning to have my doubts about Plato's Forms, too. A shadow is one thing, but this—this gasping, panting, pathetic—"

"Oh shut your face, Doc. Next time, you can philosophize on your own four paws."

✧ ✧ ✧

A few minutes later, looking out from their redoubt, Chip stared across a bitter, barren, torn, and conquered land. Miles to the north he could see the smoke trails dark against Harmony And Reason's clear sky.

Har-de-har-har. That would be the front. They were trapped far, far behind enemy lines, sandwiched between the rising red Magh' adobe walls of the enemy tunnels. In excrement deep and dire.

He shrugged and turned away. So what else was new?

Chapter 4:
A maiden in peril.

Her bed was arrayed with soft toys . . .

Virginia was the daughter of Shareholders. At the age of nineteen, even in wartime, she should have been out on the town. The social life of Shareholder children was enviable. Instead, she lay on her bed, between Mister Ted and Mrs. Wobbly, and read.

She wasn't ugly. That was just what she believed. Indeed, if she, like her Shareholder-daughter contemporaries, had employed a beautician's services she could have been almost beautiful. Not in the pinup style, admittedly, with her lean figure and elfin face. But, still . . .

Nor would Virginia have objected to being almost beautiful. Not in the least. Her indifference to her own appearance was simply that of a brain-damaged girl who had never really thought about it. True, the alien Korozhet had repaired the damage a year earlier—or, at least, compensated for it—but Virginia's self-awareness still lagged far behind her new reality. It was starting to catch up, however. She found herself staring at herself in the mirror lately, wondering . . .

Her hair, for instance, was still braided in the same way that she had had it done when she was seven. Before the accident. For eleven years she'd insisted on keeping it that way. Nobody realized that now she *might* be prepared to change. So, every morning, the maids braided it.

Her clothes, too, still reflected the choices of her childhood. Her mother had no interest, and the secluded life they'd had "our poor Virginia" live meant that there were no friends to ape either. Nor was there much hope of finding any. Virginia's parents had long since adopted the habit of keeping their daughter sequestered at home. There were appearances to maintain, after all. No proper Shareholder—and her father was preeminent in that number—wanted to be exposed to ridicule. It was embarrassing enough to have a brain-damaged child, without having the creature's slurring words, fits and tantrums exposed to public scrutiny. A seven-year-old mind trapped in the body of a teenager was not acceptable in polite society. Not in the least. So, for years before the Korozhet soft-cyber implant had liberated her, Virginia's only friends had been Mister Ted, and Mrs. Wobbly, and all the other soft and fuzzy residents of her soft and fuzzy bed. But, for all their sweet charm and kindly disposition, they were not much help when it came to giving advice to a nineteen-year-old girl beginning to wonder about her place in the world.

So she *still* didn't have any friends. Well, except for her darling "Professor" and Fluff, the galago. Fluff had been a cuddly pet before he was soft-cyber uplifted.

Her parents regarded her new improved self with vast relief. At least she was no longer throwing her fits and tantrums. Now and then, they even permitted her to join them at the dinner table in their mansion. Lately, as they'd become more confident that she would not publicly shame them, they'd even taken her to dinner in town. Her mother had ordered her Vat dressmaker to make suitable garments for that. Her mother's maid came to make her up and dress her hair for these occasions. The only thing Virginia disliked more than these rare outings was her mother's maid.

But, even so, a low public profile was still essential. What would people say about the *Shaws* having their daughter implanted with an alien-built nervous system enhancement device? The kind normally used on *animals*? Even Vats would whisper! (Not that the Shaws paid any attention to what the lower orders might say.)

Virginia didn't care. Much. After all, she had *books*. And so many! She had a whole childhood's reading to catch up on, in addition to all the adult books. There were real antique paper ones like the volume in her hand, or book-screen ones where she could blow the print up and didn't even have to use her thick glasses.

At the moment, she was devouring Regency romances from Old Earth. The download in her head had included Brontë, at her mother's insistence. Perhaps this had biased her, but she certainly enjoyed historical romances.

Fluff, on the other hand, did *not*. His objection was not to the genre as such, but to the activity itself. Because of the soft-cyber in the little galago's head it *could* read. But Fluff considered reading an effeminate pastime—and, what was worse, the *wrong* effeminate pastime. While Virginia was reading she was ignoring her far-more-important feminine duty, which was to pay attention to *him*.

He was most disgruntled. Was there anything more important to a macho hidalgo than the attentive admiration of a beautiful woman? Was there anything more natural than that she should adore him?

"Virginia, why do you read-read-read all of the time?" The little creature perched on her head and swung his long tail with its soft fur-ball at the end (that she so admired!) in front of her eyes. He knew that otherwise she wouldn't even notice him.

She plucked him off her head. Huge, limpid, dark eyes set in the tiny face of the long-tailed lemur-like creature stared back into her blue eyes. He blinked.

"So what else do you want me to do, Fluff?" she demanded. She was a bit irritated. Vernon had been on the brink of declaring himself to Frederica!

"Well . . . You could brush my fur, or"—hastily, seeing the start of a headshake—"we could dance?" This was a real sacrifice on his part. His soft-cyber had left him with a penchant for Wagner. She liked Viennese waltzes for similar reasons.

"Why don't *you* read a book instead?" she asked crossly. "I'm nearly finished with this one, and—"

"Then you will just start the next!" he protested.

Her door burst open. A ball, three feet in diameter and covered with rows of red-purple spines, came in, ambulating along on flexing spines. Virginia lowered the book and smiled broadly, her momentary pique quite forgotten.

"Professor!" There was no mistaking the delight in her voice on seeing the Korozhet. Most people found the sight of the sea-urchin-like alien somewhat unsettling. But Virginia thought the Professor was just darling. "What brings you here at this time of night?"

"Oh the relief of it! Oh, Miss Virginia! Oh, I am so glad to see you are unhurt!"

Virginia sat up straight, her eyes widening. The Korozhet's voice, transmitted through the device attached to its intricate speaking organ, expressed nothing in its tone. But Virginia, over the months, had learned to interpret many of the subtleties of the Professor's spine movements. (Much more, she sometimes thought with quiet pride and pleasure, than the Professor himself realized.) She had never seen that peculiar rattling of the spines before, but the motion and the noise practically shrieked: *anxiety!*

She began to ask a question, but the Korozhet cut her off. The Professor was already at her bedside, rattling its spines on the comforter. The hard organocarbonate points left little tears in the cotton which enfolded the down interior.

"Quickly, Miss Virginia. Quickly! Come with me. We must flee at once."

Virginia flung aside the comforter and scrambled off the bed. "What's *wrong*?" she asked. But she didn't wait for an answer before gathering Fluff and planting him on her shoulder. An instant later, she was reaching for Mister Ted and Mrs. Wobbly. *If it was a fire she must . . .*

"Leave your possessions, Miss Virginia, leave them! It is you who are in danger, not they. Come quickly! We must away! The killers may still be here!"

"Killers?" She stopped.

"Keep moving, Miss Virginia! Your poor parents have been foully murdered! I have just now stumbled upon their corpses. The dreadful manner of their dying leaves me in no doubt: *there are Jampad assassins here!*"

Virginia gasped. She'd heard of the Jampad, from the Professor. "But I thought there were none of those . . . terrible things on the planet?"

"They must have approached secretly somehow. Oh, sorrow! That they should kill such worthy citizens!" The Korozhet was now trying to drive her towards the door. Virginia resisted long enough to put on more suitable clothing. She *couldn't* leave her room in her nightgown, after all. Her parents would be furious if she let the servants see—

Her parents were—dead? She groped for an emotional reaction, but couldn't find one.

"We must leave!" The Korozhet was starting to rap her legs with its spines, so great was its agitation. "Traitors must have told them that nothing could undermine the war effort more. Oh woe!"

Now they were through the door and into the corridor beyond. The Professor's anxiety had finally transferred itself to Virginia. And obviously to Fluff as well, by the way the galago was clutching her braids. Virginia began hurrying down the hallway. The Professor rattled in her wake, babbling in a rush.

"But at least they did not kill you, my dear! Your father—bless his wise soul—entrusted me, unworthy Korozhet that I am, with a contingency plan he had made against all eventualities." The Professor paused to replenish his wind bladder. "Such foresight! But he said to me *in no uncertain terms*: 'I cannot be too careful, looking after my Virginia!' You were his most precious responsibility!"

Virginia swallowed. It sounded so . . . so romantic. But the momentary rush of affection for her father vanished almost as soon as it came. As she opened the door leading to the back staircase, she found herself repressing a sarcastic laugh. *That just wasn't her father!*

By the time she reached the first landing, sarcasm had been swept aside in its turn, replaced by affection for the Korozhet. *Such a dear, he was!* The Professor, by nature, always gave the best interpretation to everything.

The alien's next words confirmed her suspicion.

"You are his heir, Miss Virginia? I have that correctly?"

"Yes," she replied curtly. They had reached the bottom landing. She paused for an instant, pressing her ear against the door. She could hear nothing beyond. The silence left room for a sour thought. *That's my father—worrying about the inheritance.*

"It is a strange concept to us group-spawners," prattled the Professor. Frantically, Virginia waved her hand. *Shhh!*

But the alien seemed oblivious to the danger of making a noise. "I hope I can adequately fulfill your father's trust in me," said the Korozhet, talking as loudly as ever. "It is a heavy responsibility!"

Virginia sighed. The Professor was *so* absent-minded. With a quick motion, she stooped and reached a hand into the mass of spines. It was the work of a split second to lower the volume on the voicebox. Thank heavens for standard controls.

The spines froze. Then, for an instant, bristled. Virginia realized that she had startled the alien. She had never actually *touched* the Professor before. She began to whisper an apology, but the Korozhet interrupted.

"Quite all right, my dear!" The spines seemed to soften. "I forget myself, you know. I am not accustomed to such peril!"

Virginia pressed her ear back against the door. Nothing. She decided it was safe to go through. Slowly, carefully, she turned the knob and cracked open the door. The action brought a stray and whimsical thought. On Old Earth, she knew, doors were opened by electronic means. But the colony on Harmony And Reason could afford no such complex mechanisms. It would hardly do to find oneself locked in because of the absence of an electronics industry.

She pushed her head through. The large underground garage beneath the mansion was deserted, except, of course, for the multitude of vehicles parked in it. Her father was a collector of such.

Virginia decided to take advantage of the opportunity. She sped across the flat expanse, her light feet making almost no noise at all. Behind, the alien scuttled in its effort to keep pace.

"Can you slow down a trifle?" complained the Professor. "My lower spines can barely cope with this mad dash! Fortunately I do not respire through my speaking-orifice, so I am able to converse with you. Otherwise, I would be quite out of breath."

Virginia reached the vehicle that was her target, and began to open the door.

"Not that one!" protested the Korozhet. "No, no—it will not do at all, Miss Virginia. We must take the off-road landspeeder."

Uncertainly, Virginia's eyes went to the vehicle in question. She had never driven it before. In fact, her parents had never allowed her to drive anything except the golf cart. Which—

She stared at the vehicle she had been about to climb into. A half-hysterical laugh began gurgling up in her throat. *Which, I admit, is probably a ridiculous way to make an escape!*

Fluff was glaring at the landspeeder. "I hate that thing! Makes me feel sick!"

His chittering attracted the Korozhet's attention.

"You will have to leave that small creature behind," the Professor stated firmly.

Fluff's grip on Virginia's braids tightened. "No! I'll come along and look after her!" He stood up to his full eight inches—but without relinquishing his grip on her hair. "She needs male protection!"

Virginia shook her head decisively. The vigorous motion tossed the galago back and forth, squawking indignantly.

"No, Fluff," she pronounced. "If the Jampad are trying to kill me, you'll be much safer here."

The little hands clutched her hair like a vise. The galago had an amazing grip for a creature so small. "Get down, please," she said firmly.

"But Virginia . . ."

The Professor was back to its spine-rattling. "We must go quickly! Obey your mistress! Every moment we delay is dangerous!"

Moving with the same decisiveness with which she had shaken her head, Virginia reached up and pulled the galago away. She kissed the tiny monkey on his forehead and set him down on the pavement. Fluff tried to cling to her fingers with his little black hands, but Virginia forced him off.

"Go, Fluff." There was a sob in her voice. The galago jumped away with one of those prodigious leaps the species was capable of. He landed, surefooted, on the fender of a nearby luxury sedan.

As the Korozhet ushered Virginia into the passenger seat of the off-road landspeeder, the alien gave the galago a beady glare from all of the ocelli it could exude from its spines.

"Do not alert anyone!" it said forcefully. "Enemies may be anywhere." Without further ado the alien scurried around the front of the vehicle and bounced in through the driver's door, which Virginia had already opened. For all its awkward appearance, the Korozhet was remarkably agile.

Virginia had also already moved the front seat back, so that the rotund alien was able to fit itself into the space. It studied the controls. "The vehicle has automatic drive capabilities. I should be able to cope with any additional requirements, despite the fact that it is not designed for my species."

"I could try to drive, Professor," said Virginia hesitantly. She hadn't even thought of this problem. From long habit, drilled into her over the years by her parents, she had automatically taken the passenger seat. "I've never done so before, but—" She pushed her nervousness under. "Still, once a course is programmed in, the driver is little more than a failsafe. And I *did* read the instructions once, when my parents left me in the vehicle alone."

The Korozhet seemed to hesitate. But only briefly. "No. But we will opaque the windows. In case of snipers. There is great danger, and I must take great care of you. You will have to handle the security systems, Miss Virginia! The guards and the automatons will recognize you, and allow you passage. But you must be quick and careful. At least one of the guards must have been subverted to allow the Jampad in. We must give no clue that we are aware of the assassins, while being ready to race away at a moment's notice."

With its manipulatory spines exuding tiny suckers which it flicked over the expensive computerized controls, like a master pianist playing a long familiar piece, the alien set the landspeeder into motion. Virginia was deeply impressed by the sure manner of the movements. If she hadn't known better, she would have sworn the Professor was already familiar with the vehicle. They were so adept at technical matters, the Korozhet!

Despite the Professor's fears, they drove through the impressive security screen of Pygmalion House without any check or hindrance.

Virginia sighed with relief. "Four or five minutes should see us in town. We can take refuge in the police station."

The Korozhet clacked two of its spines in the motion which Virginia had come to interpret as *respectful but firm disagreement.* "We are not going into town, Miss Virginia. Absolutely not! Your father suspected enmity within the board of directors. He was right, clearly enough. That means the police have certainly been suborned."

Virginia frowned, considering his words. It was true enough that her father had enemies. A multitude of them, in fact, judging from his frequent complaints. But, if the *police* could not be relied upon . . .

Her voice was a bit shaky. "Then where—?"

"We must go to the plantation," stated the Professor firmly. It was already keying in the instructions. Within seconds, the vehicle turned onto the highway which led to the plantation, and accelerated. The huge agricultural complex was located far to the south of the capital city.

Virginia gasped. "But—the Magh' advance! On the Vid-news they said, and Papa was so angry, and . . ."

"Fortunately, they have held back the Magh' advance. Do not be concerned, Miss Virginia! Your wise father foresaw this contingency also. I assure you that his plans for your safety were very well thought out. And now, I must ask you to simply have faith in me. Operating this unfamiliar vehicle will take all of my concentration."

Virginia relaxed. Everything was very confusing, and unsettling. But if there was one thing that she *did* know, it was that she could trust the Professor.

Absolutely. The Korozhet was a rock in the sudden shifting uncertainty of her once-ordered world. Thank heavens the Korozhet had been there, and had been unhurt. She shuddered. If the Jampad had spotted the Professor, they'd have killed it. For a certainty! The Professor had told her many times of the implacable hatred which the Jampad bore for all Korozhet.

She was tired, she realized. As usual, she had awakened early that morning. It was already late in the afternoon. Now that they appeared to be safe, she suddenly felt exhausted. Her eyes began to droop.

As she drifted off, her last conscious thought was of the Professor. *Such a dear old fuddy-duddy. Like someone in one of her novels . . . Like a sort of "nice" version of Lord Bromford from* The Grand Sophy.

Virginia was jarred awake by the howling of a siren. She sat up sharply in the seat and craned her head around.

"They're chasing us!"

A pair of motorcyclists were in hot pursuit. Police motorcyclists, or she misunderstood the flashing blue lights and sirens.

"Override! Full manual control!" barked the Korozhet. With a squeal of tires the Korozhet flung the wheel hard over. The vehicle leapt from the road and bounded across a muddy field, plowing through stalks of grain.

"But they're police. Surely—"

"Suborned, Miss Virginia. Suborned! This is just what your father anticipated!" For a creature with a hard exoskeleton covered in flexible spines, who had never driven before, the Korozhet was astonishingly adept at handling the vehicle.

The landspeeder was designed for off-road work. The motorcycles weren't. Within two minutes, the motorcycles were no longer in sight. Within five, even the sound of the shrieking sirens had faded away.

The fear and excitement were making Virginia feel awfully strange. She was reminded suddenly of the nightmarish trips to the ship's surgery, back in that horrible fuzzy time before her soft-cyber implant. She felt . . . giddy. Very weak. Very confused.

Had she been shot? She couldn't feel any pain, but she had read that wounds could be unnoticed at the time they were received. Shock, or something.

Her head lolled on the seat rest. Her eyes fell on the rear window but, this time, she was not peering intently at the motorcycles on the ground. Just gazing vacantly.

As consciousness slipped away, she caught sight of a tiny, furry face, too full of big eyes. Clinging under the back sunshade of the landspeeder, Fluff looked utterly terrified.

She awoke in darkness. The bed she lay on was extremely hard. Gradually her mind assimilated that it was no bed. A hard surface, slightly gritty in texture. They must have crashed!

Her first thought was for the Professor. Virginia began scrambling to her feet. But, instantly, her head crashed into an unseen surface above. Wincing from the pain, she collapsed back onto her knees.

After a moment, she began feeling around with her hands. The space she was in—whatever it was—seemed very small and cramped. Even in the darkness, she rapidly established there was no ball of prickles in here with her. There was just no room for anyone else.

Reaching up and probing the—*ceiling?* it seemed too gritty for a ceiling—she rapidly established that there was no room for the Professor to be hanging from the ceiling either.

Sighing heavily, she lay down on her back. *Where am I?* she wondered. Suddenly her thoughts turned to the last thing she'd seen. Fluff. "Oh, Fluff! My poor baby!"

"I'm here," said a sleepy voice near her ear.

"Oh, Fluff!" she squealed. An instant later, her hands were groping for the galago. But she couldn't feel him anywhere.

"What is happening?" she demanded, fighting to control her rising hysteria. "Where are we? And where are *you?*"

"I'm here." The galago's voice was alert, now. "There is a sort of air hole here. Hang on, I'll be back with you in a minute."

Virginia heard a scrabbling noise. A moment later, the galago landed on her shoulder and nuzzled her ear.

"Oh, Fluff!" She stroked his furry-velvety little body.

"It's all right, Virginia. I, Fluff, will look after you. Have no fear. Fluff is here!"

"Where *are* we, Fluff?"

The galago seemed to hesitate. Then: "We appear to be inside the tunnels of a Magh' scorpiary."

Chapter 5:
Way behind enemy lines.

Chip stood at the head-end of the old quarry, in plain view of the advancing Maggots. There were more this time. At least there were no diggers. Most of the pursuit seemed to be the long-legged sun-spidery ones. If Chip remembered his sketchy boot camp training correctly, those were the ones called Magh'urz. According to the Korozhet who had brought the warning of the oncoming Magh' invasion, each variant and subspecies of the quasi-arthropods had a different suffix to delineate them.

But Chip hadn't paid much attention at the time, and had never had occasion to regret the loss. As far as he and every other grunt was concerned—Vat, rat and bat alike—Magh' were Maggots and they only came in two varieties: dangerous ones and all the rest. The dangerous ones always attacked and the others never did.

These, as it happened, were dangerous. Which, under the circumstances, was exactly what Chip wanted. But—

Damn! The stupid bastards!

The things had somehow not spotted him. They were veering away from the rocks, following the route the rats had taken. Chip cursed under his breath. He didn't enjoy being bait, but if he *was* going to play worm on a hook, the least they could do was *notice* him.

He took a deep breath and bellowed. *"HEY! MOTHER-FUCKERS!"*

One of the Maggots paused, as if considering the statement. At face value, of course, the accusation was absurd. As far as human xenobiologists knew, fighter Magh' had no sex life at all.

Chip blew it a raspberry. Now, it was obvious that all the Maggots had heard him. They had all stopped, skittered around, and were staring up at him.

Dammit, do they think this is one of Doc's philosophical discussions?

The last thing Chip wanted was to set the Maggots thinking. They might realize that the bait was bait. But how did he stir them into action? How did he taunt a Maggot?

When in doubt . . .

The old ways are always best.

Chip turned around, dropped his pants, and mooned them. The Maggots stormed forward, stridulating loudly. Plainly he had at last bridged the Maggot-human communication gap. It didn't sound like it was going to lead to an instant outbreak of peace. . . .

The Maggots were just beneath the shaky cliff-corner. The bats reckoned that one well placed satchel-charge would bring it all down. If it didn't, he was going to have to "please explain" that last gesture to the Maggots.

"Now!"

The explosion sounded tiny. For a moment it looked as if it would be totally ineffective. Chip's legs tensed and his heart sank. Damn those know-it-all bats! Then, with a tiny spurt of dust from the cracks, the entire cornice quivered. And fell.

Even where he stood, three hundred yards off, the ground shook and rocks tumbled all over the quarry.

Bats fluttered up, peering down into the dust. Several of the rats were leaping down already. Only three maggot-survivors had escaped the rockfall. In vain—the bats were swooping upon them.

"Heh. Got nearly every last one of the whoreson achitophel!" Fal rubbed his ratty paws. "Those flyboys know how to use their powder! Got that rockpile right on the G-spot. Did you see how it quivered!"

"Did the earth move for you too, Fal?"

The rat chuckled. Licked his lips. "Well, I must go down and grab a haunch or two before the others snaffle it all. Most of the meat is buried."

Chip shuddered as the plump rat showed what a turn of speed he could display for food. The Company biochemists *had* said that the Maggots were nontoxic, except for their poison sacs. The rats and bats came from insectivore lines. Even so, eating their enemy . . .

Chip decided he'd wait until his bellybutton was closer to his backbone.

Ten minutes later, they were legging away across country, the rats showing that table manners were not part of their download.

Chip flopped down. They were now miles further in between the high red walls of the Maggot tunnel-mounds. There was no doubt about it: away from the trench-and-heavy-shelling warfare of the front, the combined skills of the human, rats and bats could lick five times their number of Maggots. Maggots were so goddamn stupid. Well, so was frontal slugging away at each other in trenches. That kind of warfare suited Maggots. There it was numbers and sheer blind determination and ferocity. Out here, in the broken country, even right inside their own backyard, Maggots were getting their asses whipped. But they just kept on coming. That was Maggots for you. They didn't run.

"I've found another fine site for an ambush, indade. Another quarry. Fair number of quarries hereabouts. The Maggots're about an hour off." Eamon was flourishing on this diet of mayhem.

Chip staggered to his feet. "Jesus, Eamon. We can't go on like this. That cliff section you dropped on the last party was brilliant, and we nailed every single survivor. But they're back onto us again. Twice as fast, I'll swear. I've got to get some sleep. You and the rats can manage on half an hour snatches, but I'm running out of steam."

"Sleep. We'll prepare this one. I'll leave O'Niel to keep a vigil." It was a measure of the respect that the sole surviving human had won, that the big bat would even suggest this.

Chip was tempted. Then he shook his head. "We shouldn't split up," he said regretfully. "But I'd love to know how in the hell they keep on following us. And so quickly."

Bronstein had fluttered up, quietly. "It must be the smell."

"Are you suggesting that they smell a rat?"

"Belike they smell a stinking human," snapped Behan.

"Speaking of keeping together, where is the fat rat?"

"And Doll . . ."

Chip raised his eyes to heaven. "Both of them! We're in the middle of a war. Lost behind enemy lines, with half the Maggot army after us, and fat Fal's chasing tail."

"Envy makes you nasty, Connolly," said Phylla, preening her whiskers.

"*AAASKKKEEECCCH!*"

They were nearly flattened by seven of the long-legged Maggots they'd seen foraging, busy collecting literally every scrap of organic material. The running creatures paid them no attention, but ran on, fleeing as if their trousers were afire.

The bats were still fluttering in confusion and the rats scampering for cover when the reason for the panic came blundering through, stridulating blue murder. It was an eighth Maggot. And its trousers *were* on fire. Well, its hind-end was alight, anyway. Maggots didn't wear trousers, or anything else for that matter.

"Man, look at that thing go!" cheered Nym.

"Got its afterburners on!" sniggered Pistol.

Even Eamon was impressed. "Indade, 'tis not often you be seeing them from behind."

"Not often!" Melene was smiling toothily. "Why, Fal said he'd give up drinking if he ever saw one run away."

Pistol curled his own thin lips in the savage way that showed amusement. "And you said the only way he'd see them run was to give up drinking in the first place. To which he replied that he'd see a lot of other things too if he did. And then you—"

"We'd better go and look for those rats," interrupted Chip, scrambling to his feet.

The bats located the portly rat and Doll not seventy yards away, in a neat little hideaway that Fal had plainly organized. He and Doll were still lying on Chip's jacket, their tails entwined. Chip hadn't even noticed that the rat had stolen the jacket. The two were alive, and intact . . . it was just their wits that seemed to have gone begging.

For once even the fat rat was at a loss for words. And the brassy Doll's voice quivered when she finally found it. Her first question was addressed to Fal. "Art thou not hurt i' the groin?"

Fal just stared wide-eyed. Finally he shook himself. "I' faith that was bad timing!" The fat rat shook his head, untwisted his tail, stood up, and stared at the broken glass. " 'Tis a great waste," he mourned.

Pistol poked him in the gut. "Your waist *is* very great—but just what did you do to those whoreson Maggots?"

Fal paid the questioning Pistol no attention, and instead scrabbled among the rocks. "My lighter! It's got to be here somewhere."

Chip leaned over and picked up a pseudo-antique zippo. The gadget was designed for rats: smaller, overall, than the human version, but with an oversized striker to suit the relatively clumsy "fingers" of a rat's forepaws. It was inscribed: *Ours is not to do or die, ours is but to smoke and fly.* In some ways, rats were sticklers for tradition.

"That's mine!" cried Fal.

"And that is my jacket you swiped for your little bit of private whoopee-nest," said Chip, grimly. "Now, let's have the story."

"Gimme."

"Story." Chip held the lighter up, out of reach, and then, when Fal bared his teeth, he tossed it to the fluttering Bronstein.

"All right," muttered Fal. "Give it and I'll tell you. That's a genuine heirloom, that lighter."

Chip jerked his jacket out from under Doll. "After he's told us, hey, Bronstein."

"If ever," said the bat.

The plump rat glowered at them. "All right. Well, we just slipped off for a bit of . . . privacy, and I was just lighting up, after, when this Maggot stuck his face in. Well, I thought we were dead. . . . Doll threw my bottle of 160 proof." Fal looked at her reproachfully. "She missed. It hit that rock over there, broke and showered over the Maggot. The falling liquor was slow enough to go through the thing's slowshield, obviously. Then I must have lost my grip on my lighter."

"Panicked and threw it when he was trying to get up and run," interpolated Doll, obviously feeling more like her usual obstreperous self again.

"WOOF . . . next thing the Maggot took off like . . ."

"Like its tail was on fire."

"Exactly. Now can I have my lighter back?"

"I guess. So you're giving up drinking, Fal? Now that you've seen one run?" Bronstein asked.

The rat's whiskers drooped. He looked mournfully at the broken glass. "For now I am."

There were easily twice as many Maggots this time. They took one look at the quarry and, even with Chip playing bait, did not enter it but set off around. Chip and the rats and bats had to flee, the trap unsprung.

"They knew," said Bronstein, clinging to Chip's shoulder again.

Chip shook his head. "But how? We killed every single one, last time"

"Comms," the bat said, quietly.

"But they don't *carry* anything." It was true enough. By comparison the naked bats and rats were overdressed. They carried small packs and bandoliers. No Maggot lugged any hardware at all.

Bronstein gave the bat equivalent of a grimace. If anything, it improved that face. "Not that we've seen, anyway."

"Where could they hide them? I mean between you and the rats you've *eaten* whole Maggots. If there was anything there you'd have found it." Chip grinned wryly. "The rats would have shat it out by now. Like they do the slowshields."

"Maybe they're built *into* the slowshields," she said pensively, rubbing her chest over the spot where her own slowshield was implanted. "Ours don't have anything like that, but . . ."

Chip shrugged, nearly dislodging her. "Well, whatever it is, they communicate. Even when they're dying. And even if we win every fight, we're getting into a worse and worse situation, Bronstein."

The bat looked around at the tunnel-mounds that walled in the half mile wide strip of wasteland they'd found refuge in. The mounds were higher, and the strip narrower. "We need to break out of here," she said.

Chip voice reflected his tiredness. "We need to stop being chased."

"They won't stop until we're dead," mused Bronstein. Her face folds wrinkled even further. Chip thought that if there was anything in the world uglier than a bat's face, it was the face of a thinking bat. Then she said slowly . . . "So maybe we should die for them, then. Let them tell their commanders we're dead."

Chip snorted. "What do you suggest? We hold them over a fire and make them say: 'The enemy are dead, Commander'?"

"Something like that," muttered Bronstein. "I'll think of something . . ."

✧ ✧ ✧

The next ambush centered on a roll of barbed wire, either a relic of the war or a leftover from when this had been farmland. It was impossible to tell. What had once been fertile fields dotted by the occasional farmhouse had been completely ravaged—first by the fighting, and then by the typical Magh' methods of expanding their scorpiaries.

The party of Maggots that were closest and had to be ambushed were foragers or scouts. Probably scouts, because there was nothing left to forage. This area had already seen intensive work from the foragers. Not so much as one blade of grass survived. The Magh' always removed any organic material and stowed it somewhere in their scorpiaries. Metal scraps, however, were usually ignored.

Hence the roll of barbed wire that Chip had literally stumbled upon.

He swore.

"Not tonight," piped Melene immediately. "I've got a headache."

Chip grinned. "You'd be so lucky."

God help him, he was starting to enjoy his flirtation with Mel. If only she'd been a *human* female. Sigh . . .

He examined the wire, as Doc with blessed silent efficiency cleaned and strapped the slash on his leg. The wire was tightly spooled. A memory of Chip's only attempt at fencing came back to him. He'd unrolled the pig wire carefully. As he'd been cutting the stuff, the brick he'd left on the other end, to keep it unrolled, must have got up and walked away.

It was *not* a nostalgic moment. Still . . .

"Hey, Eamon!" he called out. "What about this idea?" Chip explained how the newly unwound wire sprang back.

"You cannot be using that stuff. It'll rip our wing

membranes," said Behan, one of Eamon's pack-followers.

"Indade, it's a fool you are, Behan. 'Twill tangle the Maggots up, not us." Eamon's head was a closed shop—except for taking in ideas for generating mayhem. There he was as sharp as . . . as batfangs.

"Why should we wear them, when the bats don't?"

"Because they can *fly*, Phylla." Chip knew he was going to lose it soon. The rats were being cranky about Bronstein's idea. The wire ambush had been a resounding success, but they'd been able to watch how the Maggots, dipping their long feelers to the broken ground, had been able to track them, step-by-step. They plainly followed a scent trace.

The rat-girl looked at her feet, encased in strapped-on pieces of Magh' pseudo-chitin. "But they're so . . . ugly."

"Look good on you, Phyl," Nym rumbled.

That was enough. Nym's rare comments were valued. "Do you really think so?"

"Yes. Give you a bit of extra height."

"But they're not really my color."

I'm going to lose it! Chip concentrated on making himself a pair of exoskeleton sandals, while the rats debated not the clumsiness or the slipperiness of the "shoes," but their sex appeal.

They hid out on the hillside and waited and watched. A purposeful mob of Maggots arrived within twenty minutes.

"They knew exactly where to come. I told you. Comms, built in," said Bronstein.

"It does seem the logical conclusion," concurred Doc. "Philosophically valid, too. All the great logicians agree on the supremacy of mind over matter.

I suggest we are observing, in action, Immanuel Kant's famous *noumenon*, the thing-in-itself unknowable to the mere conscious intellect."

Going to lose it . . .

"Doc," grated Chip, "would you mind giving me a translation? Before I just tell you to shut up?"

The rat reached up a stumpy forepaw and adjusted his pince-nez spectacles. "To put it crudely—inaccurately—we are seeing racial telepathy at work."

Chip stared at the Maggots. The Magh' fighters stood and muddled around their dead, or what was left of them. Eventually the mob split into little search parties, wandering hither and thither, plainly searching scent traces.

"See," said Bronstein. "They don't know where we've gone. I told you so."

It wasn't a popular statement, because it never is, but it was true. "They'll still find us," muttered Chip. "There are just too many of them."

He glanced down at G.W.F. Hegel, perched on his hip and peering over the boulder. "And if Doc's right . . ."

"Any time we fight one, the rest of them know about it," concluded Bronstein. Oddly, however, the thought seemed to cheer her up.

"But meanwhile"—she nodded toward the Maggots wandering aimlessly across the torn-up landscape below—"it gives us time."

"Time for what?" snorted Chip. "Time to sleep?" He found himself yawning.

"No," replied Bronstein firmly. "A time to die. Philosophically speaking, that is. Even—" She fluttered her wings. "*Artistically!*"

"I'm going to lose it," muttered Chip. "Completely."

Chapter 6:
Meanwhile, back at the chateau . . .

Lieutenant-General Blutin's family were second cousins to the Shaws. Even if he hadn't been overall commander of military operations he would have been an important man on Harmony And Reason. He was a short, fat, choleric man. His tailored uniform, despite the expensive material and the care and attention that his four Vat servants lavished on it, always looked as if should have been worn by a smaller, more upright sort of fellow.

But no one could argue that the uniform itself, and the avalanche of medals and ribbons which poured down its expanse, were out of place in the general's headquarters. Once a Shareholder's mansion, the huge edifice had been redesigned to the general's own detailed specifications. Damn the cost and labor! A war needs a suitably *martial* headquarters from which to be waged.

Major Fitzhugh thought the crenellations were a particularly nice touch, along with the portcullis. Completely useless, of course, against Magh's weaponry and tactics. But—certainly *martial.* Essential, no doubt, for maintaining the army's *élan vital.*

The major's attention was drawn back to the moment. Judging from the general's puce complexion—just the other side of beetroot—Fitzhugh thought the martial fellow was on the verge of completing his peroration. He'd better be, for his own sake. If the general puffed himself up any more he'd burst those polished buttons. He looked uncommonly like an angry bullfrog, without the anatomical design to make the swelling survivable.

But, fortunately, the major had gauged the affair correctly. At that very moment, the general finished his train of thought.

"So, explain yourself, Fitzhugh!" he spittled and thundered. "What do you mean—*'No'?!*"

Despite his appreciation of the superb spittling, Fitzhugh thought that the thunder was a bit spoiled by the rising squeak at the end. And while the halitosis undoubtedly added a certain charm, it fell far short of terrifying.

But the major thrust aside these idle connoisseur's musings and pulled himself even more rigidly upright. A response seemed appropriate for the moment. So—

From his towering height, Fitzhugh gazed down at the general over a long, bony, aquiline nose. As always, he kept his head tilted back a bit, giving his stare that certain panache. It was a habit they'd tried to break him of in OCS, but Fitzhugh had simply taken advantage of the criticism to perfect the mannerism. Disrespect toward one's superiors, of course, was a court-martial offense. But how could it be proved that a man could sneer with his nose?

"The word 'no' implies the negative, sir. Actually, it *defines* the negative. In this instance, the word 'no' actually means 'no.' I cannot do it, sir."

The fat general glared up at him. But, within seconds, his eyes moved away. Flinched away, really.

Fitzhugh was accustomed to that also, and was quite willing to take advantage of it. His face wasn't a pretty sight, to say the least. A Magh' claw had done for that.

Still, puff-guts had plenty of wind. He managed another little puff. "That's a direct order, Major!"

If the general's snarl was intended to abash the major, it fell very wide of its mark. To the best of Fitzhugh's knowledge, he was the only high-stock Shareholder-officer to have actively led his men, from the front, into combat against Magh' scorps. By comparison this large, plush office in Southern Front Headquarters was a cakewalk.

"Yes, sir. The order is also in direct contravention of the Military Code. Chapter 15, section 3.1, paragraph 4. 'Military personnel shall at all times remain under command of military officers.' So if I disobey your direct order, I face court-martial. If I *obey* your direct order, I face court-martial. Shall I proceed to hand myself over to the MPs?" He hefted the bangstick. "Or should I make it worth my while?"

The general scuttled back a few steps. He obviously didn't think the intelligence officer was joking. Which, since Major Conrad Fitzhugh had a certain reputation, was perhaps understandable.

The general's scuttling took him behind his desk. Given that the desk was approximately the size of a battlefield, he apparently felt a bit safer on the other side.

He plopped down into his chair. His face was as pale as it had been livid a few moments before.

"Threatening a superior officer . . ." he mumbled. He started piling the reports spread across the huge desk into tall stacks, as if creating fieldworks to protect himself from assault.

"Nonsense, sir!" boomed Fitzhugh. "If you'll forgive me saying so, the very idea is an affront to your valorous reputation. Which, as I'm sure you know, is a byword among the troops in the front lines."

Fitzhugh lowered the bangstick. "Now, if I can explain." His next words were spoken in a very dry tone of voice. "The intelligence section is comprised of four members. Myself. Captain Dulache, who, alas, has been called away again on urgent personal business. Something to do with settling another inheritance dispute, I believe. That leaves me Corporal Simms and Private Ariel, both of whom, as you know, have been declared medically unfit for further front line service due to injuries sustained in combat."

Fitzhugh decided there was no need to remind the general that Private Ariel was a rat. There was *certainly* no need to inform him that the private was in his magazine pocket right now. There was no rule, after all, that stated explicitly that headquarters staff could not wear combat fatigues, with capacious pockets.

"Between us, we are responsible for intelligence gathering on the Magh' effort. I have put in, at last count, twenty-three motivations for more staff."

"We'd all like more staff," snapped the general, beginning to recover his wind.

Fitzhugh gave the general his patented double-bore gaze. Then, slowly, he swiveled the gaze to examine the office and its polished woodwork, brassware, and thick pile carpet. More manpower went into cleaning this office than Fitzhugh actually had in the two tiny rooms that were MI.

"Yes sir. We would."

He brought the stare back to the general. Blutin seemed to shrink a bit under that scrutiny. But it was difficult to be certain, given the disparity between the general's size and the luxuriant enormity of his chair . . .

"If I may continue—sir. I have no spare staff to devote to searching for a missing civilian—sir. I have no people to give to the Chief of Police for foot patrols as you have ordered—sir."

He cleared his throat forcefully. "Mind you, General, if one of the chief's staff holds a reserve commission I shall be glad to second Captain Dulache to him for that purpose as soon as the captain returns. Whenever that might be. I should be delighted to do so, in point of fact. The word 'ecstatic,' actually, would not be inappropriate to the occasion. 'Delirious from joy' also comes to mind."

"Humph," humphed Blutin. Whatever his other failings as a commanding officer, the general had no superior at the ancient skill of spotting an escape clause. "*Hmph!* Why didn't you say so at once, then? Yes, that'll do splendidly. Captain Dulache it is, as soon as he returns. I shall so inform the civilian authorities."

He wagged his plump little hand. "Go on, now. Get out of here. And don't let me see you with that uncouth spear again!"

Fitzhugh ported the bangstick. "It is a regulation weapon—sir. I am obliged by terms of the Code to carry it—sir." Then, saluting crisply and turning even more crisply on his heel, he was out of the door in an instant. The general's sigh of relief sufficed to close the door.

As soon as Fitzhugh had passed through the outer offices—a trek in itself—he entered the mansion-now-quasi-castle's dining room. The servants were already preparing the table for the upcoming "staff lunch." Four of them were spreading the linen tablecloth, like seamen struggling with a sail, while a small army of others stood waiting with the silver service in hand. Yet another host of servants clustered here and there bearing platters of food.

Seeing Fitzhugh enter the room, the majordomo stiffened. The servant standing next to him, newly assigned to his duty here, failed to notice and was already hurrying to the major's side.

"May I have your name, sir?" this worthy asked unctuously. "So that we might set the proper card at your place."

The majordomo hissed. All the other servants in the room froze.

Fitzhugh stared down at the fellow. Then, slowly, the shark grin spread across his ravaged face. The servant paled a bit, perhaps, but managed not to flinch outright.

The bangstick was suddenly in the major's hand, pointing to the far end of the table. "I always sit directly across from the general himself," he murmured. "He finds it aids his digestion."

The bangstick flicked out and speared a honey-and-sesame-seed-glazed half-quail breast from one of the platters. Holding it upright, Fitzhugh turned on his heel and strode toward the far exit. "And the name's Banquo. Make sure you spell it properly."

Once he'd left the dining room and had reached the unpopulated regions of the corridor beyond, a long and furry nose popped out of the large pocket of the major's fatigues. Black and beady eyes regarded him. "I thought for a moment you were going to skewer that fat blue-bottle Blutin."

The eyes moved to the quail. The major lowered the bangstick. The juicy morsel was instantly plucked therefrom and began disappearing into Private Ariel's maw.

"I can't say I wasn't tempted!" Fitzhugh heaved a small sigh. "But what's below him is worse. Blutin's a bumbling idiot whose rich relations put him here to get him out of the way, back when there was no reason for an army. But if *he* goes we should automatically get Carrot-up."

The last term came with a ferocious scowl. General Cartup-Kreutzler was Conrad Fitzhugh's ultimate *bête noire*, in a menagerie of sooty beasts.

Ariel belched and began scattering quail bones on the polished floor. "So why didn't you say we'd happily go looking for this What's-her-name, then? Virginia Shaw, was it? 'Tis a fact that Carrot-up bins your reports as soon they arrive on his desk anyway."

Fitzhugh looked down at the rat. There was nothing of frigid hauteur in that glance. Ariel was the reason he had any face at all. And he was the reason she didn't have a tail.

"Because we might *find* her, dimwit."

They had reached the staircase leading to the basement where MI's offices were located. Fitzhugh took the stairs two at a time. As always, he found the confines of the former servants' quarters refreshing. Dank and dingy, true, but at least they allowed him the illusion that he was actually fighting a war.

"Christ," he growled, now striding through the basement itself, "I'm delighted to have that stupid rich-man's-burden bastard Shaw out of the equation."

There was no further need for concealment, so Fitzhugh plucked Ariel out of his pocket and perched her on his shoulder. Scowling fiercely, he continued. "You *know* that jackass was insisting on an 'oversight' of all battle plans. Christ! Half of them would be date-expired before they were set in motion."

They reached the door leading into the MI's offices. There was no need to unlock the door before pushing through. Nobody except the major and Ariel and Corporal Simms ever came here. Not since the unfortunate affair of Colonel d'Avide, which had done wonders for Fitzhugh's reputation. Captain Dulache, though he was officially assigned to MI, had set foot in the place exactly twice.

Fitzhugh laid the bangstick across a corner of his desk. That piece of furniture was scarred and worn, and the weapon looked right at home. "Maybe now that Shaw's out of the equation we can fight some kind of real war. Maybe."

As Fitzhugh lounged into his wooden chair, Ariel leapt nimbly onto the desk and began nibbling at the bowl of comestibles which the major always kept there for her.

"You're getting fat," grumbled Fitzhugh. Ariel waggled her tailless rump in cheerful agreement. "The daughter—*if found*," continued the major, "would probably be more of the same as her father. Cronies for general staff, and war-materials-contracts for buddies."

He sat up straight and reached for a pile of as-yet-unstudied intelligence reports from the front. "Good riddance to bad rubbish, I say. I wouldn't be surprised if whoever did it was trying to do the war effort a favor. Ought to be decorated, if anybody wants my opinion."

He started scrutinizing the first report. Sourly: "Which they don't."

Chapter 7:
Even heroines need to eat.

Virginia had gotten over feeling nauseated . . . eventually. Naturally enough, she hadn't gotten over being scared. But enough time in the unchanging darkness passed for her to start thinking, puzzling things out and piecing them together.

"How did we get here, Fluff?"

He nuzzled her neck. "I don't know, Virginia."

"Last I saw you, you were clinging to the back of the car."

"Um. You don't remember any more?" Fluff sounded distinctly embarrassed.

"No." She tried, but it had just . . . vanished. "Tell me how we got here?"

"I woke up here. Just like you," answered Fluff.

Fluff was definitely being evasive. "I saw you *outside* the car, Fluff. Where did we go? How did we get captured? And is the Professor all right?"

"I don't know, Virginia."

"Then how did *you* get here, Fluff?"

There was a silence. Then, in a small voice: "Inside your blouse."

"*What?!*"

"But I was unconscious! I swear it! On my mother's grave—I swear it, *Señorita*!"

When Fluff was deeply disturbed he went all Spanish. That was a side effect of his Cervantes download.

"Tell, Fluffy."

The galago hated to be called Fluffy. But—it was a sign that all was forgiven. So:

"The car stopped . . . the policemen came closer, and the Professor opened the door. I jumped in. I do not think he noticed. You were . . . asleep . . . I was a little, um, upset. I burrowed into your blouse. The door closed . . . and then I woke up with you. Here. I explored this cell and I found this hole. I looked out and there were Magh'. Then I heard you speak. That is all."

"So, maybe they don't know you're here! The Magh' must have captured the Professor, too. Oh, I hope they aren't torturing him! We must escape, Fluff, and rescue him!"

"How are we going to escape, Virginia?"

"You can get out, Fluff. You must steal the key to my cell. We can unlock the door and go and rescue the Professor."

He nuzzled her neck. "Um. There is no door, Virginia."

"But . . ."

"We are walled in. There is just the air hole. And I do not know if I can squeeze through it."

"But we'll starve!" Already, just thinking about it,

she felt hungry and thirsty. "Or will we die of thirst first?"

"Never fear, Virginia. I—Fluff!—will go out and find food and drink for my beloved!" The little creature shivered on her shoulder.

"Oh, Fluff! What's wrong, dearest?"

The galago was silent for a moment. Then: "It is all very strange. I'm frightened."

"Then stay."

"No! A hidalgo must do what he must do. Honor demands it! I shall go."

"Just be careful. Please. You're not really a hidalgo, you know. You're a galago who's way less than a foot tall and weighs hardly anything."

Fluff bounced off her shoulder. "For you, I dare anything! I will prove to you I am a hidalgo." She heard him scrabbling at the air inlet.

Then, seconds later, there was a muffled voice . . . Fluff's. "I'm stuck."

"I can pull your tail," she offered.

"No!" he squeaked. "Don't pull—*push*."

"Breathe out. I'll do my best."

The little galago's feet thrust against her hand. She knew it had to be her imagination but already the air in the hole seemed stale. Would she die in here, the air inlet plugged by Fluff?

Then suddenly he popped out like a champagne cork. She heard him land.

"Are you all right?"

"My dignity, she is bruised. Otherwise I am intact. And now—I go!"

Silence followed; a long, long silence. Virginia understood now how Cathy Earnshaw must have felt, exiled from Heathcliff. Bleak desolation.

Despite the downloaded Brontë, Virginia was basically a practical girl. She had made do for herself, largely, during the years after her accident. Later, after the Korozhet soft-cyber implant had returned her intelligence, she realized that the servants had neglected their brain-damaged charge in the knowledge that Virginia could not report their slackness to her mother. But even then she had not done so; nor had she requested new servants. Truth be told, Virginia preferred lazy servants. Less bothersome.

So, after a few weepy moments she got to her feet, bumped her head again and began to make a systematic examination of her prison, by feel. She had just concluded that Fluff was right about the lack of door or any other exit except the air hole, when he returned.

"Virginia." Never had the sound of her own name been so sweet.

Relief! "I was so worried, Fluff! Come and give me a hug."

"I don't think I can." There was real misery in the galago's voice. "I might stick fast forever. There is no one to push me through on this side."

"Oh no!" Virginia felt more deserted than ever. "What are we going to do?"

"I am just glad to be back *near* you, Virginia," said the galago, sounding piteous. "I was so scared I would not find my way. These tunnels! There are so many of them, and they are all so alike."

"Fluff! You must mark the way somehow."

"With what, Virginia?" he asked.

She was at a loss. "I suppose . . . I could tear pieces off my blouse."

"The Maggots might spot that. I scratched little marks. I just found them hard to . . . find."

"Did . . . did you find any food or any water?"

"Indeed I did." There was pride in the galago's

reply. "Great store bins of grain, and things all thrown into huge pits."

"And a drink . . . I'm parched."

The galago was silent for a few moments. "Yes. Although . . . short of bringing it in my cheeks . . . but I will make some kind of plan."

Chapter 8:
We who are about to die give you the finger.

Naturally, Maggot-mound construction played havoc with existing watercourses. And stripping the ground bare did not make for gentle runoff. Whatever the Maggot equivalents of civil engineers were, they had got it wrong in this space between their tunnel-mounds. Dry gullies turned to raging watercourses. True, thought Chip, it was probably a temporary situation. The tunnel-mounds were obviously still being built, and getting wider. Eventually the Maggot engineers would just use up the wasteland altogether and join one tunnel-mound to the next. Chip had once seen an orbital photograph of the Magh' scorpiaries. They looked like red cow patties with spiralling arms.

Chip had been glad when the rain started. His water bottle had been nearly dry. For food he was down to an "energy bar," which took more energy to chew than it provided. But he supposed if the worst came to the worst he could eat Maggot too, like the rats and bats. He was sure that if he could have cooked it, he could have made it edible—even tasty. A little garlic, some spices and a fire and it would have probably fetched four hundred dollars a portion at Chez Henri-Pierre, especially if called *Navarin de Magh' au poivre vert*. At present, however, Raw Maggot was the only choice on the menu. And that did not appeal, no matter what Fal said about it. Not even calling it *Magh' Sushi de elementare* could have sold it.

But it hadn't been a brief shower, and Chip was growing tired of being a one-man tent to a bunch of bickering rats and bats. His issue poncho had kept them all dry. Well, sort of dry. Like most raingear it had a seam around the neck ensuring a slow Chinese water-torture drip. For near on two hours they sat there, until the rain lifted in the late afternoon.

The rain was not welcomed by the Maggots, either. The minute it stopped, Maggots appeared on the outside of the tunnel-mounds, doing repairs. Clinging as they did to the outside of the tunnels, the Maggots had a wonderful vantage point. The bats flew off to disable them . . . and flew back. "They're blind. They don't have eyes. We can press on."

Unfortunately that wasn't true either. Between the hill slope of the wasteland and the scorpiary walls was a lovely new lake of muddy water.

"We'd better get swimming," said Chip, not happy with the idea. He hadn't swum much. Trips to the coast were for Shareholders. Part of his Company-sponsored education had included "swimming." But it had stopped at the level of "drown-proofing." Chip couldn't even see the other side of this body of water. It was lost around the corner of the Maggot-mound spiral.

"The water looks cold," said Melene. Gingerly, she touched it with her tail tip. "Freezing!"

"One must be philosophical about this," said Doc, looking as if this he'd rather be anything but.

"Water's not good for you," pronounced Fal, edging away. "Shrinks the skin. As pleasingly rotund as I am, I can't afford that."

Fal eyed the bats. "Can't you give us a lift?"

"You're far too heavy," said Eamon, sizing him up.

"We could sit on Chip's head," said Phylla hopefully. "He could ferry us across, one by one."

"I'm not sure I can swim that far," replied Chip. "Not even once, let alone six times." He sighed heavily. "But it's swim or die, I'm afraid."

"We bats can fly," stated Eamon. "I do not really know why we've stuck together so long anyway."

"Eamon," protested Siobhan, "we cannot just be leaving them!" She was plainly incensed, to dare to challenge the big bat directly. Normally, only Bronstein would do that.

"Be easy, Siobhan," said Bronstein, perching on Chip's shoulder. She wrinkled her face in that exquisitely grotesque manner by which bats expressed a sneer. "Eamon can leave if he has not the stomach for this."

The big bat rose to that fly beautifully. "I can fight with the best, and certainly long after you've decided to wing your way hence!"

"To be sure, you can fight," said Bronstein, dismissively. "But can you *die* well?"

"I can fight and die as well and as nobly as any son of the revolution! I can die with both courage and dignity." The bat spread his wings, assuming what he apparently considered a dramatic and heroic stance. To Chip, he looked like a miniature Dracula suffering from hemorrhoids.

"It's eating too much Maggot," snickered Pistol, mimicking the stance. "It's made *me* constipated too. Got any laxatives for us, Doc?"

Chip suddenly hooked on. "Die artistically." That's what she'd said. "Shut up, Pistol." He winked hastily at the one-eyed rat. Then he turned on the affronted-looking bat, and said "You can die with courage. But can you die with drama?"

"*What?!*"

"With great agonized howls and much flip-flopping before you are finally still," said Chip.

Eamon was affronted. "I? Die like some coward slave! Have you lost your wits, primate?"

"I knew he couldn't do it," Chip said to Bronstein in a stage whisper. Bronstein furled her wings with her own dramatic, dismissive flair. "Yes," she sniffed. "Clear enough, 'tis beyond him."

"Yeah, we rats will show you how it's done. Leave it to us!" Pistol hadn't figured out what was going on. But he could play along as well as the next rat.

"Bah!" hissed Eamon. "Anything you rats can do we bats can do better."

"Anything?"

"*Anything!*" Eamon paused. "Except drink and fornicate."

"We always master the important things," pronounced Fal.

It was, Chip decided, the finest dramatic production ever to grace the planet of Harmony And Reason. Perhaps it was the nature of the rats' downloads. Whatever the reason, the rodents were actors *par excellence*. The fight between Fal, Nym and Pistol was worthy of the Globe Theater itself. Chip was glad he managed to land himself a brief cameo appearance, "dying" quickly, so he could watch the rest, peeping as he lay still on the muddy shore.

They had a captive audience. It was certainly the best show the two surviving Maggots of the patrol would see for the rest of their lives. At the rate the water around the barbed-wire bound Maggots was rising . . . "the rest of their lives" was about three minutes off. He hoped that Eamon had finished dying by then. Even the fat lady in that opera that the Company had bussed the Vats off to watch as part of their "cultural education" had died quicker, and with less histrionics. With less noise, even.

Finally Eamon, with a last despairing shriek, flopped over backwards with Chip's knife apparently protruding from his chest. The water was rising steadily. Eamon should have chosen to die a bit higher up. If Bronstein and Doc were right, the audience was far larger than the two victims. It wouldn't do to have the late leading bat get to his feet, just because his ears were getting wet. But Eamon lay and allowed the water to creep higher and higher. The Maggot eyes were lost in the muddy water. Only Eamon's nose protruded when the rest of the dramatic company got to their feet.

"I' faith. Do you think he really did it?" whispered Doll in a hushed voice.

Chip was one of the three who ran into the water's edge to see.

Eamon sat up. Spat water. "Here's your knife, Connolly. I cut myself on the damned thing. Bah. I hate getting wet, indade. Well, could you rats have done better?"

He got the standing ovation he deserved.

Still wearing their chitin "shoes" they retreated from the scene, in case another Maggot patrol came to check on the previous one. The rats, nature's own looters, had carted away two of the Maggot patrol killed before the "command performance."

Well . . .

They carried them about thirty yards, before begging Chip to give them a hand. He did, simply because hungry rats are dangerous rats. The shrew genes gave them phenomenal metabolic rates. They hid out on the hillock, amid a slabby tumble of rocks. They chose a good high spot, but it proved unnecessary. At about midnight the Magh' engineers must have arranged some essential drainage, and the huge dam's level began going down.

And not one Maggot came looking for them.

"Now that we have shaken our pursuit," said Bronstein, "we can rest, recuperate and plan."

One of the rats burped. "Got another bit of Maggot going spare there, anyone?" asked fat Fal.

"Do you rats never think of anything but your stomachs?" snapped Bronstein.

"Hur. Of course. Are you offering, sweetie?" Pistol gave her a lewd wink.

"Nice legs," opined Nym. "Shame about the face." Bronstein swiveled her face and gave the huge rat a look that combined irritation with wariness. The trouble with Nym was that it was hard to tell when he was being serious.

"Stop teasing Bronstein, you guys," said Chip. He was a little low on humor with the guzzling rats himself. Half an energy bar had provided a challenge for his teeth, and precious little for his stomach.

Suddenly Bronstein's face broke into a nasty, toothy smile. "I hope the gluttons are enjoying their Maggot-feast. It is their last one, to be sure. You *do* realize, rats, that we can't kill any more Maggots."

"Why not, Bronstein?" demanded Fal. "Do you have a conscience suddenly? I will not stop for that!" His nose twitched. "Maggot's not a patch on a fine grasshopper, mind you, but it is still better than that muck the Company fed us in the trenches. And there is plenty of it."

"You fool. The minute we kill one they'll be after us again. And there are a million Maggots to every one of us."

She had the satisfaction of knowing she'd silenced them. Then, Doc spoke up. "Indeed there *is* more."

"What!"

"Well, *imprimis* there is eating. Then, as the ancient Pistol indicated, *secundum*, there is sex, and *tertius*—I said there was more—there is strong drink. These are the philosophical contentions of rats."

Bronstein buried her face in her wings.

Reason's moon was bigger than Earth's. Even the crescent sliver was enough for Chip to see the still-working construction-Maggots. The tunnel-mound was getting wider and higher.

"I still think it's a crazy plan," he said, looking at the dark bulk of the mound. In daylight, with ropes and things it would be hard enough to climb. They wanted him to undertake a six hundred foot climb . . . as soon as the moon was low enough to have this wall in darkness. And then, on the other side—six hundred feet down again. By that point the moon should be down.

"All right. Stay here forever then," hissed Eamon.

"Until you starve or get caught and eaten," Behan backed Eamon up.

"Until I lose my temper with you," said Bronstein, far more frighteningly. "Now climb!"

Chip climbed. So did the rats. It was easier for

them as their paws were smaller, enabling them to use tiny pockmarks in the rock. Their strength to weight ratio was also much better than Chip's. The rats' problem was simply reach. A handhold Chip could grab, they had to do three extra moves to get to. Chip just had to face up to being too big and too wide and too heavy for the climb. He still had to do it though, feeling for handholds and footholds in the darkness. The rats could see better than he could in low light conditions, and of course the bats, to whom it mattered not at all, were at home in total darkness.

They'd chosen a zigzag Maggot construction ramp, which began perhaps thirty feet above ground level. Without that they really would have battled. The ramp was about eight inches wide and zigged and zagged its way at a forty-degree angle up nearly a third of the mound's height. For the rats it was a highway. An uphill highway so that they could complain, but a highway all the same. For Chip it was sweating terror and purgatory. He edged his way along, upwards, upwards, not daring to look down . . . again. He'd nearly plummeted off into the hungry darkness when he'd risked that first brief look. He'd gone all giddy and had to clutch frantically while Siobhan flapped around him like an annoying mosquito, telling him to "be climbing not shaking."

The rats, by now near the top of the ramp, were pretty full of their climbing ability. "Easy this. Methinks 'tis like a Sunday afternoon stroll, if it wasn't uphill," said Mel.

"The uphill will waste me away," grunted Fal. "I'm sweating my whoreson chops off."

"You've plenty to spare, before your waist's away," said Doll.

Then Eamon and O'Niel had fluttered up. "Over

the side. And be quick about it! There is a builder-Maggot coming!"

"Uh. Over the side?"

"Now!" snapped the bat.

They had to cling there in the darkness, while just above them the Maggot click-sauntered past. By the time they got back onto the ledge, the rats were considerably chastened. There was nothing like hanging by your hands in the darkness over a huge drop to make you more appreciative of having something under your feet. At the top of the zigzag ramp, there was an entry into the Maggot-mound. They avoided this and had to traverse across a hundred yards or so to the next ramp.

From being near-vertical, where Chip had had to use tiny holds to hang on, the angle of the mound had eased off. He discovered that once he pushed away from clinging like a slime mold to the wall, he could actually stand on his feet on the tiny knobs. He was getting quite blasé about it when a knob of Magh' adobe decided it wasn't designed for a hundred and sixty pounds of human. He managed to jerk back. Overcorrected. He scrabbled for a real handhold . . . started to slide.

Claws dug viciously into his back. Several sets. "Get a hold, Connolly," huffed some bat behind him, obviously through clenched teeth. Whether by bat-lift or luck, his slipping foot found purchase and his hand one of the occasional Magh' adobe struts. Chip clung there, panting. From far below came the sharp sound of the knob hitting the bottom, and bouncing away.

"I nearly gave myself a hernia," grumbled Eamon, settling on the wall. "What did you go and do a silly thing like that for, Siobhan Illich-Hill?"

"You and Longfang O'Niel were already clinging to him when I joined in."

"O'Niel, for what did you do crazy like that!?"

"Foin," said the normally taciturn O'Niel, "make it my fault then. When you know it was yourself who was first, Eamon."

"Whoever it was, I owe you," interrupted Chip.

"Well, if you owe me . . . then I have favor to ask," said Eamon.

"Ask away." Chip was feeling sick. Luckily, there was nothing much in his stomach to come up.

"Just don't tell everyone. The other Batties would expel me," muttered Eamon. He fluttered off into the darkness.

Chip stared after him. He'd known the bats were divided up into a jillion factions. They seemed to compensate for their infrequent mating by devoting their energies to political disputes. But he'd never once imagined that even the surly Eamon belonged to the extremist "Bat Bund."

"Ha," said Siobhan, landing on the strut. "He forgets I am not of the Bund. And I was here too—precisely because Bronstein didn't trust him alone with a human. And he was the first to try to hold you! All big talk, that Eamon. His mouth will get him into trouble his teeth can't get him out of, one day. Now, you must go on, Chip. Bronstein reckons that you and the rats must be off the mound by first light, and that is a bare four hours off."

Chip pressed on, somehow. As the angle eased, so did the climbing. He dislodged a few more fragments of Magh' adobe, but by now it was not enough to make him fall.

Eventually, Chip and the rats stood on the very top of the Maggot tunnel-mound. They had climbed the entire way in near total moonshadow. Now they could see a last moon-sliver poking its way into a shimmer of sea, perhaps thirty-five miles off. Thirty-five miles with many many stark folds of Maggot tunnel-mounds between them and it.

The bats hung in the air, twisting about them. "It's a long way to the sea, Bronstein," said one of the rats quietly. It was Fal. Obviously the distance, and perhaps the climbs that lay between them and it, had overawed the normally bumptious rat's nature.

"I' faith. A long and wearisome way." Doll looked at her paws, as if asking whether they were up to this.

"To be sure," agreed Bronstein. "It is a long way, for you earthbound creatures. And then we'll have to wait our chances for the force field to go down. Find driftwood. Make a raft. Do you rats have any other ideas? If not, you'd better get to climbing down."

Chip sighed, and began walking forward. "No other ideas, Michaela. We'd never get through the front lines. The sea is the only option. But it is a damned long shot."

"So is our surviving behind enemy lines. And what else can we do?"

"Nothing." Chip frowned. "But a length of rope and a grappling hook or even a few spikes would up my chances of making it."

"We'll look, then," stated Bronstein. "The forager-Maggots don't take metal away. Perhaps we can find something. But I think you are wishing for a great deal."

"Right now, all I'm wishing for is getting down from here fast, without getting down *too* fast," said Chip, looking nervously into the darkness ahead of him.

The climb down was the same again, but worse. It was also nearly the end of Melene. The rat-girl was the lightest and smallest of them, and had found the climb the easiest. Then, having paused to help Phylla, she missed her footing. Plunging headfirst past Fal she frantically tried to grab him. Fal's prehensile tail wrapped around her. The plump Fal stood as firm as a pylon as she found holds.

"I' faith, my hempseed lass, I know you like exotic positions. But this is a bit too bizarre a tail-twisting even for me. Besides I'm getting a little too fat for such athletic cliff-ledge frolics. Couldn't you have waited a few minutes? Was your desire for my body just too inflamed, to even hang on for another moment?"

Mel was too shaken to say anything at first. Then she started to swear. Chip was impressed by the extent of her vocabulary.

They headed on down. Chip fell-slithered the last five yards or so, but there were no bones broken, and no Maggot came storming out of the dark to see who was making such a racket. And besides, lying there, groaning, he made a softer landing for Doc.

"Uh! Did you *have* to land on me?"

"My apologies, Chip. When I heard you fall I came with all haste to see if I could render you any assistance. Alas, thesis became antithesis. As always, the unity of opposites is matched by their struggle."

As Doc said this, Phylla landed on Chip too. "Sorry. A bit steep that last bit," she apologized. "The handholds seem to have been rubbed smooth."

"Now, are you all right, Connolly?" asked Doc, as Phylla removed her feet from his midriff. "Can you move?"

"Ooh. Damn right I can move. And even if I can't, I'm going to, before fat Fal is the next to come tumbling down!"

Chapter 9:
A brave new world.

It was a promising landscape. The fields, once overgrown with disgusting alien trash, were now suitably bare. Macroscopically sterile. The more the Expediter thought about it, the more remarkable the synergy between the two species was. The Magh' and the Overphyle came from vastly different worlds and ecologies, but it was almost as if the Magh' had been especially created to prepare worlds for the Overphyle. And in the process of farming Magh', the Overphyle also turned a handsome profit.

There was no denying that Magh' did a magnificent job of clearing undesirable alien life-forms. As far as the Overphyle knew, they'd only failed once in millennia of conquest. True, in several cases it had been against primitives, hardly worth turning a profit from.

The Magh' did an equally magnificent job of leveling terrain. When the sea level was raised the Magh' adobe crumbled. It made for superbly fertile tidal mudflats.

The Expediter knew that she, and all those of the Overphyle who had participated in this venture, expected the spawnlings of their spawnlings to live out pleasant full lives on this world. It would be well stocked with prey from home. There would be plentiful slaves to work in the factories. The Overphyle could live the life for which they were destined. It would be several generations before the Overphyle set out after the Magh' slowships again. Conquest by Magh' was a leisurely process.

She regarded the red tunnel-mounds on either side of her with some satisfaction. The Magh' were doing an excellent job with these "human" vermin. Yes, the scorpiaries were a pleasant sight, indeed.

The closer prospect made her twitch her interambulacral plates. Her optic-supporting processes clattered in annoyance. The near view was *not* a pleasant sight. Well, hopefully, if all went well, it would be all over soon. But these humans and their vassals-serfs were very trying. Very trying indeed. They would suffer for this.

Chapter 10:
Loose Fluff.

The galago is a nocturnal primate. Those huge eyes are well adapted to seeing in the leaf-dappled moonlit forest-margins of Africa. Those beautiful, fragile, erectile ears can hear a woodworm belch at fifty paces. The tiny black hands and long-toed feet are strong, dexterous, and almost adhesive. The long tail is like an extra hand. Agile hunters in the fragile branches of the upper canopy, they are capable of prodigious leaps and silent movement. They also have, weight-for-volume, the loudest voices in the animal kingdom, but this was the one evolutionary advantage Fluff did not use while moving through the dim tunnels of Maggotdom.

He was still terrified. The first time he had hung silent up near the roof of the tunnel while the Magh' streamed below him, his chattering teeth must have almost betrayed him. At least, by now, he had established that up near the ceiling he was effectively invisible.

Hanging outside the air hole of Virginia's prison he listened to her tearing material. If only he could get into her prison! He scratched at the hole, but galagos were not much good at digging, and the Magh' adobe was hard. The best he could do was to stick his long tail through the hole. Virginia would stroke that. But this time she had tied something onto his tail. He pulled it out. It was a long strip torn in a careful concentric circle from her skirt. To the end of that was tied another strip from her blouse. "If you soak these in water and bring them back to me, I can at least suck them."

So Fluff had undertaken several journeys to the water cisterns for her. He could not bring her back much to drink in the dripping cloth. He knew it wasn't enough.

Food too had been a problem, for both of them. His own natural diet was insects, gum, and fruit. A wild galago wouldn't have said no to occasional scorpions, birds or reptiles either. Of course Fluff had never had to forage for himself. The Company dieticians had made up a special-supplement diet for him, which Virginia enlivened with extra titbits, such as hideously expensive acacia gum. Of course there had also been a daily delivery of fresh termites of which he had been particularly fond.

Down here the only insect-like things were the Magh'. There was certainly no gum. He'd found ample grain, loads of harvested and decaying greenery, but other than three wrinkled lemons, harvested along with the tree and not yet rotten, nothing much either of them could eat. He'd given them to her. At least they had a little juice.

"I must go further, Virginia. I must find some more food, and some kind of container for water."

Her voice was full of anxiety. "Just be careful, Fluff. I couldn't bear it if you didn't come back."

"I will be. Promise."

It was a troubled galago that had set out. He'd actually been on one other long foray. He hadn't told Virginia what he'd found, and it was pressing on his mind and conscience. He'd found the Korozhet prisoner. Her Professor. He should go to help the alien. He really should. It was pricking his conscience terribly. He must help the Korozhet. But there were just so many Magh' there with it. He was too scared. He knew if he told her about it she'd insist on him trying to get to the good Korozhet.

Even braving a journey into the unknown was better than dealing with this dilemma.

Chapter 11:
Biter bit.

Dawn could not be far off. The mound-top was already dark against a lighter sky. "We need cover," said Eamon, looking at the skyline.

"And sleep and food," Behan added.

"And strong drink," said Fal, mournfully.

"And tickets in the Managing Director's box to see a full Monty production of *Carmina Burana*," put in Chip.

The bats fluttered off to find a spot. They came back a few minutes later and led the human and the rats to a muddy undercut bank. As a hideout it was lousy. Chip was too exhausted to care.

"Well, Fal, your tail saved my bacon. I have a haunch of maggot stowed in my pack," said Melene, with real regret in her voice.

The plump rat had been looking a bit seedy in the

dawn light. At the mention of food he perked up. He rubbed his ratty paws together. "Well, good friends, we have a place to sleep. We have food. If only we had a drink . . ."

"I have some alcohol impregnated swabs for cleaning injection sites," offered Doc. "We could suck those."

"Ah! Now, if the bats are familiar with this *Common Boo Rana*, we could just rename this tranquil rural beauty spot, 'The Managing Director's Box,' and Chip too would be satisfied," said Fal, contentedly.

Pistol peered into the muddy puddle just below the hideout. "Hey, Fal, what would a 'Rana' be then?"

"Some kind of frog, I should guess, my ancient Pistol."

Doc nodded in agreement. "Indeed, there is a genera of frog by that name, I believe."

"Ah." Pistol gave his best one-eyed wink. "There's a toad in here. That's close enough. I'm sure that would do, eh, Chip?"

Gnawing hunger awoke Chip. He'd heard if you stopped eating you stopped feeling hungry. Only he'd been eking out his rations. Eating less and less, but still eating. Now the cupboard was bare. And his stomach was not satisfied with some silt-flavored water.

Earlier presleep jokes about the toad having to be careful about not becoming a double amputee, with a chef around looking for frogs' legs, stopped seeming so funny. It was time he started to eat off the land, time he got rid of his foibles. He would starve otherwise. The thought of raw toad was still hard going though. Maybe he could toast it over fat Fal's zippo.

Then he realized he should have woken up earlier.

Only a last webbed foot protruded from Fal's face. Then, with a crunch, that too was gone.

Fal told him it had tasted awful. Anyway, Nym and Phylla had got most of it. "We're going out foraging. We *have* to. Oh. And I'm afraid we ate your shoes."

Chip looked down. With relief he realized that they meant the maggot-hide sandals.

"We've got a real problem." Chip said to Bronstein.

The bat hadn't appreciated being awakened. "Other than being stuck behind enemy lines with a crazy human and a bunch of lowlife rats, *I* have no problems. That one is bad enough. And I *love* being woken up, to be sure."

Chip closed his eyes and counted to ten. "Okay, I've got a direct problem. You can just fly away. *But*, bat, when the Maggots catch on they're going to get serious about hunting you. Really serious. They've got aerial movement detectors. We know that. The Brass got at least a thousand bats killed proving it. They zap your slowshields with rapid-fire tracking projectiles. Keep it hard so that you can't fly. And once you are on the ground, you bats are no match for even the feeblest Maggot. The rats have got to get food. If they don't, they'll turn feral. It's the shrew genes. You heard what happened in that caved-in bunker on the eastern front?"

Bronstein looked at him. "You mean . . . where they ate the others? I thought that was just a story."

"No. It was true. I knew one of the kids on the cleanup squad. The platoon was trapped in there for four days. Without food. The rats ate the humans. They managed to catch and eat the bats. Then they started on each other. There was only one left to face court-martial. We've got to feed those rats, because otherwise they'll go out of their minds hunting food.

Sure, they'll start on me. Then they'll go out hunting Maggots. And then the Maggots will be onto you."

Bronstein shook her head. "I'll get the others. It's nearly twilight. We'll see what we can find."

"Good-o. I'll start turning over rocks. The Maggots have cleaned up all the surface stuff. But I might find worms or something."

"Be careful that the rats don't bite the hand that feeds them, Chip."

Chip grinned wryly. "Never mind biting it. They'll probably eat it."

"It's about half a mile off," said Siobhan. "The farmhouse itself must have copped a direct hit. It is pretty well flattened. But the outbuildings are intact, or mostly so. The ground is stripped bare, but surely there must be some food in sealed containers?"

"There can't be less than here," grumbled Chip, looking at his muddy hands. "Let's go. It looks like it is coming on to rain yet again, and I'd rather have a roof over me, than be one for you lot."

The farmhouse must once have been a very large and beautiful one. Now it was nothing more than a masonry shell. Chip poked through the remains of the kitchen. The pickings weren't very good, so far. Three jars of marmalade, which had miraculously survived the explosion. There had been a walk-in freezer room and cold room, but these had been blown open and thoroughly gutted by the Magh'-foragers.

"Hey!" There was a shout. "Methinks we're going to die happy! Look at this, you bacon-fed knaves!" Chip went to see, visions of a secret food hoard lending him speed.

Fal had found an outbuilding such as the place where good rats think they will go when they die. It was a small winery. The rat was eagerly sounding stainless steel vats. "This one is nearly full! And there is a pot-still here! That means *brandy*!"

"There is something down here too," called Pistol. The Maggots had taken the wooden doors, leaving the dark stairway into the cellar unguarded. Here were ten thousand bottles, packed in their serried ranks.

"Well strap me, if I don't crack a bottle or two to celebrate!" said Pistol, cheerfully. "Can I offer you a drink, Fal?"

"I never thought to hear those words! Pistol offering someone else a drink, instead of scrounging it! Indeed you may!"

"*Stop!*" said Chip. "Don't touch that stuff! Do you hear me, Fal?"

"Boy, tell him I am deaf," said Fal, ignoring Chip pointedly.

"You must speak louder sir. My master is very deaf," said Pistol, obligingly, cracking a bottle neck against a pillar.

Chip snatched the bottle from the one-eyed rat. Red wine sloshed onto the floor. Pistol looked startled. "Now, Chip. There is plenty for all of us."

"Don't be fools, Pistol, Fal. You're both still starving-hungry, right?"

"Yes. But what we want for in meat we'll have in drink." The fat rat eyed the bottle greedily.

"While you're sober, you're keeping your wits. Keeping your hunger in check. Get a bit drunk and all you'll want is food, and once you're good and drunk, and this hungry, you won't care where you get that food. You'll eat me. You'll eat each other. We've got to find food first—*before* you drink."

The rats were silent.

"You can put the bottle down," said Fal, seriously. "Food first, eh, Pistol?"

"I reckon. I wouldn't want to eat Chip. Not while he owes me a crate of whiskey." The rat sniffed at the robust, berry-rich inky bouquet of the spilt wine. "And it is a lousy vintage, anyway."

"A rat! I have found a rat!" Nym bellowed.

They all ran back upstairs. The big Nym had cornered a large black rat. The real thing, too—a descendant of unwanted stowaways on the slowship, not a creation of genetic engineers. A real, non-cyber-uplifted rat. It bared its yellow rodent teeth at them.

"Dinner!"

Fal lifted his long nose. "Sexy smelling dinner!"

"Yeah. Nice body!" said Pistol, eyeing the rat lecherously. "Shame we're just gonna eat it."

Fal straightened. "Hur. That's where you're wrong, Ancient Pistol. There is something we've *got* to do first. 'Tis our soldiering duty after all. Tradition! Tradition's clear as crystal on the subject. Says soldiering's got killing, looting *and* rapine." Fal rubbed his paws and eyed the rat. "Fighting Magh', o' course, 'twas a moot point. But now methinks we've gotten lucky!"

"Hark at him, lads!" cried Pistol. "This soldiering business has really got it all!" He turned his head to let his one good eye get a proper look at the captive.

"You're a bunch of paltry rogues," sneered Melene. "Kill it and let's eat."

"Well, just now!" protested Pistol. "I mean a rat's gotta do what a rat's gotta do!"

Fal nodded solemnly. "Duty first! We're just going to have to steel ourselves to it." He smiling toothily at the captive rat. It hissed back at him.

Nym looked at the wild rat. Then at Pistol. "You know what his ideas usually get us into."

"What, good Nym?" exclaimed Fal. "Can I believe my ears? A valorous whoreson rat not willing to put up his naked weapon? What manner of rat are you?" Fal strutted back and forth before them, his paunch wobbling, his chest out and his head back. He flourished his bristly tail. "Where is your martial vigor?"

Nym still looked skeptical. "I'm remembering that time when you . . ."

"Don't be disgusting, you lot!" Phylla did *not* look amused. "Get on and just kill it. My stomach thinks my throat has been cut, while you fool around."

Siobhan had fluttered in. "You are not going to *eat* that rat, surely?!" she said in tones of horror. "Why, it is nothing better than cannibals that you are!"

"In sooth. Doth it speak? Is it a tame shrew?" demanded Pistol.

Doc had wandered in, by now, and immediately begun pontificating. "Indeed, that is the question. The morality of the deed rests on this. Does it think deep thoughts? If it does not, then wherein lies the problem? Not in the mere fleshy envelope."

"There is as much going through its mind as there is going through one of you rats' minds!" snapped Siobhan.

"Therefore," said Fal reasonably, "as you bats have assured us nothing goes through our heads, the killing of this rat is no sin."

"They're planning to rape it first," hissed Phylla.

The bat looked as if was going to throw up.

Fal put on a mournful expression. "We really don't want to, of course—but the soldierly duty's to be done, to be done!"

The fat rat, paunch wobbling gloriously as he resumed strutting back and forth, gestured histrionically and burst into a singsong rendition from *Henry V:*

"But when the blast of war blows in our ears,

Then imitate the action of the tiger:
Stiffen the sinews, conjure up the blood,
Disguise fair nature with hard-favoured
rage!"

"Tradition!" chorused Pistol. "Anyway, what difference does it make? We're going to kill it and eat it, anyway. It's a dumb animal, even it looks a bit like us. What difference does it make if, uh, we do our soldierly duty first?"

"It makes a difference to *you*!" Siobhan was practically choking from indignation. *"Rape!* How can you even think of it? I'm going to call Bronstein."

"Hmm." Doc's eyes were almost crossed, as he pondered the ethics of the matter. "But consensual sex implies and indeed presupposes an intellect. Therefore, where there is no intellect . . ."

"You know, Doc, you're about as much fun as an enema!" snarled Fal. "I'm proposing soldierly rapine! That's not a matter of intellect. It is a matter of tradition! Like pillaging and burning! We soldiers have a reputation to keep up. It is our soldierly duty!"

"Since when, you buffoon?" Chip had the average conscript's respect for his uniform, but this was a bit much.

"Always! 'Tis in my memory banks!"

Nym finally came to his own conclusion. "I know. We'll kill it first. Then it won't mind."

"Take the logic through to the end," Doc immediately countered. "Eat it first, kill it later and rape it after that."

Chip shuddered. "I'm going to kill it now and get it over with, you sick bunch."

Fal sighed. "Chip, you are a sorry gutless hobgobbin. A spoilsport. You won't let me get drunk. You won't let me force my will on this svelte little rat-maiden . . . and she rather fancies me. Don't you, my sweetness?" The plump rat reached out for the wild rat.

She bit him, and ran.

"Yow! After her!"

But they were too slow, and the rat dived down a hole.

Fal nursed his paw. "She bit me."

"Good," said Bronstein, who had come in behind them.

"Now, where is our dinner?" demanded Doll. "Get down that hole after it, you idiots!"

"That's dinner that bites. Besides I don't think I'd fit down that hole."

"I've a good mind to kick you down it!" Phylla snapped. Hunger made her very irritable.

"Hullo. What is going on here?" asked Melene, who had just wandered in.

"These stupid, randy, male sots have just let our dinner get away, in their quest for more bawdy lechery. They've let a tasty wild rat escape away entirely with their dumb oversexed behavior!" Phylla aimed a kick at Fal, who was still sucking his paw.

"That's males for you," sniffed Melene. "Come, I have found us something to eat. We'll leave them to their bit of wild-tail, seeing as *we're* not good enough for them." She linked arms with Doll and Phylla.

"Wait . . ." said Fal, hastily.

"Stick your private parts in the rat hole, you tripe-visaged sots." Doll smiled nastily back at them. "Maybe the wild one will bite them off."

Shamefaced, the male rats followed them.

"No, no, stick to your 'soldierly' duties," said Phylla, showing teeth.

"Ah, come on . . ." begged Nym.

Doll showed teeth. "Bugger off and go and enjoy your wild rat."

"We too have found some useful things, Connolly, although not to eat," said Bronstein. "I was just on my way to find you."

"Fine. Let's just go and see what the rats have found. The honest truth is, Bronstein, I could have eaten that rat myself. Raw. A bit of a come-down for a former sous-chef, eh?"

The bat chuckled. "We also need food, Chip. We aren't as voracious as the rats, to be sure, but flying is an energy-expensive exercise."

"Well, let's go and see what they've found. But, knowing their tastes, don't expect smoked salmon," said Chip, with a half-smile.

He was quite correct. The smoked salmon, presliced and inadequately preserved, had gone off. In the tasting room next to the cellar, where the wine farm had provided delicate little snacks for its wealthy Shareholder clientele, was a small fridge. Without power, much of what was inside was simply gag-making rotten. One or two of the soft cheeses had actually evolved to self-awareness, and had to be forcibly suppressed. But there were a fair number of sealed bottles and tins. And up on the wall was a cupboard full of cellophane-sealed packets of dry crackers.

A few minutes later the male rats came along. The bats, Chip, and the female rats were gathered around a table on the terrace. The trellis above, which must once have been vine hung, was now festooned instead with batforms. Their dark silhouettes were stark in the moonlight. Occasionally one would swoop down on the table.

"We can't get to it . . . have you got anything to spare?" the male rats asked from below, an edge of dangerous hunger in their voices.

Food had had a mellowing effect on the rest of

them. "All right. Come up. There just might be a few scraps left." Phylla gestured at the stairs with a slopping wine glass. "Connolly made us some fancy chow."

The male rats fairly galloped up the stairs.

Chip, on seeing what they had found, had pushed the rats and bats aside. "I'll prepare it. Go and find us a bottle of wine." This was what he had done for five years . . . well, for the first year he had scrubbed pots . . . but he had an eye for this sort of thing.

Several by now half-empty filigree-edged silver platters rested on the table, filled with an array of delicate, elegantly presented canapes. Even the starving rats could only gape.

"Here, Fal. Try one of these bits of meatloaf," said Mel cheerfully. "What's it called again, Chip?"

"*Pâté de foie gras*, with truffles and cognac." Chip winced, watching the fat rat shove it into his face and chew. Twice. Gulp.

"Methinks 'tis not bad for tinned meatloaf, really," Fal pronounced, washing down the exquisite delicacy with a draft tipped straight from the bottle.

"Hey! What do you think glasses are for, you Philistine?" demanded Nym, helping himself to a glass and a biscuit piled with slices of pickled quail's eggs in chopped aspic, topped with mayonnaise and dusted with caviared trout-roe.

"Dunno. What?" Fal had another pull at the bottle, and another piece of "meatloaf."

"Drinking out of," said Chip, raising his glass, swirling the ruby liquid and savoring the bouquet.

Fal clung to the bottle, pointedly ignoring the glasses. "A waste of time, when the bottle is handy." This time he examined the pâté briefly, before putting it in his face. He gave it a cursory chew before asking in a spray of crumbs: "What was the little black bits in it? Con nyak, it's called? Some sort of testicle?"

"Cognac is brandy, you pleb," said Nym, looking curiously at the strange thing on the toothpick.

Fal grabbed for the platter. "Gimme. Gimmeee! Food and drink at once!"

"Too late, Pistol got there first." Nym chewed the toothpick. By the looks of it, he had decided that the stick tasted better than that pickled fishy-roll.

The odd food had even mellowed Eamon. "Just watch out for those little black balls he's put on those round biscuits. Chip's admitted 'twas just buckshot softened in fish oil, indade."

"What about the big ones in that bowl? Some kind of droppings?" inquired Pistol, reaching happily for them.

Siobhan swooped down and took a spiral of smoked oyster and gherkin slivers. "Black olives," she said, distastefully. "Beware, I tell you. There are pips in them. Nearly broke my teeth on one."

"Besides, what kind of fruit is salty?" demanded Phylla. Suspiciously: "I think Chip was having us on."

"S'like t'ose snake eggs." The plumpest bat belched and pointed a wing.

"Pickled quail's eggs, O'Niel," said Chip, grinning over his wineglass.

O'Niel condemned them with a lordly flap. "T'ay taste just like the eggs in boot camp."

Melene laughed "The ones we used to bounce?"

"Myself, I like those little bits of fish with green bits in the middle." Doll burped in an unladylike fashion and swilled back some of the Director's Reserve '03 Cabernet.

"Which do you mean?" inquired Doc. "The ones with the crunchy green-bits or the dark red ones with the wrinkledy bits of stuff in the middle." He inspected the one of each in each paw, squinting through his spectacles.

"The crunchy ones. What did you call it, Chip? Oh yeah. Roll-ups."

"Are you sure you're not supposed to smoke them?" asked Fal. "And the other fishy ones? Tried those?"

Doll swilled back some more wine, dripping it down her chin. "Nah. I thought they was bad. I mean, going green in the middle. I was just being polite and not saying so."

Chip chuckled. "It's an anchovy rolled around a caper, you ass."

"That wrinkled green thing is not a caper!" Doll leaped on the table, and pirouetted clumsily. "Thish ish a caper!" Fortunately Chip caught her before she could land on the snack platter.

"Bah, drunken rat revelers!" Eamon's temper was rising. "They can think no further than the ends of their long noses. Wasters and drunks!"

Phylla fixed him with a slightly glazed eye. "You know what, Eamon? You're right."

The big bat was taken aback. "I did not expect . . ."

"And you know what else?" She winked at him.

"Er . . . what?" asked the bat, in the cautious fashion of one who has just received praise from very unexpected quarters.

"You're really dead sexy when you're angry." She hefted the bottle. "What do you shay we shlip off and get totally rat-assed together?" Another thought crossed her ratty-soft-cyber mind. "Or what 'bout flying? Never tried that. Fly 'nited." She giggled and slumped forward onto the table.

Eamon hung on the trellis wires, gaping. Bronstein and Siobhan were definitely laughing at him.

He was not a bat that took kindly to being laughed at.

Chapter 12:
A little something.

The Magh' scraper tried to do its task as far away as possible from the Expediter. The Magh' apparently found the chemical exudate from the Overphyle hard to bear.

The Expediter lowered herself into the saline recliner. The scraper continued ineffectually. Strange. The Expediter had to admit that it was odd that chemical intolerance was all that had kept the Overphyle from being dinner to the savage wild Magh', back in that primitive scorpiary. Thus one of the most fruitful partnerships in space had nearly floundered. There were many billions more Magh'—even these lowly Magh'tce, now. And the Overphyle had found the Magh' very profitable . . . to farm.

Still, this new species was proving a tougher carapace to crack than had been anticipated at first. The opposite of the Magh' in many respects. Individually, the Magh' were almost mindless. As a collective scorpiary-mind they were . . . a bit uppity. Not too uppity. The Overphyle took great care to remind them just who the masters were.

Now the humans, on the other hand, could be relatively sharp and incorrigibly disobedient as individuals, and yet were as stupid—if not more stupid, than individual Magh' when they attempted to act together. What did they call it? Mob intelligence. An interesting datum. A contradiction in terms. A shame the humans were unreliable. They were better chelate-scrapers than this purpose-bred Magh'. But implants would fix that, if the Overphyle decided any were worth keeping.

Appetite stirred in the Expediter. Changing sex involved considerable energy expenditure. Well. Chemical exudates might have stopped the Magh' eating the Overphyle . . . darts leapt from her tubes and ripped into the joints-space of the scraper's chela. Nothing stopped the Overphyle eating Magh'.

The creature twitched briefly and was still. Overphyle toxins were singularly effective on Magh'. The onset of paralysis was rapid. That was good. The digested protein always tasted better when the animal wasn't entirely dead. The Expediter retracted the barbs, pulled the harpoons back, then humped out of the recliner, dripping. She clambered over the victim. The victim was too stupid to understand more than pain, but the group-mind would know that a tiny piece of itself was being ingested. Know, and feel, and remember just who the master was.

The seven-sided mouthparts spiraled open. The Expediter poured her inverted stomach out of her mouth . . . and in through the harpoon hole into the faintly twitching victim, oozing her stomach into the narrow gap. Then, in the delicious half-digested soup inside the Magh' shell she began to secrete more enzymes, and feed. The Expediter felt herself relaxing. So what if the Magh' made poor chelate-scrapers? It was good to be back among proper subjects. And there was nothing like the feeling of a good meal outside your stomach to make you feel truly at home.

Chapter 13:
They also serve who only jump and wait.

The telephone jangled Conrad Fitzhugh's concentration. Preparing this report and these analyses was a thankless, fruitless task. Conrad still tried to turn in something he could be proud of, even if that mindless jerk Carrot-up would probably refuse to read it. Conrad had had no formal training for this. Before the war he'd been nothing but a relatively spoiled son of a Shareholder, with a penchant for danger-sports. Yes, his parents were unusual, in that Conrad's father's fortune owed far more to business acumen than to the modest size of his shareholding. But otherwise Conrad had not been that atypical. Now he wished he knew more about data analysis. The phone rang again. He ignored it.

Dammit. There's something going on here. Sector Delta 355 . . .

The phone rang again.

"Answer it, Simms."

There was no reply, except another ring of the telephone. Fitzhugh remembered that Corporal Simms was out at satellite tracking, collecting pictures. Sattrac refused to send it electronically. He was alone in the dank office. Even Ariel was out foraging somewhere. She couldn't sit still for too long. Irritated, Fitz snatched the instrument from the cradle.

"Intelligence," he snapped.

A gargantuan laugh came down the line. "Were you on the job, my boykie, that you took such a long time to answer?" The voice could have done a fair double as a foghorn.

Fitz's frown slipped. A smile actually began to ease through. "Bobby, you dumb bastard. You haven't bounced yet?"

"So long as I don't let you pack my 'chute again, I'll be all right," rumbled Major Robert Van Klomp of the 1st HAR Airborne. "Listen, *boeta*, I've got a big favor to ask. If I have to do one more damn 'display-jump' I'm going to go mad and bite somebody's balls off. I begged and kissed ass to get this unit formed. Sure, I've only got one-fifth of the men I was promised, but I've trained them into a halfway decent strike group. Maybe they've even got a bit more backbone than a bowl of herrings."

Fitz knew this translated as enormous pride. Bobby had pushed those men to the limit of his own gorilla-like endurance. The paratroopers were as tough as you could make soldiers without putting them under fire. The parachute major thought the world of them. But Van Klomp would never say that.

The parachute major sighed. "So what do we do,

Fitzy? We jump out of airplanes or helicopters at parades. Five-way linkups with pretty colored smoke for the Korozhet observers. I'm fucking sick of it, and so are my boys."

Fitz snorted. "And what do you expect me to do about it, Bobby? Tell this bunch they can't have their parades? They'd shit themselves. That's the purpose of war! Anyway, the best I could do for you is to recommend you go on doing a parade a day and never see active service. That's how well General Cartup-Kreutzler listens to my recommendations."

"*Ja*. I wondered how well you'd fit in there. But I don't need your general, Boykie. Just a set of orders from someone you've managed to bully."

It was Fitz's turn to sigh. "I'll try, Bobby. But I've blotted my copybook here already. And after last time, Carrot-up has circulated a memo to all Headquarters staff. 'In future any action recommended on the basis of intelligence reports is to be coordinated through his office and signed by his high-and-mighty self.' "

"So what are you still doing there, Boykie?" demanded Van Klomp.

"I don't know, old friend. I really don't know."

Chapter 14:
There's got to be a morning after.

The radio crackled. "*The getaway vehicle has been spotted on satellite photographs at the Shaw Plantation, which is now in enemy hands. In the opinion of the Chief of Police, Ben Hudrum, the kidnappers made a severe misjudgement in their choice of hideout. Now we cut to Doctor Victor T. Slade, an expert in Criminal Psychology at the Sydney and Beatrice Webb College for his comments on the choice of hiding place. Dr. Slade, in your opinion . . .*"

"I'm damned if I know why you listen to that Company propaganda rubbish, Chip," said Bronstein. The bat had fluttered silently up to where Chip was sitting against the wall, toasting his balls in the morning sun, and thinking wishfully about coffee while listening to his cheap portable radio.

Chip snapped the droning hot-airhead off. "Dunno

myself, Bronstein. For the music, I guess. And to remind me that there is a world and other people out there. Looking out from here you could forget that there was another life, where we could be huddled in trenches. Beautiful this. Tranquility in desolation." The farmhouse was on a hilltop. The morning mist, still hanging below them, was kind to the war-shattered and bare-foraged lands. The Maggot tunnel-mounds were red and sharp and clear above the mist-sea.

Bronstein looked. "You're a human of hidden depths, Connolly. Unexpected. I always thought you were little more than a two-legged rat. . . . Anyway, now that you've eaten and slept, come and look at what we've found." Bronstein flew off.

Chip followed. The bat led him to a large shed some distance away from the smart facade of the tasting hall and the winery. The shed must have once been hidden behind the farmhouse. Obviously out of the public eye, it was as utilitarian and plain as the other buildings were ornate. The "Public-eye" buildings must have had wooden doors that the Maggots had taken away. This had ordinary corrugated iron ones, pop riveted onto a steel frame.

"You'll have to break the lock," said Bronstein

It was a sturdy, workmanlike padlock, attached to a chain that passed through the doors.

Chip looked at it and shook his head. "I could do it, if I had two trench knives." There wasn't a grunt alive who hadn't broken a padlock or two like that. People were forever losing their keys, aside from anything else. He rattled the doors. They were neatly made and fitted tightly.

"We got in through the eaves. But you're too big. Let me go and see what I can find." The bat flew up, wriggled through a narrow gap between the roof and the wall, and disappeared. In the meanwhile Chip looked around. There was a diesel tank up on a stand. A pile of bricks and piece of rusting tarpaulin-covered machinery beneath a lean-to. Chip shook the doors again, wondering if he could lift them off their hinges.

Bronstein reappeared, just as Melene came around the corner. The rat-girl was plainly suffering from a hangover. "Will you stop rattling those things," she said, irritably.

"To be sure. Stop rattling and start sawing, Connolly." Bronstein had a hacksaw blade, a shiny new hacksaw blade, in her claws.

It was a substantial lock. Chip looked at the blade. Then at the thickness of the hasp. "Bronstein, this had better not be your idea of joke."

The bat showed her fangs. "Just get to work, Connolly!"

Chip started sawing. "Flying foxes are considered good eating," he said, dryly.

Melene took a seat and shook her head. "Bronstein would give *anyone* indigestion. She's guaranteed to disagree with you. Besides, they're only part flying fox. Can't you saw a bit more quietly? That squeak is making my ears curl."

"Why don't you just go away?" grumped Chip.

"What, and have to listen to this thumping in my head on my own?" The rat smiled cheekily at him. "Anyway, I'm curious."

Chip had a distinct weakness for Melene. "Curiosity killed the rat." He felt the blade and pulled his hand away hastily. "Shit! This thing is hot."

Melene chuckled. "As the actress said to the bishop . . ."

"What?

She winked. "Get on with it."

"Take the other side then." The rat shrugged her shoulders and did.

They sawed away. At least Chip sawed, with the rat steadying the blade. Rat-paws were lousy for any work that required dexterity. Still, the cut went faster. "We should be able to snap it now," said Chip, flexing aching fingers.

Of course they couldn't, but did it at the next try. The metal doors swung open.

Aladdin's cave could not have been more full of treasures.

It was the farm workshop, and included all the essentials of a *good* farm workshop. It had everything from the really important dark, oily tins of mysterious miscellaneous bolts and bits, to unused, shiny-new workshop manuals. There were several coils of the most essential of farm-mechanics' equipment, used to fix everything from wristwatches to combine harvesters: eight-gauge wire. There were two engines in various states of disrepair. There was a cutting torch, an arc welding unit and enough scrap metal to justify a slowship shipment back to Japan on Old Earth. The bits ranged from rusty sections of reinforcing rod to the inevitable pieces of expensive stainless steel mesh, cut-to-measure, just slightly wrong.

There was a whole wall devoted to tools, complete with hooks and spray-painted patterns. One or two of the tools were even still on the hooks. The rest, of course, were in their natural place . . . in a wide radius around a dinky little vineyard tractor. The teensy narrow tractor must have been someone's pride and joy. It was probably the main working tool of the farm and even had a little hydraulic blade. The left front wheel was off, but otherwise the tools seemed to have been engaged in putting it back together. Quite a lot of fresh eight-gauge wire had obviously just been judiciously applied.

"There. Next to that stack of fertilizer. There's a whole load of rope!"

Well. It was rope all right. Typical farm rope. Not exactly the right stuff for a budding mountaineer, and not particularly light or oil free. But there certainly was plenty of it. About a thousand feet, at a guess, in various untidy coils. "Well, gee, Bronstein. Now that's really worth the blister I got cutting my way in here. Now, if I just take that crop-sprayer tank off the trailer, I can carry it all."

There was an audible sound of clicking teeth from Bronstein. "Then it is without it you can damn well do! Useless, ungrateful human. If you don't want my help, don't ask me for it!"

Chip sighed. "Sorry. I was out of line. Look, I appreciate the rope. We'll even find some we can use. And we'll use some of the metal junk for anchors. It was just . . . well, I was working it out. We found a little food. We've got . . . oh, say enough for a week with the rats on rations. Did you see how many tunnel-mounds we've got to scale?"

The bat nodded. "To be sure. I counted them. Thirty-two."

Chip grimaced. Felt his bristly chin. "In a week?"

"Ha." Melene appeared from behind a pile of metal junk. "First you're going to have to persuade Fal and the others to move. They think they've died and gone to heaven. Except for the food, of course."

Chip couldn't help smiling. "What's wrong with the food, Mel?"

"Well, no insult, Chip. It can be eaten, yes. But it isn't a good plate of curried pigs' tripes."

Chip bowed his head, humbly. "Alas. It isn't. We'll have to go looking for pigs. Mind you, I thought you rats were doing a fine imitation."

Mel took him seriously. "Well, I was thinking we

should at least go and scout for some ordinary provender. Use this place as a base. We're bound to find some stuff. Stock up, equip ourselves and be in a decent shape to make a long, fast bolt."

"To be sure, that was what I myself was going to suggest." Bronstein was plainly impressed.

"You bats aren't the only ones who can come up with a bit of elementary strategy," said Melene loftily, rat-nose in the air.

"Ah. But we are the only ones who *do*."

"What! Go out foraging? But we just found all this prog!" Pistol had a bottle in one hand; in the other, a three cracker Dagwood of anchovies, quail eggs, pickled onions and caviar with marmalade. Plain to see, he was not keen to move.

"I'd liefer put ratsbane in my mouth," agreed Fal. "Pass that salad dressing, when you've finished hogging it, Nym. I shall try some with fish-oil soaked buckshot. It might make it edible."

Chip had to resort to bribery. "Curried pigs' tripes."

The rats sighed in unison. "Now, I'd go foraging for *that*," said Fal.

"Well, the shop here is closed, you gluttons." Chip started gathering crackers, jars, cans and bottles. He realized just how big a dent in the supplies the rats had already made. "So you might as well go foraging for that."

"Says you and who?" demanded Pistol, his one eye gleaming dangerously, as he clung to a pickle jar.

Eamon had fluttered over. "Says me. Never mind anybody else. Just me. Want to make something of it?"

Red-tipped rat teeth flashed at him, but Pistol parted with his pickle jar. "Don't like gherkins much anyway."

Chip took the jar. "Sleep. We're all short of it. This

afternoon I'll provide a *frugal* meal and we can go out scavenging in earnest."

"Not too frugal, I hope?" said the smallest rat-girl.

Chip grinned. "We've got to make it last, Melene."

Pistol eyed her and grinned toothily. "Eh, my pretty little rat-maid from school. We can't eat, but we can drink and do other things. We can make that last too."

"You should have hung onto one of those little cocktail gherkins, Pistol. You'd have been so much better equipped."

Chip spent a couple of hours in sleep, and a couple of hours fossicking about in the workshop. He was surprised to find Nym there too. "Got a liking for mechanical devices," the big rat admitted. "I know it is not very ratly, but they fascinate me."

It was he who clambered up on the tractor and, while fiddling around, gave the key a twitch. The engine actually burped and gave a bit of a grumble. The rat was already out of the door. . . . The nose came back first, timidly whiffling around the door. Then Nym followed it back, doing his best imitation of casualness. "Gave me a slight start, that," he admitted.

"And how fast can you move when you get a real fright?"

"Methinks you should consider that I'm at about the right height to bite one of your balls off," growled Nym, walking a bit closer to where Chip sat. "So what happened?"

"You turned the key. The motor nearly started. The battery is probably flat, and that was the last bit of juice in it."

"So why don't we blow up the battery, pour some more juice into it and start it up?" The rat was bright-eyed at the prospect.

"You don't know one hell of a lot about these mechanical things that fascinate you, do you, Nym?"

"Give me a break, Connolly. Four months ago, I woke up with all sorts of things inside my head and boot camp to get through. I've been in the trenches since then, and from before that I sort of remember a big cage with a lot of other rats."

Chip swallowed. It was a longer speech than he'd ever heard Nym make in the whole month they'd served together. He'd never really thought about where the rats came from. "Um. Didn't think. But it doesn't work quite like that."

"So how does it work?" Nym asked eagerly.

"Jeez. I dunno. I was a trainee sous-chef, Nym. Not a mechanic or a farmer. Big Dermott could have told you." That last just slipped out. He had been very carefully trying to avoid thinking about her since they'd arrived at this farm. She would have loved the workshop.

He turned away. The rat wouldn't understand and he didn't want him to see.

"She was a good kid, that," the big rat said quietly, which showed Chip how wrong he could be about rats too.

"Yeah." His voice was a bit thick. He fumbled blindly through one of the cupboards. Nym discovered other things to poke and pry at. Chip found himself staring blankly at a packet. "The Wonder flexible emery-wire saw." For no good reason he thrust it into his pocket. "I'm going out to get some air. Don't do anything dangerous, rat."

"Go and have a drink, Connolly."

"You think that's the answer to everything, don't you, rat?" Chip was suddenly bitterly angry.

Nym shrugged. "Nah. But 'tis the sort of answer a good rat would give. And I don't know what else to say."

Once again Chip was embarrassed at how wrong he had been. Considering that Nym's intelligence stemmed from a piece of plastic-like stuff the size of a lentil, and that the rat had only that and a few months of life experience, the rat was remarkably humane . . . and remarkably human.

In the gathering dusk the foragers went out, following their keen noses. Well, Chip blundered around. For what his effort was worth, he might as well have stayed back at the ruined farmhouse. By comparison to the natural equipment of the bats and rats, even his sensitive chef's nose and surgically enhanced eyes were feeble.

After they'd wandered through the debatable lands an hour in the dark, a thunderous eruption roared just next to his ear. Chip dived for cover.

Eamon had the grace to sound embarrassed. "Sorry. 'Tis that bedamned bottled sauerkraut."

Chip stood up. The bats had taken to the pickled cabbage in big way. "I've come to tell you that we've found the smell of much food," said Eamon.

"With luck there won't be any more ruddy sauerkraut," Chip muttered. He sighed. They would not just come and inform him for fun, or out of politeness. "Where? Is it far? Must I come and carry?"

"You must come to council," said the big bat sententiously. "We need to talk."

Now Chip's suspicions were truly aroused. "Why?"

"Because it is inside the Maggot tunnels."

Chapter 15:
The great pantry raid.

"So . . . you say somewhere down inside there, there is lots of food." Chip pointed to the tiny aperture, about a finger-width in size in the side of the Magh' mound. It looked like a black speck in the moonlight. Chip put his nose to it. It had the typical Maggot-tunnel fungus-and-hint-of-Gorgonzola whiff. He was damned if he could smell anything exceptional about it. "You're sure?"

Fal raised his eyes heavenward. "Your nose is not worth a gooseberry, Chip! If it were written in ten-foot neon letters, it couldn't be clearer. Some of it is spoiled. Down there lies the Maggot's pantry."

Chip shrugged. "So. What are we going to do about it? I'd say that in there it is out of our reach."

Eamon spread his wings. "If we could get in, we could fly down, raid their store and be away, with the Maggots none the wiser. We bats are the quietest of fliers. We can drift in, silent as autumn leaves."

"Unsmelt by any Maggot," said Chip, waving his hand in front of his nose. "Phew, are you rats sure that 'spoiled' bouquet is coming from down *that* hole? If you ask me, it's the inside of Eamon that has gone bad."

"Um. That was me, actually," Bronstein admitted quietly, in the reluctant voice of the inherently truthful. "That is one of the reasons we need other food."

Chip wrinkled his nose. "Best reason I've come across yet. Mind you, I still think you're crazy. Listen, you'll be caught for certain."

"Indade, *you* would be caught," said Eamon, dripping scorn.

"We know it is risky. To be sure, otherwise we'd just have done it." Bronstein's tone was more conciliatory.

"Ha. Methinks they just called you because they couldn't work out how to get in through the mound-wall," said Doll, "otherwise they'd have just gone ahead, instead of telling you about it."

There was a brief, embarrassed silence.

"No!" and "Never!" said two bats with equal insincerity.

"Oh well, in that case," said Chip, "as you don't need anything from me, besides help in your decision, I say 'do it.' Don't let me stop you. Now, can I go back to the farmhouse?"

There was a longer silence, finally broken by Bronstein. "Damn you, loudmouth rat!" She flapped her wings with irritation. Then, sighing: "All right, Chip, how do we get in?"

"Well . . ." Chip looked at the wall. Tapped it. It was brick hard. He breathed in deeply. Stuck his hands into his pockets. Encountered something. Pulled out the packet he'd thrust into his pocket in the workshop, earlier. "As it happens I have just the thing here. Unfortunately, I'm going to need to go back to the workshop and fetch a drill and a piece of wire."

Among the many, many things which Chip had always wanted and known he'd never get around to owning was an electric screwdriver. He'd spotted one, back at the workshop, as well as a little case of ninety-six "useful" bits for it. Of course the only two really useful ones were missing, but obviously the mechanic had had little use for drill bits. Those were still all there.

With those and a piece of wire, Chip came striding back. He'd show them.

The battery pack of the neat little cordless screwdriver lasted about thirty seconds. He cursed. Fortunately—so to speak—the dinky gadget could be reset for manual operation. The drill struggled to bite into the hard Magh' adobe. It wasn't brick or concrete, but it was as hard as hardwood. Chip went on drilling and swearing in darkness. Eventually he got through. Then he did it again.

"What is takin' you forever, begorra!" demanded O'Niel, eventually.

"I've bent a curve in this wire, attached this emery-wire. I've pushed it through from this side. Now I'm trying to get it back." Chip spoke through gritted teeth. Being manually dexterous was supposed to be what humans did well.

"Indade? So why is it taking so long?" Eamon was dancing with impatience.

"Because I can't see the goddamn other hole," answered Chip tersely.

"I' faith, you should ask fat Fal to help. With that great girth of his it's been years since he's been able to see the hole," grinned Doll wickedly.

Just then the wire encountered the hole. "Ah! Here it comes."

Mel cocked her head sideways. "Funny, isn't that just about what Fal says too, eh, Doll?"

There were two little lead balls on the ends of the flexible saw. Handles keyed over these. Chip clipped them in and began pulling the saw to-and-fro. The saw positively hissed through the Magh' adobe. Then Chip had to push the wire through the other hole. Saw, saw and then again. Soon he was able to hook a neat triangular little "door" out of the Maggot-mound wall.

When Chip finally had the piece out, he took a long, careful look it. Then he did a spot of swearing. He could see now why he'd struggled so with the drilling. The convenient indents on the surface, which had stopped the drill bit slipping around, marked the solid struts in the hollow-block material. He'd chosen to drill six inches instead of one inch, then an air space, and then another inch. Still, it could have been worse. There was a foot-thick stanchion next to one of the holes.

Well, it was no use crying over wasted energy. Chip bowed, flexing his tired hands. He pointed at the hole with an elbow. "There you go, *messieurs et madames*. Be pleased to *entair*."

"Who ate madames?" asked Fal, ever hopeful.

"I dunno. Wasn't me. Must have been the bats. Do you think that's what giving them such gas?"

The bats fluttered down into the hole, from which Maggot-lumifungus cast a wan light. Chip rigged a string onto the little door of Magh' adobe, and replaced the triangular piece. The bats would knock to come out, and the keen-eared rats would remain on standby to listen for them.

They waited in the darkness. After a while even the rats' banter died away. Chip decided he'd rather take risks than wait while others took them. A lousy attitude for a soldier, but his own. Anything was better than this waiting.

The silence and darkness grew more and more oppressive. Time dragged. Finally, Fal said what was on everybody's minds. "They've been caught."

Doc assumed his favorite professorial pose and spoke in a doom-laden voice. "Lost in the tunnels. Fated to wander for ever and ever . . ."

Knock-knock.

Chip pulled open the door.

The bats emerged . . . sans food.

"What the hell kept you?" demanded Chip and the rats in unison.

" 'Tis a foine welcome back, indade," said O'Niel, clinging tiredly to the mound-wall.

Chip counted bat heads. All present and correct. "Where's the food?"

"We couldn't find it. 'Tis a long way down, and that whole level smells of it. We found spoiled stuff being shovelled into Maggot fungus beds."

Fal voiced the general rat disapproval. "Your noses could not smell their way to a privy. We'll have to do it for you."

"For once, rat, I'd say try it, and welcome. It's a maze down there," said Bronstein, tiredly. "But how do you think you'll get down? The Maggots are chewing rock down there, it's so deep."

For once Pistol came up with the answer. "We could abseil."

"What?" The bat looked at him as if he was a talking brick.

Pistol shook his head pityingly. "Abseil. Rappel. Slide down a sodding rope. Don't you bats know anything?"

Chip knew what they were talking about. He remembered with shuddering horror having to do that on the two-day "adventure experience" Company school had sent them to. The "adventure center" had been controlled by a major Shareholder, so of course it had been a part of their curriculum. The expense was naturally charged to a vatbrat's account for later repayment. Since it was considered a "luxury," the charge had been steep, too.

Hell's teeth, Chip thought gloomily. That had been a foretaste of the army if there ever was one. "Do you rats know how to do that?" he asked.

"O' course," said Nym. "Part of basic training. Buggered if I know why."

Pistol nodded. "Yeah. Like most of the rest of boot camp. Dafter than bat-logic."

"Be watching your tongue, rat!" snapped Eamon. The big bat bared his fangs for an instant. Then, his temper easing: "Not that I can't but agree with you about the craziness of that institution called 'boot camp.' But don't call it bat-logic. 'Tis an affront to our intelligence."

"What are you going to use to abseil down?" Privately Chip agreed with them about boot camp. In this army the surest ticket out of active service was to be an instructor, and the best way to be sure you stayed one of those was to be a brainless sadistic asshole. That was what the Powers-That-Be, who didn't know combat from a hole in the ground, expected of an instructor. Discipline! That was the thing. But if they got onto the subject they'd be here all night. Best to move along, even if he'd like to ask if they'd also had to brush the hairs on their blankets. It was vital to military skill that the left-hand side of the blanket's hairs faced left, and the right-hand ones right. How could one defeat the enemy otherwise? And starching and ironing of the corners of the bed to knife-edge creases was of course essential. That meant you quickly learned to sleep under your bed, rolled in a spare blanket, which made sleeping in the mud in the trenches quite homelike.

"There's a big spool of braided nylon back at the workshop," said Nym. "Methinks it wouldn't support you, Chip, but it'll be fine for us. There is nylon webbing the farmers must have used for tying down loads. We can make harnesses out of that. There is plenty of chain. We can contrive harness links and descendures out of that. Piece of cake. Now, tell me, did they also make you humans do all that stupid marching stuff?"

"Yep. And you?" Chip couldn't imagine rats marching while some company drill sergeant bellowed.

Fal laughed. "Hah. Tell you about it as we go back. The drill sergeant's father was a bachelor. We used to have to march with our tails straight. Do you know what that does to your balance?"

It was Eamon's turn to laugh. "Hah! Soft you had it, indade. We use to have to march too. Sheer insanity! 'Swing those wings!' I can hear still the loudmouth shouting it."

"I believe both the logic behind it, and the methods used, to be ridiculously archaic. Rooted in formation combat. In terms of phenomenology, a classic confusion between self-certainty and Reason."

Doc, as usual, silenced them all for a while.

Then Bronstein continued. "To be sure, 'tis a system which is all well and good for incompetent fighters, like most of your species, Chip. It makes mediocre fighters of the bad. But to try and teach hunting creatures like us to fight like clockwork-men, is a sure waste of talent. It assumes the enemy will fight like clockwork too."

O'Niel snorted. "And that's like these foine 'battle plans.' They nivver survive a moment's real battle. And why for should hand-to-hand combat be any different?"

"Oh, but we cannot make as many holes in an enemy's battle as in a woman's petticoat. *That* would take intelligence." Sarcasm was definitely Phylla's strong point.

"*Military* intelligence?" demanded Chip. "Don't make me laugh!" There was the conscript's love of the army in his voice.

Phylla laughed. "Ha ha. The fool who taught us to abseil made one intelligent statement."

Chip's curiosity was aroused. "And what was that?"

"He promised us we would hate him. And we did. I believe he lived."

"Hey, Chip! Remember you said you charged for giving a rat a lift?" prompted Melene.

"Yeah."

"Well, would you take payment in kind? My feet are killing me," said the rat-girl.

Pistol whistled. "Woo-hoo! You got a roll of sticky tape, Chip?"

"You rats are really disgusting," said Siobhan, and fluttered off, before she had to listen to more.

The cord was discovered. Generously, the rats allowed Chip to saw the chain links from which they made up descendures. They tied their own webbing-sling harnesses, and told Chip he'd be fortunate enough to be allowed to haul them back up. As even fat Fal plus his wobbly paunch weighed only a few pounds that was plausible. With a piece of angle iron to brace across the hole, and an empty woven-plastic fertilizer bag for loot, they went back to the hole. A bat took the line down, as it would not be a straight abseil.

"Go carefully," said Chip to Nym.

"Oh, certainly. We shall steal upon them with catlike tread." The rat promptly fell over the angle iron and nearly disappeared down the hole, without being attached to the rope. He landed next to the edge with a thump.

"A fly's footfall would be twice as loud," said Phylla, dryly.

"Don't worry. We're just swapping soldiery for burglaree," said Fal. "Seeing as you disapprove of us doing soldiery properly."

One by one, the rats untied the rope, threaded their homemade descendures—because snap links were beyond Chip's limited skill as a machinist—retied the rope, and stepped through the small doorway. Then they were gone, down into the Maggot-mound.

Chip was left sitting alone in the darkness again. He liked it even less this time.

Chapter 16:
A brave caballero!

Bronstein was glad to have the rats along. She would never have admitted it out loud, of course. There were a number of places where the bats had had to alight and wriggle through a gap. The lead rat at the first of these paused, wrinkled her nose, and said: "Over there." They pulled the rope up and moved it across to a far wider adit. This brought them to a wholly different level where even the bats could have found the fresh food. Unlike the bats, the rats worried not at all about the mazelike nature of the place. They could smell where they'd been and also how long ago. In addition they seemed to have a sense of direction the bats could not match.

They also had the gift of nearly walking into sleeping Maggots. The hours between midnight and early morning appeared to be "quiet-time" in the tunnels.

A Maggot would just stop right where it was and catch some shut-eye.

"Back," whispered Eamon, shooing the rats with his wings. "There is another Maggot."

"This place must be fairly crawling with them when they're up and about. This burglaring lark isn't as easy as a-lying in the sun," whispered Fal. "But I'll admit you bats make fine brothers in filching," he added, to Eamon's chagrin.

Finally they came to a long chamber. There was yet another Maggot asleep at the partially sealed mouth of it. "There is good stuff in there," whispered Melene, hunger in her voice, her long nose twitching.

"To be sure," Bronstein said. "There is also a Maggot in the way."

"We could fly over it?" ventured Behan.

"Risky," vetoed Bronstein. "What's left of that entry is particularly narrow."

Siobhan nodded. "But the echo beyond it says the chamber behind is huge."

The fat rat grinned. "Let's go as far as we can from the Maggot and make a rat-hole."

To Bronstein's over-tense ears the digging rat was making more noise than a cross between a steam shovel and an oompah-band. Still, no Maggots had arrived on the scene yet.

"Make it a decent size," whispered Fal, "we'll have to get the food out."

Mel snorted. "Not to mention you in."

Eamon fluttered back. "Be keeping the noise down, you fools," he hissed.

Melene, from inside the hole said, "There is a waxy layer here now. Easy to get through."

"Come out." Nym hauled at her tail. "Methinks we

should make the hole through the hard stuff wider first."

Bronstein's patience was sore tried by now. "Move it up, rats."

Pistol lifted his long nose at her. "If you can dig faster yourself, come and do it. Otherwise, shog off."

She snarled. "If I bite your tail, you'll dig faster."

"Bullying witch," grumbled Pistol, nibbling at the hole edge.

"We're through!" said Nym. "Keep guard. Come on, rats."

The rats bundled through the hole, the smell of foodstuff beyond drawing them on as if they were on a string. Warily, watchfully, Bronstein checked out the passage. It would be just their luck to have some Maggot trot along now. She was totally and utterly unprepared for the shriek of pure fury from *inside* the hole.

"What the devil!?" she said, and then began issuing orders. "Go for the Maggot on the far side, Eamon, Siobhan—and you, Behan! You stay here, O'Niel. I'll get in there!"

Bronstein struggled through the hole. She was not designed for creeping and crawling, but whatever monster was in there sounded far bigger than a handful of rats could handle alone.

The creature standing on top of the pile of looted human foodstuffs could only be described as large of eyes and voice. The animal and its red frogged waistcoat would have fitted into a big human soup mug. But could it *bellow*! Right now it appeared to be virtually incoherent with rage.

"HOW DARE YOU!? THIEVES! BANDITS! MURDERERS! DESPOILERS OF THE INNOCENT!

LOOTERS! I'LL HAVE YOU ALL SHOT, DRAWN, QUARTERED, CRUCIFIED AND HORSEWHIPPED!"

"Shut *up*!" hissed Bronstein.

Doc shook his head. "It won't listen. Not even to epistemological discourse."

"It'll listen to *me*, all right." Bronstein couldn't understand why the Maggot at the proper entrance hadn't arrived. Perhaps Eamon & Co. had nailed it. Still, she wasn't going to take any chances.

"*WHY HAVE YOU TAKEN SO LONG TO GET HERE? AND NOW YOU DARE TO STOP FOR LOOTING! HOW DARE YOU?*" The volume that the creature could muster would, *must* call the Maggots down on them.

Bronstein took to her wings. As she swooped down on the noisy little thing, it leaped away. It was faster than she was, and that leap had taken it a good fifteen yards.

It stood up on its hind legs, blew her a raspberry and then roared at her. She'd heard less noise coming out of a drill sergeant.

"*WHAT HAS TAKEN YOU STUPID, USELESS SOLDIERS SO LONG?! MY VERY IMPORTANT AND WONDERFUL MISTRESS IS QUITE SICK WITH WORRY—AND YOU ARE PLAYING AROUND, LOOTING! SANTA MARIA! SANTA THERESA! IS THERE NOT ONE REAL MALE AMONG YOU? NOT ONE HERO? MUST I DO IT ALL MYSELF?*"

Melene applauded. "He's dead sexy, isn't he?"

"He'll be dead, never mind sexy, if I catch him," said Pistol grimly, mounting the pile of boxes.

"And so *masculine*," said Phylla, lasciviously.

"Handsome *and* well hung, into the bargain." Doll licked her rat-lips and leered at the little primate.

"Effing Hell! *I'm* going to hang him, if he doesn't

shut up." Fal began heaving himself up a clumsy stack of bales. "Come on, Nym. You take the right-hand side."

Bronstein tried again. She'd give him "macho" when she caught him!

The galago easily evaded the bat, and chittered mockingly at her from a pile of grain sacks that would have fed half a regiment. It opened its mouth to start bellowing again.

"Will you be shutting *up* in here? There are about fifty Maggots coming this way!" Eamon shouted from where he was trying to squeeze through the rat-hole.

The little creature paused in its bellowing, and seemed to consider this news. Then, in a hiss: "Only if you will agree to go and rescue my mistress. And take me to your human-in-charge!"

The galago bounded away from Bronstein, and clung to the tiny knobbles on the wall with seeming ease. He was now out of reach of the rats. His long-fingered black hands were plainly very strong. They were surprisingly humanlike, those hands. "I will shout really loudly, really REALLY loudly, if you do not agree."

"All *right*!" said Bronstein. "Just *shut up*."

"Do you promise?" demanded the galago.

"Yes. I promise. Now keep quiet! Eamon, did you kill that Maggot at the entry? Are they coming because of that?"

Eamon struggled the rest of the way through the hole. "No, indade, it had finished its job and gone before we got there. But the Maggots seem to be waking up. Now hush!"

They waited. Then Siobhan said, through the hole: "All clear. But we must be going. Quickly now! The Maggots are getting going."

Bronstein nodded. "To be sure. Come, put some of those boxes in that bag. Take some of those concentrate bars, all of you. You too, little creature."

The little creature raised itself up. "I am not your 'little creature'! *I* am a galago, *and* I am a hidalgo. Treat me with respect, I warn you!"

Bronstein did not take to this. "I don't care what or who you are. Carry food or go hungry."

"I am no beast of burden," sneered the galago.

Bronstein gave him a look that promised plain and fancy murder. Later. "You're a big mouth and a small brain. Carry food. We don't have any to spare."

"Yeah, and we girls would hate you to lose your sexy figure," said Doll, lowering her lashes. "You might need *all* your strength."

"And *lots* of stamina," added Phylla, winking.

"That tail of his is just too, too *gorgeous*!" Melene hugged herself, quivering.

"And those dreamy bedroom eyes!" husked Phylla throatily. "Wow!"

The male rats were not enjoying this. Not even one tiny bit. The galago, on the other hand, was strutting his stuff. He was also gathering provisions.

Of course, Doll was the first to make a move. "So what is your name, handsome? Heedalgo-go?"

The galago took Doll's paw and bowed over it with an extravagant flourish of his long fluffy tail, before kissing it delicately. "*You* may call me Don Juan, *señorita*. My name is Don Juan el Magnifico de Gigantico de Immaculata Concepcion y Major de Todos Saavedra Quixote de la Mancha."

"Ooh! I don't think I'll ever wash this paw again!" Doll said breathlessly.

Melene looked on with longing. "Ooh! He fair makes my insides turn to jelly! *So* romantic!"

"Huh. I'll turn *him* into jelly. Effing cream puff," muttered Pistol.

✧ ✧ ✧

As best they could, the rats hid their hole. Then they had to lug several bags of looted food back through the waking corridors of the Maggot-mound. It was no sinecure.

"You've overfilled this thing," Fal moaned.

Nym grunted. "Well, we can't exactly pour some out here, can we?"

"Why not?" Fal was ready to suit action to the words.

Nym tapped Fal's head with his tail. "Why not just leave a signpost for the Maggots, smooth-pate? Anyway you'll be the one complaining that you cannot compass the waste."

Fal shook his head and tried to wrap his tail around his bulging belly. "I cannot even compass my own waist, but with this sweating I am forced to do, I'm fain to be melting away."

"You've got a fair bit go still, Fal. Umph. And you're letting your corner down," said Nym.

"Hey you, whatsisname . . . Don Gigolo, come give us a hand," said Fal, ever hopeful.

A bat fluttered up. "Back. There are Maggots coming. Quickly, fools!"

They hid. Scampered. Hid again. Dodged off down a new passage. And finally reached the down-rope.

"What is this?" The galago eyed the rope with suspicion.

"The effing way out, Don Gigolo." Fat Fal might have sounded grimmer than usual because he did not fancy it. Or perhaps he was just tired.

The tiny galago strutted into Fal's personal space. "If you call me that again, I warn you, I shall challenge you to a duel."

"I'm shakin'. I'm shakin'. Oh, Pistol, I'm tho thcared, big bad Don Gigolo will prong me."

The galago was beside himself with fury. "Name your seconds, sir!"

"You leave Don Juan alone. You bunch of big bullies. Don't pay any attention to them, DonJee, sweetie." Doll took him gently by the arm, showing Fal her teeth.

"Will you be stopping this tomfoolery and tie those bags on so Chip can haul them up," hissed Eamon, "before I bite all of you. He's still got to haul you up."

The galago paused. "Who is 'Chip'?"

"He's the human member of this circus," replied Bronstein.

"There is a human up there? Then I will go. My mission, she brooks no delay. *I* am a galago of action." The little primate saluted the cluster of rat-girls and began to climb the rope with consummate ease.

Phylla sighed. "He's sooo masterful!"

Nym shook his head. "He's a complete ass."

Bronstein rolled her eyes. "Siobhan, fly up and tell the silly creature not to go out past the last level. Chip's not expecting him. Chip'll probably turf him down again if he suddenly appears. Now, let's get these bags tied on."

"We could have used the bigmouth. His hands are better for this sort of thing than my paws are."

False dawn had faded the stars. Chip was a very nervous man by now. He couldn't leave his post, or the rats would be unable to get back up. On the other hand, Maggot constructors were already visible in the distance working on the tunnel-mound. Some of the Maggots were sightless, he knew, but some them weren't. It was getting lighter by the second, and he felt very exposed out here in the open, next to the mound. It had been a long, cold, anxious wait up here in the now disappearing darkness. The line began to thrum under his hand.

What could that be? His imagination conjured a climbing-Maggot.

His hand went to the Solingen. If he cut that line now . . . Splattermaggot. But he couldn't. What if he was wrong? He'd trap them down there. No. He'd have to deal with whatever monstrous thing was climbing as it came through the opening. He waited, nerves as tense as a cheese-slicer-wire.

The little door popped open. Chip lunged forward, knife first. He got a sudden view of cute, huge, dark eyes set in a tiny gray-white furry face. There was a squeak of terror and the face disappeared.

"Dammo!" panted Siobhan. "You daft beast. Come back! Hell! Now I shall have to chase it. And it can climb so fast. It beat me flying up here. Did you have to frighten it out of a year's growth, Chip?"

Siobhan fluttered away, back down into the mound. The three sharp tugs Chip had been awaiting came, and he began hauling. The thin line, with added weight, proved to be hell on the hands. He wrapped his jacket around them and went on slowly hauling. Next thing, the little cute-face came up again. In the improving light he could see that it was a lemur-like thing, complete with what must once have been a delicately embroidered red velvet waistcoat. It looked very, very wary. Siobhan was with it.

"See, you idiot. He's a human, not a monster."

Chapter 17:
The hero to the rescue!

"Explain," said Chip. Bronstein would have added, "and you'd better make it good," but Chip was feeling guilty. The little fellow looked more like some kid's soft toy than a problem. He'd frightened it into a wide-eyed silence because of his own nervousness. He might easily have killed it.

"You are the commander of the rescue force?" The galago sounded doubtful.

"Commander?" Chip shrugged. "Hell, we've never got around to having one of those. Bronstein is the highest ranking of us, but as a human I could claim I was in charge . . . if I was that stupid."

"Better to make it my fault, to be sure," said the bat, from where she hung on the miraculously intact crystal light-fitting in the tasting room.

"And as for being a rescue force," Fal picked his teeth, "belike what gave you that idea?"

"Indade, we're in need of being rescued, but I don't see how or why it would happen," Eamon chipped in.

The little creature's face crumpled. "You have not been sent to rescue my princess?"

Chip shook his head. "We just got ourselves trapped behind the lines in the last push. We haven't been sent to rescue anyone."

"Yeah. We'd just like to get out alive . . . Don Gigolo," said Fal, pausing in the very act of getting outside the contents of a bottle of wine.

The big eyes sparkled dangerously. "I warned you before, you fat mouse."

"Mouse?! MOUSE?! Who are you calling a mouse, you . . . you . . . whoreson caterpillar!" Fal tried to grab the galago, who leapt onto one of the wall-fittings.

"That's enough!" Chip and Bronstein bellowed in unison.

The galago didn't think so. "He insulted my honor!"

Neither did Fal. "He called me a mouse! And he's trying to seduce our girls!"

Phylla sneered. "Methinks you should grow up, Fal! We're *not* 'your girls.' " There was a very dangerous edge to her voice.

Chip sighed. "Here we are, refugees trapped in the middle of enemy territory, and you're calling each other names and fighting. Now will you both *QUIT IT*."

"In heaven's name, just don't start the little one bellowing," said Bronstein wearily. "He has a louder voice than you have."

The galago was practically hopping with fury. "Nobody calls Don Juan el Magnifico de Gigantico de Immaculata Concepcion Major de Todos y Saavedra Quixote de la Mancha a—a *gigolo*!"

"Make me stop," swaggered Fal, his paunch wobbling and his tail doing a little wave.

Chip sighed again. "If I have to, I will, Fal."

"And if he doesn't, we will," said Doll. "Hey girls?"

"And if all that fails, there is always me," added Bronstein.

"You all gang up on me," whined Fal.

"Okay, we all gang up on you," agreed Chip. "Now leave off calling him names and you—Don Whatsisname—you leave off calling fat Fal a mouse. He's an ugly rat and proud of it. Now tell us, Don, who did you think we were here to rescue?"

"But of course I thought you had come to rescue my fair princess from the durance vile and clutches of the wicked, evil Magh'. I was wrong. But, of course, now you will volunteer bravely to do it. You will become heroes!"

"Dream on," snorted Chip. "We're conscripted grunts, sunshine."

"Methinks heroes are the humans with the gold bird-dropping on their shoulders. We just want to stay alive. And out of any volunteering." Fal's nose was plainly out of joint.

"And anyway, we need no other humans," added Eamon. "The one we have is *more* than enough."

The little galago rocked on his heels, furled its mobile delicate ears, and stared at them. In quite a different voice, with a sob lurking in it, he addressed himself directly to Chip, "But surely—*señor!*—you cannot leave a beautiful girl to die? Slowly and horribly, she will die! She will die without water or food, walled up, alone, desperate, in the darkness . . ."

Chip looked at the Maggot-mound. Hell's teeth! He was no hero, damn it. Not one of these handsome devil-may-care idiots whom the Company spent like water to stop the Maggots. He was just an ordinary conscript grunt who kept a low profile and kept himself alive.

"Bugger it . . ."

"Then I will go back . . . by myself," interrupted the galago. There was both despair and determination in his voice.

"Let me finish, will you?" grumbled Chip. "I was trying to say—bugger it, I wouldn't leave a dog to die trapped down there. A . . . friend died like that. Buried." He sighed heavily. "I'll give it a go."

"You, sir, are a hidalgo! A true knight! A Siegfried!"

"I'm a sucker, never mind this Siegfried character. Or was he a sucker, too? Are you sure this girl's still alive?"

"Oh indeed. I was fetching food for her when I met your—" The galago sneered and looked down his nose at animals taller than himself. "Brave companions."

"You watch your mouth or I won't come along," snapped Nym.

"You are coming, *señor* rat? You are one of great courage!"

"Oh, we'll be there too," piped Melene. "We girls could hardly refuse to follow such a brave—and sexy—caballero."

"Are you all loons?!" Fal was incredulous. "Here we've got away, safe, and you want to go back in again and risk your lives down there?"

Phylla sniffed. "We got away with it once."

"The contentions of this frail mortality in the light of absolute . . ."

"Oh shut up," said Fal, sourly. "I suppose you're going too?"

Doc pushed his wire pince-nez back on his snout. "Yes. It is not logical, but yes."

Bronstein tapped her head with a wing-claw.

"You're all crazy. Crazy. Loony. Mad. Insane. You're rats. RATS. Rats do not volunteer, ever."

"Well, look at it this way," said Pistol, "We either go, or let that little Molly in the pooftah red jacket show us all up."

"It's a very elegant waistcoat, Pistol," said Phylla, "and you're just jealous."

"What, me?" Pistol gave her the full benefit of his eyepatch. "Jealous of a namby-pamby thing like that? Ha!"

"Well," said Chip, getting to his feet. "I never thought I'd see the day that rats were crazier than bats. What the hell." He gave Bronstein and the other bats a stiff little bow. "It's been nice knowing you guys." To the rats: "I just want to get some stuff together from the workshop before we go."

Bronstein looked amused. "To be sure, who said we weren't going with you?"

" 'Tis a foine and noble lost cause to die for!" O'Niel put in.

"Wrap the bat-wing round me, boys . . ." Siobhan quavered.

Fal turned to Eamon. "I can't stand you, and you can't stand me. I suppose we'll have to join them or I'm fated to be left here with you. But I'm going to stock up for the trip too. With brandy."

Chip stood in the workshop, checking his gear. He didn't want to admit, even to himself, that he was putting off going underground again. "Flexible saw, I've got. I'll need to cut a bigger door. Rope I've got. That'll have to do for an anchor." Chip tossed his attempt with some rusty reinforcing rod and the vise on the pile. It wasn't going to win him any prizes for practical engineering, but he might have gotten one for modern sculpture.

"I better test this idea first, though." He picked up the backpack herbicide sprayer. "I'd back off, you lot, in case the whole thing goes *whoof* along with me."

He pumped up the pressure. Gingerly, he lit Fal's zippo, held the flame up and then squeezed the trigger to his homemade flamethrower. He'd taken off the original spray pipe and replaced it with an eighteen-inch-long brass pipe, with the spray nozzle from the paint spray gun hammered into the end of it. He'd used a piece of wood to buffer the hammer, but, even so the nozzle was not quite what it used to be. It sprayed diesel rather skewly.

Nothing happened. The mist of diesel drifted back toward him . . . nothing happened. It probably wasn't atomizing the stuff finely enough. He gave up.

"We will need you to carry a couple of bags of stuff for us," said Bronstein, as Chip stared morosely at the failed flamethrower.

"Sure. What?"

"Two of those. Unless you can manage three or four." The bat pointed a wing at the bags of fertilizer.

Chip shook his head. "For what, bat? It's *fertilizer*, for crying out loud."

The bat ground her teeth audibly. "I know it is fertilizer, Connolly. It's ammonium nitrate. Don't you know *anything* about explosives?"

Chip chuckled sourly. "Sure. I'm an experienced sous-chef. If you put an unpunctured squash into a microwave, it explodes."

The bat hissed breath through its long teeth. "Listen. Just take it from me. *I* know explosives. Using our satchel-charges as detonators we can make that explode."

"You listen, and just take it from me, Bronstein. Those bags probably weigh a hundred pounds each.

I know heavy lifting. I'm not going to stagger down into the Maggot-tunnels carrying even one bag."

"Half a bag?" she asked, her voice hopeful and wheedling, hardly like Bronstein at all.

It made him feel guilty. "Half a bag split into two bags."

"Are you sure that's all you can manage? We could do so much . . ."

"Destruction. Eamon's idea of a good time." Chip turned on the rats, lounging against the tractor. "And you? Anything *you'd* like me to carry? Besides your idle selves, that is. What about that dinky little tractor to lean against? I could put that on one shoulder, and then take a stainless steel vat of wine on the other."

Fal grinned at him. "Don't take it out on us because those bats want you to hump a ton of fertilizer. Anyway, what is the use of carrying wine when we've discovered a vat of brandy? Here, try some of this."

Chip took the proffered glass of clear stuff. Took an unwary mouthful. Spayed it out, coughing. "You stupid bastards! That's lighter fuel!"

The rats seemed to find that very funny. "A bit over-proof, eh?"

"And you don't have to carry it," said Doll. "We'll carry it ourselves. Or in ourselves," she added, with a ladylike belch.

"It's probably wood alcohol," protested Chip. "Methanol. It'll make you go *blind*, for God's sake."

One-eyed Pistol replied loftily. "No use trying to keep us off the drink, Chip. Can't be done. We're good and proper rats, us."

"It's for your own good, you asses!"

Nym looked at him speculatively. "Tell you what. We need a volunteer to try the stuff out. A bat, that's the ticket! They're loons to begin with. They volunteer for everything. And they're blind as bats, anyway, so if it turns sour—"

All the bats set up an agitated fluttering of their wings. "Begorra! It is sick to death I am of that foul slander!" Even the taciturn O'Niel was stirred into speech. "*Blind as a bat!* Are ye daft? We see as well as you, or better in low-light conditions. And we don't drink!"

"They don't drink! Hear that girls? So what else is making them blind, methinks?" Fal gave a lewd wink to Phylla.

"Check the palms of their feet," Pistol sniggered.

Chip shook his fist at all of them. "Will you bunch of stupid rodents stop this?"

"Who's your 'rodent,' primate?" demanded Behan. "It is more cheek than an intelligent life-form you've got! I am Chiroptera and proud of it!" He folded his wings with affronted dignity, like a magistrate tightening his robes of office.

"And *we're* macrosceledia/insectivora," chipped in Doc. With a casual wave of his paw: "With a mere dash of rodent thrown in. Couldn't give a toss about it. The term 'rat' is purely an honorific."

"Well said," hissed Fal and Pistol in unison. Nym rumbled his own wordless agreement.

Chip shrugged. "All I was trying to do was persuade you not to kill yourselves."

Melene took pity on him. "This was a wine farm, Chip. And believe me, even distilled, I can smell the grapes."

Chip knew it was no use arguing further with them about drinking the stuff. The beggars chorus already had a fair amount in them, by the sounds of it. Not enough to incapacitate them, but enough to make them very troublesome. Rats were very good at attaining that level. The high metabolic rate allowed them to drink more than you'd think they could. And practice kept them from incapacitating themselves. Rats liked drink. It was the one method the army had found to get them to fight. They got a daily issue of grog, much as sailors once had.

Of course, one of the bats still had to try to stop them. "But why take the daemon drink with you?" cried Siobhan. "It'll be the ruination of you! Take things to keep yourselves alive, not to kill you."

"Molotov cocktails," snapped Fal. "That's what we're taking. Do they normally get served with an olive in them, Chip? We're not sure of the traditions, here."

Siobhan seemed shocked. "But surely you cannot just take drink?"

One of the rats picked up a spool of baling wire. "This is heavy enough. Useful stuff, wire."

Chip was still dwelling on his failed flamethrower. An errant thought of flambéd crêpes went through his mind. "Is there really lots of that . . . raw brandy?"

Doll grinned. "I' faith, enough to swim in or to keep Fal drunk for a month!"

"Take me to it."

The rats looked shifty. Very shifty. "I suppose there is enough," said Melene finally. Grudgingly.

At a guess, Chip thought that the stainless steel tank had about four or five hundred gallons in it. The rats were still scandalized when he poured the diesel out of the backpack sprayer and then tapped raw brandy into the tank.

"It'll give it a horrible taste, Chip," whined Fal.

"Watch!"

He pumped up the pressure. Lit the lighter and squeezed the trigger. With a sudden BOOM, it caught. Chip held a six foot flame-torch. That would show the Maggots!

"Keep the tip down!" Siobhan fluttered clear, shouting advice. "The thing is dripping! The drips are running down the nozzle—and the flames are following the drips! You idiot!"

Hastily, Chip stopped squeezing the trigger and pointed the nozzle down. After an uncooperative minute, the flames died.

Well, it worked. But as Chip's previous experience with flamethrowers had been caramelizing sugar with a blowtorch, he was more than a bit nervous of the gadget. The whole thing struck him as a recipe for disaster. But if it scared Maggots . . .

"Where's Don Whatsisname?" he asked.

Nym shook his head. "Dunno. The girls have been looking for him."

"He's probably gone into hiding then."

They found the tiny galago asleep. Deep asleep.

"It is daytime, 'ginia. Not waking up time." The galago curled tighter under his tail.

"Nocturnal," muttered Doc. "That explains the big eyes."

"What sort of guide is it that I have to carry because he's flat out?" complained Chip, picking the creature up.

"He's probably been through a lot in the last while, poor mite," said Bronstein. "He's obviously some rich woman's plaything. Not used to this sort of life. He's probably having the first decent sleep he's had ever since they were captured."

"You falling for him too, Bronstein?"

The bat snorted. "Hah. I'm not one of those oversexed rats. Likely the next time he holds forth about needing a real male for the job, his pretty little ears

I'll notch for him. Still, though he was as scared as a rabbit to go back into the Maggot-tunnels, he was still ready to try. That took courage, real courage, for a pampered little thing."

Chip sighed. "That's true enough. But this is a stupid idea, Bronstein. We're never gonna get away with it. Maggots are up and about now. They were asleep when the others went in."

"True. So I think we should wait. Eamon and I have an idea."

"Which involves blowing something up."

The bat had the grace to look faintly abashed. "Uh. Yes. But only if it is needed."

"Oh. You mean Eamon is going to give up a chance at mayhem? Explain that one."

The bat snarled. Restrained herself. "I'll explain what we have in mind! Look, when Siobhan flew after the little fellow, she found out that there are tunnels which go straight across . . . from one side of the mound to the other. And at the other end there was a down chute . . . I don't know, an air hole, whatever, identical to this side."

Chip raised his eyes to the twinkling force field that was between him and heaven. "Oh wonderful. Now all we need to do is find that there are ones going along as well as across and we can set up a toll booth, or walk straight to the middle of the whole Maggot nest!"

"Will you *listen*, Connolly? Springing this human, which Eamon and Behan are none too keen on, I'll tell you, is bound to alert the Maggots. If we get out, we will want to come back to the farmhouse. That's where the food is, *and* that's the right direction for the sea. So what we want to do is to go across to the far side. Set up a shot pattern to get us out into the valley we escaped out of originally."

Chip cocked his head. "Which is the wrong direction."

"Right," Bronstein said, in the tone used to humor a small and annoying child. "We'll set things up so that the Maggots can chase off to where we *aren't* going to be. That'll give us a head start, at least."

Chip rolled his eyes. "So you're going to cross the whole mound and set up a dummy first. Don't let me stop you."

Bronstein looked uneasy. "Well, we need you to come along. You'll be carrying the fertilizer. And quite a lot of diesel. And that would save us from having to use more than one satchel-charge."

These bats had bats in the belfry and no mistake! "I see. And doubtless you want a couple of rats along for hole digging. Forget it, Bronstein. It's a good idea, maybe, but there is more chance of my falling pregnant than the rats agreeing."

"We . . . took the liberty of getting Melene and Doc to put a cold chisel and a four-pound hammer in the bag. Those hollow blocks give us really quick shot holes . . ."

"You're crazy Bronstein, damn you! I'm not doing it!"

Well, at least he was carrying much less weight in fertilizer and less diesel because he'd argued before giving in. He'd been able to talk them down to half again because of having to carry the cans of diesel. And now that the things were set up, what was left in the fertilizer bags couldn't weigh more than twenty to twenty-five pounds. It was nice to have insurance, even if he *hadn't* agreed to that second booby trap they'd set. And at least they'd waited until dark. It did appear that Maggots slowed down at night, coming to a virtual halt in the wee small hours. But crossing the six hundred yards of mound had been scary as hell, even with the bats flying interference. Still . . . it was easier than climbing over it. He'd gotten there. He'd even gotten back.

Now he was going to have to abseil down, into the depths. Shudder. There would be no safety rope, this time. At least there would be no instructor screaming at him to stop being a wimp.

He steeled himself. The descendure had better work or he would be strawberry jam. He leaned back, knuckles white on his rope-clutching hands. . . . Through gritted teeth, he whispered: "Here goes nothing."

He stayed dead still. He forced himself to relax his clutching hands. Still no movement. The problem eventually proved to be getting the oily old hawser-laid rope to go through the descendure to allow him to move at all. His previous experience had been on a smooth, braided-perlon sheathed rope. The descendure the rats had designed for him made the twisted rope twist more below him. That formed knots he had to spin loose before he could go down at all. His slow descent gave him plenty of time to observe his environment. He was pretty sure this was an air shaft. Little tunnels gave off it at ridges which were probably floor levels.

By the time he got down, the rest of the crew were in foot-stamping impatience. The galago had descended by calmly climbing down Chip's rope, regarding the cursing human *en route* as a sort of slow-moving rest stop.

"Right. Where now?" Chip didn't want to think about the plan for getting back up. Not so soon after that descent!

"Are you sure you wouldn't be liking to stop for nice cup of tea then? Or maybe a nap?"

Chip was in no mood for sarcasm. "Shut up, Siobhan. Where do we go? Back to the food chamber?"

"Oh, but we need to go back up two levels," said the galago.

Chip missed.

They crept along as silently, Bronstein acidly informed them, as a herd of dancing elephants. The galago had led them up one spiral ramp when the inevitable happened.

Either the Maggot was coming down anyway, or it had heard something.

Bronstein waved them back. They retreated into a side passage.

Scritch, scritch, scritch. It kept coming after them. And this was a dead end . . . some kind of adobe-closed store chamber. Nobody breathed. Then the galago gave a sudden squeak and skittered away up the wall.

There was a thump. Bronstein appeared. "Be using that four-pound hammer to provide us with bit of masonry, Chip. I don't think it saw me. We better fake a natural death for it."

Chip reached up and knocked a spur loose. "Here. But I think the shit just hit the fan. We'd better move it up. Where is that galago?"

"I am here," replied a small voice from the roof shadows. "I was just about to strike when the wonderful Bat Lady beat me to it."

Bronstein lifted a lip.

"Come on, Duke of Plazo-Toro," chortled Fal. "Let's move out."

The galago drew himself up. "What did you call me?"

"That elevated, cultivated, celebrated gentleman,

the noble Duke of Plazo-Toro," replied Fal. His voice was perfectly level.

Bronstein shooed them along, flapping her wings. "Move, move, both of you! And leave that Maggot alone, Pistol! They'll smell a rat for sure if the limbs are missing."

At a dogtrot they continued. Fifteen minutes, and another successful circumvention, brought them to the place where the girl was walled in. The galago suddenly bounded ahead and bounced up to the tiny aperture near the roof.

"It is I, Virginia! I have brought the rescue!"

"Oh—*Fluff!* Dear God, you've been gone so *long*. I thought you were dead!" The voice on the other side of the wall was young, female, and sounded thoroughly miserable.

"Fluff?" Fal grinned broadly.

Chip was relieved that it hadn't all been a wild goose chase. He was also not mentally prepared to speak to her. He had privately suspected the "princess" would prove to be some ancient-Shareholder-bitch . . . if there was going to be anyone at all. "Uh, ma'am . . ."

The reply was a few seconds in coming, as if she was thinking it over. "Is there somebody else out there . . . ? I heard voices. Am I hallucinating? Fluff?"

"Indeed, it is I, Virginia," said the galago with pride and reassuring affection. "Really. Here is my tail. I have brought some brave soldiers. We have come to rescue you!"

"Really? You've come to get me *out*?" There was wild hope in her voice.

"Yes. Really. Please keep it quiet, ma'am," begged Chip. "Here, Don Fluff, push this end of the flexible saw through."

Bronstein took charge of the rest of the operation.

"Okay, the rest of you. While Chip saws, I want you rats to get to the corners. Find somewhere to duck out of sight if possible. Siobhan, you and Behan take those passages. I'll take this one, and Eamon and O'Niel can stake out the others between you."

"Bats always get to do the risky work, indade." But Eamon fluttered off to do it readily enough.

The carborundum-toothed saw hissed through the Magh' adobe. It was easier with two of them working—or it should have been. The "princess" kept jerking his fingers against the wall in her eagerness to be free.

"There's a bunch of digger-maggots down in the big passage coming this way," warned Behan.

"They're coming to get me!" The girl's voice sounded on the edge of hysteria.

She probably was, poor kid, trapped in there for God knows how long. Chip looked at the cut. It was about eighteen inches down, by ten inches across. "How far off are those diggers if they're coming here?"

"At least three minutes." Behan, like all bats, was an expert at time estimation.

Chip looked at the cut; turned to the hovering galago. "How big is she?"

The galago gestured with wide arms. "Immense. Compared to me, that is. Humans are overgrown."

"Compared to me, you ass!"

"Perhaps a little taller," said the galago.

"Stand clear in there," Chip whispered into the hole. "I'm going to shoulder-charge this, to see if I can knock it down. Then be ready to run."

He hit it. The wall cracked. His shoulder felt like it had cracked as well. He tried again, and the whole section fell in. The air, already dusty from their sawing, was full of swirls.

Light reflected off heavy-framed glasses. The girl-prisoner had missed a lot of meals, apparently. Her face was muddy and tear-streaked. With her hair pulled back tightly from her angular face, she looked about twelve years old . . . except that she was distinctly taller than he was. "Quick! Take my arm. We'd better move out."

Eagerly she scrambled through the hole. She was all ragged clothes, thick glasses and long legs. She struggled to get out of the hole, hooked a foot, and fell out into his arms. Chip found himself being hugged fiercely. "Oh, thank God!"

Poor kid. Poor damn kid. "It's all right." She nuzzled into him. He kissed her cheek, gently comforting. Her lips found his. Parted eagerly . . .

Chip started back in alarm, but she held onto him.

Chapter 18:
The hero's regrets.

The piece of masonry fell. Lumifungus light streamed into her dusty darkness. He stood there framed by the light. A hero. *Her* hero. He was Heathcliff, Heathcliff—to the life! She climbed out and fell into his arms. . . .

"Will you two stop behaving like rutting *rats*!" snapped someone. "We've got to move!"

She looked up. Focused with difficulty though her dusty glasses. And screamed. Briefly. Her hero clapped a hand over her mouth.

It was a huge bat, with a wingspan the size of a full arm-stretch. A satanic apparition, black and evil in the eerie tunnel-light. The monster's long canines gleamed white and cruel. She cowered against her savior.

He was quite muscular, she noted with satisfaction.

Just like a hero should be, if perhaps a tad on the wiry side. But why was he pushing her away?

"It's only Bronstein," he gruffed. "Come. We don't want to get you captured again."

"But it's a bat! A giant bat!" She shuddered. "Won't it get into my hair?"

He picked up his pack. "Don't call Bronstein an 'it.' And I don't know about *your* hair, but she can certainly get up *my* nose."

"Stupid humans," muttered—Bronstein?

What kind of name was that, for a monster?

"Call the rats, Chip, we must go."

They began jog trotting down the passage, the hero hurrying her along. Virginia was a bit nonplussed. The hero was called—Chip? What kind of name was that for a hero?

She started at the sight of the cat-sized rats that joined them, but managed to refrain from comment. Now that she thought about it, she'd heard about the rats and bats that humans had bred to fight against the Magh'. These looked like fighters, just in the way they moved. Not just fighters, but battle-scarred and battered fighters. They all wore harnesses, packs and bandoliers. Briefly, she wondered where their leashes were.

Fortunately, they hurried her onwards before she asked.

"And Fluff? Where is Fluff?" Virginia asked anxiously.

The galago leapt onto her shoulder. "I said to you, 'never fear, Fluff is here,' *mi* Virginia. Now we must run, before the Magh' come."

"Hear that girls?" sniggered Pistol. "Don Macho-shrimp is called Fluff!"

Fal laughed. "Heh heh. Fancy a bit o' Fluff on the side, eh, Phylla?"

"Don't you mean a Fluff on the bint?" asked Nym.

"Come on, rats!" said Chip. "Time for that later. We want to get out before the Maggots stir."

The girl looked at him, startled. "But why are we going out? We must still rescue the Professor."

Chip looked her. "No, Miss Muffet. What we've got to do is get the hell out of here. Now."

Virginia gasped. "But . . . he's my tutor. You can't just leave him here." She stared in fury at Chip.

"Tutor!" Chip laughed. "I'm not surprised you're a bit crazy, having been stuck in there."

She stopped and stamped her foot. She was not used to being disobeyed. She vaguely remembered that the servants used to play mean tricks on her, before . . . But no one would ever have dreamed of directly countering an order from her. "You *WILL* go and rescue him now!" she shouted.

He grabbed her shoulder and hauled her onwards. "I *will* give you a smart slap if you don't shut your face, and get a move on."

She wrenched herself free. "*Do* you know who I *am?*"

He lowered his head and shook it, looking like an irritated, if small, bull. "I couldn't give a toss if you are the Queen of Sheba. Or even the Managing Director's daughter, for that matter!"

"Well, that is *just* who I am," she informed him imperiously.

He snorted. "The Queen of Sheba? Well, get a move on, your royal majesty—or you'll be Maggot-crap."

"I am *Virginia Shaw*! And you'd better listen to me, you . . . you . . . Vat-born scum!"

He looked into her face, and gave her a crooked-toothed grin. "Oh yeah. Tell me another one, *made-moiselle* Shareholder." He snorted derisively. "Your teeth are a giveaway, kid. So you're the only Shareholder on the planet with skew teeth."

Virginia tightened her jaws. How could she tell him that before the implant she'd been too impossible about the orthodontic brace? That her parents had given up, when she utterly refused to cooperate. "I *am* Virginia Shaw," she repeated sullenly. "Ask Fluff."

"I wouldn't trust that little thing's piece of head-plastic to speak my weight," he said dismissively. He tugged on her arm, trying to get her to walk.

She hit him. She'd never hit anyone before. It made a very satisfying *swat* noise on his cheek and stung her hand.

Then—she was instantly contrite. "I'm sorry. I'm really sorry. But you *mustn't* insult Fluff. I am Virginia Shaw. Really."

"S' okay." Chip grinned at her. "I wasn't insulting the little fella. Just that alien-built rubbish in his head. Let's at least keep walking."

She swallowed. She *definitely* wasn't going to tell him there was a soft-cyber chip in her own head. "I know it doesn't look like it, but I truly am who I say I am! We must rescue my tutor."

From his perch on her shoulder the galago supported her. "She is, *señor*. Is absolutely true. Ask her about Pygmalion House if you do not believe."

"*I* wouldn't know what that looked like," said Chip. "So she could tell me anything. Good try, little one."

Dejectedly, she said: "It's true, Fluff. I don't look like a Shareholder, do I? I could tell him about Pygmalion House, or Maxims or Chez Henri-Pierre . . ."

"Ha! Tell me about *that*. If you can tell me about that I might believe you, indeed." His tone was again derisive.

She decided to ignore the tone and give him the

answer. She had to do *something*. "Well, it has mirrors everywhere, these delicate little tables and spindly little bentwood chairs with velvet cushions."

He looked startled. "What color?"

"The cushions?" He nodded. She thought a moment. "Sort of red-pink. I didn't like it much."

"Cerise," Chip growled. "Hated it myself."

That was startling too. He should have no idea . . . "How would you know? Vats didn't . . . I mean . . ."

He gave a wry, bitter grin. "You mean Henri-Pierre had a 'no dogs or Vats' policy. I worked there. Tell me about the food."

She'd swear she'd never seen him before. He couldn't have been one of the waiters or he would surely have recognized her. Her heart fell at the mention of the food. It was always so . . . fussy. Besides it reminded her just how hungry and thirsty she was. "You haven't anything to drink, have you?"

He slapped his forehead. "I should have thought. Here."

The water in his issue-waterbottle was tepid and silty. She'd never tasted anything so wonderful. "The food all had those long French names. I had the duck breast with mango slices, sometimes. The breasts were cut into this fan. Somehow, some of the slices were slid out to make a butterfly. The mango was cut into a flower around it. It was always so pretty it seemed a shame to eat it."

It was his turn to stop. "I used to do the cutting . . . my God, you really must be . . . I heard about it on the radio." He stepped back, away from her. "Hey, Bronstein. Guess who we just rescued."

The bat gave an impatient flutter. "To be sure, some stupid human who wants be caught again. Keep the noise down and keep moving, Connolly."

"It's the arch-enemy, Bronstein. The Company in

person. The Goddamn managing director's daughter!" Chip edged away from her.

The bat snorted. "Stop fooling, Connolly. We don't have time," she said impatiently.

Chip shook his head. "I'm *not* fooling, Bronstein. It's true. She knows Chez Henri-Pierre. And who else would have a fancy talking pet? Think about it."

Virginia had had enough. "When you've *quite* finished insulting me, can we go and rescue my tutor? NOW!"

The bat spat on the tunnel floor. "Come on, Connolly. Let's get moving."

"Are you going to do what I *ordered* you to!?" she shouted.

"No. I wouldn't do anything for *you* even if you asked me nicely. And if you shout again I'll kill you," added the ugly bat, in deadly earnest.

To Virginia's shame, she started to cry.

If she hadn't started to cry, thought Chip savagely to himself, they wouldn't be having a confab in one of the alcoves. A whispered one-way argument instead of running. He should never have comforted her. Let her have her drizzle and get on with it. It was all very well her claiming that she had nothing to do with the Company's policies. That was true, he supposed. Like her claim that the Company had been set up to build a new and better world for humans. That was true, in concept, even if as far as he was concerned, the practice was flawed to hell. But the idea that they couldn't abandon her precious tutor was going to drive him to drink.

He tried patience and a reasonable tone. "Look, kid. We can't. We need to get out of here. I'm sorry but whoever this guy is, it's just too bad."

"Heighdy! Lack-a-day-dee! We're not sticking our

noses out to help some old geezer," said Fal, being honest instead.

Neither approach had any effect. She sniffed. "How can you refuse to help one of the Korozhet? They've done so much for us."

Chip was rather taken aback at this, if no more interested in rescue. "Your tutor is one of *them*? Those pricklepusses?"

She stamped her foot. "Of course he is! Don't you know anything?"

"We must set up a search pattern," said Eamon.

Chip's mouth fell open. The big male bat had been all for summary justice when he found out who she was. Now he was talking about searching. "Are you crazy? We need *out* of here."

"She says her tutor is a Korozhet. Is that true, little one?" said Eamon—who had insisted on not being out on flutter patrol because he wanted to scotch any plans this vile human might try to get them to agree to.

"Upon my honor, *señor*, it is," said the galago.

"We'll take the lower passages," said Fal.

"Has that piece of plastic crap in your heads fried?!" demanded Chip furiously. "It's a Korozhet. So what? You're all behaving like they're something great. What the hell have they done since the war started but sit in that ship of theirs?"

"They provided weapons, slowshields and soft-cyber units," snapped Virginia. "Humanity on Harmony And Reason would be history without them!"

He wasn't buying it. "At a price! At a hell of a price! Anyway, we have absolutely zip chance of finding the alien. We might as well get moving and head out, collect chow, and head for the sea."

The galago raised himself up very erect on her shoulder. "You must not insult them like that, or I will challenge you to a duel!" He slouched, slightly. "And I know where the Professor is."

"Oh Fluff! I knew I could rely on you!" Virginia hugged the small primate. "Where is he? We mustn't waste another minute!"

"There are many Magh' guarding him," he said doubtfully.

She clapped a horrified hand to her mouth. "Oh, Fluff! We must rescue him, at once!"

"You are utterly insane," pronounced Chip.

And found himself a voice in the wilderness. For no reason he could understand, all the bats and rats were entirely in favor of the girl's idiotic proposal. Insane!

They followed the galago. He led them up. And up.

"We're nearly at the level where we came in," muttered one of the rats. Their sense of direction was uncanny.

They crossed the wide main passage hastily. There were few Maggots about, but there was no sense in looking for extra trouble.

Just on the far side of the tunnel in the side passage, Melene paused and sniffed. "Mothballs. And diesel. We must be near that booby trap of yours. What did you use the mothballs for?"

"Didn't. You're smelling something else," insisted Siobhan.

"Hush, we are nearly there, *señores*. Prepare to fight! There were Magh' here in numbers last time."

Pistol twitched his nose. "Doth think perhaps we've got lucky?"

Indeed, they had. There was not a Maggot in sight. "He was in there." The galago pointed to an open chamber.

"They'll have hauled him hence," said Behan gloomily.

"Let's check it out. If he's in there, there'll be Maggots." Chip took out the Solingen. "Stay back, girl."

"I want to help," she said.

Chip restrained her gently. "You'll be in the way. Please . . . stay out."

She noticed their postures had changed. Suddenly they looked like a very deadly crew. The big bat said: "Okay. Let's go."

Nobody ran. That didn't help with slowshields. They just moved fast.

There was a terrible scream.

Virginia and Fluff ran into the room. The Korozhet, sitting in a shallow bath, shrieked again.

"Professor! It's me! Virginia! We've come to rescue you."

"Eeeeeeeee!!!!!"

"Shut up or I'll knock your goddam spikes in, Picklepuss!" Chip swung the four-pound hammer in a menacing arc.

The Korozhet at least stopped screaming. "Virginia! Oh, Miss Virginia! I was so overcome with excitement. We Korozhet are so emotional. I could not contain my delight at seeing my saviors! Have you come to rescue me from this terrible torture?"

Chip looked at the alien in its shallow waterbath. How did you tell whether a ball of prickles is in pain? "What's wrong?" He sniffed. The place smelled like the clothes he'd taken from the poor box, before he'd been apprenticed. The smell brought back a flood of unpleasant memories.

"This liquid immobilizes my spikes," the Korozhet explained.

The rats were already trying to lift the alien. He

was too heavy for the efforts of Virginia and the rats, and Chip had to give a hand.

Lifting it by the base of two of the hollow spikes was the closest Chip had ever been to one of the aliens. Sure, they'd given the colonists at least a breathing space, and a chance to halfway prepare for the Magh' invasion. They had even visited Chez Henri-Pierre, in the early days, before the war. He, along with several of the other kitchen-vats, had risked thick ears from Henri-Pierre to steal a closer glimpse than they'd gotten as part of the cheering crowd at that first Korozhet motorcade.

Like most Vats, Chip had seen the arrival of an FTL ship as the end of the Company monopoly. *Hah.* When it had arrived the Korozhet ship's engines were apparently virtually still smoldering from their race to beat the Magh'. The ship had lain in state till weeks ago, being repaired. He'd heard over the radio that it had lifted at last. Well, if this Korozhet was here, they must surely be coming back.

He began to help Virginia dry the spines with some cloths that had been piled near the tank. Not much of a critter if it could be trapped by a bowl of water. Still, it seemed to be well-spoken. It also seemed innocuous enough, although he wished like hell it hadn't screamed like that.

"Maggots!" Siobhan called from the entrance. "Maggots coming."

"We've got to run," said Chip to the alien. "Can you move fast?"

"Yes, the Professor is wonderfully fast on his spikes," Virginia informed him cheerfully.

The Korozhet mournfully contradicted. "Alas, not now, Miss Virginia. My joints are still very stiff. Also I have changed sex. I am now female. Please remember that."

Chip grabbed Virginia's spike-caressing arm. "Come on. Take one side. We're going to have to carry it, even if it is a little double-adaptor. The rest of you will have to deal with the Maggots."

It was possibly the most awkward bundle Chip had ever carried. They were sure as hell not going to make good speed like this. Glancing back hastily, Chip saw Eamon dive onto a Maggot-scorp. There was no way they were traveling around the scorpiary undetected any more. "Hell, Crotchet, I'm going to drop you any minute! Stop wriggling those spines."

"I am most sorry. I am trying to get life back into them!" It sounded most contrite. Chip would rather it had just stopped wriggling.

"Down this side passage! Quickly!" called Behan.

They bundled off at right angles. "With any luck Siobhan and O'Niel will lead them straight past!" said Chip, grinning.

"Eeeeeee!!!!!!"

Chip's grin vanished. He menaced the Korozhet with the hammer again. "Shut up! You damn fool creature . . ."

"Eeeee! The pain. I cannot help it! The pain. My limbs are in agony!"

"Move it up!" The rats staggered into the passage, carrying one of their number. "We didn't shake them. Phylla's hurt."

"Here. Get her into my magazine pocket." Soldiers in this war might have no use for spare magazines, but the uniform trousers still had the big thigh pockets.

"Just a cut." Chip could hear the pain in the rat's voice as she climbed into his pocket.

"Run!" shouted Bronstein.

Chip was taking strain. Looking across at his companion, he saw that she was doing well, comparatively.

It wasn't just that the alien was heavy, it was also just so awkward to carry. The spines kept poking into him, and the two he held were constantly twitching. Whatever they'd done to this poor creature must have been hellish.

They were crossing a ramp-bridge, above a Maggot aqueduct and lower roadway. "Try to stop twitching, will you? If we drop you here you'll go splat. And we're both close to dropping you." The creature was stilled.

Looking at Virginia, Chip saw it was a question of whether she dropped her burden or fell over first. Her face was looking transparent, she was so pale.

"I believe I can manage to ambulate now," said the alien cheerily.

They put it down with great relief. Ambulate it could. But damned slowly. They got over the bridge less than twenty yards ahead of the Maggots. Never had bat-placed explosives sounded so sweet as when they took the pylon out of the middle of the bridge.

"*Yes.* Way to go!" cheered Chip.

It bought them minutes. But the alien was just so damned *slow*.

"How far? asked Chip. He'd like to kick that prickly football along. In his pouch Phylla gave a slight groan.

"Quarter of a mile, more maybe," replied Bronstein. "We've just passed the booby-trapped wall."

"I'm buggered. Gonna drop the rest of this fertilizer."

"There's a hole. Drop it into that." Bronstein waved a wingtip.

Chip didn't argue at this stage. He just did as she told him. Twenty-five pounds lighter, legging it was less of a strain.

"There are some ahead of us!" someone cried.

"And they're closing in behind us. But not for

long." Bronstein held a detonator trigger-bar in her claws.

"I'll get the ones in front." Chip groped in his pocket for Fal's lighter while sorting out the hose of the backpack sprayer. He ran out in front, ripped the backpack off, and rammed the pressure plunger up and down. He realized he wasn't going to have time to get it on again. With a shaking hand he flicked the lighter, and pulled the trigger. The flame-torch was just in time. Grabbing the backpack by the straps he took off after the fleeing maggots.

"*Run*, you fuckers, run!" It was good to be on the chasing end for a change.

Behind, the bats triggered their booby trap. Hah! It was all going like clockwork! Chip brandished his torch, pointing upwards and forwards with the triumphal flame. A thin trickle of alcohol ran down the metal pipe. A little flame followed it.

Chip shook the pipe hastily before the fire got to his hand, suddenly remembering he must keep the flame nozzle pointed down. The little tongues of flame went out. Then the flames leaped back again. They were very little flames and mostly followed the drips, so long as he held the pipe slightly below horizontal. The homemade flamethrower was working really efficiently now, the flame-tongue at least six feet long.

WeeeeWOOOOOMH!!

The hammered-in spray-gun nozzle exploded out of the brass pipe. It ricocheted off the next bend in the passage thirty yards away. A huge gout of eyebrow-singeing flame leapt down the passage after it. Before, the alcohol had merely been atomized and burning. Now the small flames had vaporized the stuff inside the pipe. Chip dropped it and danced away from the flames still coming out of the pipe. The backpack was wet with alcohol . . .

"Back off! RUUUNNN!" He suited action to the words.

The heat still licked at his back. Chip swore. It was all his own fault for thinking it *could* go like clockwork. In combat, battle plans are by definition screwed. If the enemy didn't mess it up for you, then you did it for yourself. Brilliantly synchronized movements were great for dance companies. *Of course* getting to the break-out point they'd set up to mislead the Magh'—with the enemy cooperatively doing just what they were supposed to do—had been doomed from the start.

They came back to the caved-in section where the bats had set their "distraction" booby trap. There was a dusty hole through the wall, and the ground underfoot was pure mud. The explosion had resulted in at least one crushed Maggot. A limb twitched at them. Typically, a rat bit through the joint-tissue, and thrust the leg into his pack-straps.

"Through here," called Fal. They slithered up the muddy slope and out of the narrow lumifungus-lit tunnel into a huge hall full of long tanks. The nearest tank was leaking, obviously cracked in the blast. A group of Maggots with large hairy paddle-palps were frantically milling around the crack, trying to stop the crack with their paddles. Their entire attention seemed focused on it. Despite this, Virginia stopped dead at the point where the new adit opened into the hall.

"Go!" Chip pushed.

"I can't," she said, fear in her voice.

Chip could see why. The creature in her way had obviously escaped from a tank—it was alternate rows of tentacles, pincers and spines. And big evil eyes.

The Korozhet flicked the thing aside with a spine. Chip was justifiably grateful.

The Maggots were a lot more interested in their problem with the tank than with a fast leaving bunch of aliens. The newcomers dogtrotted warily past them without any obvious moves from the paddle-palps. The bats scouted ahead as they moved down the long hall full of tanks. Big hungry eyes gazed from the weedy water of the tanks. Occasionally a tentacle would wave from the water.

"You okay, Phylla?" Chip asked when he had the breath.

"I've stopped the bleeding." The rat-girl's voice was subdued. "But I think I've lost half my tail too."

That was serious. Not only was the tail a major part of the rat's balance, but it was a rat's sex symbol, the equivalent of nice legs, a large bust . . . or well-filled trousers to a human. Chip guessed the rat-girl would rather have lost a limb or an eye.

"That trick of yours with the flamethrower may have turned out for the best," said Eamon, grudgingly. "We've come out nearly at the place we set the charges. No Maggots in sight. All we've got to do is go up a level. Then across six hundred yards and we're out."

The Korozhet sighed. "You'll have to leave me, good human, Miss Virginia . . . my spines can take no more. Leave me. Save yourselves."

Virginia was shocked. "But we can't leave you."

"Indeed you must! Save yourselves," said the alien, nobly.

Chip looked at Prickles. Carrying it like they had before would slow them down terrifically. He pulled his shirt off, ripping a button in his haste. He tied the two sleeves together, then cut two slits into the material near the tail. He laid it on the ground. "Get onto that, Crotchet."

The Korozhet twitched spines at him. "I do not understand . . ."

"Just do it!" shouted Chip, pulling the hammer from his belt loops. Whether it understood, or was intimidated, the Korozhet complied. "Right. Now we've got a stretcher, let's go. Take the sleeves . . . Miss Shaw."

For the first time since they'd rescued the Korozhet, they were able to really get a move on.

"Maggots coming!" shouted Siobhan.

They legged it. At first the Magh' gained on them. Then they began to drop back. "Unfit, these Maggots," said Melene.

"They cannot run for long. They respire through booklungs, which are less efficient than yours," the carried Korozhet explained. "They accumulate oxygen in the respiratory system slowly during normal sluggish movement, and use it rapidly in bursts of speed."

Bronstein fluttered in front of them. "Here we are, comrades. Up . . . Where are you rats going?"

"Span a bit of wire," said Nym. "There is a narrowing back there around that last corner."

Doll sniffed. "If we go up one layer, up that air flue . . ."

"Take this cord up, bat. We'll have to haul the Korozhet."

Virginia looked at the narrow hole in the wall. "We go in there?"

Chip pointed. "In there and up. Somehow. See that hole there? That's full of explosives."

Siobhan came along, shooing rats. "For what are you still waiting then? Up! Up! Eamon has already started the timer. We've got barely a minute now."

The galago bounced off her shoulder and across to the far wall. "Come, Virginia, *mi* gorgeous, it is easy."

With obvious trepidation she entered the hole, putting a foot across onto the far wall, into the hole Chip had punched with the cold chisel. Chip followed. He edged up the flue, his back on the inner wall, his feet braced against the outer, and a long way down between his knees. It was *not* sweet, knowing that a detonator was ticking away inside the hollow-block wall underneath his feet. If he moved fast, he'd fall. If he didn't move fast, he'd fly. He crawled out onto the next level with relief. Virginia was already trying to haul up the shirt bundle with her precious Korozhet tutor in it. Chip added his muscle to the task, and, accompanied by bats, the Pricklepuss arrived.

"Move!" shouted Bronstein. Twenty-five seconds later the side wall of the tunnel blew out.

He could see darkness out there. The floor behind them had cracked too, and fallen in to within ten yards of them.

"Phew! That was too damn close. Let's go," said Chip.

"Not so fast. First, Nym, give Chip that Maggot-leg. Can you cut overshoes, Chip? Then we can travel without a scent trace."

"Let's try the flexible saw on the stuff."

It was easier to cut than Magh' adobe. Virginia was nearly sick when he thrust pieces of meaty Maggot-leg over her hand-tooled expensive leather shoes. There was no time to clean the stuff out first. If Chip had looked at those shoes first instead of her ragged clothing, he would have been a lot quicker to believe she was Virginia Shaw.

He stood up. "Right. All aboard."

The rats chose to cling to him rather than her . . . except Melene, who ignored Virginia's involuntary shudder and climbed up to the opposite shoulder from Fluff. Why miss an opportunity?

"Right." Bronstein fluttered in front of them. "Siobhan and Behan will run interference for you. Eamon, O'Niel and I are off to sow a bit of confusion along the way we're supposed to have gone. We'll see you back at the farmhouse."

Chip shook his head."Not more bombs?"

Eamon pulled a face, somewhat improving his gargoyle looks. He held out a bag in one foot, gingerly. "Worse! Rat droppings."

Virginia had never realized how sweet the feeling of the night wind on her face could be. She couldn't believe that they were out and free! She could feel the lessening in the tension with the sudden tired-voiced banter among her rescuers.

"No more explosions! I don't understand why you bats are so set on bangs when you never have any," said a rat from the moonlit darkness.

"We're not sex obsessed like you rats," said a bat loftily, from above.

"But you do reproduce sexually," said the odd rat with the wire frame glasses. "It is in my medical datafile. Once a year, and you practice sperm storage."

This produced a stunned silence from the rats for a few moments. Virginia found herself stifling a giggle. Then the one-eyed one said, "I've a theory why bats think once a year is enough. It's the hanging upside down. Don't get enough blood to their privates to shag."

"No blood to the brain is what you rats have!" snapped a bat-voice. That was the female one that Virginia had come to realize was called Siobhan.

The plump rat beside her chuckled and strutted in the moonlight. "Why would we want our *brains* engorged and swollen?"

The badinage continued as they stumbled their way across the war-and-Magh'-ravaged landscape.

"So tell me about this sperm storage," piped one of the other rat-girls. Melene, Virginia thought. She was getting better at distinguishing the odd synthesizer voices. "Does that mean you can have an instant poke whenever you feel like it, Siobhan?"

The walls of the ruined farmhouse loomed out of the darkness. Two minutes later the party was in the tasting room.

Chapter 19:
Military Intelligence: an oxymoron.

Fitzhugh stood waiting in the antechamber of General Cartup-Kreutzler's office, a sheaf of painstakingly prepared analyses and reports in his hand. The large-busted blond receptionist at the desk was doing her best to ignore the tall scarfaced intelligence officer. Conrad Fitzhugh was prepared to bet she'd never worked so hard in her life as she did while the intelligence officer was doing his weekly champ at the waiting-bit. Well, she could have been worse off. He'd wanted to report daily. Then she might have had to learn to type.

Fitzhugh knew that his "promotion" to the hallways and offices of Southern Front HQ had been punishment for offending the powers-that-be. Besides that, it got rid of an embarrassment to his fellow officers. His piece of the front-line hadn't been pushed back when theirs had.

When he'd been injured, his commanding officer had seized the opportunity to be rid of him. Still, Military Intelligence was a unit with a purpose, General Cartup-Kreutzler had assured him when he'd arrived. He knew that now. The purpose of this department was to take the shit when anything went wrong.

Major Fitzhugh was a rare Shareholder. He'd *volunteered* for active service. He had actually gone through boot camp with a sea of Vat conscripts for three whole weeks, before a shocked camp-commander had come and personally hauled him out and sent him to Officer Candidate School. Even that hadn't stopped Fitzhugh from getting a front-line posting, where he was supposed to be conveniently fragged or get killed by the Magh'. When he'd failed their expectations, they'd "promoted" him here.

A hearty laugh came from behind the general's door. The beautiful relic-of-Earth polished oak door opened, revealing the joyous sight of the general affably slapping the shoulder of a brigadier with a large curling handlebar moustache. "Heh, heh! I must remember that one, Charlie, old boy. 'And the Vat said . . .' Ho, ho! Jolly good. I must remember that one."

The general caught sight of the waiting major and his expression turned to one of distaste. With pride Fitzhugh successfully kept a poker expression while saluting.

"I'll be seeing you, Charlie. Come in, Major Fitzhugh." The general's tone of voice shifted between the thought of a pleasant afternoon's golf and root-canal work in the span of two short sentences.

The major went into the sumptuous office. It always struck him that Carrot-up put up with the army, but really yearned for cavalry. The gilt-framed horsey pictures that lightened the rich maroon wallpaper certainly showed where the general's interest lay. There was enough expensive horsey-leather hung about the place to start a tack shop. A very exclusive tack shop.

A willowy captain in an elegant tailored uniform leaned an idle elbow on a tasseled velvet-upholstered chair. Although it was just ten-thirty in the morning, the room reeked of whiskey and cigars. Fitzhugh hoped like hell the ambience wouldn't make Ariel sneeze. The decanter and glasses on the acres of gleaming desk bore mute evidence to a hard morning's war-planning.

"The week's intelligence reports, sir." Fitzhugh attempted to hand them to the general.

"Don't give them to me, for God's sake. Give them to Captain Hargreaves. Why you can't just leave them with Daisy, I don't know." The general flopped into his leather-upholstered lounger.

The captain reached a languid hand for the dun folder. Fitz gave him the full benefit of the bad side of his face. With sudden insight, Fitz realized he must have looked like that once. Tall. Blond. Blue-eyed. Features carvedly aquiline and aristocratic.

Bah. Wet tissue paper.

In the glare of Fitzhugh's arctic gaze the aide wilted. The reaching hand pulled back.

"I must discuss certain aspects of this with you, sir," said Fitz.

"Oh, you must, must you?" demanded the general mockingly.

Fitz chose to ignore the sarcasm. "Yes, sir. I must. Satellite imaging shows that the concentration of Magh' troops in sector Delta 355 has diminished. This is the ideal time . . ."

The solidly larded general stood up. He was as tall

as Fitzhugh. He pulled the painstakingly prepared reports from the major's hand; tossed the dun folder into a scatter of mixed papers on the floor in the far corner; and then turned his back on the intelligence officer.

Fitz wondered if his knuckles or the shaft of the bangstick would go first. Carrot-up had him pegged perfectly. He would *not* give in and stab the man in the back.

The general turned around. "Now hear this, Major who is on the verge of becoming a captain. You presume too much. Understand this. You do not ever again presume to advise me on military matters. You have no grasp of military strategy and your opinions are of no interest or value to high command. Your job is to organize the data the Korozhet's probes bring to us. That's all. Do I make myself clear?"

Fitz restrained himself. He didn't scream "but it's a lot of fucking crap!" His one disciplinary hearing to date had been for daring to question Korozhet data. Events had proved him perfectly correct, and the Korozhet data misleading, but that had been beside the point to the tribunal. "Sir."

"As for that withdrawal, I've already been informed. It is a feint. Since Shaw's death I have been given the honor of having a Korozhet adviser myself. Now, pick up those pieces of paper and give them to Daisy on your way out. Hargreaves, you and I must get on with planning that parade to celebrate our Korozhet allies' return after their victory over that sneak attack by those other aliens. What are they called again, Hargreaves?"

"Jampad, sir," responded the captain, making no move to assist Fitz.

"That's it. Imagine if we'd had to fight off another bunch of damned aliens? Go on, Major. Get on your bike. Leave that folder with Daisy on your way out."

"Sir." Fitz hated to beg. But there were men, rats and bats he'd fought beside, whose lives were riding on this. "Please read it, sir."

The general sighed. "I'll get Hargreaves to read it and give me a summary. But, Major, stop deluding yourself that you have a grasp of military strategy. You should do some reading on the subject. We have excellent field officers to deal with little troop movements. Chaps like Brigadier Charlesworth, who was here just before you came in. People with more know-how about tactics and strategy in their pinkie fingers than you have in your whole body."

"Very well. I'll do some reading, sir," said the major, in the flat even tone that might have made wiser men than the general wary.

But, a small part of his mind reasoned: *The useless bastard might just have hit on something. Someone, somewhere must have had to deal with this situation before.* And thinking about that beat thinking about that stupid son of a bitch, Charlesworth. The brigadier, according to one of the analyses of losses in that folder, was possibly the worst commander on the front. And that was out of an amazing collection of incompetents.

"Do that. Now get along with you."

And Major Conrad Fitzhugh had to obey.

On the way past he put the folder on the general's receptionist's desk. She chewed gum at him.

" 'Tis exactly as I said." The rat in his magazine pocket didn't even stick her nose out. "We'll have to do it my way."

"There has got to be another alternative," said Fitz grimly. "Sure, we'd get away with it—once."

"Well, I am still going to sneak in tonight and piss in his whiskey decanter. Try and stop me."

The scarring had done all sorts of things to Fitzhugh's facial muscles. When he smiled now, he looked like an incoming shark. He didn't smile often. It tended to frighten the hell out of people. The two idling typists in the corridor suddenly found good reason to get back to work. "I could withhold your chocolate."

A loud sniff came from his pocket. "You don't love me anymore."

Fitz raised his eyes to heaven. Inescapable female logic! Still, since she'd lost her tail, Ariel needed constant reassurance. "Of course I do."

"Then I want chocolate. *Now.*"

"You'll have to settle for a piece of cheese."

"Don't want cheese! That's an arrant stereotypical slander. I'm an insectivore. Not a dairy-productivore." Another sniff, more like a snuffle. "If you really loved me, you'd give me liqueur-chocolates all the time."

"You'd pop."

"I know. But 'twould be a wondrous way to die!"

Chapter 20:
A *stairway to Valhalla.*

"Now I finally understand what Hegel really meant," Doc said quietly. He adjusted his pince-nez and then, in a slight singsong, recited: " 'Spirit conceived in the element of pure thought is meaningless unless it also becomes manifest in something other than its pure self and returns to itself out of such otherness. The Absolute is a relation of pure love in which the sides we distinguish are not really distinct. But it is of the essence of Spirit not to be a mere thing of thought, but to be concrete and actual.' "

He began to adjust his pince-nez again; but, instead, simply took them off and wiped his snout wearily. "It was too late. Without surgery it was always too late. Even with it, too late by hours."

The group standing around Phylla's still body were all silent.

Then Nym sighed. "Out, out, brief candle. Well, I suppose I'd better go and fetch some brandy. Or would anyone prefer some wine?"

"You're going to get *drunk*?" Siobhan's voice rose to a squawk of outrage.

Doc nodded. "Of course. The observance of rites for the dead are what set us apart from the animals."

"But that is to behave like animals, indade!" Eamon sounded genuinely appalled.

"Methinks if we behaved like the animals we came from, we'd eat her," replied Fal reasonably. "Besides, I thought you'd be in favor of a wake. It is a fine Irish tradition."

"It is?" This obviously made a strong impression on a bat who felt himself to be, among other things, heir to the mantle of De Valera.

Fal nodded vigorously. "You don't have to attend, but not to do so is a mark of scanty respect for the dead."

Even Bronstein was caught half-cocked. "But it is not our custom . . ."

"It is ours," said Pistol with finality. "And our Phylla was first and foremost a rat."

Virginia sidled up to Chip. "What are they doing to that dead rat?" she whispered, staring in fascinated horror.

"Laying her out. Maybe not the way we humans would understand it, but the way a rat would." Chip's tone was very dry. "Phylla would have appreciated it. Sort of a rat joke."

"What do *I* do?" she whispered, unable to stop looking at the bizarre rite.

"Well, you can behave like a typical good little Shareholder, look disgusted at the antics of the proles and go off and sleep somewhere. Or you can stay and pay your respects. She only died because she went to rescue you and that smelly Pricklepuss." Chip walked away, leaving her between anger and tears.

"Are you *sure* I have to drink this filthy stuff?" Eamon eyed the glass of colorless brandy with extreme suspicion.

Nym nodded. "Phylla would have appreciated it. Some with each toast. It's tradition."

The bat looked wary. "Toast? Are you going to cook her . . ." the bat shuddered, "and then eat her? Or do you mean *drink* a toast? And since when is it tradition?"

"As far back as anyone can remember," came the sententious reply from Fal.

"About six months," added Nym. "We didn't have soft-cyber implants before that, so no clear memories. And now hush. Pistol is about to start the toasts."

The one-eyed rat raised his glass to the dead. "Phylla was as near to a wife to me as we rats have. I chose her because she was the best screw in boot camp 301. Ask *anyone* in Alpha Company."

"To the best bonk in boot camp!" The rats raised their glasses and drank. Except for the one-eyed rat. He took his glass and poured some into the mouth of the deceased.

Eamon watched in horror. " 'Tis debauched and debased you rats all are. Just like that rat was in life!"

"Hear, hear! Well said! What a fine eulogy! Go and give her a drink then."

The big bat looked stunned. They weren't joking. He flapped over to the corpse. "To the rat that propositioned even me." He poured some of the firewater into her mouth. At least it got him out of drinking some of the stuff. All round the circle rats cheered and drank. "To the rat-girl that even propositioned a bat!"

Standing next to Eamon, Pistol sniffed. Wiped his long nose with a paw and said, thickly, "Thank you, bat. I'd forgotten about that. You know, you're not a bad fellow for a bat." He sighed. "Such a lovely corpse did you ever see!"

Fal began to tell a story about Phylla, which, were it true, would have frightened Casanova and Don Juan into early retirement and made Dicey Riley look like a temperance union member.

Chip looked at the late-Chairman's daughter. She was still standing there. Red as a beetroot, with eyes nearly as wide as her Fluff's. But she'd stayed. And she managed to take a small sip from the glass with each toast. Well. She had more steel in her than he'd thought. He walked over to her. "Have you got your toast ready?"

"Me?" she squeaked.

"Yes, you, Miss Chairman's daughter. They'll be very insulted if you don't. I notice Pricklepuss has sloped off."

"Will you *stop* calling me that! I can't help who my father was. And I'd better go and see that the Professor is all right."

"Siobhan had a word with him, I mean her, on her way out. She'll have told him, her, it, not to go too far because of the booby traps. The alien'll be fine here. This place is safe enough. And at least you had a father."

"If you could call him that! I would have given *anything* for a real father, a father who loved me. Even after—" She fell silent, not wanting Chip to know about her own soft-cyber implant. The bitter thought never passed her lips. *A real father would have cared for me even after a horse-riding accident left me brain damaged. My father might have had all the means in this world, but he didn't give me the only thing I wanted in those blurred days.*

"All of us Vat-kids wanted that too," Chip said sourly.

"You had that! You had fathers or mothers who cared enough, dreamed enough to send their children twenty-four light-years to found a new utopia, away from the interference and bureaucracy of Earth." Even as she said it she realized she was echoing her father.

"The tissue donor wasn't my father. He was myself. And if this is Utopia for anyone but Shareholders, then I'm a rat's backside."

She pinched her lips together. Then she said, "Anyone can become a Shareholder, Connolly."

He snorted. "Not in *my* lifetime. Now pay attention. Melene is about to finish her toast. I reckon Pistol will call on you or Bronstein to say something next."

"But I don't know what to say!"

"How gutless and ineffectual can you be?" snapped Chip, cutting her to the core. "Think of something. She died to keep your Professor alive."

"—on the bar counter in the enlisted-rats pub. Three of them!"

The rats cheered. Even a few of the bats did.

"I'll just ask Don Fluffy to say a few words," said Pistol.

The tiny galago rose magnificently to the occasion. "She was a symbol so sexy! And also of an appetite the most insatiable—*magnifico*! too *magnifico*!—and a tail so enticing and enchanting." Fluff planted one little hand over his heart and waved the other about dramatically. "Yet! She was a heroine—of courage the most great!—and her heart was as big as a lion! In my dreams she will dance for me, the dance of the extreme privacy. My machogalagohood is rampant at the very thought—but my heart is rent! Torn in my breast!" He began plucking at the fur on his chest. "Ai! Woe is me!"

"Well shed, little one," O'Niel said thickly. "As foine as a bat she were in that last fight." Hiccup. "Calls for shong, me boyos! 'Wrap the bat-wing round me boys . . .' " He fell off the perch he hung from. Brandy was something the bat had never met before. But nonetheless the bats began to sing, "*Wrap the bat-flag round me boys, to die is far more sweet, with batdom's noble emblem, boys to be my winding sheet. . . .*"

The bats couldn't sing very well. But they sang with feeling. The rats even joined in. And sang along with "We Shall Overcome," "The Rifles of the IRA," "Solidarity Forever," "A Nation Once Again," and their own version of an old Scots favorite:

> "We were bought and sold for Company gold,
> Such a parcel of rogues is a nation . . ."

Virginia found herself sobbing quietly, and joining in the chorus of songs she'd never heard before. Outside of books this was her first encounter with the emotions of real—people. She found herself singing the words with fervor, even though she barely understood them. When Pistol called on her it was not hard at all to go forward, and simply embrace the dead rat, tears streaming down her face. The fiery brandy was a libation freely given and a prayer for forgiveness.

"We should give her a send-off fitting of a bat," said Eamon thickly to Pistol and Chip.

"She was a rat, all rat. Not a bat."

"Indade, 'twould have to be some thing a rat could appreciate too. A low joke. But she died like a true bat even if she was a rat."

"I'd like to have buried her under a pile of dead Maggots, to take with her for travel-food," growled Chip. "And good bottle or two for the road."

"Why don't we do just that?" mused Bronstein slowly. "What would you say if we gave her the explosive send-off of a bat, with a booby trap rigged so she takes a fair number of Maggots with her. With a couple of quarts of alcohol so she burns along with them."

Melene, swaying slightly, joined them. "I'd say it would be a fine and fitting send-off!"

Pistol nodded. "Heh. She'd have loved it. And it *would* take a fair number of the blue-bottle rogues with her. Where are we going to do it?"

Bronstein, as always, had been thinking ahead. "On the other side of the mound. That'll help the Maggots to believe we're heading in the opposite direction. We'll fly her body over. If you can rig us some kind of harness, Chip? Somehow we can spread the load between all of us."

Chip looked across at a plumpish bat sitting on the floor with a wing around Doll's shoulders, a glass in the other wing-claw and the bat version of "The West's Awake" on his lips. "Do you think O'Niel is fit to fly?"

Midmorning, and Chip's sleep was disturbed by a distant explosion. So. Phylla had some Maggots for the road on that long staircase to Valhalla. The way those bats used explosives she was probably a fair way up that road already. And it *would* buy them some time.

Chapter 21:
A joint misunderstanding.

Virginia was gazing out at the high ridges of the Magh' mound that hemmed them. Chip, standing a few feet behind and to the side, studied her for a moment. He was beginning to realize that the girl—young woman—had the sort of looks that grew on you. On him, anyway. Now that she was not frantic with fear, her face was more very-pretty-elfin than gaunt. And while her figure was tall and slender, it was most definitely female. Almost uncomfortably so, in fact. He did *not* need to get himself—

She must have become aware of him watching her. She turned to him. "Last night I thought we were out. But we're just as trapped, aren't we? Trapped between those." She pointed at the mounds.

"So we go over the top," he said, with an easiness he did not feel. "I've been over the top of that one.

Or maybe we'll go through. We've been through, too. Thirty-two more humps and we're at the sea."

"The sea!" She seemed aglow at very idea.

"Yep."

"That's *so* romantic!" she said, dreamily. "The sea . . . and freedom!"

He realized she had a hand on his arm and was staring into his eyes, her head slightly tilted to one side. He reacted like a man who has just found a rattlesnake in his path. He backed off, and kept backing. "Uh. Got stuff to do."

He retreated to the workshop, where he found Nym fiddling and Doc contemplative. He was relieved it wasn't Fal. But Nym was good value, for a rat.

"I've got a problem, guys."

Doc nodded. "The human condition is problematic."

"It's worse than a human problem, Doc," said Chip, despondently. "It's a woman problem."

Doc squinted at him. "Preposterous. How can there be a problem between thesis and antithesis? Simply resolve it with a synthesis, which in this case is obviously—"

Chip scowled fiercely. "Thanks, Doc! With friends like you, I don't need enemies." He turned to the other rat in the workshop. "Nym, that woman is driving me crazy!"

The big rat looked up from his oily fiddling. "They like to tease, to fain disinterest. But she fancies you, Chip."

"Disinterest!" Chip buried his head in his hands. "She can't keep her effing hands off me. She *paws* at me."

Nym was distinctly puzzled. "Well, what is the problem then? If it's lessons you need, Fal's your man. . . . Mind you, I'd have thought that Dermott gave you sufficient instructions. She used to call them out loud enough for the rest of us to appreciate."

"Will you leave Dermott out of this?" Chip's voice had a dangerous edge to it.

"Surely. I did but mention her gentle instruction." The rat grinned.

"I don't know why I bothered to speak to you," muttered Chip, turning to leave.

The rat took his sleeve with an oily paw. He pointed with his nose to an oilcan-armchair. "Tell us, Chip."

"You wouldn't understand."

"You'd be surprised," said Nym.

That was true enough. He had been surprised by Nym before. "Okay. Well, do you understand the concept 'fraternizing with the enemy'?"

Nym looked at him quizzically. "Giving the naked weapon to a Maggot?"

Chip smothered a snort. "That . . . wasn't quite what I meant. Um. But say I was doing that. You'd say I was a traitor, right?"

The big rat snorted. "I'd say it was a dead Maggot, or you're in grave danger of . . . coming short." Nym clutched reflexively. Doc grinned.

"Besides, I have seen excretory orifices on them but no reproductive organs," said Doc, pushing the pince-nez back on his nose.

"You haven't gone strange on us and want to bugger Maggots have you?" Nym asked warily. "We haven't been under shell-fire for days. What does this have to do with Dermott or that Virginia Shaw?"

"As far as I'm concerned, the *enemy* aren't just the Maggots," said Chip fiercely. "Look at it this way. Why the hell do you think we're conscripts? A good kid like Sandy Dermott is dead, instead of back at school, but 'Miss Virginia Shaw' is living it up in her mansion, eating at Chez Henri-Pierre, having a good life. We're cloned cannon fodder to the goddamn Shareholders. And then she has the cheek to say, as if butter wouldn't melt in her mouth: 'Anyone can become a Shareholder.' Oh, yeah. I can buy a basic share as soon as I'm debt free. All I've got to do is pay off the cost of turning me from a tissue scrap to human, and of educating me into cannon fodder to die for them. Which would take me the rest of my life, even assuming I don't get killed in the war."

"You could be worse off. Such conditions are relative. You could be a rat, created for a war in the Company laboratories." Doc stretched himself out, leaning against the tractor's wheel.

Chip thought about this. "And how do *you* feel about that?"

"Philosophical. If there was no war there'd be no rats . . . or bats. But that is the nature of we short-lived creatures. Though the bats find it a bone of sore contention."

Nym got back to the point. "So if I understand this right, you don't want to prong this wench because she's Company."

"Yep."

The big rat grinned. "But you do, because you're as lecherous as a monkey."

Chip looked embarrassed. "Uh. I'm not used to being chased. Hell, I'm not much to look at. I've never had to fight a girl off before."

Nym wrinkled his forehead. "So why do so? 'Tis not hurt you'll be doing to yourself."

Chip blinked. "Because . . . it'd be treachery to Dermott. Besides, if we ever get out of here, the Shareholder's dear family would see me going over the top, on my own, at a ten thousand Maggot charge, just for touching her. She doesn't understand. To her it's just a game. Something to idle away the time. Nothing to it but a quick bit of amusement."

Nym scratched his long nose. "Your Dermott is dead. And you humans make life hard for yourselves by not having a rattish outlook on life."

She was puzzled by his reactions. She knew she wasn't very pretty, but there wasn't a lot of competition. And he was the most heroic man she'd ever met. Not that she'd been allowed to meet many men . . .

But Virginia had decided. He was her beau ideal! She'd have to make him notice her, at least. He'd called her gutless and ineffectual. Well, she'd show him that she wasn't. He seemed to like that bossy bat. So, if that was what he wanted . . .

She went inside and found several bleary-eyed rats and bats eating. "Right, let's get moving. We've got a long way to go before we reach the sea. Bat, I want you to organize the food into manageable parcels."

The silence was absolute. The array of bats and rats looked at her. She'd assumed Chip must be in the alcove. Now she realized that he wasn't.

Fal leaned back and put his paws behind his head. He yawned artistically. "Pistol, tell her I am a trifle deaf."

"I would rather tell her to shog off, Fal." The one-eyed rat put his feet up on the table. "Who do you think you are, wench?"

"I am Virginia Shaw, and I'm a *human*, rat. And you've got to listen!"

"Oh! Hear that, Fal?" demanded Pistol. "She's a Virgin Shore. Her face hasn't had boat keels up and down it, after all. It must look like that naturally."

Fal snorted. "Are you Shaw she's a Virgin? Mind you, with that homely face and bad complexion . . ."

"And she reckons she's *human.* Couldn't be!" Pistol sniggered.

This was all going badly wrong. *"You'll do as I tell you!"*

"She's got nearly as loud a voice as the Duke of Plazo-Toro," said Fal, with no obvious sign of cooperation. "So where is your ridiculous little fanny-licker, Virgin-ear?"

Pistol laughed coarsely. "Heh. When he's on top, it must be Ridiculous on the Virgin, instead of Virgin' on the Ridiculous!"

Virginia felt herself blushing from the roots of her hair to her toes. She grabbed for Pistol and snatched him up.

Pistol made no attempt to dodge. He just showed a row of sharp teeth, ready to sink into her thumb. "Well," he said conversationally. "Now you've got me. What are you going to do with me? You want me to come and sort out that ear of yours, my sweet wench?"

"Screw some sense into her head," said Fal, scratching himself.

"Belike if ever there was a human that would have benefited from a soft-cyber, it's this one," Behan commented.

This was all going wrong! Virginia, to her horror, found herself bursting into tears. Behan's remark had cut right to her heart.

Fortunately, Bronstein intervened. "That's enough! Leave her alone. You let go of Pistol, girl. When you attack something either kill it immediately or incapacitate it so it can't hurt you." The bat unfurled her wings. "Now come," she commanded. "It is high time you and I had a talk. And stop that drizzle, right now."

Meekly Virginia followed after the fluttering Bronstein, leaving the derision behind her—but taking resentment and misery along.

They came to a place that commanded a view across the landscape, an old veranda. The bat hung herself on a trellis wire. "I like to perch here. It allows me to keep an eye out for Maggots. We are still in enemy territory, you know. Now, it's high time someone explained a few facts of life to you."

Virginia looked at her sullenly, wiping the tears away. Then she sat down cross-legged with her back to the wall. "I don't have to listen to you."

Bronstein hissed, showing teeth. "Human brats appear short of a few lessons in elementary survival, never mind manners. Now, listen or I will bite you. It is a lot of silly human ideas that you seem to have about leadership and the right to command. Maybe they work for you humans, although for the life of me I cannot see how. Why who your father was, or how much money you have, should gain you *any* respect, I myself cannot see. But if that's the system you humans wish to use among yourselves, that is your problem. But here, you are among rats and bats, and respect is earned. Leadership is conferred by those who respect you, not by some piece of metal or cloth or right of birth."

"But I'm a human!" protested Virginia coming up with the age-old defense . . . which is no defense. "We made you!"

The bat shrugged. "So? We may be artificially engineered creatures, with what Chip calls 'head-plastic' in our brains. But it doesn't matter what we came from, it is what we are now. Now for heaven's sake stop trying to push everyone around, especially the rats. You won friends and respect last night. Your arrogance has lost it for you this morning. Just because you're a human, and I have a soft-cyber implant doesn't mean . . ."

"I've got one too," said Virginia, her voice scarcely audible.

Bronstein was a bat. They can hear crystals grow. She cupped her wings to her ears. "*What?*"

"I said, I have a soft-cyber implant too."

"But . . . but . . . you're human!" The bat nearly lost her grip on the trellis wire.

"Not if *you* define someone with an implant as not being human. By that definition the rats were quite right. I'm not human. I'm just a piece of head-plastic," Virginia said quietly.

"But . . ."

"You don't believe me. But it's *true*," Virginia blurted bitterly. "I was brain-damaged in an accident. My parents thought the soft-cyber implant would make me a good little robot, and no embarrassment to them. But I'm not! I'm a person! I'm still the same person I was before, it's just that I can think again. I *am* the same . . . but more."

The bat stared silently at her for almost a minute.

Virginia got up and stared back. "Well. What are you staring at? I know I'm a freak, but you don't *have* to stare. It doesn't show on the outside."

Possibly for the first time ever, Bronstein sounded apologetic. "No, to be sure, I am staring at the first human being who can really understand that we are neither trained animals, nor cattle for slaughtering in a war. We are people, even if we are not human."

Virginia had never thought of it that way. Even Fluff had just been a clever and beloved pet in her eyes. With sudden insight she realized he wasn't that in his own eyes. She'd bitterly resented the fact that her parents considered her to simply be a less embarrassing talking doll now that she had the implant. She *wasn't* a doll, and Fluff *wasn't* a pet.

"Well, this is going to be something to tell the others." Bronstein's tone said she was both delighted and excited by the prospect.

Virginia cringed. "Please don't tell Chip. Please!"

The bat scratched her head with a wing-claw. "Why not?"

This was terribly difficult, Virginia found. More difficult than admitting she had an implant. "Because . . . because then he'll think that I'm just a talking doll. And I . . . want him to like me."

The bat nearly fell off her trellis wire again and had to flutter both wings to regain her balance. She shook her black head. "You humans are nearly as bad as the rats. You should be more like bats. Take a longer-term view of things. Connolly! Holy Erin! I mean, he's a decent enough human as humans go, to be sure, but it isn't like his face has interesting and attractive folds. He's rather ugly, to be honest with you, girl. Under that rat's-tail fur his face is quite smooth, I promise."

"Just *don't* tell him," Virginia begged. "And, um, *I* don't think he's ugly."

The bat looked the human female up and down. The black crinkled face crinkled some more, in sympathy. "Well, maybe some nice facial folds will still develop. You haven't got many yourself. Anyway, I suppose the important thing is that you like his face. What does he think of yours?"

"Most of the time he doesn't even know I'm alive, never mind notice my face. And the rest of the time he treats me like a bad smell." Virginia twisted her slim fingers.

"Then you must make him notice you." Bronstein, as always, was good at decisiveness.

Virginia grimaced. "That's just what I was trying to do, in there. All I managed to do was to get those two rats to be beastly about my name. And then he wasn't even there."

The bat looked at her with wide, dark eyes. "Why

in Erin's name did you think that would impress him? And pay no attention to those foul-mouthed rats. That's just the way they are."

Virginia finally ventured a small smile. "Because he likes you. And that's the way *you* are."

Bronstein's mouth fell open. "Me? ME!! You think *I'm* bossy? That's RIDICULOUS, I tell you! I'll not hear such talk!"

"Yes, ma'am. If you say so." Virginia looked down demurely.

They were all gathered together in the tasting room, even the Korozhet, when Chip came back from his long sulk.

Eamon was holding forth. " . . . so, indade, I reckon we should go through, rather than over. We'll battle to get the Korozhet up and down."

"That is most wise," said Pricklepuss, as if it hadn't nearly got them all killed, and, in a way, been the death of Phylla.

Chip was feeling distinctly otherwise, a common male problem when the testicles are going one way and the mind another. "NO."

"What do you mean 'no'? It's decided." Behan's tone was as snappish as the words.

Chip looked at Behan with distaste. Of all the rats and bats, even surly Eamon, Behan was the only one Chip genuinely disliked. The bat was a camp follower if there ever was one. "I mean there is no way I am taking Pricklepuss screaming-mee-meemy on a sneak back through the Magh' tunnels. We go over, and one mistimed shriek or squeak and I'll let go of the ropes."

Siobhan shook her head at him. "Don't be ridiculous, Chip. Tell him, Bronstein."

"I don't want to interfere," said the bat.

Chip almost choked. *Bronstein?* Not want to

interfere? *Ha!* So she didn't like the idea either. He wondered why she didn't simply ride roughshod over it, then, like she always did.

He decided it must be more bat politics. Chip knew that Bronstein was neck deep in one crazy bat faction, whereas Eamon was a mover-and-shaker in the other. Knowing Eamon, the shaking was probably done with a nice firm grip on someone's throat. Well. Bronstein had backed him up often enough. He'd be glad to be her hired lance for a change.

Chip folded his arms across his chest and said: "You can't do it without me. And I won't do it. And that's final."

Knowing Bronstein was solidly behind him, Chip stood as firm as any pylon, through all the threats, imprecations and cajolery. The truth was that he held the trump cards. Without him to do the camel work, carrying the food, carrying the Korozhet, doing the dexterous work like cutting holes, they couldn't do it. And Bronstein must have wanted his support badly, because, after not saying anything—would wonders never cease?—she fluttered out while the argument raged.

Eventually he won. "Look. We aren't being chased. We can follow the space between the mounds back towards the front. The mounds are much lower there, and not as steep. We can do three a night. The bats can fly the line up—it's thin and light enough for them to carry—the rats and the galago follow, and when they're up, they haul up a decent anchor, and then a rope. Miss Shaw and I climb up, using the rope as a safety line. We'll use those sliding prussik loops—you know, those knots that slide one way, that Nym was telling me about, the ones we didn't need to use getting out last time. Then we haul Old Crotchet up. Lower him down the other side. Easy.

Whereas if we cut our way through, we're bound to get caught sooner or later."

Then, just when he'd won, the Crotchet turned the whole thing on its head. "I have been thinking. Miss Virginia, and other good allies in this fight against the vile Magh' scourge, the human male is right. We *could* escape. But *should* we? We have within our spines' grasp the most stunning victory. We should not seek to save ourselves, but indeed, strike a blow for our peoples! Never before has a battle-capable group stood *within* the force field. We can strike at the brood-heart itself! We can strike a brave, heroic blow for Humanity!"

Chip snorted. At least he knew where he stood as to allies. He could just *see* the bats striking a brave blow for the sake of Humanity. As for the rats, they had a sensible grunt attitude towards volunteering, never mind volunteering for suicide missions. "Oh, that's really a fine idea, Mr. Pricklepuss," he said sarcastically.

"Okay!" piped Siobhan. "So we're all agreed, then?"

Chip was startled to realize *she* wasn't being sarcastic. Then his startlement turned to outright shock when all the other rats and bats immediately chorused their own support for the Crotchet's loony scheme. For all the world, they sounded like fanatic enthusiasts!

"All right then," he said coldly. He played his trump card. "I'll just go and find Bronstein and tell her that the Korozhet has decreed that we all go on a suicide mission."

He stormed out to find her. She'd put a stop to this nonsense!

Bronstein was on her favorite terrace, peering into the distance. Before Chip could tell her how ridiculous everybody was being, she turned on him. "Do you find me inclined to enforce my will on others?"

Chip grinned. "Yeah. So what?"

"It is a bad tendency in a neo-anarcho-socialist," said Bronstein morbidly. "Down that path lies totalitarianism."

"For foxache, Bronstein! What has got into you now? Sure you boss people around. So what? Has Doc infected you with his philosophical crap? We're in shit and someone's got to make decisions. So you do. Somebody's gotta do it, and you do it pretty well. No one is making us listen to you."

"But do I interfere too much?" asked the bat querulously. She seemed to be seeking comfort from Chip.

But Chip had other things on his mind. "Is piss warm and wet, Bronstein?" he snorted. "Interfering is what you do best—and naturally. Like Eamon thinking of ways to blow things up. He wouldn't be same big stupid bastard if he didn't, and you wouldn't be Bronstein if you didn't interfere. Now can we quit thinking about eternal verities and get you to come and interfere in the insanity that the dumb Korozhet is talking them into now? He wants us to forget escape and go and attack something called the 'broodheart.' "

"The Korozhet said that? I think it is a good idea, then. Like going through instead of over was."

Chip gaped at her. The whole world had gone mad!

The Korozhet used one of her spines to scratch on the dirt. "My species have spent many years studying the Magh' and I too have gained great insights as a captive. I am an academic rather than a warrior, and I know I am too emotional and frail for such exploits, but we must impale the opportunity!"

The alien tapped the diagram. "The Magh' tunnels are built according to a rigid pattern. We know from our victory and conquest of a scorpiary on

Korozhet-prime that they are built like this. Each spiral arm has 'highways' which follow a central passage to the middle of the scorpiary. Every three hundred and two yit—that is about one point three of your yards to the yit—there is a cross passage and a spiral road leading up and down. The largest of the highways is always just below ground level. If we can follow it, it will lead us to the brood-heart where the Magh' group-mind breeders are."

Virginia shook her head. "Group-mind?"

"Indeed, Miss Virginia. It is one of the things we Korozhet have long suspected, but it was confirmed while they were torturing and questioning me. All the Magh' within this scorpiary are effectively one being. The 'head' of that 'being' is the breeder-caste."

"Then how come one of you Crochets gave that talk on forces radio saying they were a number of allied species?" demanded Chip. His tone was both skeptical and sarcastic.

The Korozhet was not at a loss for an instant. "This has been an ongoing argument within Korozhet ranks for many years. I can now confirm that the multi-speciesist theory is quite wrong."

"So you're telling us that if we get to the center of the scorpiary, kill the breeder-caste—we win the war. Ha. Tell me another one!"

"No. That might have been true when the Magh' ship landed, but they rapidly began growing new scorpiaries. That is what the long tentacles of conquest do: Seed new brood-hearts. But you will destroy several million Magh' as an effective enemy. Now, your trip to the brood-heart will require that you traverse considerable distance . . ." The alien poked at the diagram.

"Shtupid idea." Pistol was distinctly full of alcohol. But, at least, thought Chip, he'd come to his senses.

The idea wasn't just stupid. It was insane. They'd go round in ever-decreasing circles to get to the middle of the scorpiary. Many miles to try and sneak into the group-mind "brood-heart." Of course, they'd be detected. Then, if the Crotchet was right, the whole damn lot would be trying to stop them.

"Hear, hear!" exclaimed Chip.

"Yesh." Pistol blinked owlishly. "Why go round, and round, and round like a whoreson Maggot? Take a short cut!" And with the tip of his tail he drew a straight line across the dusty whorls.

"He's drunk again," sneered Behan. "Never mind being killed by Maggots. If we stay here much longer the daemon drink will have away with those rats." His tone suggested that might be a good thing.

Bronstein, however, looked thoughtful. "To be sure, but he's right though. If we blew down a few walls we could make what looks like a long way . . ."

"Roughly one hundred thirty-two miles," Virginia put in, looking up from fiddling with the standard issue mini-GPS. Some Shareholder family had the contract . . . Chip had to acknowledge that the Shareholder-girl was terrifying with numbers. She seemed to have an innate grasp of formulae that made Chip's brain hurt just looking at them.

"Yes. Say one hundred thirty-two miles, to a short distance, say . . ."

"Roughly seventeen point two miles."

Chip looked at her in amazement. *That's what I call mathematics. How she does it, I don't know. I'd still be here next week counting toes.*

The Korozhet tapped the drawing in the dust again. "Taking a short cut is an excellent idea, but unfortunately that is impossible. You do not have sufficient explosives, and even if you did have you couldn't carry them."

Chip smiled nastily at the Korozhet. He *still* thought the whole idea was nuts, but he couldn't resist the chance to stick it to the snooty alien.

"That's where you're wrong, Crotchet. We've got all the explosive in the world, *and* we can transport it!"

Eamon looked startled. "Er, Chip, even you and Virginia can't carry *that* much."

"Would a tractor load do? I'd think that would be enough even for *you*, Eamon."

Chapter 22:
The gathering.

The Korozhet made a little *humph* noise and pointed two of its thick spines at him. "Ridiculous! If you cannot be sensible I shall go back to my rest." Exuding a kind of sea-urchin haughtiness, Virginia's tutor prickle-ambulated out.

Bronstein cocked her head at Chip. Chip reflected, not for the first time, that the gesture was disconcerting coming from a creature hanging upside down.

"That's crazy, Connolly."

Chip stood his ground. "Why is it crazy? Listen, I know you agree with me on this, Bronstein. The way this war has been fought by high command is to use us—rats, bats and Vats alike—as if we were Maggots. Has it worked? Can we Maggot better than Maggots?"

He glared around at them. "And who's been advising them? The Crotchets, that's who. To hell with what that critter thinks is crazy. I'm telling you this may not work, but—shit!—it'll work better than trying to blunder a hundred miles of tunnels on foot."

They were silent. Chip waited . . . and then continued. "Think about it. We know Maggots can't run for long. We can outrun them. Well, at least we can for a bit without the Crotchet. We can't *keep* doing it. But that little tractor can outrun them and we can lug along plenty of explosives and every booby trap you can think of. We can even take Pricklepuss in comfort, faster than we can run with her."

He squatted down and started to draw his own diagram on the floor. "We don't do this like Pistol said. The cross tunnels won't line up anyway. We go as far as we can here between the mounds, blow our way in. We can run down the main tunnel until we find a cross tunnel. Through the wall, and back onto the main drag. You know Maggots. All of the Maggots in creation will be chasing along behind us, and charging from further inside the mounds to be in front of us. If we do it right, we can come out behind them again. And keep doing it."

"I like it," Nym pronounced. "Besides, I want to ride that thing. Can I drive?"

"Myself I t'ink it a foine idea." O'Niel was the most taciturn of the bats. His support surprised the others.

"To be sure, like all military plans 'tis bound to screw up," said Bronstein gloomily. "They never survive contact with the enemy."

"So what else do you suggest?" asked Chip, trying to be reasonable.

The bat shrugged. Like the head-cocking, the

upside-down gesture also struck Chip as weird. "Nothing. We just take plenty of booby traps along, and be prepared for the worst."

"Let's go and have a look at this little tractor again." Eamon swung to wing. "I'm thinking of a fair number of ways to deal with Maggots, given what we've got. And I agree with you, Connolly. Human high command have always fought this war as if they wanted the Maggots to win."

"This is something which my history-download suggests humans have often done," Doc said. "I can only put this down to the intrinsic conservatism of the human intellect, which, in turn, judging from Hegel's remarks on—"

Chip raised his eyes to heaven. "Oh, put a sock in it, Doc."

Fal nudged Pistol. "Do you think he gets girls to let him work his wicked will on 'em by threatening to go on talking?"

The one-eyed rat chuckled. "Or do you think they think all that hot air makes him rise better?"

"Ha, Ancient Pistol," said Fal assuming an attitude of profundity. "He's so windy he probably floats above them."

"It is a good thing no one's sticking a prick into *him*," cackled Pistol. "He'd whizz around the room."

Fal and Pistol heckled on cheerfully as they walked across to the workshop. Doc, as usual, paid them no mind.

"Are you sure this thing will fit in the tunnels?" Eamon peered doubtfully at the little tractor.

Chip nodded. "Yep. And yep again to the trailer."

Eamon's interest was definitely pricked. "Well, then. Here is some barbed wire . . . There are many possibilities here." You could almost see more ways of generating mayhem boiling out of Eamon's head as he fluttered around the room.

Chip began to rummage among the pieces of angle iron.

"Why are you doing this?" asked Doc curiously, from a perch on the chain bin. "I know you think that this idea is flawed in concept."

Chip snorted. "I think it is barking insane, never mind flawed. Think about it, Doc. A handful of rat, bat and Vat grunts, and we're going to go and take on a couple of million Maggots. As if that wasn't bad enough, we've got an alien who claims to be 'an academic rather than a warrior,' a useless Shareholder girl, and a little big-eyed half-rat-sized monkey as passengers. We should be running and hiding. Doing our best to get out. We've found out all sorts of things about the Maggots that could change the war. We could take flamethrowers to the Maggots . . . we also know now it is no use trying to trick them, because what one Maggot knows all of them do. Kind of explains why all of high command's 'big pushes' have gone spectacularly wrong, doesn't it? And with Shaw's daughter someone might even listen to what we've found out. Instead we're going on this suicide plunge. A mission that can't work."

The rat looked thoughtful, wrinkling his forehead. "Then why have you not decided to go your own way?"

Chip rolled the front wheel of the little tractor up to the axle hub. "Why are *you* going along, Doc? You sound half crazy spouting that Hegel stuff, but I've noticed there is some good sense underneath it all."

Doc thought over his reply for some time. "Hegelian philosophy contains the essence of logical thought," he mused. "But I do this . . . because I feel compelled to do it."

"If you ask me, that Crotchet-built crap in your head isn't working properly. Well, if we're gonna do this, then let's do this so that the tractor at least works. Pass me that spanner."

"Virginia, this is no occupation for a gentlegalago!" Fluff rubbed his pinched fingers and stared balefully at a pair of pliers nearly bigger than himself.

Virginia could sympathize. She'd never worked with wire before. Her hands felt raw. Yet there was no way she was going to stop. Everybody was working. Well, except for the Professor. He couldn't really manage this sort of thing, and it wasn't fair to expect him—her—to try, no matter what Chip said.

The problem wasn't just the work force, however. It was also a lack of knowledge and dexterity. Chip was the only one who had even been in a workshop before, and that had been simply been basic Vat workshop training. His knowledge of internal combustion engines was limited. When he'd been little more than a pot scrubber at the restaurant, he'd sometimes been chased off to go and help the jack-of-all-trades-mechanic who kept Chez Henri-Pierre and its vehicles running.

The mechanic had been a large, lazy, fat man who'd made his grease monkeys do as much as possible. That was why, when it came to vehicles Chip had the beginnings of an idea. . . . At least when it came to complicated stuff like "put the wheel on the studs and tighten the bolts." He just hoped like hell the rest of his "knowledge" was accurate. Experience suggested it wouldn't be. . . .

Chip decided that responsibility shared was probably responsibility quadrupled, but he'd try it anyway. "Bronstein. We need to plan this lot out. Here,

Nym. Come and join us—you're as near to a mechanically inclined rat as the universe has ever seen. I've got the wheel back on the tractor. Virginia and Don Fluff have made a whole load of snares. Eamon wants eleven bags of fertilizer. We need to make brackets for putting fertilizer bags, the barbed wire and other stuff onto the vehicle. Eamon also wants holes drilled in pieces of wood for all the bangstick cartridges. We need to drill, and most of all we need to weld. The trailer has a broken hitch. We're going to need power."

Nym chuckled. "I'll just run across to the Maggots' place with a cable, shall I?"

Chip eyed Nym savagely. The rat had the grace to look embarrassed. "Nym hath heard that rats of few words are the best rats," he muttered. "Sorry."

Chip continued. "Now, there is a little generator here . . ."

"We should be careful if it makes low-frequency sounds," said Ginny. "The Professor says the Magh', particularly the Magh'tsr and Magh'evh, hear low-frequency sounds over great distances."

Chip tried glaring at her. She hadn't been invited to this conference! But she was distracted just then, by Fluff landing on her shoulder, so he wasted a perfectly good glare.

Bronstein, however, gave attention instead. "So what does that mean? Does this generator thingy make low-frequency sounds? What can we do about it?"

Chip shrugged. "Muffle it in something, I suppose. I'm not too sure what a 'low-frequency sound' is. Vibrations and stuff, I guess?"

"There are a couple of battered mattresses half under masonry over in the farmhouse," Virginia volunteered brightly.

"Right, Miss Muffet. Get them," said Chip, pointing at the door. That would get rid of her.

She went, eager to help, and that left Chip feeling bad again. How the hell did the scion of all that money end up being so like an eager little puppy? It was hard to kick a puppy . . .

His mind turned to other forms of eagerness. She must have some kind of problem. Vat-shagging was a favorite male Shareholder pastime. He'd even heard of Shareholder girls slumming it with a Vat for a night. He'd never heard of a happy outcome though. Not for the Vat involved, for sure.

He pulled his mind back to the task in hand. "Anyway, what I was getting to is this: we need to line up all the projects we need power for. There's a fair chance we'll attract Maggots. We need to get the stuff ready, get the tractor going, and move out."

Bronstein nodded. "As soon as it gets dark we're going to fly up this 'valley' and locate the best place for an access hole. Then we'll get everything ready. Siobhan and O'Niel are going to go and sow some more rat droppings, and maybe a booby trap or two."

"Look for a route we can drive the tractor down," said Chip. "It can't be too narrow a hole. And how are you going to find the cross passages?"

Eamon smiled nastily at him. "Relax. We have a length of string for that very purpose, indade. And now that we know of the regularity of the thing, the pattern is just too obvious. Oh, and I have been meaning to ask. You *do* know how to drive this thing, don't you?"

"Um, yes." There was doubt in Chip's voice. "I know how it works. I've driven something similar. And Miss Muffet will have lots of driving experience. Cars are for the rich."

But when Virginia returned, her glasses dusty and

with a nasty scratch on her arm, dragging two still-damp foam mattresses, she had to disappoint them.

Chip found it weird. She must be the only Shareholder kid in existence who didn't drive. Oh well, the Shaws were the top of the heap. Maybe once you got up there you always had someone to drive for you. She went off to ask the Korozhet if he could. Apparently he'd driven the landspeeder all right. Why didn't the idea fill Chip with glee? He went and set up his little radio. They might as well have some music while they worked.

The music helped to lift his spirits. He could see the funny side of a list of booby traps being written on a wine label. A commando-style raid which had a bunch of reluctant grunts planning and executing it was a bit of a joke too.

Heh. It surely would have high command's elegant silk underwear in a twist around their nuts. No carefully orchestrated stuff where everything had to be dead on time and go absolutely right. No elegant strategy which sure as hell they had read about in some book. He could have told the stupid bastards that those plans never had a cat in a dog pound's chance of working, off paper.

"Synchronize your watches, gentlemen." Snort. Yeah. He'd been in one of those operations. Total balls-up. Well, that couldn't happen this time. Nobody had a watch, except the girl. High command could surely have learned from Bronstein: *Do it when you have to, or when it's ready. And prepare for the worst. Don't expect things to go right, and when they go wrong, seize the gaps.* Not that they'd ever listen to a bat!

"Yoww!"

Something on the high shelf had seized his

exploring fingers. It was a mousetrap. Stepping up onto a box he saw there was a whole row of them. Some joker had left this one cocked.

"What's the shriek about, Chip?" Nym and several of the other rats peered at him from where they'd been attempting to maneuver pieces of steel pipe.

"I just found something I have a real use for." He waved the mousetrap at them.

Nym bared his teeth. The others just looked at him with reproachful black beady eyes, their upturned pointy faces filled with horror.

"How low can you sink, Connolly?" Melene couldn't have crammed more disgust into her tone with a shoehorn.

"For Pete's sake! I mean to use it as a detonator, not a rattrap!" Chip's tone was defensive.

Fal was not mollified. "Shogging whoreson! Next he'll be talking about 'Rodent operatives.' Bah. Smash the things."

Chip's fingers hurt. "Oh for . . . crying out loud, you lot aren't even rodents. We had a whole goddamn speech from General Focnose on how calling you rats was derogatory and not to be tolerated because you were insectivores."

"Still disgusting things . . ." Fal was interrupted as the heavy metal doors creaked and Virginia came in, sunlight reflecting off her thick glasses.

Behind her, the Korozhet prickled along in the dust, bringing its bouquet of old clothes. "No, you will have to abandon your plan to use this thing! I can only drive things with automated controls. Miss Shaw cannot do it either. A shame. You will have to abandon your plans. We will have to resort to stealth after all. A pity indeed. I had almost come to see the merit of your plans. If you climb down into the lower regions there are very few Magh' down there . . ."

"Oh, it's all right, Professor," Virginia said sunnily. "Chip knows how to drive." The cheerful words were accompanied by a very broad smile. She had a nice smile, Chip noticed. *Very* nice. Something in his stomach went *urp*.

"Um," he said. Swallowed hard. "Um."

"We interrupt this broadcast of Forces Favorite Radio with a news-flash. Celtis Observatory reports . . ."

Crash. The Korozhet had turned abruptly and its spines knocked the radio off the workbench. Then, to add insult to injury, it stumbled and splintered it. "Clumsy me! Oh woe! It is for this reason I am not a technician! Forgive me, all! I did but turn suddenly to see who was speaking to us. A thousand apologies!"

"You did that on purpose!" Chip grabbed the hammer.

"Don't be a loon, Chip," snorted Fal. "How could he—she—plan to do something behind it? Her."

"Of course it was an accident. I saw. I had considered doing it on purpose myself," said the galago. "At least that horrible caterwauling she is stopped. Not one piece of Wagner has been played on it."

"No Strauss waltzes, either. Don't you like classical music, Chip?" Virginia apparently thought any subject was safer than the Professor's clumsiness.

"What I *don't* like is that self-admitted klutz near this workshop. Get her out of here, Ms. Shaw. And of course I like the classics. I'm a big Jimi Hendrix fan. And I like The Doors and Eric Clapton, too."

"An assembly line is what we need." Bronstein began organizing the rats while Chip still fumed over his smashed radio. "Fal, you and Doc can try to manage the sawing. We need fifty pipe sections. Eamon has marked where the pipe must be cut."

"But we have paws! We're not dexterous." The rats were clearly disgruntled.

Bronstein hissed impatiently, like a bad-tempered kettle. "You can manage a hacksaw between the two of you. It is only plastic pipe, for heaven's sake! Now, while they're busy doing that, I want a window-putty plug, the diesel and ammonium nitrate in and the top full of metal junk. Doll, Melene and you and O'Niel can get to filling those one gallon and five gallon cans with diesel. When you finished that, come back to me."

"Dictator," muttered O'Niel. "Tyrant." But he and the two rat-girls started lugging cans out.

Virginia followed Melene, offering her help. "Load the cans into that barrow, and I'll take them out for you."

"Good idea," said Mel. As soon as they were outside, she added: "Then you and I can have a little talk about males. Bronstein said you had a girl-problem."

Virginia blushed. "Okay," she squeaked.

Bronstein turned on the galago, who was surveying the scene with thumbs stuck in his waistcoat pockets. "And you, little one. Are you up to a man's job?"

"Of a certainty!" he said with pride.

She smiled. "Excellent. You can hammer in nails."

The galago was taken aback. Plainly enough, that wasn't what he'd had in mind. "But, *señorita*-bat, a man's job is to sit in the shade and watch the girls dance or wash the clothes."

"Not while there is breath in *this* 'señorita-bat's' body, it isn't." Bronstein's tone would have intimidated a pro football player. The galago got busy, hastily.

"It would have been nice to have some music with this lot," grumbled Chip.

Virginia came back in just in time to hear the last

statement. "Seeing as the radio's broken, we could sing," she suggested brightly, while loading more cans in the barrow.

"And what would you be after having us sing, Miss Shaw?" demanded Eamon. The big bat's tone of voice was surly. " 'Four Green Fields'? Or 'Joe Hill'?"

"I don't know either. But I'd like to learn both," was her earnest reply. She hefted the handles of the now-loaded barrow, straightened, and pushed it through the door. The effort brought out all the curvature in her slender figure.

A moment later, she was gone. "Humph," grumbled Eamon. Chip said nothing. He was preoccupied with the memory of the departing figure. In the sunlight . . .

Humph. *Forget it!*

"Pull the pump handle for a bit," said Melene. "Now, what is the problem with you and Chip? Bronstein actually came to me, believe it or not, and asked me to advise you. She seemed to think you had a rat-type problem."

Virginia blushed again. She'd brought the barrow load of cans out to the diesel pump and now Melene was giving her the fifth degree inquisition. She didn't even know what the problem was herself.

"You can tell me all about it. Bronstein says you're one of us." The rat-girl's tone was kindly.

Virginia swallowed. One of *them*? Then she realized. She was. And they did not consider themselves inferior. "I'm in love!" she blurted.

"So what's the problem? Can't he get it up? Generally I found if you get them before they have too much to drink . . ."

Melene continued onward, into anatomical detail that nearly had Virginia's eyes popping out.

Finally the girl interrupted. "Uh. That, um, wasn't

what I meant I was having problems with. I meant . . . um . . . *Romance*."

Melene looked puzzled. "Romance? Isn't that what we're talking about?"

Virginia felt her face must be a fiery beacon. "No. You're talking about sex."

The rat-girl was definitely mystified. "What's the difference?"

Virginia felt like a very inexperienced swimmer caught up in an undertow. "Well sometimes, um, romance *does* lead to sex."

"Methinks it seems an unnecessary complication," said Mel, dismissively. "But tell me then, what it is you're wanting?"

"Well . . . I don't know." Ginny wrung her hands. "I've never had a boyfriend. Um, in books they bring you flowers or . . . or candy."

"Instead of giving you a drink? Seems strange to me. Still, humans *are* rather odd. I don't think Chip has any flowers or candy." She paused. "You say you never had a boyfriend? Does that mean you've never . . ."

Virginia couldn't do more than nod.

"Whoreson!" Mel giggled. "Don't you tell Fal that. He'd get ambitions!"

Virginia shuddered.

Melene laughed outright. "Don't you let Fal push you around. Bully him back. Tell me, is that the problem? Chip wants to and you don't? That's males for you . . ."

"NO! It's not like that." Virginia said fiercely. "My nanny told me all men just wanted to . . . But he doesn't. Doesn't even seem to want to touch me."

Melene put her head on one side and surveyed the miserable human girl. "You mean you would, if he wanted to?"

Virginia stopped pumping. Bit her lip. Wrung her hands. "I suppose so. Yes. If he wanted to. I don't understand. Am I hideous or horrible?"

"Nonsense! Not to humans, anyway," Melene reassured her. "Chip used to behave almost like a rat with that Dermott-girl. And she also had virtually no tail, and an even shorter nose than you."

That news didn't seem to cheer Virginia up.

The organizing had taken some time. Everything that could be done by hand had been done. Now the welding machine had been trundled out and stood ready. The little five-hundred-liter tank trailer with the one severed bar of the Y hitch had been manhandled into position. The plate Chip was going to try to weld on to secure the hitch was clamped in place. The generator reposed on the one mattress, like some oily yellow mechanical baby. The extension cords had been located and, in one case, fixed. Next to the drill press lay the box of cartridge mines-to-be and the pieces of angle iron Chip wanted to bolt onto the trailer. They needed, somehow, to make a rack for the huge and growing pile of stuff they wanted to take along. The windows had been blacked out. The door was chinked. Chip needed his headlight to navigate towards the jenny. Well, in a minute they'd have power and there'd be an extension light on.

He grasped the little handle on the generator and pulled. *Fud-dududu . . . duh* again. Again. Again. And again. Sweating, Chip checked the SOB thing out. Ah. Choke. Ooops. On-off cutout.

Fud-dududu . . . fffopoppop pop.

Well, he'd achieved a curl of smoke. Nearly. So he went back to pulling . . . and it didn't start. He tried it with the choke both in and then halfway in. Not for all the swearing and sweating in creation was the cantankerous thing going to start.

"Methinks it needs a drink," said a fruity rat-voice from the darkness.

Chip shone his beam savagely at Fal. "Shut up," he snarled. "Anyone else with bright ideas can try pulling it themselves."

"I'll try." Virginia said, eagerness glinting off her glasses.

Chip knew exactly what would happen as soon as he gave her that starter cable. The goddamn thing would start.

Which, of course, it did. First pull.

Maybe the thing had been flooded by his previous attempts . . . At least it had the decency to die when they put the load on, and then to fail in starting again for her.

He put the choke in, and it started on the second pull. "Now leave it running for a bit before we plug it in."

And then . . . there was light. A sunrise is a joyous thing, but Chip hadn't realized just how much he'd missed the normalcy symbolized by an ordinary incandescent globe. Once long ago—in a life that seemed to have belonged to someone else—it had been something so . . . accepted. He hadn't realized how much he'd missed it.

"Right . . . weld first, I think." His voice was a bit thick.

"It's just so lovely to see the light," whispered Virginia.

Chip felt a twang of sympathy, surprised at the common ground between them. But all he said was "Don't look at the arc light," as he slipped the welding mask over his face. He spoke with a confidence he was far from feeling. True, "Armpits" Jones had showed him how it should be done. Armpits had even let him *try*. He felt himself blush and was glad of the mask.

"I'm going to try to muffle the sound from the generator," she said.

"Fine." Chip was concentrating on working out the best approach to the welding job. He tapped the rod against the metal. The rod sparked actinic arc light, hissed and . . .

Stuck. Welding hadn't miraculously gotten easier in the intervening years.

"Well, let's get on to the drilling then," said Nym professionally, rubbing his paws. "Come on, Pistol. You hold that short piece of steel in place. I'll pull the handle down."

The one-eyed rat looked at the drill press nervously. "I'd liefer wait for Chip."

Nym looked at him with scorn. "Stop blithering, rat. It's a basic piece of machinery, for goodness sake. I pull that lever down. The drill comes down. What could be simpler?"

"Get Fal to hold it," suggested Pistol.

Nym's icy gaze would have withered polar lichen. "Tch. He can hold your hand if you like."

Even Pistol wasn't proof against that. "No, if you're sure . . ."

"Well, we'll do those small pieces first," Nym condescended. "Start with the easiest."

He started the drill. Virginia tried to hold the second mattress wrapped around the generator with two hands, while she tried to tie it in place with a third and a fourth hand she didn't have.

The big rat hauled at the press handle. "Whoreson! This bedamned lever is stiff." He threw his giant-rat weight and strength into the project.

The high-speed drill bit came down fast, and bit into the mild steel. The piece of steel proved an efficient transmitter of torque.

What followed was the first airborne rat-strike in history. A process that went something like—

"AAAAAHHHH!!!!"

THUD. Fortunately, Pistol hit Virginia's mattress and rolled to the floor unhurt, still clinging to the steel section. He was paralyzed with fear and shock.

Well . . . except for his mouth.

"YOU FUGGING BACONFED WHORESON RATCATCHER!"

Virginia stood there, wide-eared with amazement, while Pistol shredded Nym's character and morals, etc. etc., unto the fifteenth generation back. He was working on the sixteenth when he stopped abruptly.

The mattress, alas, had caught fire.

Stamping on it was ineffectual. Oil had seeped into the mattress, and it burned even though it was still partly wet. The workshop was a hell's-cauldron of smoke, steam and little dancing flames. Virginia bolted from the Dante-esque scene.

Chip cursed her under his breath as he stamped on the mattress. *Just like a fucking worthless Shareholder bitch to run!*

She was back an instant later, armed with a fire extinguisher.

Some time later, the place still was acrid with burned mattress and the ozone smell of welding. Virginia gazed admiringly at the hitch-wishbone. "You're brilliant!"

It really wasn't a bad piece of "hedgehog" welding. There weren't more than seven stuck welding rods cut off with side cutters. There were even a couple of really nice spot-welds. Chip had skilled hands and exceptionally fine motor control, as befits a master chef. Still, you don't learn to weld very well in ten minutes.

"Hey, Chip! Is this thing supposed to come off again?" Nym wrestled with the C-clamp. "Because I need it for the drilling."

Chip looked. "Um. No. That clamp is now a permanent fixture."

Chapter 23:
Baring the Brontë.

The drill was silent at last. So was the generator. Careful bat-patrols had shown no sign of Maggot-awareness. The bats had flown off to trail some more droppings and trigger another explosive . . . two valleys away.

The rats were off filling Molotov cocktail bottles with alcohol. On a "one-for-me, one-for-the-Maggots" basis, Chip suspected. The dexterous galago had gone to screw on lids—Melene and Doll were still keen to get him to screw on anything and anywhere. That left Chip alone with Virginia, who had appeared to have the same in mind earlier. But he needed the strength of another human for these jobs.

Chip and Virginia began maneuvering the little tank trailer out of the workshop. The task was difficult, since the new rack of bolted-on pieces of angle iron kept catching on the doorframe. In addition, the trailer was festooned with a tangle of barbed wire rolls, on top of knee-buckling loads of fertilizer bags, on top of diesel drums. Once empty fertilizer bags were now bulging full of wire snares, pipe bombs, homemade caltrops, and everything from aerosol cans to a gallon can of floor-tile glue. The remaining space was taken by bundles of hinged ceiling planks set up with tenpenny nails and bangstick cartridges. There were still bags of Molotovs to come.

And the insecticide bombs, which consisted of powder stuffed into the condoms which Virginia had found in the back of a desk drawer in the workshop. Someone had obviously believed in the colony policy of increasing the human capital—as soon as they'd got this reproductive act perfect, which, of course, required practice.

Virginia had asked him why anyone would need rubber balloons in a workshop. Chip had managed to choke out some kind of preposterous answer, which she had accepted without question. He was beginning to realize that, for all the girl's evident shy passion for him, she was an utter naif. The odd combination was giving him . . .

Fits.

He could feel his defenses crumbling. For all his detestation of Shareholders, Chip could no longer fool himself into thinking that the girl was simply toying with him out of idle-rich-girl ennui. Now, watching her wrestling energetically with the trailer, he felt his defenses crumble some more. Virginia's forehead was beaded with sweat. Trickles of it coursed through the dust and grime on her face. Her lips were pulled back in a grimace, exposing slightly-skewed front teeth. For all the world, she reminded him of—

Dermott. Except *this* girl was prettier—a *lot* prettier—and . . .

Sigh. Smarter, yeah. A lot smarter. And . . .

Virginia noticed him staring at her. Her grimace turned into a smile. Not a coy smile, or a coquettish one. Just—a smile.

Sigh. His eyes shied away from her and came to rest on one of the insecticide bombs. The sight of that bulging container triggered off a rapid free association in his mind.

He drove those thoughts away, fiercely, almost frantically. That road led to disaster!

Finally, they got the trailer outside. Next came filling the tank. They found a hose. Now all they had to do was start a raw brandy siphon. Oh, and calm the rats. They were going to get hysterical about Chip swiping their booze.

In the gray dawn light Chip caught sight of the distant flicker of returning batwings. He couldn't but feel relieved. Funny. In those far off days, about a week ago, bats, rats and humans shared a war and little else. Now . . . they were welded together by their struggle to stay alive. Even this Shareholder girl. She'd worked like a Vat. Chip had to admit she looked a bit like a Vat. The glasses and the skew teeth did it. A good Shareholder had those made-of-plastic-looking regular teeth and contacts or eye surgery at the specialist unit in the ship. "Toss me that rope."

She did.

"I've been meaning to ask—why do you have to wear glasses?"

"Because I can't see much without them," she said shortly. It was apparent he had trodden on a nerve.

He proceeded to make a bad thing worse. "What

I meant was, what about surgery? They implanted infrared lenses into us soldiers. They do stuff with lasers . . ."

"My corneas are too thin. Back on Earth they could transplant. Here I'm stuck with it." Her tone said: *Talk about something else. Don't ask me about contact lenses.*

Tact was Chip's strong point, only if compared to his ability with seventeen-dimensional theoretical geometry. But this warning-off was clear enough to anyone, and it finally even got through to him. He kept his mouth shut. She must have realized that he was backing off. She initiated another subject, hastily. "What are you going to do after the war, Chip?"

He smiled. "First thing—get out of the goddamned army. If I live that long. Go back to work I suppose. Henri-Pierre would probably take me back. The SOB hates my guts, but then he wouldn't have to teach a new Vat from scratch."

"Did you like working there?" she asked, timidly.

"I couldn't *stand* it. But I was serving my apprenticeship. Apprentices do what they're told."

The grimness in his voice spoke volumes. But, after a moment, he relented. "I enjoyed cooking well enough. I just couldn't stand Henri-Pierre, or his ideas of food. Silly fancy overdressed stuff. Some of it was pure poison, honest. And such small portions."

He paused, uncertain whether to continue. But the friendly interest in her face sparked him onward, almost against his will. "What I always dreamed of doing was opening a steakhouse. A steakhouse and a pizza place. Where I could cook *real* food. Good robust stuff, chunky and tasty. Italian food, too. The only French thing I'd do is fries. And I'd like it to be just across the road from Chez Henri-Pierre. Just upwind of it, so people in there with their little bitty portions of pretty can appreciate the smell of ribs and french fries."

She began to laugh, a delicious sound, and it was a laugh which even twinkled her eyes. It would have turned stronger men than Chip to jelly.

Crumble, crumble. *Disaster!*

"Sorry," she choked, "I wasn't laughing at you, honestly. I was just remembering Daddy taking me to Henri-Pierre when I was a teenager—and being *so* hungry *after* lunch. His customers will go *mad* smelling that. That's beautiful!"

There was a flash of teeth in the predawn light. Chip used the reminder of coming mayhem to haul himself back from the precipice.

"Yeah," he said gruffly. "Enough talking! Let's get a move on."

Bronstein swung to hang under the eaves of the ruined outbuilding. "All right. What is it you want to speak to me about, Eamon?"

The big bat looked about the dawn uneasily, before hanging beside her.

"We have a chance to be free," said Eamon. "A chance to cast off the yoke of humanity forever. No more in slavery's chains to labor, and shed our life-blood for tyrants."

"I've heard it all before," she snapped. "It would be a betrayal of trust."

"But the end justifies the means, Bronstein. We do this for bats, all bats. You can't make a revolution without breaking a few humans."

She was silent, her head turning. Then: "I can smell naphthalene. The Korozhet is somewhere about. We'll talk later."

✧ ✧ ✧

Chip was doing his best to be persuasive. Calm, reasonable.

"Look, I don't want to be a wet blanket, but you're going to be a hindrance in combat. Distract us from keeping ourselves alive. You and the Crotchet would be safer here. You've some small chance of escape."

Virginia shook her head. "No chance at all. There is a statistically increasing probability of us being caught, each step we take away from this place." She seemed almost inhuman when she got onto math. . . .

She stood erect, her chin upraised, defiant, determined. "No, I am *not* staying. This is my war as much as it is yours." She smiled at him. "*To die is far more sweet . . .*"

"Bullshit, lady!" So much for his calm reason, thought Chip. "Pardon my language, but that's pure, pure bull. No kind of death is sweet. Death in war is just plain ugly, mostly."

"Surely you think dying nobly for a good cause is better than starving to death slowly?" she retorted, staring at him challengingly.

"Indade!" said Eamon.

"Hear, hear!" Siobhan clapped her wings.

"*Anything* is better than starving," added Fal, with feeling.

Chip tried a different tack. "What you and the Shareholder high command don't understand is it takes a lot of skill to kill a Maggot in a slowshield."

Virginia sniffed. "I must show you what I found when I ran for the fire extinguisher."

She walked into the workshop, her head held high, her fine-boned face set in a determination that shone in those glasses-magnified eyes. She emerged with a serious weapon. A chainsaw. It was a small one, perhaps intended for vine trimming. "I've seen these used. I don't believe I need much skill. And if I have to walk behind you all the way, I'm coming along. Accept it."

She was a mystery to him. Like lace on a suit of armor. The first bit might be froth and tears and romanticism, but there was a steel underneath it all that he could not match. Chip wasn't a fool. Short of tying her up he saw no way of stopping her. That wouldn't stop him trying. Still, the rats did their best . . .

"Methinks 'tis—Virgin Chainsaw-chick!" cheered Pistol, giving her a lewd one-eyed wink and a ratty-wolf whistle.

"What about giving our Chip a quick circumcision of the puissant pike?" sniggered Fal. "Just to prove to him you know how to use it, you lusty jade."

"But do it properly, my sweet little rouge. Don't take any short cuts!" Pistol laughed so much he fell off his perch on the trailer.

She bent over and put the chainsaw down. Pulled the cord. Miracle of miracles, it started. She picked it up and gunned it. Her heavy glasses shone through a cloud of blue two-stroke smoke, and her slightly skew teeth were revealed in a feral smile. "I'd rather use you as an example, rat. How would you like an instant sex change?"

Pistol scurried away.

"You're learning, Ginny," approved Melene.

"It'll roll." Chip kicked the tractor wheel. "The damn thing is heavy, sure, but I can move it on my own. The two of us should be able to push it easily."

"So? What's the problem then, Chip?"

Virginia studied him as he stared at the wheel. She was learning to read him. That realization both pleased and surprised her. The romances had never mentioned that necessity. . . .

Chip never approached a situation with a "how-shall-we-do-it" question. Instead he always stated the possible facts that pertained to the problem. Set out the building blocks for his solution . . .

He breathed in, sucking air across his teeth in a pensive hiss. "So just who is going to drive?"

That was a question! Ginny thought about it. "We could put Nym on the brake pedal?"

Chip shook his head. "In most respects, he's an exemplary rat. But entrusting Nym with mechanical devices is like giving a backsliding alcoholic a bottle of gin to look after. The mad rat would try to drive the thing."

There was a lot of truth in that, Virginia acknowledged to herself. She'd seen Nym perched on tip toes on the saddle of the tractor, clinging to the steering wheel, making odd *brmm-brmm* noises. When he'd realized she was looking at him he'd pretended to be clearing his throat. Nym seemed to assume that since he adored mechanical devices they returned the affection. Virginia started to snicker, until she realized that she had made much the same mistake with her romantic inclinations toward Chip.

"Doc, then? Or Melene? She's very sensible." Virginia felt herself blush remembering the very frank talk Melene had had with her. . . .

Chip pulled a face. "Doc would probably get distracted by the philosophical contentions of whether to push the brake pedal or not to push the brake pedal. Melene would be good, but she's by far the lightest rat. That's a stiff pedal, that. I think it'll have to be fat Fal."

"But Fal . . . he's so . . . so like Hindley," she shuddered.

"Who?"

"Oh, you wouldn't know," Virginia spoke as lightly as she could. "A character out of *Wuthering Heights*."

"I do, actually," came Chip's morose reply. "I had to read it at Company school. I guess you did, too. Shame. I didn't realize they did that sort of thing to Shareholders as well. I thought it was torture reserved for Vats."

"That book is part of me!" she started to protest. But she managed to choke off the words. It was part of her download, but she couldn't explain that to *him*. Chip had made clear enough his suspicions of "cyber-intelligence."

"Oh? I hated it, myself. That Cathy was such a total wet-lettuce. Five minutes of guts and there would have been no book." He didn't realize *he* was being Heathcliff to the life.

Fal stared distrustfully at the pedal. "This had better work, Connolly."

"Trust me, Fal. There's nothing to it." Chip almost crossed his fingers behind his back.

"Are you sure it's the right pedal?"

"Of course," said Virginia indignantly. "You think Chip wouldn't know something like that? Just be sure to stop the tractor when it gets to the hill."

Chip held his tongue. There were three pedals. He'd worked out clutch easily enough. The other two *must* be brake and accelerator. Must be.

The moon was up, the charges laid, the tank trailer full, the last supper eaten and the waiting hour . . . done.

Nym had stalked off in a huff.

"A-one, a-two . . ." The tractor began to roll. Glacially, and then more easily. More easily. More easily.

It was rolling down the hill, picking up speed. Picking up speed.

Fal was *not* a happy rat.

"Whoreson!" he shrieked. "Why isn't it stopping?"

The rat had both feet thrust hard down on the pedal. The pedal was flush with the metal.

"Put the blade down!" shouted Chip, heels dragging as he now tried to hold the tractor back.

"HOW?" The rat frantically grabbed levers . . . Pressed pedals.

Crunch.

The wheel hit the rock that Nym had rolled in the way. The big rat had picked the biggest he could move. Even so it wasn't a very large rock . . . she was going over . . .

Over the rock . . . and the tractor stopped. Virginia hadn't tried to stop it by arm-strength. When the tire hit the rock she'd jumped up, and, not knowing what to push or pull, had grabbed the gear lever at the same time that Fal had jumped off.

A few gear teeth the poorer, the tractor halted.

" '*Trust me*,' he said. 'There's nothing to it,' he said." Fal's fangs glittered wickedly in the moonlight as he stalked closer to Chip.

"Look, rat. *This* is the clutch. *This*, on the opposite side, where I put you, is the *brake*," snarled Chip. His own teeth were bared.

"Look yourself, you—you . . . tripe-visaged shogging rascal! I tried that one first. Then I tried the one next to it. Then I tried the grab or clutch . . ." He dug in his pack. Produced a clear-fluid filled half-pint bottle. "Here . . . Ginny. Do an old rat a favor. Open this screwcap for me."

"Fine bloody lush that can't even open his own bottle," Chip growled.

"Methinks you're walking on a thin edge, Connolly. I just wanted to give the lady a drink for saving my tail." Fal's lofty tone was betrayed by a slight shake of the paws that were holding out the bottle.

Chip snorted. "You're going up in Fal's estimation,

Virginia. 'Lady,' now. Weren't you a lusty jade earlier?"

She handed the rat his bottle, ignoring Chip studiously. And, with great ceremony, he passed it back to her. "No. You first. I insist. Have a good belt!"

She wished like hell he hadn't insisted. That hasty mouthful made her glasses mist up. Still, it was warming . . .

Maybe that was why she was so ready to urge Chip into that saddle. In the moonlight he was dark faced, his features stern and heavy browed . . . his eyes and gathered eyebrows were ireful now . . . the book words flowed unbidden into her mind. *He wasn't Heathcliff. He was Edward Rochester. How could she have not realized it?*

That made her . . . Jane Eyre. Well . . . well. Jane was courageous. Cathy was a wild headstrong child and a tearful emotional adult. He was *Edward.* . . .

She took another swallow. *But in some ways he was more like Heathcliff.* . . .

Again, the tractor was rolling down the hill, bats following in its erratic wake. In the stillness of the night she heard Chip swear. But there was still no ignition. She followed the pack down the hill.

There was a small rise on the downhill road, before it plunged steeply again. The tractor had paused just short of the top. Chip was off and examining it.

Well . . .

Off and kicking it.

"What's wrong?"

"In case you hadn't noticed, 'lady,' " he snarled, "it hasn't started. And Fal was right. *Neither* of those two pedals work as a brake. Maybe they're not connected, or maybe they only work when the engine's running."

He walked around the little tractor, poking and prodding in the eternally hopeful fashion of the nonmechanical. *Must be sumkinda magic* . . .

"I'm sure these wheel things should be joined. Attached to this propeller thingy. At least I think so."

"A fan belt?" offered Virginia

He snapped his fingers. "That's it. A fan belt! I remember. We broke one when I did that trip to collect coalfish with Dieter. He was our mechanic. He took a pair of panty hose off Alette. Alette cried. She only had the one pair. Um. I don't suppose you have . . ."

"They're rather laddered," Virginia said.

She saw the flash of teeth. "I don't care if they have escalators. Gimme."

She blushed fiercely. "I, um, I'll go back up and get out of them."

"Just go around the other side of the tractor," Chip said impatiently. "We haven't got time."

She could swear she could feel herself bathed in infrared torchlight. Then there was a clatter up behind her, and something fell onto the roadway. She whirled, undergarments in hand, between anger and fright.

"What the hell do you stupid bastards think you're playing at?" Chip had scrambled halfway up the front cowling. He was wrestling a bottle from the grasp of a portly rat-form. Pistol was trying to help Fal pour liquor into the air filter.

"We're only giving it a drink, Chip," protested Pistol.

"Tis true. We just wished to give it something to live for." Fal's ratty voice was full to overflowing with generosity. He pointed at Virginia, who was trapped in Chip's instinctive follow of the headlight. "I mean, isn't that what *you're* doing?"

"Methinks it would have preferred a stripshow from

another tractor," said Pistol, leering as only a one-eyed rat could leer.

"Will you dumb, oversexed, drunken bastards get the hell out of here!" snarled Chip.

"We were only trying to help," they protested, in a mutual chorus of insincere innocence and affront.

"Did you pour any of this muck into it?" demanded Chip, withholding the bottle.

"Barely a stoup for a miserly knave," insisted Fal virtuously, reaching for it.

Chip pondered the matter. The bottle really didn't seem to have much out of it, and he had other things to do besides fight with them. He gave it back. Forgetting that Virginia was there, Chip came hunting the top section of the air filter. Fortunately, she'd finished, and was able to give the metal plate to him, along with her pantyhose. In tight-lipped silence.

To find the wingnut which had fallen off the top of the air filter took the rats' senses of smell, however. For which arduous self-created labor they extorted another swallow from the bottle.

A few minutes later, the makeshift fan belt was in place. Now, they considered another small technical problem. With five yards of slight uphill, Virginia and the combined rat-weight couldn't budge the tractor with Chip on it. It was going to take both of the humans to push it again.

"Fal! Front and center!"

"Oh *no*. Never ever again, Chip! Thou whoreson knave! You can thrust me into base durance and contagious prison first. You can even take away my drink." The portly rat backed off with a surprising turn of speed.

"I'm sure they're just power-assisted brakes," insisted Chip. He sneaked closer to Fal, cooing: "It'll be fine when the engine is going; all we've got to do is put it in gear as soon as we're over the hill . . . and I'll jump up and do it."

"Shog off, Connolly!" Fal was now a good twenty feet away.

"I'll do it," offered Nym eagerly. "Machines like me."

Chip snorted. "Oh yeah. Do you think we're stupid, Nym?"

"No, honest," said the rat. He pointed a stubby foredigit. "All I'll do is stand on that clutch pedal, push the gear lever up, and then jump off the clutch pedal. Nothing to it. Simple mechanical device."

"That's what he said about the drill press," muttered Pistol darkly.

Chip tried for other volunteers. "Well, Pistol? Mel? Doll? Will you do it?"

"Not shogging likely," replied Doll and Pistol in unison.

"I'll go with Nym," said Melene warily. "And let's take Doc, too. We'll make sure he does the right thing, Chip."

Chip realized he wasn't going to get any better offers from the rats. And the bats were conspicuous by their silence. Mechanical devices—well, nonexplosive ones, anyway—were a closed book to them. Which they obviously intended to *keep* closed.

"A-one, a-two, a-threeee . . ."

It was a far steeper slope.

Their panting was drowned in a sudden roar. A flame, fully twenty feet high, leapt out of the air filter. In its sudden stark light Chip saw Melene and Doc clinging for dear life to the steering wheel. The still valley was filled with an over-revved tractor bellow.

"Told you what it needed was a stoup of good strong drink!" boasted Pistol.

"To be sure," said Bronstein drily. "And do you think there might possibly be a single Maggot, on the whole southern front, that doesn't know exactly where we are now?"

Chip was running after the tractor, shouting, oblivious to the danger of alerting the enemy. "*Get after them, bats, and tell them to put the brakes on!*"

He and Virginia started gaining on the tractor, which had left the road and was now careering wildly in a drunken madcap fashion. Jumping up onto the back stabilizer, Chip seized the wheel around the clutching paws of the manic Nym. He thrust his foot down on what he had decided was the brake pedal. Hard. Nothing happened.

He hauled at the mess of hydraulics levers. The blade came down with a clunk and started rectifying the shell damage to the terrain. The tractor still didn't stop. Virginia, panting, jumped up next to him. Belatedly, he thought of taking it out of gear.

They stood, stationary at last, in the middle of a war-torn field, the tractor still roaring away at full throttle. Chip vainly searched for a stuck accelerator pedal. Whatever that other pedal was, it didn't affect the throttle. Trust them to find a buggered tractor. Oh well. They'd just have to do their best.

Eamon fluttered out of the darkness. "Maggots!" he shrieked. "Maggots coming fast! Get up that hill and get the trailer."

Chip pulled wildly at the hydraulic levers again. The blade started to lift the front end of the tractor. Hastily he pushed the other way. The blade came up and the tractor began to roll downhill again. Desperately, Chip tried to thrust it into gear. Remembered the clutch. Tried again and let the clutch out . . .

With a jerk that nearly threw them all off, they began their blundering passage back up the hill.

"Faster!" yelled Nym, bouncing wildly on the tip of the saddle between Chip's legs, endangering Chip's family jewels. Still under the happy delusion he was driving the thing, the big rat was clutching the wheel with one paw, and belaboring the dashboard with a short stick.

"*Faster!*" shouted Eamon. "*The Maggots are gaining!*"

Chip ignored them all as he grimly hunched in white-knuckled fifteen-mile-an-hour concentration over the wheel. He proceeded up the once elegantly raked and graveled curve of the winery driveway. Doing his bit for aesthetics, he reduced the last three surviving plump-cherub statuette-befouled pillars to eye-pleasing plaster chips as he wove his way back up to the workshop. There he dropped the blade onto the cobbles in a screaming streak of sparks before getting the tractor out of gear.

He and Ginny leaped down from the still-roaring tractor and began manhandling the loaded trailer up to it. The rats scrambled to help—all except Nym, who stayed on the saddle, shaking the wheel.

They'd just got the linchpin in, when the bull-throated bellow of the over-revved diesel was muted. Reduced to a throaty chuckling thrub-thrub. Nym stood on the saddle looking as if he'd just burned his paw. "I just . . . um, pulled that lever."

"For God's sake, get off there," shouted Chip. "This time you found the throttle. Next time you'll probably blow the whole thing up."

"Not I!" protested Nym. Smugly: "Just as I said. Methinks I'm a natural with machines."

Chip's bellow showed he was sergeant-major material in one way at least. "GET down here! Give us a hand with this drive shaft. We've got to move!"

Ten seconds later, they'd figured out that it couldn't

be done, short of losing fingers. "We'll just tie the trailer end of the drive shaft out of the way! We don't have time. There must be a way of stopping it turning—but I don't know how!" Chip's voice was sounding a tad desperate, even to him.

"I'll find out," said Nym serenely.

"No you won't!" snapped Eamon. "Tie it up and out of the way. We'll go and arm the mines."

Half a minute later it was done. And not half a minute too soon. A huge mass of Maggots was streaming up the hill from three sides, dark in the moonlight, except where the light flashed off snapping chelicerae.

"Okay, chilluns! All aboard the Maggotdom Midnight Express!" yelled Chip, caught up in the manicness of it all. "Grab your toys and let's go go GO!"

"Where is Fluff?" cried Virginia. "And where is the Professor?"

"Never fear! I am here!" The galago stood rampant in the moonlight on the trailer-top. Head back in a noble pose, he beat on his chest with tiny fists.

"Where is the Professor, Fluff?"

Chip would have shouted "leave the stupid bastard," except he knew by now the others cherished stinky-prickles. The rats and bats fanned out, searching and calling. Chip followed his instincts to the cellar, with a piece of cargo netting. The Korozhet was lurking behind the farthest vat.

"You must flee, human. The enemy approaches," said the Korozhet.

"Come on," cooed Chip. "We have the tractor waiting."

"No, no. I will just delay you." The Korozhet retreated farther into the corner, rattling spines at him.

"It's all right. I've got a wonderful safe hideaway

for you, Crotchet. We must look after you. Come." He quietly laid down the piece of netting. It was dim down here, and he'd noticed that the Crotchet wasn't very good at spotting obstacles in the dark. The Pricklepuss came wandering out of its dark corner. When it was half out and on top of the net Chip flipped the other side over it. Virginia, Siobhan and Melene came running in as he caught the corners.

"Chip," Virginia yelled, as she tripped down the stairs, "the bats have mined this place! It is going to blow sky-high in less than four minutes. We've *got* to find the Professor and get out of here."

"Grab a couple of corners," said Chip. "I've just arranged transportation for your Pricklepuss. Hey, Pricklepuss?"

The Korozhet seemed to be undergoing a sudden change of heart. "Indeed, Miss Virginia! Let us flee!"

The Crotchet was tied to the trailer like a bag of onions. Chip thought it an excellent place for him. And then the first Maggots came spilling into the yard. Bats dived into the attack as the tractor took the only open way out—back into the shed . . .

"Heads down!" shouted Chip, thrusting the tractor into second gear and pushing open the throttle. They took off with a wild jerk and sway, bouncing off most of the contents of the shed before crashing into the corrugated iron wall in the back. In a terrible, tearing din, the wall shrieked off its rivets and clattered aside.

They were out, free, and into the open. The tractor switchbacked down the hill through the barren fields as Chip kept frantically overcorrecting his overcorrections.

"That was a brilliant idea," shouted Virginia above the engine roar. "Going through the shed like that."

Chip didn't realize that it *wasn't* sarcasm. "Yeah. Sorry. Didn't realize how much space it took to turn the thing."

"I thought you knew how to drive one of these?" demanded Nym, from where he clung to the saddle.

"Um. In theory, yes. I've driven something similar."

"What?" demanded the rat.

They swerved erratically around a huge boulder. "A delivery truck. *Hold tight!*"

They bumped and swayed wildly down the cut to the roadway. For an ugly moment the tractor's balance clung . . . narrowly. Then they were down on the road. "And how much driving did you do?" demanded Nym, terrier-like.

Chip's grin gleamed in the moonlight. "I reversed it up the garage ramp. Went over the edge. Cracked the sump. Dieter never let me drive it again. Hold tight again. I'm going to try another gear. There is a half a sea of Maggots coming down that hill after us!"

In a cloud of dust and bats, the tractor and its trailer bumped, surged and swayed erratically down the road.

The hilltop behind them erupted. Melene, perched on Virginia's shoulder, blew a raspberry at the Maggots. Fal, perched on a cushion of insecticide-filled condoms, blew a raspberry at the tractor.

Action; reaction. Fal's sharp claws punctured one of the containers. A cloud of insecticide enveloped him and the road behind.

"Why I—never use—the damn things!" he coughed. "Can't be trusted!"

Chapter 24:
A sign from above.

In his small dingy basement office, Major Conrad Fitzhugh sat staring gloomily at his desk. On one side was a tottering pile of book-disks, and on the other the pile of new grim paper reports from the front. As usual he was working late.

The military history and strategy book pile told him they were doomed to lose this war. Fitzhugh had known that from first-hand observation, even without the terrible confirmation hidden in the nondescript report language of the paper stack.

He hadn't really needed to read the books. What the book pile told him was that high command's strategy was outdated and ridiculous. Even twenty-five hundred years ago Sun Tzu had established more sensible premises. The other thing the book pile had shown him was that, historically, the military had made just these same mistakes time after time.

In particular, the descriptions of Earth's First World War were eerily familiar. But Harmony And Reason just didn't have the manpower, not even with rat and bat troops, to slug it out with the Magh' as the damn Korozhet advised.

And it seemed things weren't about to change. When Shaw had been killed, Fitzhugh had been sure things would get better at last. He'd thought that without Shaw and his cronyism they'd *surely* get a new General Staff.

Hah. How wrong could he have been? The next tier of major Shareholders was now bickering about sharing out the spoils. This war was just something to profit from. Didn't the stupid bastards see this was the road to perdition? As for the General Staff . . . Well, they might get a new overall commander, but Carrot-up had been doing his scurrying and brown-nosing too well. He looked set to rise.

God damn them all.

The little Vat corporal burst into his office as fast as the gammy leg that kept him out the front-lines could carry him. "Major Fitzhugh! Sir! This just came in! It's sector Delta 355 again—*Look!*" He thrust a printout of a satellite picture under the major's nose.

The major stared at it. The shark's grin spread across the ruined visage. "Yesss! Hey, Ariel! Come and have a look at this."

Ariel hopped across from her terminal in the ballet leap that rats were capable of.

The picture showed a blossom of flame in the dark Magh'-held landscape. After examining the pic, Ariel showed her teeth. "Something just went bang. Deep, deep inside Maggot turf."

The major turned to the Vat. "Johnny, I want

daylight pics—close-ups—and if you can get an infrared scan . . ."

The corporal pulled a face. "I'll try, sir."

Major Fitzhugh knew what that meant. The satellite-monitoring staff wasn't going to accept those requests from a mere Vat-clerk. He stood up, plucked a bangstick from the corner, and held it like an old, old friend. "Come on, Ariel, Johnny. Let's go and persuade them a bit. Some of ours *must* be alive and fighting in there."

"Could just have been an accident, sir." The corporal's tone showed how much he hoped he was wrong.

"How much money do you want to put on it?" asked Fitz. His fearsome smile hadn't wavered an inch.

"Don't bet with him," said Ariel from her pocket perch. "He cheats."

The major snorted. "I thought you were on my side, Ariel."

Ariel looked up at him and fluttered her rat-eyelashes. "I am, darling, but Johnny Simms gives me chocolates too."

Fitz assumed a stern expression. "He's trying to usurp your affections. I'll have his stripes."

The corporal just grinned. The odd-looking trio moved through the corridors at a speed they hadn't mustered for six months.

"Where is Captain Dulache, by the way?" Fitzhugh's smile was now utterly sharklike.

"Off sick again, sir," said the corporal, his voice carefully bare of expression. "A strained leg muscle, I believe."

"Ah. Such a pity we'll miss his wise counsel." Fitzhugh clucked his tongue. "Brutal sport, polo."

Chapter 25:
Once more into the breeches.

Debris rained down around the tractor. The shower included small items like the three-ton shed roof which narrowly missed them, and tiny things like whole slowshielded Maggots. It also included big things, in small pieces--like the whole of the hilltop. The bats dived for shelter and clung under the trailer. Chip wished he could do the same. Instead he was obliged to hunch his shoulders, think turtle thoughts, and keep steering around the fallen rocks.

Fal, clinging now to the wheel arch, looked back at the crown of leaping flames around the once-winefarm and sniffed, his dark eyes clouded with sorrow. "The waste is very great," he intoned tragically.

✧ ✧ ✧

The moon was down, hidden behind the mound-walls, with only the high ground of the far ridge still bathed in its brightness.

None of them saw the hole until Behan cried a warning. "*Stop!*"

Chip dropped the blade as his foot found the clutch. With a screech and sparkstream they halted. The front of the tractor hung over the edge of a vast crater where the road had once been. Now the blade had nothing to act as a brake on . . . and they were rolling slowly forward. With eyes like saucers, Chip frantically fumbled for reverse gear. With a jerk that nearly stalled the tractor, they backed off.

Fortunately they went back a good nine yards from the crumbling lip before the trailer jackknifed. Still more fortunately, Chip was riding the clutch. The impact pushed his foot flat, and stopped them from breaking the hitch.

There was just enough space to edge forward and around the crater. After struggling across the earth and tar debris, they were able to get back onto the road.

"That's it," said Chip with finality. "We'll have to slow down. We just can't travel that fast." The back of his shirt was wringing wet, for all that it was a cool night. "Second gear, and that's max."

They pressed on, much slower now. A few minutes later the first bat returned.

"Chip, you've got to go faster," Siobhan pleaded, tugging at his shoulder with a wing-claw. "Maggots are coming in diagonally. They'll get ahead of us if you don't move it up."

He ignored her.

She put her wings over his eyes.

He swatted her away. "Will you stop that! I can't go any damn faster! I dare not. Goddamn helmet batteries are dying."

"And the Maggots are coming to cut us off. Choose, Bezonian," said Pistol, peering into the dark. Even with only one eye he could still see better than Chip. After that last incident all eyes strained to see the dark road.

"I can't see properly," said Chip, angrily. "Are you going to tell me where to drive?"

Pistol nodded "Yes. Methinks that's a fine concept."

"Are you fucking mad?"

"We cannot continue with this drive in the darkness," the Korozhet piped up. "It is not safe!"

"You're right," agreed Siobhan.

"Yes!" Chip opened the throttle. "We might be hurt or killed. Oh, thank heavens Professor Crotchet is here to guide us."

"Methinks there is no need to be sarcastic to the Professor," reproved Doll severely. "He's just trying to look after all of us, because you can't see where you're going."

"Left, left. Bear left. Hard!" shouted Siobhan from where she clung to the headlight.

Cursing, Chip swung the wheel over.

"Army left! Moron!" bellowed Eamon.

Chip swung the wheel the other way.

"Why don't we just put the headlights on?" asked Virginia.

Chip had no immediate answer for that. "Um. Er. Maggots might see us."

"More left!" yelled a bat.

They skidded onto gravel. "Not so much!" shouted a rat.

"Even if they see us, we'll crash without light. I think it is one of the buttons on the dashboard." She felt for buttons and hit them. The one working headlight lit up and . . .

"*HEEEHAW! HEEEHAW!*"

The horn brayed electronic jackass. The joke of some dead Vat-mechanic nearly had them all off the tractor. Fluff jumped from Virginia's shoulder to the rear of the swaying trailer and back again, squealing all the while. Very poor form, actually, for a machogalago.

In the backlight from the dash, Virginia saw Chip crack a grin. "Not a bad battle cry for us. Effing appropriate." For all the fright of the moment, she felt her heart suddenly leap. There was nothing Heathcliff-heroic about the dirty, wiry man sitting next to her, his hands wrestling with a steering wheel. Just—

Hers. By damn—and she would see to it!

Bronstein came diving in. "To be sure, let them find out how hard the jackass can kick!"

"And bite!" added Melene, showing teeth.

They came to an upgrade. Now, had Chip been even slightly more experienced at driving he would have downshifted the gears, or accelerated sooner. Instead he just kept hoping. . . .

Their gallant steed was losing revs . . . She wasn't going to get to the brow of the hill . . . She was going to stall. Chip gritted his teeth. The diesel coughed, spluttered, missed. He hastily put his foot on the clutch.

Well, that stopped them from stalling. But . . . they were rolling backwards already. He got the blade down hastily. They stopped.

Chip realized that he faced that nightmare of all inexperienced drivers: The hill-start. And worse . . . The hill-start without a handbrake . . .

"Get some rocks, quickly! Put them behind the wheels."

The rocks were in place. The bats fluttered about like anxious dishcloths. Chip wasn't a religious man, but he did some praying as he put the tractor into first. Trying his best to let the clutch out gradually, he did it a bit too fast. She jerked, and the blade gave a metallic screech against the paved roadway. The tractor hiccuped. Chip thrust his foot on the clutch again. "Ginny, you'll have to lift the blade while I deal with this clutch."

She bit her lip. "Just tell me what you want me to do."

" 'Tis not everyday you get that sort of offer, hey Chip?" Pistol winked from his post next to the air filter.

Chip ground his teeth. "Oh, shut up! There must be some time when you don't think about sex."

Pistol gave that fair consideration. "Well, I'd liefer think about sex *and* drink. But two things at once is beyond you, eh, Connolly? Still, I must care for the whoreson who owes me ten cases of whiskey . . ."

"Just ignore him," Chip said to Ginny. "Here. It's these two levers. I'm going to count to three. Start pushing this one up first; then, up slowly on two. Then the other fast on three. Can you manage that?"

Virginia could do calculus in her head. This was far more alarming. "I will do my best to give satisfaction, sir."

He snorted. The rats chortled. "You do choose your words, don't you Ginny?"

She was desperately glad he couldn't see her blush. She *didn't* choose her words. Something in her head chose them for her.

"One. Two . . . three . . ." And, with scarcely a jerk, they were off, and lumbered over the top. He gave her an unconsidered hug. "You were great. We're the 'A' team, huh?"

She smiled like a child and hugged him back.

" 'Ware Maggots!" shouted O'Niel.

"WereMaggots! Argh! Not wereMaggots!" shouted

Chip. Snarling: "If we shoot them with silver bullets do they turn back into Shareholders?" The tractor was going straight for the fifteen long-legged spindly stilt-runner-Maggots.

Virginia ground her teeth and dropped the hand from Chip's waist. He was as sensitive as a brick! *On good days . . .*

He hit the horn. And it brayed out a challenge.

The slowshield has a perimeter area in which incoming kinetic energy is absorbed. Inside that is the area where that energy is dissipated as a temporary "hard" shell. The shield is shaped to fit the wearer—in a closest-fit ovoid shape. Low-slung Maggots inevitably included a substantial piece of the ground in their shield. Upright humans didn't have much of the ground in theirs. The argument against tank warfare was that hitting Maggot shields would be the equivalent of hitting concrete bollards.

In broad theory, especially if the Maggots acted in concert, that was true. Chip proved, at least in the case of these thin upright Maggots, that in practice it was a lot of crap. Accompanied by the bray of the horn, the tractor sent the Maggots sailing like so many tenpins hit by a strike.

Eamon dropped in. "Slow down. If you get there in less than two minutes there won't be a hole to drive through."

"Speed up, slow down," grumbled Chip. "Will you make up your minds?"

He eased the pace.

They came around the corner just when Eamon wanted them to. A hundred yards farther up the valley stood a choke of solid Maggots. They stood stark and sharp-edged in the headlight beam. That lot *would* be enough to stop a tank.

When they were thirty yards from the Maggot-mass . . . the wall of the mound blew. Through the settling dust a hole full of lumifungus-green light beckoned. This was no time for finesse and careful aiming. Chip didn't even dare ease back the throttle. At the last minute he closed his eyes.

And he didn't scream alone.

Fortunately the bats had erred on the side of caution with their shot placement. The hole would have taken a six-lane freeway. Chip barely brushed the edge on the way in, before they started falling . . .

The tunnel floor was a good fourteen inches lower inside than the outside ground level. They bounced. Bounced again. And then, humping and mounting, galumphed their way over bits of fallen Magh' masonry.

"Deploy a roll of barbed wire!" shouted Bronstein, above the racket of their blundering progress.

Nym and Fal were on the trailer in a bound. Between them and Fluff the first roll of barbed wire was spooled out, with a rock tied onto the end. It was released—and snapped back into anything *but* a neat coil.

"Molotov," called O'Niel. "And light for me, Fal. And get more ready!"

Glancing back, Virginia saw the first Maggots, trapped in the tangle of rusty wire, firedancing with limb-tearing frantic effort.

The horn brayed. "Maggots. In front of us!" shouted Chip. "Hold tight!"

They bounced and bounded onwards, belching diesel smoke into the maze. Deeper and deeper into the tunnels of the scorpiary. Chaos trailed along behind them. And in front of them spread panic. For the first time in many years a scorpiary-organism knew fear.

Chapter 26:
On the outside looking in.

The technician at the slowship's satellite tracking unit looked sullen and unhappy about this invasion of his domain. Most of the colony's technical resources were still centered on the huge skeleton of the ship that had brought them here. The technician wasn't going to complain, however.

Not just yet, at least. For now he was going to be wondrously cooperative. His collar was still wet with his own blood. That had been the rat's teeth on his throat. Those teeth were *that* sharp. He was intensely grateful to the major for stopping it from going through with its threat.

He silently showed the pictures from the computer cache for the night. The terrifying looking major had had him focus on sector Delta 355.

"There. To the left." The tailless rat with the

mismatched fur patches and the missing ear pointed imperiously. The Earth-built satellite cameras had been intended for precision surveying. The resolution was excellent. The rat's eyesight was marvelous too.

"Zoom in on that point," said the major.

The technician did. There was a pinpoint of light in the darkness of the screen. Conclusive proof that tractors need strong drink to give them the will to live, though the two men and the rat staring at the screen did not know it.

"A flare!" Fitz smiled. "That's when it started. Match those coordinates with a daytime pic of the area."

The technician obeyed, willingly enough. Curiosity was now driving him as much as the rat's threat. An aerial picture of the road from the ruined winefarm appeared on the screen. Unbidden, the tech followed the road to the buildings and gave them max zoom. He looked at the text scrolling onto the screen.

"Clos Verde. It was a wine farm before the war. I went there once."

"Methinks I'm right. 'Tis a bunch of rats," said Ariel.

Fitz snorted. "Goddamn likely considering the choice of hideout. But the explosion is more like bats. One of them could have survived by being aloft when an assault started." He sighed. "Looks like they blew themselves sky high a few minutes later. Okay. Let's go on with the time series."

The explosion came up on screen. Fitz could see that even the sullen technician's interest was caught by now. "Do you think they committed—what-do-you-call-it—hari-kiri, sir?"

Ariel goggled. "*Rats?* Are you *crazy*?"

✧ ✧ ✧

Corporal Simms looked at the explosion's print carefully. Prewar he'd been a clerk for a demolitions company. He was a bright man, and the company had ended up getting him to cross-check all the calculations. He'd made it his business to learn as much as possible about explosives. In the natural fashion of military organizations, after drafting him the army had put him as far from the sappers as humanly possible. "If they did," he said slowly, "I reckon they might have taken a lot of Magh' along. That was a huge explosion. In the five or six tons of TNT bracket."

Fitz nodded. "That flare beforehand—away from the explosion—makes the whole thing look planned to me. Let's continue with the time series. Just zoom out."

They did. And once again it was Ariel's eyes that picked up the light trace. "It's moving at . . . what would you say, Johnny?"

Corporal Simms studied it. "Too fast for too long and too steady for a running man. Besides, too much light. It must be a Magh' vehicle."

The technician's hands flickered across the keyboard. He squinted at the display. "It's moving between seventeen and thirty-two miles an hour. Averaging twenty-eight. It slowed right down and stopped here . . ."

"Steep hill?" Fitz asked.

The technician checked. "Yep."

"And they veer here and disappear. Let's just backtrack the time on that place where they disappeared." Fitz tapped the big screen with his bangstick.

The bats knew how to place their shots. It was a small flare, but now they were looking for it.

There was silence as they stared at the screen. Then the major whistled.

The technician could no longer restrain his curiosity. "What does this all mean, sir?"

"It means that those aren't Maggots," said Major Conrad Fitzhugh, slipping back into grunt slang. His voice approached reverence. "Maggots don't blow holes in their own damned nests. Those are some of our lads there. And they're heading straight *into* the nest."

Even the technician was caught up by it now. "You mean they're a sort of special services raid? Right inside the enemy's force shield?" His eyes shone. Clearly enough, he'd quite forgotten the cut on his neck.

Fitz blinked. "No. I wish like hell they were," he said quietly, regretfully. "Most likely they're just a bunch of grunts on the run. Not a clue what they're doing."

Corporal Simms looked at the second explosion. "A bunch of grunts heading straight into the Magh' spiral. Brave, whoever they are."

"Not rats," said Ariel quietly. "They're not that stupid." She also sounded regretful.

"But . . . what are they trying to do?" The technician pointed to the screen. "I mean, you said yourself it all looked planned. Look at the way that wall blew up just before they got there. That's really skilled timing! 'Synchronize your watches' sort of stuff. Like in old DVDs!"

Ariel shook her ratty head. "That stuff always goes wrong."

"It looked like it worked to me," said Fitz, slowly.

"So what do you think they're trying to do?" the technician persisted.

Fitz shook his head. "That's anyone's guess. What they *are* doing is pulling tens of thousands of Maggots off the front. We'd already noticed that. What I wish they *would* do is destroy a force field generator. We could take the offensive then."

✧ ✧ ✧

The technician, Henry M'Batha, turned out to be a decent sort of fellow. Ariel was even beginning to regret having chewed on his neck.

Like most skilled technicians, Henry was the holder of a solitary share. Boredom and frustration had made him a touch officious and petty. But *this* made him feel as if his work had real purpose at last. That can change attitudes dramatically, so he persisted some more. "So what do you think they're trying to do?"

Fitz looked at the screen. "At a coarse guess, die young. You're looking at the evidence of some very brave soldiers."

"Can't we do *anything* to help them?"

The major ground his teeth audibly. Then he shrugged. "We'd have to move fast. But unless the force field goes down . . . *nothing*. Except salute them." He did.

The technician noticed that the rat and the corporal did the same. He found himself imitating them. "You wanted max-res infrared tracking," he said.

"Yes. We might pick up something," said Simms quietly.

"I'm supposed to get signed authorization from the satellite monitoring manager." M'Batha waved a piece of paper at them. "But if you wake her up now . . ." He drew a finger across his throat. "The hell with her. Those guys in there are risking their lives. I'll risk a reprimand from a sarcastic old bitch who can't replace me anyway." Decisively: "I'll set it up for you."

Simms smiled slightly. "Good for you. But I'll give you a signed order if you've got a blank form." On the blotter, the corporal neatly produced the head of satellite monitoring's signature. "Would that do?"

The major and the technician stared at the corporal. Simms held up his hands defensively. "My boss had to countersign the demolition orders. But he was always drunk by ten. Um. So I learned to do it for him."

Fitz eyed him speculatively. "Let's see you do my signature, Johnny."

The corporal blushed, but signed a sprawling scrawl. "I only used it when you were too busy, sir."

"He used it to requisition me chocolates," said Ariel reprovingly. "Which proves you could have done it yourself." Sniffle. "If you still loved me."

The major put his face in his hands. "Argh. I'll be locked away for chocolate black marketeering. Give him your form, tech. And thank you."

He gazed reprovingly at the rat. "Sorry about that little nick she gave you. On a sugar high, she's practically a homicidal maniac. That's why I ration her chocolate."

Ariel sniffed. Henry smiled. "It's nothing, sir. Given myself worse cuts shaving. If there is anything else, you just have to ask. Shall I call you, or send the printouts to Military Headquarters?"

"You can get me on my beeper." Fitz scrawled the number hastily on the blotter. "Or Johnny back at HQ. I'm going to go and wake up a general."

"Do you think they might have a chance, sir?"

Fitz was silent for a moment before he spoke. Then, his voice a little husky, he said: "None."

He gathered himself. "But still, they've hurt the Magh'. They're doing a thoroughly professional job of it. We owe it to them to follow up as professionally as we can too. And *I'm* going to see it happens."

There was iron determination in that voice. The major left the satellite tracking station like a shark leaves a lagoon. Heading for deep waters, where bigger prey could be found.

Chapter 27: *Blow-by-blow.*

Metal screamed. A glass reflector shattered. And, worst of all, they stalled. The silence was sudden to ears accustomed to the over-revving-in-too-low-a-gear of a learner driver.

"That we should be cursed with a bedamned amateur driver!" said O'Niel. That bat was becoming very fond of mechanical transport. It beat flying, he said.

"Oh, shut up," muttered Chip. "It was your idea to turn down here."

The little tractor was wedged. Jammed good and solid. Maggots didn't build in straight lines. This cross tunnel was no exception.

"Let me out of the net," said the Korozhet. "We must flee on foot. The machine has ceased to function."

"Don't be stupid, Crotchet," said Chip, his heart

in his mouth. How would they ever get the tractor out of this jam and then push start it down here . . . ?

He twitched the key, just knowing it was not going to work. She started perfectly.

As usual, Bronstein took charge. "Fly ahead and see if it gets any wider," she commanded O'Niel. "Behan, you and Siobhan go back to the main tunnel and scout ahead. Eamon, let's you and me take those spray cans and see if that'll slow them— *What are you doing?*"

Eamon was attempting to wrap a piece of white rag with a red splotch on it around his head. "Indade. Just something I have a fancy to," the big bat said sullenly. "Here, you—Don Whatsisname—tie this around my head."

"Of a certainty!" cried the galago. Despite the apparent enthusiasm of the words, Fluff seemed doubtful of the project.

"Stop wasting *time*, Eamon!" snapped Bronstein. "Chip. You're to go on if that's possible. Otherwise try and reverse."

Chip looked appropriately nervous at the thought of reversing fifteen yards. "Hope like hell we can go on."

Even as Bronstein and Eamon flew off, cans of spraypaint clutched in their feet, O'Niel returned.

"Begorra, 'tis narrower ahead!"

Eamon turned and shouted: "Join us then, O'Niel! Time we'll need to buy for them!"

The plump bat looked startled. Eamon's somewhat skew white headband with a red paint spot in the center looked bizarre on his evil blackface. "Are you injured, then, boyo?"

"No. 'Tis my new image," came the proud reply.

O'Niel clucked. " 'Tis right daft you look."

✧ ✧ ✧

Chip peered at the gear lever to work out—again—where reverse was located. He *thought*—

"Hang on, Chip," said Fal. "Methinks we'll go and set some snares. Come on, you swashers!" said Fal. The rats baled off.

"Hey, don't leave me alone," whined Chip.

Pistol stopped and grinned back at him. "Tradition! Rats are deserting a stinking ship!"

Chip grit his teeth. "Here goes nothing."

He was dead right. They were stuck fast. All that moved was a little wisp of steam that curled up from the engine. He tried; stalled again. "Where the hell are the rats and bats when I *need* them?"

"I will do my best, *señor*!" piped the tiny galago. "How may I help?"

Chip shook his head. "Can you dig through Magh' adobe or blow it aside? No. I need rats and bats . . ."

"I'll run and fetch them," said Ginny eagerly.

"No, stay. Let's try it with the blade," he said.

"Yes, Virginia," said the Korozhet. "Stay. You must stay near me."

Ginny looked affronted. "You don't have to be so protective, Professor. I'm a big girl now."

"You tell him, girl. And get that chainsaw of yours going in case." Chip's tone was deeply approving.

He started the tractor again. With care, accompanied by the smell of a burning clutch and various wild efforts with the hydraulics—the tractor came free.

Of course, the trailer started scraping along the wall. But at least it couldn't jackknife.

They scraped through a trail of fertilizer from a torn bag. Back out into the main passage, where terrible war raged.

The rats were sitting back, against the wall, watching it. Placing bets.

"Three to one on the greens," said Pistol, pushing forward a small pile of money.

"Pass the bottle. I'll take you up on that!" Melene's voice was cheerful. "Methinks the oranges have the edge in skill if not the numbers."

Fal was in the act of putting a suggestive tail around Doll's waist. "Hey Doll, we have time, doth want to slip away for spot of tail-twisting?"

"With you, Fal? But where are my flowers and candy?" Coyly, Doll pushed his tail away.

Fal's jaw dropped. "Flowers? Candy? *Candy?* I offered you a drink!"

The plump rat's tone was shocked, shocked. He caught sight of Ginny and the galago and began shaking his fist. " 'Tis your fault! Yours, say I!"

Chip, Ginny and Fluff stared at the bizarre scene. Some seventy yards away the tunnel seethed with Maggots. Some of them were rather decoratively spray painted . . . particularly across the eyes. And Maggots were shredding Maggots. The blinded ones blundered into the rest. Contact initiated attack; attack spawned counterattack.

Siobhan fluttered in. "Ah, you're out. The next passage is wider. Behan's gone on to be checking it out further up the main passage."

Chip thumped the horn, which brayed obligingly. "All aboard! All aboard. Settle your bets, Gentlerats and Ladies. Let's go!"

Indeed, it was a good time for it. The group-mind had obviously figured out what was happening, and the painted-eyed Maggots were lying down, allowing the others to come through. Chip already had the tractor in first gear, and Virginia was off, chainsaw in hand, chivvying the rats from their argument about who'd won.

It was just as well she'd taken the chainsaw, and

that she'd already pull-started it. One of the Magh' was a sprinting type. While all around its companions staggered and ripped off legs in the rows of snares the rats had set up, this one came through. It was lightly armored, but fast.

Virginia barely had time to shove the chainsaw in the Maggot's face and squeeze the trigger. The chainsaw was either inside the Maggot's slowshield or it didn't have one. The creature grabbed at it with its long chelicerae. The blade screamed through pincers and the biting mouthparts and on into the creature's head, spraying the three set-on-rescue rats with Maggot juice.

The Maggot fell, losing control over its legs, nearly dragging the racing saw out of Virginia's hands. It ripped through the carapace instead. Virginia managed to stay erect—barely—panting, a dead Maggot at her feet.

"Come on, Ginny!" Melene, Nym and Doc dragged at her.

She stood frozen in shock.

Chip had leapt off the tractor along with Fluff. The tractor was left to decide on its own course, guided by nothing but a net full of squalling, protesting Korozhet. Truth to tell, the mindless machine was actually doing better without Chip interfering with its steering.

He grabbed Ginny, and pressed the chainsaw cutoff. The next thing Virginia knew she was over Chip's shoulder, still clutching her chainsaw, as he staggered off after the tractor. Fluff clung to her shoulder and chittered anxiously into her face.

"Put me down!" she shouted. "They're coming!" But Chip just staggered determinedly on.

Claws reached for her . . .

. . . and Ginny got a near-face education into why

the rats were this war's equivalent of natural-born samurai. Fal and Pistol took the first one, tag style, with that apparent lack of effort which sets the masters apart from the tyros. Then the bats joined the attack. Between aerial mastery and rat fangs the far bigger Maggots were outclassed.

Chip had seen Nym sprint for the tractor. The mechanically-inclined rat must have gotten it out of gear. It had only been puttering along anyway, but it slowed now. A few more steps and he'd be there.

Next thing, Nym appeared on the top of the trailer and flung a Molotov over their heads. Ginny's clamor for Chip to put her down finally got through to him. He did and dived for the tractor. "Come on! Up everybody, up!" He scrambled into getting it going again.

With a jerk they were moving forward. He risked a glance back, nearly hitting the wall. "All on?"

He caught sight of Ginny wacking at a Maggot with the shovel he'd put on the trailer. He should have thought of that earlier, when they were stuck.

"Yes! Let's GO!" someone yelled.

"Okay! Second gear! Let's go go go!" And they surged away.

"Next left, Chip," shouted Siobhan. "And be watching where you're driving!"

"You're getting as bad as Bronstein," he grated, over-revving and, by way of a grating venture into first, changing into third.

They did the corner very well. On two wheels—well, three, if you counted the trailer. There was an annoying lot of screaming.

"Stop!" shouted Bronstein.

"All right. All right. I'll take it slower!"

"No, you fool! I mean *'stop.'* Barbed wire must be

deployed, and then we'll blow this entry down. Use up the rest of that leaking bag."

"I hope like hell we don't have to come back!" said Chip, thrusting the tractor into neutral and putting the blade down with almost-skill.

Eamon fluttered up. "Here, take this damned thing. Indade, it was near the death of me." Eamon thrust his makeshift headband at Ginny.

She took it. "Uh. Why?"

"It slipped over my eyes when I was dive-bombing them," the bat said angrily. "To the very divil with fashion and image! It could have killed me! Pure suicide wearing that thing."

"I mean why did you wish to wear it in the first place?" she asked, staring at the red splotch.

The bat scatched his head and nearly fell out of the air. He corrected and explained. "I saw a picture of this dive-bomber, from human history somewhere. It struck me as remarkably stylish. I've had a fancy to try it for some time. And this may be my last flight . . ."

"I'll try it instead." She smiled at him. "I thought I was going to lose my glasses back there."

"And welcome!" said the bat fervently. "Now, let's have that barrel of diesel up there."

"Chip! Come and knock us a few holes with the four-pound," shouted Bronstein. "And let's set a few expedient mines on this side."

"You all right?" asked Chip, with unprecedented solicitude, when he got back to the idling tractor. Virginia was staring at the chainsaw.

"Yes," she said quietly. "I've just never killed anything before. Not on purpose."

She didn't know how she was cutting him to the quick right then. How he'd comforted Dermott after the first bloody fight, when that big tough farmgirl had started quietly weeping. "Get used to it," he said, shortly. "It's them or us."

Less than two minutes later, the first two runner-Maggots charged into the barbed wire . . . as the tractor drove away. The explosion behind them was a sweet, sweet sound.

Some time later, they slithered to a hasty halt against the inner wall of the spiral arm of the tunnel. Naturally, Chip miscalculated. There was a *crunch*.

Bronstein immediately began giving orders. "Right! I'll need shot holes . . ."

"Er, Bronstein." interrupted Chip. "I can see darkness though that wall. We hit it quite hard."

Bronstein looked. "So reverse off and hit it again."

"Indade, 'tis a black shame not to blow it to glory," groused O'Niel.

Fal snorted. "Methinks it is not as much of a shame as that, that . . . otter, telling our women that we should give them . . . candy, when we wants a bit of slipping of the muddy conger."

"Otter? Which otter?" The bat looked puzzled.

"Her." The rat pointed with an elbow to Virginia, as he dug for his bottle. "Why, she's neither fish nor flesh; a man knows not where to have her. Want a drink?"

"She looks fairly human," said the bat, half-uncertainly. He was speaking about the affronted Virginia as if she weren't there. "To be sure, 'tis always hard to tell by looking. I could have a feel, I suppose. As for the drink, well—after last time, begorra, Bronstein gave me hell. She said I could choose between drinking or flying. So I decided to give it up."

Fal took a deep pull from the bottle. "Rather you than me. It's a rat's life, and then you die. Alcohol simply makes the getting to be dead a bit more lubricated."

O'Niel shook his head. "No, I meant the *flying*. I far prefer this mechanical transportation to the hardworkin' flapping o' the wings. Pass the bottle, then."

Behan stared at him in horror. "You're not fit to be a Batty!"

"Ah, the divil take you and your politics," said O'Niel, wiping his lips and passing the bottle back, as Chip attempted to cautiously reverse. The trailer made it a nightmare.

Siobhan fluttered up. "You've got to move faster, Chip. They'll be through here any minute."

"I can't!" said Chip through clenched teeth. "She jackknifes."

"I have an idea," said Nym. "Switch her off."

Without thinking, Chip complied. Then he realized who was giving orders. "Nym! What the hell are you doing?" The rat was fiddling with the ropes tying the drive shaft in place.

"Come and cut the drive shaft loose, Connolly. Methinks, it'll not jackknife so easily if it is hooked up."

Chip concluded that he was probably right, and jumped down to help. Of course he was damned if he was going to say so to Nym. The rat was bigheaded enough about his mechanical genius.

It proved correct, too. The trailer was still tempted to go where its own inclination took it, but to a far lesser degree.

Three thumps, and a large section of the wall fell in. Most of the big bits missed them.

It was bliss to drive out into the open night air again, as the bats and rats set booby traps behind them. They'd moved a great deal farther into the spiral. The gap between arms was smaller, a mere thirty yards wide. Bats flew ahead to locate the next cross passage, as the tractor chewed along the muddy strip toward it. The bats set charges and they were in. Unopposed.

"Begorra. This is the way to fight a war, boyos!" said O'Niel, from where he reclined on the top of the trailer.

"I wish you hadn't said that," Chip muttered gloomily.

"Sometimes things *must* go right," opined Ginny. But she didn't sound very convinced.

"It is my contention," Doc speculated, "that the Magh' have never come across the military philosophy entrained in the word, 'Blitzkrieg.' " He peered through his pince-nez at the empty passage ahead.

Chip snorted. "I dunno what that means, but if it means 'things only go right so that they can get worse later,' or 'if one thing is going right, it's only because another is going wrong'—then you've got it in . . ."

The rest of his statement was lost in a shrieking mechanical wail-gurgle. The noise could be described as a teething baby being drowned in shallow engine oil.

O'Niel proved it was possible to launch from flat on your back into powered flight in three microseconds. The shrieking came from inside his backrest. And then it stopped.

They were all silent. Edgy. Ready to jump. Then Ginny started to giggle. "This time it didn't go wrong! It's the pressure valve, on the trailer. Look at it! When you guys hooked the drive shaft up you must have started the pump running. You're ready to start spraying your crops."

"Dunno about crops, but there's a cropper coming!"

Chip pointed ahead. The group-mind had had its construction teams building earthworks. They'd arrived while the builders were still on the job. Chip lowered the blade to just above ground level and dropped the tractor into low gear. The 'dobe was still wet. They plowed through it like . . . like a small vineyard tractor through sticky mud—with much slithering and near sticking.

Meanwhile, Ginny had clambered across to look at the pump. There was a galvanized pipe with a red valve handle. She moved the lever across, into line with the pipe, more to see what would happen than anything else. A thirty-five foot mist-wall of seventy-four percent alcohol is what happened, before she hastily turned it off. The Maggot-soldiers who had been waiting in the side passages charged straight into the mist. The tractor blundered on through the earthworks, speeding up now as Chip determinedly thrust it through gears. And then Behan took it into his head to fly back and fry a few more Maggots.

He never even dropped the Molotov, before the atomized alcohol in the air ignited.

WOOOOOMPH!!!!!!

The shockwave hardened slowshields. It spun bats from the air like autumn wind-torn leaves. It rocked the tractor. It fried hundreds of Maggots. It seared and panicked twice that number . . .

And it took Behan away to the great belfry in the sky.

"I killed him," said Ginny, in a small wooden voice. "I killed him."

Chapter 28:
A romantic little place in the country.

The pager bleeped insistently. Fitz was glad to pull over to the side of the road. He was not relishing this little trip.

"Major Fitzhugh? It's Henry M'Batha from satellite tracking here. We've just picked up another explosion. About five miles from the last one. They're heading southeast and inwards, sir!" The technician sounded as pleased as if he'd infiltrated the Magh' scorpiary himself.

"Thank you, Henry. Well done! Keep me updated, will you? Can you contact my office and send printouts to Corporal Simms?"

"Yessir. Right away!"

Fitz gritted his teeth. Well. They were still alive. So he would just have to go ahead. But M'Batha would have sounded less cheerful with his "good news" if he'd understood that it meant waking General Cartup-Kreutzler. Fitz was under no delusions as to how the general was going to feel about this . . .

"Got any food in this rattletrap?" asked Ariel, yawning.

Fitz grinned wryly. "In two minutes you can start on Carrot-up. How's that?"

Ariel made a face. Which, on a rat, was something to see. "Blech! A little lard goes a long way."

The gate guards were no match for Major Conrad Fitzhugh at his most glacial.

"Halt!"

"Private. I am going to count to three. If you don't take that damnfool firearm out of my face, I'll *inspect* it." Fitz's tone was cold enough to make liquid nitrogen seem like bathwater.

The rifle was hastily lowered. "Uh. Nobody is allowed in here, sir."

Fitz raised an eyebrow . . . on the bad side of his face. "Do you know what happens when you use a high-velocity automatic rifle within interpenetrated slowshields?" he asked quietly. His voice was terrifyingly even.

His eyes swept the small squad of soldiers. After a moment's hesitation, one of them spoke. The corporal in charge.

"Uh. Nossir."

"Have you heard the word 'ricochet,' Corporal?" Fitz spoke between clenched teeth. "It means both of us end up dead. Outside the shield it is totally useless. Inside you've got just one shot. What sort of defense are you against the Magh'?"

"Uh. Major dien Thiem had us issued us with these, sir."

"He and I will have words in the morning." There

was now helium frost in the major's tone. "Now, stand aside. I need to see General Cartup-Kreutzler on a security matter of the highest urgency."

"Erm. He . . . he's not alone, Major Fitzhugh."

The major smiled. The guards cringed. They knew who he was. Sometimes a reputation helped. So did a shark's smile. "He needs to see me. And see me he will, even if he's entertaining Shaw's daughter to a private soireé. Now, open those gates."

They did.

He drove past them, down the long curving avenue to the door of the general's little country retreat, just outside of the town. The general had a handsome mansion in town too . . . with a wife and children in it. That didn't have armed guards at the gates.

The pager bleeped again.

"Can't a girl sleep around here?" muttered Ariel.

The major pulled up. Took the communicator out of his pocket. "Yes?"

"The infrared scan, sir! Definitely a vehicle, sir, and, and there was a huge heat trace further in. Really big."

"I wonder if that was them buying it," said Conrad with a trace of regret. "They can't go on like this . . ."

There was a moment's silence. Then a gleeful: *"NO! They've just come out in between the next two, sir. They're REALLY giving it to the Maggots, Major!"*

Chapter 29:
The paradigms of war.

Chip had to hold Ginny and steer. Words just seemed pitifully inadequate.

And then they rounded the corner. The floor was solid wall-to-wall Maggots and there was no way to slow down or stop. Chip knew that hitting two or three hundred slowshields at that speed was going to be like driving into a thirty-foot thick concrete wall.

Only . . . it wasn't.

"Brace yourselves!" He shouted. They hit the Maggots. And kept plowing through. Crunch and splatter. Ginny was knocking them back with a shovel. The Maggots weren't slowshielded. And they weren't warrior types either. They were mostly small, weird-shaped specialists drafted into line as a solid cork.

Eventually, though, the tractor was brought to a stop by the sheer weight of crushed bodies. Chip grabbed the chainsaw from where it hung, ripped the pull cord and thrust it at Ginny. "Take this! Gimme that." He snatched the shovel from her and belted at a pick-snouted Maggot. Beside him he heard the chainsaw ripping and growling.

A glance showed him Fluff belaboring a Maggot with a piece of pipe. *"AIEEE! GET DOWN, YOU FILTHY BEAST!"* Either pipe or galago-volume was enough.

Pistol, clinging to the air filter, was flailing at the mass with a length of chain. All he needed was a biker jacket. Beside him Fal fought tooth and claw, until Nym, from the trailer, tossed him a piece of reinforcing rod. Up on the trailer, all with bits of reinforcing rod, Nym, Doll, Melene and Doc were smashing Maggots away. These Maggots weren't fighters. Just endless.

The bats, except O'Niel, had dived to war. O'Niel sat calmly on the middle of the trailer, took a drink from a bottle, then popped a wick into it. Then he held it upside down to soak, while flicking the lighter with his feet. Then, using both wings he tossed it. "Duck, you suckers!" Fire still caused pandemonium.

O'Niel shouted to Fluff, a lid in his mouth making him sound even more bog-Irish. "Ghet oop here and ohpen bhattles, damn ye!" With a leap, the galago complied.

The Magh' could still overwhelm them, but only by sheer panic and numbers and the slipperiness of the ground. Nym came up with a new crowd-clearer. Some of the scrap brought for shrapnel in the expedient mines yielded a couple of huge nuts, which the big rat hastily strung onto ten feet of nylon, bitten from the roll. He scrambled forward over Chip's head and onto the front edge of the radiator grill, where he clung by toes and tail. He whirled it around his head. He nearly got Pistol on the first arc, but then he got the angle right. The Maggots were mostly small and Nym kept the thing whirling at the height of the waving limbs. Knocking limbs off didn't even slow the weapon down.

One of the whirling nuts howled, and that put the horn into Chip's mind. He dropped the shovel and set the tractor going again, leaning on the horn. It brayed and brayed, as they began to slither and crunch their way forward through a flaming fleeing mob. The tank pump chose this moment to add its own drowning-baby shriek. Something about that seemed to frighten the Maggots even more.

And then . . .

They were through. Out on the far side. Rolling along the open Maggot-way. Nym dropped his makeshift flail and began cheerfully tossing insecticide bombs behind them.

"We did it! We did it!" shouted Siobhan. "Holy mother! I think we just beat more Maggots than the whole army ever has in any one battle!"

"No shields," murmured Chip, wonderingly. "Imagine going to fight with no shields."

"I haven't got a shield," said Ginny. "It didn't stop me."

It stopped everybody else on the tractor.

They stared at her openmouthed—except for Fluff, who jumped up on Virginia's shoulder and put his long fluffy tail around her throat. "It is true! And I do not have one of these either. Bah, a true knight does not cower behind a shield!" He adopted a Napoleonic stance on her shoulder.

Chip shook his head. "You're a loony. In fact, you are a pair of flipping loonies. It didn't occur to me that you didn't have shields. *Everybody* in the army has shields! I . . . forgot you were civs."

"I'm not sure if that's a compliment, or an insult," Ginny said dryly.

"*Au contraire!* It is a *revelation*." Doc leapt up on the engine cowling. His ratty beady eyes glowed with an inner fire. "You have shifted the entire paradigm of war."

"Oh, put a sock in . . ." Pistol began.

Doc turned on Pistol. "You shut up! And listen for once, you fool."

The astonished Pistol shut up. And *everyone* listened.

"Our thinking tends to operate within the bounds of a set of preconceived premises. Every now and again those premises are shown to be flawed, and then the entire structure built on them must be rebuilt." The philosopher-rat cleared his throat and then continued with the dignity of a rat addressing the prestigious Shareholder's Society for the Advancement of Science. "The humans entered this war with one of the basic premises *wrong*. Their species has, for a long time now, fought with projectile, long-range weapons. They assumed that that was the way any civilized species would fight, if given the choice. They assumed that if their troops were unshielded the Maggots would use projectile fire. It was an *incorrect* premise. The Maggots *bodies* are their weapons."

"We still can't use guns while they have shields," said Chip.

The rat shrugged. "You are still thinking within the terms of reference of the projectile weapons premise. The point is: while Maggots use shields *they* can't use guns either. The strength of human armies wasn't always projectile weapons. It was that they were *armies* relying on numbers, not on individual strengths. Believe me: Shields and the small AP mines our bats sowed helped the Maggots, not ourselves. They isolated individual humans. They made you do what your history shows that very few of you can do well: They made you fight on your own, instead of in mass attacks. We are better off without shields and AP mines. A mass of shielded Maggots couldn't penetrate a solid wall of humans with pole-mines . . . if the humans stood shoulder to shoulder, unshielded, without interpenetration of the human and Maggot shields. There is no good reason why an unshielded human is worse off than a shielded one, in a fight with a shielded Magh'. For one thing you can run away faster."

Chip saw the truth of it, clearly. But he had a feeling—a certainty, actually—that some desk jockey back at high command *wouldn't* see it that way.

"He's a broth of foine thinker, that," said O'Niel. "Whould you be hafter a small drink to be whashing down all of that dry preaching, Doc, or Georg Hegel, as you style yourself?"

Doc took off the pince-nez. "Not any more, I do not. I see now that that too was a false premise, rooted in the past. Henceforth I will call myself . . . *Pararattus*. I will build a new philosophy . . ."

Pistol snorted. "I reckon I'll still call you Doc. For all that, methinks, you may have something . . ."

"Yes," said Bronstein. "I hadn't thought about the projectile weapons . . ."

"But the Magh' do use projectile weapons! Have you forgotten their artillery?" demanded the Korozhet from his bag. "You are wrong, rat!"

Doc regarded the spiny mass of alien. Then he shook his head. "No. I'm not wrong."

For a moment the only noise was the tractor's thud-thudding diesel.

"What we need is an on-off switch for slowshields, Professor," said Ginny.

"Like I wish we had for Pricklepuss," muttered Chip.

Eamon and Siobhan came back from scouting. "Next left."

Siobhan settled on Chip's shoulder. "You should look after Chip better, Virginia. 'Tis troubled he looks. Give him some chicken soup."

Siobhan was, however, more concerned about the rest of her flock. "Why is everyone so quiet and troubled looking? To be sure it is to certain death we're going . . ."

Chip made a wry face. "Doc just told the Crotchet he was wrong."

The bat nearly fell off Chip's shoulder. "That's surely not true?"

Chip saw the corner. Dropped a gear, and took it in what—for him—was consummate skill. "Surely is. And I agree with him."

By now the gap outside the walls was a tight, narrow spiral. Chip started to turn back in toward the heart of the spiral—his own heart reaching for open moonlight-bathed heights. It felt like hours that they'd been traveling and fighting their way underground. It should be morning by now, surely?

"The other way," Bronstein commanded.

"But that's out!" Chip protested.

Bronstein shook her head at him. "Stop thinking like a Maggot. Never try the same trick twice. Tell him, Ginny."

"She's right, Chip. The group-mind will know."

Chip put his foot on the clutch. "*Right!* Now I feel like Doc. Breakthrough. All we've got do is *keep* changing the pattern! Come on, Ginny. Turn that tap on and let's fog this whole passage with alcohol."

Even in the dashboard light he could see she'd

turned pale. He didn't pretend not to understand. "It wasn't your fault, Ginny," he said softly. "And it will keep us alive, if we play it right. The expedient mines will trigger it."

The rats were already busy setting them. Each hinged plank had a tenpenny nail which would strike a cartridge percussion cap as soon as a Maggot stood on one. The cartridge was buried in a pile of diesel-wet fertilizer and covered in "useful" metal junk from the workshop.

As soon as the rats were back up on the tractor, Ginny filled the back-tunnel with atomized alcohol. If it affected the Maggots the same way it did humans, they'd be too drunk to ever reach the expedient mines. Then Chip drove out, away from the heart of the spiral, before breaking in again.

There were already Maggot sentries on the entryway to the main passage. The group-mind was learning. But there were only two of them, unshielded. Not warriors. Child's play to this group. But now the tractor's position was known to the group-mind. What it *didn't* know was the convolutions of Bronstein's mind.

"Straight across," she ordered. "And rats, set some trip wires further up the main passage. Quickly! Chip, you keep her running down this passage, slowly. We'll catch up."

"You do your thing, Bronstein. And tell Eamon not to nip back and watch the big bang," said Chip.

"Methinks it must be ooh, hours, since I last had one of those." Melene cheekily rubbed a furry thigh against the galago.

But Fluff had an answer for her. "Alas, *señorita*, I should love to oblige, but I am entirely out of candy."

Fal nearly fell off the trailer laughing.

Chapter 30:
To Banbury Cross.

That was definitely a feminine squeal. And rather a lot of panting coming from the other side of the door.

There'd been no answer to the major's demanding knock on the outer door. Being who he was, Conrad had tried the door before starting to kick it down. It wasn't locked. The keys lay hastily tossed onto the ormolu hall table.

Ariel had said: "They're upstairs."

The major hesitated for an instant at the upstairs door. Then, gritting his teeth, he knocked.

No answer.

"They're busy, from the sound of it," chuckled Ariel. "Won't pay no attention at all to a measly knock."

Fitzhugh shrugged, and opened the door.

His timing was exquisite.

The general's gum-chewing secretary Daisy was occupied in an equestrienne pursuit. Or that was what she was dressed for. Well, half-dressed for. There were parts of her distinctly undressed. She shrieked.

Her steed definitely needed more exercise. He was rather paunchy . . . and very undressed.

For a moment Fitz nearly retreated and slammed the door behind him. Then his sardonic humor asserted itself. "I seem to have come at an inopportune moment. Unfortunately, General, my business is pressing and won't wait."

Ariel stuck her head out of his pocket. "Methinks, your general won't be coming at this opportune moment." She giggled nastily. "And I don't think *his* business is pressing any longer."

Daisy shrieked again. "A rat! A rat! In his pocket!"

Ariel showed her teeth. "Shall I get out of this pocket and give you a reason to jump on the table and do some *more* shrieking? I could nibble your toes instead of your bare tits."

The general found his wind at last. "*What is the meaning of this outrage?*"

His rider suddenly realized that her excessively generous frontage was exposed. Maybe Ariel's nibble comment had gotten through. Fitz had always suspected it took ideas a long time to penetrate all that hair. She tried first to pull her inadequate jacket to cover herself, before remembering that it had been designed *not* to cover the cleavage. She snatched the frilly continental cushion from behind the head of her gray steed. His head thumped onto the wall.

This was all too much for Fitz's gravity. There were men dying out there, sure, and a war to be won or lost. But walking in on the pompous ass being boffed by his bimbo-secretary, playing mount-the-(snort)-stallion, was truly priceless.

"Sir. I'll withdraw for thirty seconds, to allow you time to assume a more dignified—ah, position. I've no desire to disturb your private life, but I need to talk to you about urgent military business." He almost managed not to smile.

The red-faced general almost managed not to look at the telephone.

Fitz unplugged it, and walked out with it. "Don't infuriate him," he hissed at Ariel.

The rat just winked. Fitz sighed. She'd do it her way. She always did. He put the telephone unit down on the parquet floor and they went back into the room.

Daisy had fled to the bathroom. The general had obviously given up his frantic search for his trousers. He was wrapped in the sheet, looking like a very irate Roman senator.

"This had better be good, Major," he hissed.

In a voice of perfect urbanity, Fitz replied. "Sir! I would not have dreamed of disturbing you for anything less than something of major importance. And—*of course*—your private life is of no relevance."

"What is it? And why didn't you just call or call my second-in-command, General Fertzengu? In fact, why did you override the chain of command?" The general was fast working himself up into the fury of a man caught in a compromising position, with nowhere else but temper to turn to.

Fitz looked down his long nose at the man. Then he realized he was doing just what he had asked Ariel not to do. He attempted to answer without any sign of irritation. "Firstly, sir, my orders are to report directly to you on matters of intelligence and not to attempt to influence junior officers. Those are your exact words, sir. Secondly, your 2 I.C. is out of town on a shooting trip and is not available, according to his household staff. Thirdly, I *tried* to call you. You have not drawn your pager, sir. I called your office. I called your home." A look of discomfort crossed the general's face. "I then called on Captain Hargreaves, sir. He provided me with this number, but the phone was not accepting calls. I had little alternative but to come here in person."

The general ground his teeth audibly. "You had no call to burst in here. You should have waited . . ."

Fitz lost it. "While you play your stupid philandering *games*, men are dying!"

"And rats too," put in Ariel.

It was perhaps not what he'd asked her to do, but it gave Conrad a second to cool.

It hadn't done that for the general. "Don't you dare shout at me! I'll have you stripped of your rank and back in the trenches before you can say 'knife.' And now get yourself and that animal out of my quarters. You're dismissed, Major. *Dismissed!* I will see you in my office at nine tomorrow, morning. Sharp."

Inside Fitz something finally snapped. He had tried to work within the framework . . . He knew that there was now only one real course of action open to him. But he would have a last attempt. His voice was very cold, as it always was when he was really angry. "You'll listen to me *now*. I'll see you in your office, later. And then you can do your worst."

A sensible man hearing that tone would have shut up. It even took a *little* bit of the bombast out of Carrot-up. "I've given you your orders, Major."

"And I'll obey them. *After* I've finished, so you might as well let me make that quick. Now, I have interrupted your . . . rest, to tell you we have satellite information coming in that indicates that some of our men—"

"And maybe rats, and probably bats," interrupted Ariel, dropping out of his pocket to the floor.

"Yes, and possibly other troops, are behind enemy lines. They've attacked a scorpiary. The result is that on sector Delta 355 all the Magh' forces have been pulled back inside the force shield to deal with the insurgents. They're wreaking havoc in there, General. Three major explosion traces so far. They have some kind of vehicle and they're going through the scorpiary like a dose of salts. If they succeed in knocking out the power source for the force shield we must be ready to move in with speed, sir. The Magh' side of the line is undefended, sir. We should have whatever troops we can muster waiting in their earthworks. Even if the insurgents fail, which, of course, there is a good chance that they will . . ."

The general stood up, nearly losing his toga. "You dared to disturb me with this *rubbish*? It's a complete and utter farradiddle! And even if it wasn't, I don't care if there are a handful of other-ranks blundering around behind the enemy lines. It won't change the war, Major. These 'glamour' actions never do . . ."

The pager in Fitz's pocket beebled insistently. The major calmly interrupted. "I must answer that, sir. It is either my office, or the satellite center." From the dressing table came the clatter of a bottle being knocked over. As he pulled the pager from his pocket, Fitz saw the general's tunic top being dowsed in expensive single malt.

It was the satellite center. M'Batha didn't even wait for him to speak. He actually had to hold the pager away from his ear.

"They've done it again! We measured a tongue of flame in excess of a hundred feet less than four minutes after we'd tracked them leaving the spot.

They've gone back in, sir! Our boys are pounding the SHIT out of them!"

Fitz smiled. There was more than one voice in the background. It sounded like M'Batha had half the tech-services on the slowship in there with him. Well. It wouldn't do any harm at this stage. "Thanks, Henry." He held his hand over the pager mike. "Satellite tracking, sir. Reporting another explosion." There was no way the general couldn't have heard anyway. Daisy, with her ear to the bathroom keyhole, could probably have heard. "Would you like to speak to them, sir? Confirm it for yourself?"

General Cartup-Kreutzler wasn't buying it. "Pah. Do you think I don't recognize a put-up job. You think you can fool me! Satellite tracking is there to monitor the damned weather. Crops and things. They do not do this sort of thing. I do not know what you hoped to achieve by this . . . ridiculous performance, but you've failed. *Failed, d'you hear? NOW GET OUT!"*

Fitz clicked the pager off. "Is that your last word, sir?"

"*Yes*. Now GET OUT!"

Fitz shrugged. He couldn't bring himself to salute. "Enjoy the rest of your . . . entertainment, sir. Come on, Ariel. Let's go."

"We'll meet again, Carrot-up," said the rat cheerfully. She clambered up Fitz's leg, clutching a chocolate she'd just looted from a heart-shaped box on the dresser.

As they walked out, Fitz carefully put his heel down on the phone and crushed it. Ariel scrambled out of his pocket again, pausing to wipe her chocolaty paws on the flap. "Methinks, I'll deal with the wires just outside the house. There might be another phone. You check the other doors. And see that you pick up his trousers on the way. They're at the foot of the stairs. You humans are as good as blind. Typical of that stupid bimbo to like—*bleah*—strawberry creams."

Fitz smiled to himself. Rats, and Ariel in particular, were terrible rank-and-file soldiers. Nature's own samurai had far too much initiative. "I'll deal with the lights, too," Ariel added. "See you at the car."

"Fuse box is just outside the portico," reported Ariel with satisfaction. "So that tradesmen don't have to come inside, and lower the tone of the place."

"I know. I used to live like this," said Fitz grimly. "Convenient enough, of course. But it makes for easy sabotage."

Ariel scrambled up into the fatigue pocket. *Her* pocket. Not two seconds later, her head popped out, beady eyes filled with baleful outrage. "What's this?" she demanded, holding up the offending object.

Fitz smiled. "Called a distributor cap. Relax. We'll pitch it once we get off the grounds."

"Oh." She studied the gadget. "Okay. As long as it makes Carrot-up's life miserable, I'll tolerate the encroachment."

The guards at the gate saluted.

"Quite a party your general's having back there," said Fitz, dryly. "I wouldn't disturb him if I were you. Or let anyone else in to disturb him. Or pay too much attention to the . . . shouting."

"Can't really hear anything from here anyway, sir," said the corporal.

One of the privates sniggered and then realized that the major wasn't laughing. "No, sir," he said, absolutely rigid. "Anyway, we won't see anyone until the household staff get in, sir. They always come on just after the general leaves."

"Ah. And what time is that? I want to take up the length of your stint with your Major . . . diem Thien," said Fitz.

"We only do four-hour stretches, sir. Whoever's on the last stint just covers until the general leaves. Just before eight. We only have to do about two a week, sir. It's not a bad billet," added the soldier hastily. He knew perfectly well that when officers catch flak they pass it down.

"Compared to the front, it's heaven," agreed Fitz. "Just see your relief doesn't let anyone in—not anyone at all, understand? Tell them it is my specific orders, relayed from the general."

"Yessir." They saluted, and Fitz drove off.

"Oh dear," said Ariel. "You forgot to give them the keys."

Fitz smiled in the darkness. "It's got his office key on it. I thought I'd have to ask you to climb in through the ducts, but I won't need to now."

"You take away all my fun," she said. "Got any more food?"

He pulled a ration bar from a pocket. He knew just how fast that metabolism was. "Here."

"Yuck." She took it anyway. "You forgot to give him his trousers too."

"I'm planning on wearing those," said Fitz.

Ariel chuckled. Then she asked: "Why are we doing this? Not that I mind. But why?"

"We?" said Fitz.

"Methinks I should bite you on what's left of your balls," she said quietly.

Fitz sighed. "Because if we never win . . . we never can. Maybe if I prove they can advance . . . They'll learn."

"I doubt it," said Ariel.

"I know," said Fitz quietly. "But I've reached point-non-plus. I'm sorry, Ariel, to have dragged you into this."

She nuzzled him. "I love you." A moment later, remembering, she pitched the distributor cap out the window. "Even if you do let squatters move in on me."

Chapter 31: *Constipative Innovation.*

They'd broken out, and, this time with difficulty, broken in again. The space between the spiral arms was getting narrower and narrower. There just wasn't the sort of turning space a tractor needed. Then they'd knocked over the guards. And hastily turned down another cross tunnel.

The bats and rats had had to hold off the Maggots while Chip hastily knocked holes. Ginny and the galago poured fertilizer and diesel and inserted the primacord, before clipping on the bat limpet. Chip adjusted it, one minute twenty second fuse . . .

They were getting to be pretty fair sappers, with all the practice. Still, even the tiny HE bat-limpets and thick-cotton primacord were getting low. Chip had the can of floor-tile glue ready and bellowed for the rats and bats as soon as he clicked the limpet relay shut. Ginny, bright girl, was already up getting the tractor started. The Crotchet was holding forth at her again. Well, at least Chip didn't have to listen.

Bats and rats hurried past, as Chip poured glue. Then he dropped the can and ran. A Maggot was coming and, besides, Nym had managed to get the tractor going. In the interest of the poor tractor he had to get back to it. Somebody tossed a Molotov past his ear.

Panting, he made it to the stabilizer bar, hauled himself up onto the seat, and took over the driving. Even getting the tractor to move along faster was easier now.

Behind them came the sweet sound of detonation.

"Foine! More of the same?" asked O'Niel, a bottle in hand. Maybe he was just getting a Molotov ready.

Chip smiled, his crooked teeth matching Ginny's. "Nope! Always more of something different. This is like the restaurant trade. Your customers get sick of the same meal again and again, no matter how good. So innovation is the name of the game. First, you bats 'ud do us a favor if you'd check on whether there are any live Maggots in our tunnel. If not, we can have a little rest."

Siobhan fluttered up and touched a wing to Chip's head. "To be sure, the boy's brain's overheated."

"Methinks, 'tis too little sex," sniffed Fal. He leered at Ginny. "Eh, girl?"

Her dusty glasses twinkled at him. "Why, sir, he never gives me candy."

It was a joke, but Chip detected just a touch of wistfulness under it all.

"Or flowers, I suppose," added Melene, dryly.

"Or even a drink," said Doll.

"Ahem." Doc cleared his throat. "He's right, you know . . ."

Pistol clapped. "I agree. I'd liefer get off this candy scale."

Doc sighed. "Explain to him, Bronstein. The Maggots do not expect us to stop. So therefore we must."

But Bronstein and Eamon had already flown back down the tunnel.

They came back a bare minute later. "Indade," said Eamon cheerfully, "there are no sounds of digging. And 'tis awful conceited those few Maggots who got through were. They couldn't even defend themselves."

"Conceited? Did they think they could beat you, Eamon?" asked Chip.

"I think he means they were stuck-up," said Ginny. She had soft-cyber language experience on her side. "Now what?"

Chip grinned. "R and R time. We give it . . . say five minutes. Then we go back out . . . the way we came in."

He dug the GPS out of his pack. "If we're right about where we're going, we've got less than a mile to go."

"Just the last little bit," she said. "Isn't that great news, Professor?"

Chip answered, his voice serious now. "The last bit is going to be the worst. It'll be wall-to-wall Maggots in the inner part. I honestly never believed we'd even get this far. Eamon, I think you'd better wire up a limpet to the trailer. We might as well go out in blaze of glory."

Eamon looked at him appraisingly. "Indade. You're thinking almost like a bat. You're an odd human, Connolly."

Chip shrugged. "Where do *you* think all those odd ideas in your head came from, bat? Have you still got some of those distance-trigger mines left?"

Eamon shook his head. "I've still got two," said Bronstein. "But you're wrong, Chip. Some of the words—and words color your thinking—I'll grant you, come from humans. But we are still bats at the core."

"Indeed. It would be impossible to segregate the physiological and evolutionary from the implant . . ." Doc Pararattus had barely got started when Pistol, Nym, and even Melene, who usually listened, all said: "SHUT UP."

Fal and Doll's voices were absent from the chorus. Chip decided it was a poor time to ask where they were.

Doc sighed. "I don't suppose anyone brought any food, did they?"

"The Maggot back there is full of glue," replied Eamon gloomily.

Chip dug in his pack. Produced two bottles and three small tins with snaptops. "Sauerkraut. A couple of tins of smoked mussels in cottonseed oil and a bottle of Roll-mops. And I've got some biscuits."

The condemned woman, man, rats and bats prepared to eat a hearty meal. Only the galago looked miserable. Chip looked at him. And dug deep in his pack. "Fruit, huh?"

"Or insects or acacia gum, *señor*," said the galago wistfully.

Chip pulled out a jar. "Here. Try these preserved green figs. They're traditionally served with fine cheese. But I can't oblige you there."

The galago looked longingly at bottle. "*Señor* Chip, I love figs. But they have on the insides of me a most distressing effect."

Chip handed him the jar. "Eat them. You probably won't be alive to worry about the aftereffects."

They even saved a bit of food for out-of-breath Fal and Doll.

"What happened to candy?" Both of them gave Chip a filthy look, before diving on the food.

"Now let's get out of here." Suddenly Chip saw the weakness of his strategy. He had a good three hundred yards to reverse. He peered back up the tunnel. It was long and curved. "Goddamn stupid bastards. Why didn't they build it like a wheel with spokes? Nice straight spokes going to the middle, instead of this damn spiral. Now I've got to reverse this trailer."

Doc took up an oratory pose. "My hypothesis is that they are like us."

That was a curious enough statement not to get him shouted down. "Methinks not even humans build in spirals," said Melene.

"No, I mean they are trapped within an evolutionary and construction milieu. This was once a defensive structure."

Chip edged the tractor backwards, and spoke through gritted teeth. "Bull, Doc. It's a disaster, defensively."

"It is now, against us. But once it must have effectively channeled and split their foes. And insured that if an enemy did get into the tunnels the guard stations along the way would stop them. Note how easily and neatly the entries fall—every time. They were built to collapse. They were built as traps. I will bet you would find a keystone in each, that they do not need explosives. You see, explosives and the tractor alter the equation. Their previous foes did not have those."

"It's a trap all right, to reverse out of. By the time we get out of here, even Maggots will have figured this out."

"Hey Chip. Methinks you could just go forward and turn around," said Fal.

"No space," said Chip shortly, putting the tractor into first. He was trying to get into a better position to reverse from.

Fal chuckled. "Just keep going forward. There's a sort of chamber, a bit ahead, that Doll and I, um, found."

"The candy store no doubt," snorted Chip.

Even the rats had the grace to look embarrassed. "Well. It might have been our last chance."

Chip noticed Virginia was looking at him very speculatively.

Chip eyed the chamber. It might have looked big to the rats. "I can go in. But then I can't turn around."

"Go past. Back the trailer in and then go out again forwards. Or go in forwards and then come out backing the trailer the other way," said Ginny.

"You know a hell of a lot about it for someone who can't drive," said Chip sourly.

"Just do it!" snapped Bronstein. "And be quick about it."

So he drove the tractor in cautiously, dropped the blade—with some skill by now—and started cranking the wheel over.

"No," said Ginny. "The other way—if you want to reverse."

He kept turning his way. "That doesn't make sense."

"It does mathematically. *Please*, Chip."

He shrugged, and tried it her way. "Holy Mackerel! So that's how it works! Why didn't you tell me before?" They were around! He pushed the throttle out a bit fast for the last bit, before they could drive back down. And the trailer jackknifed in earnest. Shaft-snapping earnest.

Fortunately, the drive shaft snapped at the link. If

it had snapped at the pump it would have killed the Korozhet. The piece of ricocheting steel just touched across Ginny's high forehead. Even a quarter-inch closer and she'd have been dead. A sudden line of red appeared, and then beaded with blood.

Chip stared at her in open-mouthed horror. "*Oh, shit!* Are you all right! I didn't mean . . ."

"I'm fine," she said faintly. "Just drive." This time, when she put an arm around him, he did not pull away.

Chapter 32: *Orders.*

When Conrad and Ariel checked in to the headquarters-parking-precinct, Corporal Simms was waiting for them. Hopping with impatience.

"You'd better get home, Johnny. Be sure you sign out." Fitz spoke before the car had even fully stopped. This was a good man. No point in dragging him down into what was going to be a hell of a mess.

Simms simply ignored the comment. "I've got the G23-A signed and waiting. I've got current troop deployments up on screen for you. I think the division at Cressy could be mobilized within the hour. The only problem is that Brigadier Charlesworth is in charge of it. Still, they're the nearest. I took the liberty of going ahead and organizing transport vehicles. They've got farther to go. The dispatch riders have gone with that one, and I've got three others on standby."

For a moment Fitz could only stare at him. Swallow. *How the hell?* "Johnny, you go and get yourself signed out of that gate, *now*. PDQ! You've a wife, and a kid on the way, you fool. I want you out of this."

The corporal twitched a grin. There was no humor in it. "Let's get to the office, sir. There are lots of other men with wives and families. Sometimes, a man just does what he has to do."

They hurried down the passage. "How the hell did you know what I was going to do . . . and where the hell did you get redeployment orders?"

"Yeah. Well done, Johnny," said Ariel. "Saved us some trouble."

Simms sighed. "I'm a Vat, Major. I don't have delusions about Shareholders. I knew Carrot-up wouldn't do a thing, even if he believed you. The Kreutzler family has the main artillery-shell contract. Not in the family interest to do anything to disturb cost-plus. I know you. I knew what you'd decide to do."

Fitz stopped, removed his cap, and ran his fingers through his hair. "I'm a Shareholder too, Johnny."

The corporal grinned. "Nossir. *You* are a lunatic."

Ariel laughed. " 'Tis true. Hey Johnny, I wish you could have seen Daisy horse riding. Tell him, Fitz."

But the major was still intent on the subject in hand. "And the G23-A's? Redeployment orders live locked up in the general's safe."

"Yessir," said Simms. "They are well locked up. They're *still* well locked up. But only after Daisy orders the forms from central stationary stores. I walked into there and helped myself . . . about a month ago."

Once more Fitz found himself without a word to say.

"That's just how the army works, sir," said the corporal, obviously by way of further explanation.

Fitz had to admit that there was quite a lot of truth in this. "We're going to get court-martialed, you know."

"Yes, sir. That's unfortunate, sir."

Fitz made notes off the screen as Corporal Simms filled in the troop redeployment forms in a neat, precise hand . . . totally unlike General Cartup-Kreutzler's sprawling signature. "No word in from the satellite guy?" he asked.

The corporal looked up briefly from his meticulous detailing. "Nothing, I'm afraid, sir."

"Shit. They've bought it. Well, if we move fast maybe we can still salvage something from the price they've paid."

"If that idiot colonel has got his troops into position in the Magh's lines . . . and if they can hold until these troops get through," muttered Simms.

The phone rang. The corporal picked it up and answered in his best Shareholder drawl. His written counterfeiting was much better. "General Cartup-Kreutzler's office. Liaison Officer Simmons . . . Excellent! No. I'm afraid the general's unavailable right now. Yes, sir. I'll pass that on, sir. Yes, he is a genius, sir."

With huge smile, he turned to Fitz. "They've just pushed forward into the Magh' earthworks on sector Delta 355. They're totally unoccupied. He hopes the backup he's requested gets there soon. He says the general is a genius."

"And here is the A.33-1," said the returning rat. "Do you know how many stupid forms there are in that rat's-nest of an office? It's a disgrace! And what a mess they're in! The only reason that Daisy keeps her job is . . ."

Fitz grinned affectionately at her. Of course, most

people would have found it a frightening experience. "Ariel, there is a box of chocolate cointreau straws in my top drawer! You are a rat past price. A darling."

"I love you too," said Ariel. "Even when I don't get my favorite form of chocolate for giving you the pleasure of shafting Brigadier Charlesworth."

Fitz looked at the forms. "Forget the dispatch rider, Johnny. I'm going to take these myself."

"Yesss!" Ariel cheered.

Corporal Simms looked worried. "What about the satellite stuff?"

Fitz pulled a face and spoke quietly. "They're dead, Corporal. They went damn well. All that is left now is to see that their effort isn't wasted. I'm going to *see* that that happens."

The phone rang again. Simms answered as previously . . . and then: "Henry! Sorry, didn't realize it was you. Yes, he's here."

Corporal Simms smiled beatifically, and held out the phone. "You're fucking well wrong, sir," he informed his commanding officer with glee.

Fitz reached for the phone. "Then I have some more organizing to do. But I'm still going."

Chapter 33:
Onwards and inwards.

"Next time you want to use glue, for the holy Mary's sake don't use it when we're going to double back. It was a foine idea, but messy." "Preparing" Molotovs was making O'Niel positively loquacious. But the bits of sticky Maggot flying off the wheels were obviously upsetting him.

Melene fastidiously wiped her fur. "Yes. My pelt doesn't look fit to be seen dead in."

The tractor started pushing its way back into the adobe debris. Chip shook himself. "Good thing they'll probably skin us when they catch us then, huh? Come on. All off! You lot clear some of this stuff."

"Methinks *you* can get off and clear stuff," said Nym. "I'll drive."

"Oh, come on!" said Chip impatiently.

"No. It makes good sense," said Bronstein. "You

humans are bigger. Besides, I have heard that those who spend all their time sitting behind tables become constipated. We must do our bit for your digestion. Get to it."

"Huh?"

Ginny started to giggle. "Chip, you said 'desk jockeys are full of shit.' Soft-cyber translation can be a bit literal. Come on. In first gear, the tractor won't run away from you. And Bronstein's right."

Chip sighed. "I suppose we are bigger."

At least four voices said, "No, we mean you're full of shit."

Chip hopped down, and started hauling adobe pieces. "It's just bits of sticky Maggot, honest."

The push through the area they'd blasted earlier had taken longer than Chip had anticipated. Maybe Doc was right and this was a very sophisticated trap. All he knew was it had taken a hot sweaty twenty minutes to dig their way out. And they were not more than a minute late, at that. Ten minutes earlier and they'd have had a clear run. As it was the Maggots were at least either ahead or behind. But not very far behind. It was obvious that Papa-Maggot was calling all his children home. Or maybe, by the way they were running, Mama-Maggot. *All* the children, back to the middle of the hive.

That was about all that had saved them. There were just so many Magh' that the warrior types couldn't get through. Tractors, while wonderful vehicles in many ways, were not known for rapid acceleration. And there were just too many Maggots to fight off. But they got in each other's way. Then Ginny had the bright idea of playing "roll-the-barrel" with a half-empty twenty-five-liter diesel drum. It was a great knock-on game.

Thus the few scorps who reached the tractor were possible to fend off as the tractor gathered speed. The creatures were determined, though. Fire used to cause pandemonium. Molotovs still fried them, of course, but it was just bug-popping now—noisier and more splattery than popcorn. They came on, as if driven. Barbed wire was simply trodden down, along with the unfortunate Maggots entangled in it.

Eamon looked regretfully back. "Indade, a pity we can't mist-and-burn this bedamned passage. Stop them catching up on us, now that they know where we are."

O'Niel dropped wire-loop Maggot caltrops. "Aye. If they do catch up we'll be the mayit in the sandwich."

"Methinks I've never tried it in a sandwich," said Doll, with a bit of regret.

"Open the tap on the trailer. The stuff will burn anyway, even if it isn't misted," said Chip.

Bronstein nodded. "True. Let's set a few more expedient mines, eh Chip?"

Chip shook his head. "I don't think we can stop. We'll have to drop the stuff, and you'll have to fly to catch up."

"Okay. We'll do just that. You—Fluff! Open the tap." The galago looked at Bronstein and went off to comply. A minute later, a sack of fertilizer and a drum of diesel narrowly missed the tiny hidalgo's delicate ears. He ducked—getting splashed by the brandy river—while avoiding a bundle of hinged cartridge planks.

"Fluff, I *do* like the aftershave," said Melene, when he reappeared. "But Bronstein said, 'please close it now.' "

The galago shook his head, mournfully. "My best, she is done. Already I have tried with great effort. The tap, she leaks."

✧ ✧ ✧

Ginny clung with one hand to the ropes of the wildly swaying trailer. Her feet were carefully tangled in the cargo netting that she and Chip had tied there . . . several lifetimes ago. The abrasive, bumpy Maggot-tunnel floor blurred past as she struggled to close the tap. The alcohol must have gotten to the seals . . . hardly surprising, really. It was close to rocket fuel, as she well remembered. A thin stream of seventy-four percent trailed behind them, despite her best efforts with the recalcitrant tap. If she fell now she'd be dragged to hamburger meat.

She managed to pull herself up. "It will not be stopped!"

"Oh . . ."

Bats came hurtling in, and of course the explosion followed.

Then the hot wind came rushing along the tunnel . . . the alcohol wasn't rapidly going *woof* as it had when atomized. Instead it was burning steadily. Looking back on their curving trail she saw that even if the Maggots weren't catching them . . . the flames were. A little firetrail was leaping and hopping down the path laid by the leaking tap.

"Flames are catching up with us!" yelled Nym.

Chip risked a glance backwards, nearly sending the tractor into the wall. "Stop the alcohol!" he shouted. "If those flames catch up with the trailer, it'll blow us to shit!"

Ginny resolutely stuck both feet into the cargo net again, and lowered herself over. Facing out, back the way they'd come. Then she let go with her first hand, and then the second. The ends of her long hair swept through the dust as she cupped both hands under the tap. She knew that all she had to do was to break that alcohol line, but hanging by her heels, seeing the flames leap closer, was terrifying. The trailer bounced and the libation in her cupped hands spilled. A small stick-up knob of Magh' adobe plucked violently at her hair. Her legs and feet screamed with the effort.

And then a huge force plucked her upright. Hauled her onto the top of the trailer. All he'd been able to reach was the front of her blouse, which would never be the same again.

"Are you fucking crazy?" Chip shouted into her face. "You could have killed yourself! You silly little idiot!" Then he dived forward to help Pistol, who was attempting to restrain Nym's driving efforts.

Well! Apparently he *did* care . . .

Bronstein flung herself into flight. "Come on, Siobhan. Let us see if we can get ahead of these speeding lunatics. See what joys lie in store for us."

Ginny peered at the GPS figures. Less than a half a mile to go! She looked at her spiky-haired, stubble-faced love, his face dirty and sweat streaked, his gaze intent on the tunnel-road.

He wasn't very tall, she had to admit, and his torn-sleeved shirt showed arms that were more sinew and scar tissue than beautifully sculpted muscle. Well, he might not be the cover picture from her favorite romance. Actually the thought of him in elegant Regency knee-smalls and a swallow-tailed coat . . . was enough to provide her with a welcome snort of laughter. She'd never again be able to imagine a romantic figure in quite the same way.

He glanced at her and she smiled. And he smiled back.

She was looking at him. He could feel it, and it made him feel guilty. He had had no call to shout at her like that. It had just come out. She really was a good kid for a Shareholder. In fact it was hard to believe that she was a Shareholder. More like a mixture between a crazy bat, and a pragmatic rat. With twice her share of plain old-fashioned guts. Pretty too. Yeah, okay. A bit skinny. And she'd torn a bit much off that blouse and skirt for a man's imagination. But she had the kind of face that grew on you . . . even those glasses. That cascade of thick dusty gold hair tied up with that ridiculous bandana. Shit. Just when you got to like someone—they were bound to die. Hell, they were all bound to die, and damn soon too. The barriers between Vat and Shareholder seemed very irrelevant right now. In the midst of this lot, the boundaries between bat, rats and humans seemed virtually imaginary. The only thing he couldn't identify with was that Korozhet. At least the alien had kept its mouth shut, although someone had said the damn things spoke through their asses anyway. Its voice wasn't very loud. Maybe it couldn't make itself heard above the tractor.

He looked at Ginny. And she smiled at him, that trusting, generous smile of hers. He found that his answering smile came very easily. He also found himself bitterly regretting some missed opportunities . . .

"Why don't you come and stand over here?" he said, looking at her uncomfortable position.

"I need something to hold onto."

"You could hold onto me."

The Korozhet addressed her repeatedly in the next little while and she didn't even notice. Chip, of course, had no trouble ignoring its demands to be set down.

Idylls never last.

Siobhan called from ahead. "Bronstein says next left. Maggots are coming."

They turned in. Blew the entrance down. It was a good strategy. Except . . .

Eamon and Siobhan came fluttering back frantically. "The back end of the tunnel is solid Maggots. It's a trap!"

Chip swung the wheel hard over. It was simply an instinctive act because the tunnel was far too narrow for them to turn. The blade gouged into the wall before the tractor stalled. Fal had fallen off in the crash. He stood up swearing. "*You whoreson mother-shogging baconfaced . . . !*"

And then he stopped. Darted forward through a hole. He stuck his head back. "You're driving's not worth a gooseberry, Connolly. But you found us a way out, if we can get through the wall."

Bronstein took charge. "Expedient mines. Diesel. Ginny, get down with that chainsaw. Chip, you'll have to hammer a few more shot holes.

"Let me out," demanded the Crotchet.

Chip thought Bronstein gave this more consideration than it deserved. She paused her work for a moment. Then she spoke decisively. "No. We don't have time. And we certainly don't have time to get you back up again. You'll be safer there."

"Move it up, Bronstein," said Chip impatiently. "Tell me where you want the next shot holes. You can chat to Smelly later, if we're alive." Chip noticed how the Crotchet flexed and pointed spines at him, but then he was too busy working to watch any further.

Down the tunnel came the sharp crack and boom of the first expedient mines. "Behind the tractor, everybody!" shouted Bronstein. "I've used small charges."

She was a master of demolitions. The gap would take the tractor. Eamon came fluttering up, rats running in his wake. "Let us begone. I've set the timer for forty seconds on the big one further back. We'll have the lead Maggots here in less than that!"

Chip scrambled up. Started the tractor. And it was good and stuck. "I'm going to have to move the trailer." He jumped down and started trying to drag it by main force.

"Bounce it!" shouted somebody. He heard the snarl of the chainsaw. As he bounced the trailer an inch, he saw Ginny cut into a big scorp. And then take on a second one. And rev the chainsaw one second too early. The blade hit the slowshield. About ninety percent of the chainsaw blade was inside the shield. The chain, totally stopped at twenty-two thousand rpm, snapped in half. The section inside the Maggot's slowshield played ricochet blender with the Maggot. The piece outside whizzed into the fibreglass of the trailer. Chip suddenly found he had the strength to lift and bounce that trailer a good eight inches.

"Drop it, Ginny, we can go now. RUN everybody!"

Head down, he drove the tractor through the gap . . . behind them another forty pounds of fertilizer blew. This wasn't an entryway, so it didn't fall to seal, but it certainly restricted access.

"Barbed wire!" Bronstein shouted.

"And a can of diesel and a Molotov!" yelled Eamon.

Chip had his first proper look at the place they'd broken into. It was a shock to realize that even parts of Maggotdom could be beautiful.

The whole place was one enormous alien hothouse. Or, by the looks of it, alien fungus-cellar. The basic color of the tunnels was mud, doubtless in many attractive Maggot-pleasing shades. Here the basic color was . . . bright. The tangle of spindly-stemmed nodding-capped plants came in every shade from pale chartreuse to deepest burgundy. And the air was sharp with a ferment of strange bouquets, some edging on the not-nice side of cumin-spicy, others lush with overripe esters.

Part of Chip's soul rose. This was a vision into a distant place, a place where a strange sun gleamed pale on an enchanted fungus-world.

Pistol fanned his nose. "Whoreson. This place doesn't half pong. Phew!"

"Come on, Chip!" yelled Bronstein. "Open her up! Maggots are coming along. We're probably driving through their sewage farm."

Chip had little choice but to plow on through the delicate stems, wreaking havoc. But when he saw a spiral downramp, he took it without a second thought. Rats might have no poetry in their souls, but this was too much like destroying a cathedral. The downramp took them out onto a cross passage . . . and that to a clear tunnel heading inwards.

"That place was so . . . so beautiful," said Ginny in a quiet voice. "Elfin. I don't know how something as horrible as the Magh' could come from a place like that."

Chip gave her a glowing look which she missed because she was looking at the Korozhet. "They don't," the Crotchet said. "Those are rare plants from a world previously visited."

The rest of this enlightenment was lost to them because they had arrived at the central well. In the middle of the well stood a Maggot tower. A Magh' adobe spike separated from the circles of incoming spiral tunnel arms by a gap sixty feet wide. Off to the right, two levels up, were the remains of a single bridge. The Magh' were busy destroying it, leaving a single spar to a doorway into the tower. Across the gap in the tower, workers were blocking the doorway, working with frantic haste.

Looking at the four circles above them Chip realized this must have been the finest entertainment in all Maggotdom. The circles were solid Maggot.

Actually, Maggot on top of Maggot. Heh. It was a good thing the Crotchet had told them they needed to go down to the base of the tower, or they might have tried to hack their way through that lot. And that would have been impossible.

Chapter 34:
Calling out the Cavalry.

"We upped the detection levels in the infrared. One of the guys from over on technical . . . uh, I hope you don't mind, but half the nightshift is watching . . ."

"I had gathered," said Fitz dryly. "Go on, Henry."

"Sorry, Major. This is just the first time anything exciting has ever happened. I mean, we all thought nobody ever actually *looked* at satellite data. Everybody is so pleased to be, well, involved in something useful. And it is so great seeing our guys really hit back for a change. You don't know what it has meant to the people here!"

"Believe me, I do," said Fitz. "I just hope this doesn't land you all in trouble. Anyway, tell me—you've obviously tracked them a bit further?"

"Yep. They haven't come out of the mound again, but they're still alive and heading inwards. With slow time-exposure infrared we've picked up what must have been a massive fire. Ambient temperature of outgoing air from vents went up by about fifteen degrees in spots. It looked like little flowers on the screen. It must have been one *hell* of a fire." Henry's delight was plain.

Fitz understood the psychology. "Every time I think that must be all, these guys pull another rabbit out of the hat."

"YESSS!"

The cheering was so loud Fitz held the phone away from his ear. "We've got another explosion, sir. Smaller this time."

"Keep me posted, Henry. And tell the tech who used his initiative, well done. If more people used their brains, we'd get somewhere."

"I'll tell him, sir. He just thought he was losing money! The guys are betting heavily on your commandos, sir."

Fitz rolled his eyes. "They're not commandos, Henry."

"Well, Special Services or whatever, sir. They're great guys, sir."

"They're not Special Services . . ."

"If you say so, sir." Henry's voice indicated he was very happy to go along with whatever story the major wanted to spin for him, but it would be a frosty Friday in hell before he believed a word of it. "We'll keep you posted on how your . . . non-commandos are doing."

Fitz put the phone down. "That's how bloody myths are born," he said, savagely. "Well, let's see if the real thing can do anything to help them." He dialed.

"Airborne." The voice on the other side sounded irritated. Well. It *was* going on 1:00 am.

"Evening, Bobby," said Fitz cheerfully.

"It's bloody morning, you mad bastard." The irritation had been replaced with obvious pleasure.

"Okay. Morning, then. And as it *is* morning, are your lads up and ready to go?"

"*What?*" Van Klomp nearly deafened him. "Don't fuck me around, Fitzy! Have you got a us a real mission at last?"

There was too much hope in that voice for Major Conrad Fitzhugh to tell his old parachute instructor anything but the absolute truth. All of it . . .

"So," he concluded, "if the force field comes down, I want you lads ready to get in there. That's the only hope those boys on the loose in there have got. Besides anything else, they'll know more about the inside of a scorpiary than any man alive. I'll cut you some orders. They'll be fakes, but . . ."

"Screw the orders, man," said Van Klomp. "If the field doesn't come down we go on sitting on our *tuchis*, doing displays at parades. If it does . . . we probably won't be answering any questions. We'll try to get to them, but I've only got sixty men." There was a momentary hesitation; then: "Fitzy, you're in for the high jump, unless this goes right and your dear general decides he's going to claim the credit."

"So I'm for the high jump. This could just be the big chance, Bobby. Now, if you do go in, you just hold on. I'm not hanging around for the court-martial. Ariel and I are on our way to the front. We'll push the troops along."

"You still got that mad rat? You want a chopper ride to the front?"

Ariel jumped at the phone. "And fuck you too, Van Klomp!"

Fitz grinned. "The chopper would solve a lot of problems. And I warn you, I'm jealous. Ariel obviously wants your body."

"I'll have a chopper with you in fifteen minutes. You'd better get your satellite boykie to report to me." The man on the other end of the line paused. "Good luck, Fitzy."

"Yeah," said Fitz quietly. "And sorry to drag you into this shit, Bobby."

There was another longish pause. Then Major Robert Van Klomp replied, also in a quiet voice, quite unlike his normal bellow. "This is supposed to be the Army's elite unit, Fitz. I just hope to God I've finally got a chance to prove it. Now, I'm going to stir asses out of sacks. Go to it, my boy."

The lump in his throat stopped Fitz saying goodbye. It was possible he'd just sentenced an old friend to death.

Chapter 35:
What address were we looking for?

The trailer slewed wildly. So did the tractor driver. So did the tractor. Instead of completing the turn the right-hand front wheel went over the edge of the spiral downramp next to the well.

Chip looked back at the hitch-wishbone. It *would* snap now. Well, it'd probably only been the C-clamp and the wire he'd wound around the porcupine-weld that had held it together for so long across very rough terrain. And there was no time to do anything now. The tractor and the trailer were not going anywhere—except possibly over the edge and all the way down.

"All off!" shouted Bronstein. "Cut the stuff we need off the trailer and toss it over the edge. We're going to have to run."

"Alas, I cannot run," complained the Korozhet. "My poor spines are so cramped from this bag. Abandon me! Virginia and I will hide here and the rest of you can draw pursuit."

"No," said Siobhan, "We must look after you. We'll lower you down first."

Chip cut the Crotchet's bag free with a single swipe of the Solingen. "Come on. You're the only one who claims to know where we're going. Grab me that rope, Ginny. I'll get him down quick."

"But I do not wish to be lowered." The Korozhet clacked his spines at him. "I will run."

"Tough shit." Chip pulled the rope through the top loops of cargo net.

"Methinks we rats will abseil with you," Melene comforted, while rolling a drum of diesel to the edge.

Doc, bent nearly double under a bag of alcohol bottles, agreed. "Yes. We have to use original ideas. I was going to lower these bottles. Once I have done that the logical thing is for us rats to abseil down too. We are needing to go down, Madam Korozhet, you said. . . ."

Chip swung the alien over the edge and began lowering. Siobhan flew down alongside her.

Meanwhile, Bronstein was furiously organizing, and Eamon was fiddling with last-minute touches on a trip wire attached to the limpet-mine on the jammed trailer. Chip saw O'Niel pat their doomed steed with a gentle wing. "You're a foine, foine device," the bat said thickly. "Eamon, you'll be seeing it be quick, will you now?"

" 'Tis not a bat," gruffed Eamon, as he tensioned the wire.

O'Niel gave a mournful sniff. "I know. But it was a fine and a gallant companion."

Eamon shook his head. " 'Tis a machine, O'Niel. But she'll go out wi' glory. A fine fiery send-off, fitting of a bat. And a number of her enemies with her. Now lend me a foot."

The Crotchet was down, and Chip and Ginny came to help carry the heavy stuff. One of the few things the humans could do better than anyone else was porter. They carried fertilizer bags and turfed them over the edge twenty yards from the rats' abseil-point.

On his second trip, Chip noticed that Nym was sitting quite still, pouring brandy down the air intake while patting the little tractor awkwardly. Snuffling all the while. Chip took his grappling iron in one hand and the rat in the other along to where the others were abseiling. Cursing all the while.

"They're on their way. *GO, go, go!*" shouted Bronstein, from higher up the ramp.

Chip realized with horror that he was going to have to abseil again. And worse, Ginny had no homemade harness, or any idea what to do.

He took a deep breath. "You'll have to get onto my back," he said, hoping he sounded calm to her. Trying to ignore the small booms of the expedient mines higher up the ramp, he rigged himself. He knew he couldn't afford to make any mistakes now, or they'd both fall and die. On the other hand, if he didn't move fast they'd be blown to glory along with the tractor and trailer.

She walked up close. "How do you want me to hold?" she asked with perfect faith.

Chip found that hard to deal with. "Tight. And you, Fluff, go down that rope. Chop-chop. Send it."

As calmly as possible, he lowered the two of them over the edge. Her body was warm against his. Very warm, very firm, very soft, very—very—

He forced himself to concentrate on the rope.

At least abseiling with double the weight was easier. But he'd swear he didn't even hear the vineyard tractors's last blast.

He did notice pieces of Maggot and masonry falling past. And then, they were falling too. Something had severed the rope. Fortunately a five-foot fall onto a pile of fertilizer granules wasn't going to kill them. And he managed, somehow, to spin them so that Ginny landed on him rather than vice versa.

The plump rat regarded them with a wry rat-smile. "Methinks that was definitely virgin on the ridiculous."

"Oh shut up, Fal," muttered Chip.

Fal chuckled. "Only if you'll tell me how you get it right in that position. Or is that the explanation for the virgin part, eh, Ginny?"

Just in time she realized he was teasing. She had been about to start on an impetuous tirade against Melene not being able to keep a secret. But he really *didn't* know. And, with a sudden shock, she also realized he wasn't really trying to be nasty. He was just . . . being Falstaff.

"Fal, you are ugly and your mother dresses you funny," she said sternly.

He grinned. "That's the spirit, girl. You'll make a proper rattess yet. Now get off the muck heap."

"What do you mean 'muck heap'?" grumbled Chip.

Ginny laughed. "Fertilizer. That's the way soft-cyber logic works."

Chip grinned. "You understand it better than I do. Anyway, Fal, I'm sore, and bruised, and I'm tired. Why shouldn't I lie in the muck if I want to? Got nice company." Despite the words, he was trying to stand up.

Not fast enough to suit Fal. "Up, up!" he shouted. "I'm supposed to be collecting the muck into these bags while the rest of the thinner rats are off laying charges with the bats. Even your galago has gone along . . . with Doll, I think. Bronstein says that this brood-heart bit isn't likely to be unguarded, and we might want to blow it up. Besides, we need something for you humans to carry. To keep your feet on the ground, and your minds from wicked thoughts."

Pistol scampered up. "They can always carry us," he proclaimed. "I mean, when a human's in debt to the tune of fifty cases of whiskey, the least he could do would be to provide transport."

Ginny realized Chip might have more luck at getting to his feet if she let go of him. Still, it seemed a pity.

"Will you two get up so that I can collect the explosive, or are you just going to bang right there?" demanded Fal. "And, as you're back so quick, Pistol, you can help."

"Bang?" The one-eyed rat laughed wickedly. "Old Chip doesn't need any help. Does he, Ginny?"

She realized that she'd somehow passed imperceptibly from being an outsider, to being one of them. The thought brought a fierce glow. This was the first time in her life she'd ever felt that way.

The others began trickling back, as they gathered up as much of the fertilizer as possible.

" 'Tis to be hoped t'ose Maggots aren't fast runners," said O'Niel. "I set mine on three minutes."

"Indade, you're a fool, O'Niel," snapped Eamon. "I said to you—plain as day—two and a half!"

"Oh, foine. 'Tis a fool I am, now. Just because my claw slipped," muttered O'Niel.

"Indade?" said Eamon. "A drunken fool!"

"Will you two stop bickering? Let's go." Chip had shouldered two half-bags of fertilizer and was rolling one of the three dented twenty-five-liter drums of diesel that had made it down.

"We're waiting for Siobhan and Doc," said Melene.

Fal looked around. "And the Korozhet."

Ginny looked alarmed. "Where did he go? Och. I mean she, the Professor, go?"

Pistol pointed. "He went with Doc. They were arguing about—'the dialectic,' or some such."

Chip put his load down. "We'd better get after them. When Doc gets going he's unlikely to notice a little thing like a time fuse."

They found her first. By smell. Something very unpleasant had happened to Siobhan. Murder. Murder most foul. The twisted body lay just inside the access-tunnel mouth.

Bronstein bristled. "Her pack is missing. No Maggot ever takes anything."

With a terrible feeling in the pit of his stomach, Chip ran past the bats. The little body of Doc lay on top of the pile of fertilizer. For a moment he stood, frozen. Then he noticed a minuscule twitch of the nose. Fal and Melene arrived, full tilt.

"Whoreson! What the hell killed him?" demanded Fal.

Melene, who had dived onto the philosopher, was listening intently. "His heart is beating. But it is very faint."

Suddenly, it all fell into place in Chip's head. He grabbed Doc, and gathered Melene up too in the same armful. "Fal—*Run!*"

They sprinted. At the tunnel mouth, the remaining bats and remaining rats were congregated with Ginny and the galago.

Ginny looked up. "You've got Doc! The Professor must be in there too!" She turned, hastily, toward the tunnel.

Chip dropped his burdens and dived on her, bringing her down.

The galago shrieked as he flew from her shoulder. "I will go . . ."

Chip saw Pistol, moving like a blur, knock the little galago down.

Then, as he had foreseen, the charge in the tunnel went off.

"The Professor!" Virginia tried to scramble to her feet.

Chip hung onto her fiercely. "Don't you see, you little fool, the goddamn Crotchet killed Siobhan—and tried to kill Doc. It's a fucking murderer!"

She struggled. "NO! Never! He couldn't be! Korozhet are *GOOD*."

Bronstein's gargoyle face twisted. "Yes." The word sounded torn out of her. "But we can't go in there. The rest of the charges are due to go off at any moment. We must finish what the Korozhet wanted us to do."

Ginny struggled some more. "You go on. I must go back and see."

"You'll come with us," Chip said, half dragging her. "If I have to knock you out and carry you, you'll come with us now!"

"I won't!" she struggled hysterically.

He hit her. In the solar plexus. Hard. As her breath whoofed out, he grabbed her and began to run for the dark tunnel where the Korozhet had said their destination should be. He had a sinking feeling about that, too, now.

Chip dumped her, groaning, in the entry tunnel. He turned on the rats who had followed with Doc. "You let her out of here, and I'll kill you. Got me?"

"And if he doesn't, I will," said Bronstein grimly.

Chip ran to gather the bags they'd dropped on their way in. He'd just made it back when the various tunnel charges went off.

✧ ✧ ✧

"I never ever want to speak to you again," Ginny said fiercely. "You left the Professor there to die, you . . . you *Vat.*"

"Suits me, Shareholder bitch," he said, dragging the bags along past her. He didn't even look at her.

"Uh. Ginny." Someone plucked gently at her elbow. It was fat Fal, being uncharacteristically quiet. "The Korozhet wasn't in there. Honest. The only sign he'd ever been there was that smell. Ask Melene. And if Chip had let you back into that tunnel, methinks all that would have happened, would be that you'd have been killed too."

She sniffed back the angry tears. The inside of her head was a confused and miserable mess. Not a small part of her was wishing that she *was* dead. "He shouldn't have said that Professor had murdered people." It was a subconscious slip. They were "people" to her now.

Fal shrugged. "Chip's a valiant little whoreson, but he speaks his mind. I know it couldn't be true, but . . . be fair, Ginny. That is what it looks like."

"It's *all* so unfair!" she sobbed. "Thanks, Fal." She found herself hugging the most unlikely rat in the world.

"Gently, gently," said Fal, in faintly crushed tones, but speaking gently himself. He comforted: "Never mind Ginny. It'll all come right. If we ever get out of this we'll steal you the biggest box of candy in the whole world to give to him. Meanwhile, have a drink."

Bronstein fluttered up. "Come on, girl. Come on, you fat-rat. We must finish this now."

"Methinks 'tis typical of a bat," grumbled Fal, getting to his feet, "letting a little thing like an unfinished job get in the way of drinking and kinky sex."

✧ ✧ ✧

The tunnel into the tower was typical of a Magh' structure. It was a wide spiral inwards. After about fifty feet of cautious advance they found something that wasn't, in their experience, typical of Magh' architecture.

A door.

It wasn't a human-type door, though. It was a circular structure, with a spiral of interlocking black plates. Chip reached out and touched it. At this stage he was still so mad he didn't care if that had got him killed. He'd saved her damn life! And all she cared about was that murderous ball of prickles!

The door certainly wasn't metallic. It felt more like some kind of gritty hardwood.

"To be sure if there's a door this must be an important place," said Bronstein. "Well, let's blow it. Shot holes . . ."

"Why bother?" Chip asked, pushing the panel upwards. It had moved when he'd put his hand to it. It opened like a camera iris, the plates spiraling into the wall. Warm, sticky air gushed out. The air carried a prickly "green" scent with it, reminiscent of fresh-cut bell peppers.

Chip stepped through the gap. And stopped. The tower was perhaps six hundred meters tall. The roof of the chamber they stood in was fully half that height. And it was full of racks. Endless vertical racks about a foot apart, going almost up to the roof. A soft champing noise came from the quarter-mile high grub-racks of the scorpiary. "Oh, fuck me," said Chip.

And not even Doll said "not now, I've got a headache."

Eamon came fluttering up. "Maggots are coming down the walls. Pouring down, like, like . . . Maggots."

O'Niel fluttered up as well. "Well, boyos. I hope

this was where you'd be wanting to go. Because, indade, there's no going back." There was an explosion.

"Just the tunnel mouth," said Eamon.

Then there was a long slow rumble. Ginny and the galago hastily bundled in. Nym spiraled the door shut on a last view of the tunnel filling up with fine sand.

There was a long silence. Then Chip spoke quietly. "Well. That's it. We're stuck. This is the wrong address. And that was obviously the last ditch defense. I'll bet the whole thing has a double hollow wall, full of that fine stuff. We can't even dig our way out."

Bronstein looked around. "To be sure, we won't be lonely. It looks as if we have several hundred million baby Maggots due to join us, shortly."

"I wonder if they're born hungry?" asked Chip.

Chapter 36:
Taken at the flood.

As the chopper roared through the occasionally light-pricked darkness, Fitz found himself wondering if he was out of his mind. Then the radio crackled in his headphones. Van Klomp probably didn't even need a radio, he was bellowing so loudly.

"Fitzy, you ugly bastard! Your satellite boykie just called in. Your lads have just blown something else. A big one. And he says that if he reads the signals right, there were a couple of smaller bangs after that! Over."

"I wish they were my lads, Bobby. Over."

"Heh. Your satellite boykie doesn't believe they can be anything else. Enjoy kicking that ass Charlesworth's butt for me. Over."

"I'll do my best. Over and out."

They roared over a snaking column of headlights. Well. Transport was on its way.

The brigadier's headquarters were in a now-abandoned country "chateau." Typical of the jumped-up slimy bastard, thought Fitz. The rows of tents outside it were a model of early morning tranquility, until Colonel Van Klomp's favorite chopper jockey buzzed the place at about twenty feet.

The chopper jockey dropped them to a neat landing barely thirty yards from the ornate *porte cochere* of the phony chateau.

It was a fine imitation of a disturbed ants' nest. With added lights. Through all of this Fitz walked like a giant iceberg passing through a turbulent sea. Unperturbed and unstoppable.

The biggest wave around, in the shape of Brigadier Charlesworth, washed ineffectually against the 'berg. "What is the meaning of all this?" Charlesworth demanded.

The chopper roared off into the night. When the noise had faded Major Fitzhugh stopped gazing icily at the glorious apparition in a frogged dressing gown. Fitz didn't answer. Instead he patted the neat briefcase he carried.

"Brigadier Charlesworth. Assemble all your staff, in full battledress, within the next ten minutes. I have here orders signed by General Cartup-Kreutzler for your immediate redeployment. Issue orders to get the enlisted men up and into full kit. Get your quartermaster to start issuing ammunition and combat rations. Your transport should be here within fifteen minutes. Where is the communication officer?"

"Sir. That's me, sir." A mousy one-pip lieutenant saluted.

Fitz looked at him with the bad side of his face. "There is a total communication blackout. As of this instant. We've discovered that the Magh' have tapped into our communications network. There will be *no* calls out. *None*. Not even by your commanding officer. Do you understand me clearly? You are to prevent it by deadly force if necessary. Detail a guard. *Now*."

"Sir!" The mousy individual left at a run. Something about that "*sir*" said he'd really enjoy it if someone dared to try to use the comms.

Charlesworth had finally caught his jaw and started to recover it. "Here! You can't *do* this! I need to speak to the general . . . I refuse . . . I demand an explanation. This is an *outrage*!"

Fitz took out an "official" sealed envelope, and handed it to a bleary-eyed man who'd at least gotten as far as his dress-uniform jacket over his pajamas. "Colonel Nygen. Read this."

Somehow no one dared to interrupt. The colonel opened the envelope and began to read. He passed from half-asleep to wide-awake in the process of silently reading one line.

Then the colonel looked at his commanding officer. "Brigadier Charlesworth. You are relieved of your command." He handed the document to the brigadier, who was doing the most remarkable imitation of an indignant toad.

The brigadier ripped the single sheet of paper in half. "I refuse . . ."

"Destroying official documentation. A court-martial offense!" Fitz had his bangstick against the brigadier's belly. "Colonel, I suggest you have the brigadier confined to his quarters immediately, under guard."

Colonel Nygen looked alarmed. "Er. A fellow officer . . ."

Ariel popped her head out of Fitz's magazine pocket. "Do it, bumsucker! He's got a set for you, too."

Chapter 37: *We have already decided: don't confuse us with the facts.*

Doc groaned. Ginny bent low over the rat on her lap. "Otherness without subject is not-being, and this sort of not-being is omnipresent like Melene's tail . . ."

The rat suddenly sat bolt upright, with his eyes wide and unfocussed. "Siobhan! *Look out!*"

Then he keeled over sideways, muttering, "Necessarily utterly capricious . . . that's rat-girls."

His audience didn't hold it against him. Melene appeared too worried to take it out on him anyway, and far too relieved that he was showing more signs of regaining consciousness. The smallest of the rats had been untowardly silent since Chip had emerged carrying Doc in his arms. She simply patted him gently.

Other than that, only O'Niel was near at hand, as all the others had gone to explore the huge brood-chamber. The bat was busy rigging demolition charges and a webwork of expedient mines around the iris-door. Opening it was going to have devastating effects on whatever came through.

Ginny and Melene waited for more words or movement, but Doc had slipped back into unconsciousness.

"There is no way out of here." Chip flopped gloomily down next to Melene, Ginny and the still unconscious Doc. "Look, Ginny. I've got to say something. I'm really sorry about what I said . . . and did . . . back there. I just didn't want you to get killed."

She started to ease her frozen expression. Then he duffed it again. But he'd been brooding on it. Brooding on apologies when you don't think you're wrong is really a poor idea.

"It was that stupid Crotchet's fault."

Her face twitched and she assumed the expression of a perfect ice maiden. Her aristocratic nose came up. She surveyed the scruffy Vat as one might the discovery of a cockroach at the bottom of a milkshake. The worst of it was that a small part of her mind said that he *might* be right.

Chip proceeded to make a bad matter worse. "I don't understand why you can't see that Pricklepuss was bad news. I mean I daresay all of these guys with 'Crotchet-made' chips in their heads *can't* see anything wrong with the Korozhet, but you're so bright . . ."

"GO AWAY!" she said fiercely.

He got up, his resentment plainly burning with a thousand-candlepower flame.

She saw him kick a towering Maggot grub-rack. And heard him swear and clutch his foot.

A bat swooped down from the roof. It spoke briefly to Chip, and then fluttered away upward. It kept going up and up and up until it was joined by the other two. She watched them head for a corner. And then they disappeared.

Bronstein was sure that it was a ventilation gap. It was only desperation that had gotten them to try sonar on the roof. There was certainly no other obvious way out, except for a long narrow chute that spiraled down from the center of the roof. There was a problem with going up that way . . . a steady stream of what could only be Maggot-eggs was coming down it. The eggs, of course were overflowing the ramp. Obviously their tenders had been summoned away.

Getting in hadn't been easy. And getting along was at first worse for the bats, who did not find themselves well designed for this rough crawling.

"Indade. These walls will be having the wings off me. Then what will I be?" complained O'Niel, who was distinctly the fattest of the bats. Eamon was larger, but not around the waist.

"To be sure, you'd be a rat, which is what you've been behaving like," snapped Bronstein. She did not like crawling, and what they were doing made her feel uncomfortable. They had talked about it often enough before, and she'd always resisted or avoided it. But her party was a minority back on the other side of the lines, and it was a minority here. A minority of one, now her dear Siobhan was dead. Bronstein was a committed Demobat. Eamon's Batty party policy on this was clear: Humans were the enemy and the interests of bats would be best served by getting rid of them.

Of course they'd had to be loyal to the Korozhet, but now that it was gone, well, bat-interests must come first. Eamon had been quite eloquent about it, for once. "Indade, it *must* have been a rat who killed her. There was nobody else who could have taken her pack. It was probably that Doc. I've no trust in his pontifications."

The argument had been unanswerable. Who else? The other plausible answer nagged at her, but that was impossible. Absolutely unthinkable.

Eamon had been unable to accuse the humans. But humans, other than Chip and Ginny—and she cringed even thinking about them—had abused the bat-folk. Abused them terribly for their own evil war. Enslaved them.

She was glad when the tunnel widened abruptly into a narrow shaft. She could concentrate on flying and stop thinking so much.

The air vent was a long one. There was no guarantee that it would lead out. There was no guarantee it would lead to where Eamon suspected either. But by following the air current it was not hard flying. And it beat thinking.

"I've no liking for this," panted O'Niel.

"Oh, it's much rather you'd be riding a tractor than flying as a good honest bat should," said Eamon sarcastically.

"Tractors . . . are foine beasts . . . Eamon. I'll . . . no' have you say a word against them. Anyway . . . that' no' . . . what I meant."

Eamon was by far the strongest flier amongst them. He had the wind to hold forth an argument and fly at the same time. "The Magh' must be genetic engineers of great skill. Look at the endless varieties of Maggot they produce. The humans have cruelly made it so that we cannot breed without their intervention. They hold the bat-folk in a vise. We need an ally that can free our bat-comrades from these human chains."

He certainly was full of wind, thought Bronstein. She wrinkled her pug-nose. By the smell of it he was getting some extra from that damned sauerkraut.

"The Maggots . . . have tried . . . to kill us," panted O'Niel.

Eamon showed long fangs. "They did but defend themselves against human imperialism, and against ourselves, why, we invaded their home. 'Tis but justifiable aggression and the conduct of honorable enemies."

Eamon pointed a wing. "Here is a cross tunnel. It must lead to the breeders. The eggs come from above. The Korozhet said that the breeders were the brains."

They flew into it. This tunnel was wide enough to fly through, but now they had to push against the air flow. It was none too easy. Bronstein was relieved when the tunnel opened into a big hollow space full of stanchions. They were in a ceiling full of hot, Maggot-scented air. It was of course largely dark, which didn't worry the bats. There were small pinpricks of light from below, however. O'Niel simply flopped. Bronstein was glad to do the same. The plump O'Niel dug into his pack and produced a small bottle.

"What are you doing with that daemon drink?" snapped Bronstein. Eamon had proceeded to one of the pinpricks of light some distance off. Let him. She needed a rest.

" 'Tis mine! 'Twas given to me by Doc. A foine feller that rat . . ."

"He killed Siobhan!" said Bronstein angrily.

O'Niel snorted. "Hwhat nonsense! Why I heard

Doc myself, with his poor wits a-beggin' show how he'd tried to cry warning to her!"

"*What?*" Bronstein sat up. "That can't be true!"

O'Niel looked at her. "Oh, indade 'tis true, I was after being wonderin' hwhat was goin' on meself, when I saw him try. His wits were wanderin'. There'd be no fakin' of that. Now, would you like a drink?"

Eamon suddenly flapped over to them. "Come! Quickly!" His voice sounded very odd. Very, very odd indeed.

The vent was too narrow for them to squeeze through. But it did allow excellent vision to the three pairs of bat-eyes.

The huge chamber below was everything ordinary Maggotdom was not. Quilted and padded with rich fabrics. Well supplied with what were obviously electronic devices. Lit with lights, real lights, not Magh' lumifungus. Around a central pool lounged things which truly looked like real Maggots. Bloated and occasionally twitching. Tended by smaller scurrying Magh'.

There was one other unexpected occupant in the chamber. Seen from above, the Korozhet simply looked like a ball of red spines. The Magh' were a healthy distance off. "A prisoner!" whispered O'Niel.

Eamon's voice was as cold as ice. "Look on the ground next to the Korozhet."

There were two small scruffy bags on the ground in front of it. One was a batpack. Open, and with the contents scattered on the ground. The Korozhet poked through the debris as they watched.

"Siobhan's." Eamon's voice was so quiet it was almost inaudible. "What you'd not be knowing, Michaela Bronstein, is that she was my lifemate."

"She told me, Eamon," said Bronstein, quietly. "She loved you, even if she could not abide your politics. She said you were the handsomest bat in all batdom."

"The other bag is Doc's," said O'Niel, in a choked voice.

There was silence. Then, eighty feet below them another scene enacted itself. They heard the Korozhet speak, in a language they *should* not have known. Yet obviously the language-coprocessor in their heads had no trouble with Korozhet. "I am hungry, client-species. I want fresh food."

Even hidden eighty feet above in the vent, the three bats all felt the compulsion to fetch it something to eat.

One of the little Magh' which was tending a huge-Maggot, detached itself. Watching from above it was obvious that the creature did *not* wish to approach the Korozhet. But it did.

The bats above became the first part of the human alliance to see a Korozhet kill—and live to tell the tale. They watched as the Korozhet humped its way onto the twitching victim.

Bronstein was the first to speak. She sounded if she was going to be sick. "The creature is still alive!"

O'Niel just scrabbled at the opening, trying to force his plump body through.

Eamon hauled him back. "No! You'll not fling your life away, O'Niel. Vengeance—bloody vengeance—I swear will be *mine* and mine alone. Treachery!"

"Enough!" snapped Bronstein. "Your vengeance is but a small thing. I'll not deny it to you. But we see the whole of the bat-folk betrayed here. Treachery, I agree. Treachery as black as . . . blood. An enslavement both vile evil and insidious. An enslavement of our very minds and wills. The bat-folk *must* know of this . . . treachery. And I swear our vengeance and hatred forever against the . . ."

The words dried in her throat. But she could not and *would not* be defeated by the whiles of soft-cyber bias. She could not proclaim hatred for Korozhet. So she would fight them stratagem for stratagem. "Crotchet." She spat out. She could say that. And she could hate and believe "Crotchets" capable of *any* vileness.

O'Niel nodded. " 'Tis true for the rats too. They are as betrayed as we are."

Eamon stood up and shook his wings. "Yes. Even the rats! Even the *humans*. We must ally with them! Common cause against a greater evil."

If Bronstein had not still been so choked with anger she'd have fallen on her back, laughing. Who would have thought Eamon could ever even think of an alliance with humankind?

"O'Niel, I do believe I would be liking some of that brandy after all," said Bronstein, quietly.

"Indade. I'd be after having some meself," muttered Eamon.

The plump bat handed them the small bottle. "Drink up. We must go back to our comrades."

Eamon paused in the act of raising the bottle. "Indade. My fellow bats . . . forgive me that I ever thought to desert our comrades-in-arms. I was wrong."

Bronstein choked on her mouthful of vile brandy.

Eamon wiped himself fastidiously. "That was not called for, Michaela. Now I shall smell like a wino's hat."

"Indade, and a waste of a foine vintage," grumbled O'Niel.

Bronstein smiled. "I just wanted you to smell like our rat-allies. Come. O'Niel's right. Let's go back."

"We can't tell them what we have seen . . ." said O'Niel.

"And explain that we came to betray humans—to Chip and Ginny?" said Bronstein, distastefully. "No. Least said, soonest mended. We can fight and die bravely beside them instead."

"Amen to that!" said Eamon, fervently.

Chapter 38:
There is just time for . . .

"Where the hell have you lot been?" demanded Chip, as the bats fluttered down from the ceiling. "If I didn't know you better, I'd have thought you'd flown off and left us."

He turned and began moving toward Ginny and the rats. "We need to have council-of-war, and that needs you, Bronstein. Otherwise these head-plastic-for-brains bastards expect *me* to make decisions."

If he'd been setting out to make the three bats look utterly hangdog and guilty, thought Bronstein, he couldn't have done a better job. Fortunately he'd looked across at Virginia, just then.

"You're a good leader, Chip," Bronstein protested.

Chip was hearing the words, not the tone. "Don't be crazy, Bronstein. Have you been drinking or something? I'm a grunt. Even Ginny is a better leader than me. When she's not being illogical about her damned Crotchet, that is."

"Indade, now, that's not true . . ." began Eamon tentatively.

"Don't you start defending the goddamn prickle-ball! I don't know what you've got into your heads about that fucking thing." Chip stopped, sniffed. "You *have* been drinking!"

"No. I meant I thought you had leadership skills," said the big bat, humbly.

Chip shook his head in amazement and raised his eyes to heaven. "You're as pissed as a newt, Eamon." They'd arrived at the huddle of rats, Ginny and the galago near the doorway.

The self-elected grunt announced in a voice of gloom: "Well, folks, we are in excrement deep and dark and dire. Really deep. Twenty feet over nostril. Deep enough to have Eamon getting so totally rat-assed pissed that he's claiming that *humans* make good leaders."

"That is an illogical contention," said Doc in a weak voice.

Melene put her tail protectively over him. "Now don't strain yourself. Rest, dearest."

Doc gazed rheumily at her. "I've died and gone to heaven." He choked. "That's philosophically awkward. I thought atheists went to hell, even if they'd been blown to bits. Will I disappear if I say to God I don't believe in him? I suppose it is bit late for the acquisition of religious convictions."

"He's got his wits back," said Fal.

Nym snorted. "Unfortunately."

"You leave him alone," said Melene, in voice that could cut glass.

"Logical extension of the perceptual facts say I cannot be dead and in heaven, despite Melene's most exquisite tail being wrapped around me, because I see Pistol's unbeauteous face. Aspects of heaven and hell belong in mutually exclusive . . ."

"Oh shut up, Doc. Have a drink. It'll fix you up." Fal held out a bottle.

"Indeed, I am in need of that . . . purely for its restorative properties." Feebly, Doc reached for the bottle.

Mel swatted the bottle away. "You're not having any of that until you feel better!"

Doc sat up hastily. "I'm feeling *much* better," he said, in a far more cheerful voice than his earlier die-away tones. "And I really, really, need a drink. My mouth does not taste good, Melene dearest."

Fal passed the bottle again. This time Melene made no attempt to stop him taking it. But the scholarly rat didn't take an immediate drink. Instead he passed it to Melene. "Have a drink, my dear."

Melene managed to look coy, which is quite an achievement for a rat. "I didn't know you cared, Pararattus."

"Doc, you Bartholomew boarpig! That's *my* bottle. Get your own bottle or candy!" Fal managed to snatch back the bottle, but not before Doc had had a pull at it.

Doc shook his head and said, mournfully: "I can't get my own bottle. The Korozhet took my pack."

"How can you say that?" demanded Doll, hands on her ratty hips.

Pararattus gave this rhetorical question serious consideration. "It is difficult. But I find if you consider the term Korozhet according to Plato's Forms . . . then it is quite possible to say that the Korozhet gassed me, and placed me on a pile of explosives. Then, while I lay between consciousness and unconsciousness, it killed Siobhan when she tried to come to the Korozhet's aid. She believed that it was helping me."

"Oh, nonsense!" piped Fal. "You got hit on the head and you were seeing things."

"Oft times this happens with too much heavy thinking," said Melene, gently. "Your brain's overheated. Too much blood in the brain. When you're feeling better methinks I have a wondrous way to redirect it." She twisted her tail around him.

Doc forgot philosophical contentions. "I'm really feeling just fine!"

"Still thinking the good Korozhet could have done that?" asked Melene fluttering an eyelash at a hypnotized Doc.

"Er." For a moment Doc wavered. But you don't get to be a rat-philosopher without guts. "Yes. It did."

Melene looked at him fondly. "It must have been a terrible blow on the head."

Bronstein wished like hell that she had some of those forms that this Plato must have filled in. Trying to talk around the soft-cyber was leaving her unaccustomedly tongue-tied.

"I'm surprised," said Ginny to Chip, forgetting that she wasn't ever going to speak to him again, "that you aren't supporting his delusions."

He shrugged. "What good would it do me? It doesn't make any difference now, anyway. We're trapped in here. The Maggots will eventually get in and kill us all. That is, unless the bats have found a way out."

Eamon assumed a heroic bat-pose. "We'll stand beside our good comrades! And bravely fight! Aye, and die too. What can we do more but vow to fight with heart, claw and fang?"

Pistol looked at the bat with amused tolerance.

"Well, methinks we could have a baby Maggot barbecue, get drunk, maybe get lucky, and then, with any luck, run like hell."

Ginny couldn't help smiling. Bats and rats! "You didn't answer the question, Eamon. Did you find a way out of here?"

The big bat was silent.

Bronstein answered for him. "Yes. But not for you."

The silence spread like jelly.

Chip stood up. "Well. You lads had better get moving then. Can the rats do it? Or do you have to be able to fly?"

"Well, maybe with that cord," said O'Niel. " 'Tis a vertical shaft, to be sure. But a human wouldn't fit."

"And where do you come out at the end?" asked Virginia. She was stroking Fluff, who had started to shiver.

Eamon shrugged. "Indade, we have no idea. We didn't go all the way."

Chip snorted. "How like bats, eh, Fal? I wonder if that comes under the heading of rat-teasing."

He got no response from the plump rat, except for a slight twitch of a smile, which immediately disappeared. In fact, nobody said anything. So Chip continued. "Well, fortunately I grabbed that roll of cord. What's left of it is in that fertilizer bag. I'd guess there must be at least seventy yards left on the reel."

"Well, we could get the rats up to the shaft with that," said Bronstein slowly. "Then we're coming back."

O'Niel took a pull at his bottle and began to quaver in a mournful tenor, "*I had four belfries and each one was a jewel . . .*"

"Ah, well," said Fal. "I'm too heavy for that cord, really. The rest of you'd better get on with it."

"To Lucifer's privy with that idea," said Nym. "For

myself, I can't see the point of being stuck at the bottom of a shaft. As well to be stuck here."

Rat after rat chimed in with perfectly ridiculous excuses not to leave. Doll said there wouldn't be room for their drink, and Melene claimed to be scared of heights. Pistol said he'd be gone like a shot, but Chip owed him a hundred cases of whiskey, and the minute he was out of sight the damned bilker would do something to get out of it . . . Die, or something equally careless. While this went on the three bats continued with their dirge-like renditions of bat-adapted revolutionary songs, until the last rat had finished.

Well, all the rats except Doc had finished.

The rat-philosopher stood up, a solicitous Melene holding his arm. "*ENOUGH!*" he said in a voice like thunder, loudly enough to impress even the galago. "I will have none of this sophistry and these silly excuses!"

"Well, we'll take you up to the first stage," said Bronstein.

Doc looked down his long nose at her. "I didn't say I was going. I just said I would have none of this pretense."

"I'm sorry guys. But you're all going." They hadn't heard Chip speak in that tone of voice before.

Doc looked at Chip. "We rats are not naturally brave, or loyal. We're fast, and we're good Maggot killers. But our loyalty *can* be earned. You've earned it. We *won't* leave you."

Chip found speaking difficult. "I'm grateful. And I would hate to leave you guys. Honest. I've . . . I've sort of forgotten that you aren't really human. Hell. I think you're . . . better than human." He paused. "But you must get out. You *must*. Ginny and I can't. Firstly, you must get back over the lines. All the Maggots in creation are around here, nowhere else. If you go right now and hide just inside the shield, some of you should manage to get out when it goes up. You bats especially. You should be able to tell our side so much. Stuff that'll keep grunts who are just like me and Gin—Dermott alive. And . . . you could tell them Doc's story. I'm not saying anyone will believe you. Just tell them."

He sighed. "Secondly, if you feel that way about leaving Ginny and me, we feel just as bad about you staying. Hey, Ginny?"

Behind her glasses her eyes sparkled with tears. "Yes. Go. Please. Please, please go. I couldn't bear it if any of you stayed. You all been my first ever real . . . friends. And Chip is right. So many sacrifices have been made to get us this far. For Phylla, Siobhan, and Behan's sake you *must* get back to the human side of the lines. For our sakes too. Don't let all of this be in vain. Please . . . dear friends."

There was another one of those jellylike silences.

Then Eamon said. "You're right, indade. We'll get the rats out, and then return to stand by you. Wing to shoulder, eh!"

Chip shook his head gently. "No, Eamon. You must go with them. Without you bats they'd have no chance. You couldn't abandon them while there was still hope, could you? With you, especially you, because you are biggest and bravest, they have *some* chance. We know we can trust you and rely on you."

The big bat promptly hid his wrinkled face in his wings.

The farewells were done. The bats had taken the line up to the ventilation hole.

Fluff had just clung to Virginia's neck, big eyed and miserable. Besides the contents of sixteen Molotov-cocktail bottles, every single rat except Doc had given

Chip a bottle. The thought that the two of them would at least not have to die sober appeared to mean a great deal to Fal. Doc had made up for his lost alcohol with a snippet of philosophical thought that Chip would have found comforting and brilliant . . . if he'd understood one word in ten.

Finally, they went.

Eamon had fluttered down at the last, when the cord had already been pulled up. "If we do get back . . . we'll immortalize you in song. Batdom will never, never forget you."

They were left staring at the roof. Finally, Chip sighed, and drew the Solingen.

"What are you planning to do with that?" she asked, her voice a little tight.

"I dunno. See if I can sharpen it? Maybe I'll get a few more Maggots with it that way."

"What does it really matter?"

"I dunno. I couldn't just give up."

"Um." She spoke now in a very small voice. "I've got something to give to you." She reached into her pocket and pulled out a small shapeless lump of what might once have been silver paper. "Melene . . . gave me this to give to you." Her voice was almost inaudible.

Chip looked at it. "Er. Just what is it?"

She looked into his eyes. He saw there were tears starting in the corners of her eyes again. She sniffed. "It was her most precious possession. She'd . . . only ever had one before." Ginny's chin quivered. "It . . . it was a chocolate."

Chip stared at her, open mouthed.

Ginny sniffed determinedly. "Rats don't really understand. I told her, you . . . Uh . . . Anyway, she said I must give it to you. She insisted."

Chip took Ginny in his arms. "Quite a girl, that rat," he said reverently.

She sniffed and held tightly to his tunic. "She's the first girlfriend I've ever had. And she was the best I could wish to have. She said not to waste this time . . ."

"Funny, that's what Nym, Pistol and Doc said. Fal said I should get drunk too, but not too drunk."

Ginny gave a choke of laughter. "Do you know that was almost exactly what Doll said?"

Chip grinned at her. "I can well believe it. That's one wild, bad rat-girl, that!"

She looked at him with big serious eyes and said quietly, "*I'm* not a wild, bad girl, Chip." She looked down and then looked him straight in the eye. "I don't know what to do. I've never even been *kissed* before. I don't want to die before I've even been kissed properly."

"But all you Sharehol—" *Fortunately*, this time he caught himself. "This is how you do that."

After some considerable time had passed, he managed to speak. "Seeing as we are going to die anyway, why don't we go ahead and take the rest of that rat advice?"

She opened her eyes and looked at him. "Oh, yes. *Oh, yes!*"

He looked up. "Well. Let's move away from here a little. I wouldn't put it past Eamon to come back. He really wasn't happy about leaving. And he has a habit of doing his own thing."

Chapter 39:
The waiting.

This was always the worst part. The waiting. Fitz hated it with a passion. The sky was definitely pale now. He looked at his watch for the third time in as many minutes. At first it had been . . . like going back to boarding school. What had really got to him was the smell. Somehow, perhaps because all vertebrates were once scent oriented, that stirred deeper and more evocative memories than anything else. In the dark, the smell had been especially noticeable. Mud, feet, urine, humanity, and the sharper animal scents of rats and bats, along with the smell of fear. Yes. Fear smelled.

But he'd come over the top. Out of the trenches, walking, with no enemy to fear. As long as he stayed between the flag-and-cord marked lines he was safe from those AP mines too.

Colonel Nygen had demanded an explanation during the drive. "It's simple, Colonel," said Fitz. "Part of the Magh' front line has been deserted. They've pulled all their troops back inside the shield to deal with a problem. Some of our MIAs have gone on the rampage in there."

The colonel was silent for a bit. "Are you sure?"

Fitz nodded. "Absolutely certain. Your precious Charlesworth had a request for support from sector Delta 355 when Colonel Abramovitz moved his men in about midnight. I checked with Lieutenant Guerra, your comm officer. He got his ass chewed for waking up the brigadier."

"Stupid bastard," Nygen said grimly. "No bloody wonder HQ sent you down." He turned his head. "Driver. You never heard me say that."

"Sah!" said the big Vat.

Nygen continued. "Good—but what I actually meant was about the MIAs. I mean, to pull the Magh off a whole sector . . ."

Fitz interrupted. "Colonel, we've been able to follow them with satellite tracking. They got hold of a vehicle and, heaven knows how, a hell of a lot of explosives. You won't believe how hard they've knocked that scorpiary."

The driver nearly had the ten-ton truck off the road. "Shit! You mean some of ours are alive on the wrong side of the line? Oh! Sorry, sir. Spoke out of turn, sir. Lost some friends, sir."

"If you don't mention speaking out of turn, I won't," said Fitz, dryly. "And don't get your hopes up for your friends. I don't know what the boys back there got into their heads, but they've tried a suicide mission. We think they're trying to blow the shield-generator."

"But you should have seen the explosions they

pulled so far on the satellite pics," said Ariel enthusiastically.

Colonel Nygen's tone was sharp. "What does HQ think they're playing at? We're been dragged out in the small hours for this? Those MIAs are *never* going to succeed. That must surely be the most guarded installation . . ."

"Colonel, succeed or not, we've occupied their lines," Fitz snapped. "Do you know how often we've managed to do that in this war? Three times. And *never* across a whole sector."

"We'll never hold it," said Nygen sulkily.

Fitz ground his teeth. This sort of thinking was ingrained. "We're not going to try. When that force field comes up we're going to punch columns hard *into* their force-field area."

It had sounded convincing back then. Now, waiting in the predawn, he could have used some convincing himself. His bangstick rested against the invisible inviolate barrier. Human gunners had proved that the Magh only raised it about three feet. And on average for less than two minutes.

"Have you got any booze with you?" asked Ariel.

Bobby Van Klomp was no better at waiting. And there'd been nothing from the satellite crowd for over an hour now. He sighed and checked his gear one more time. His own guess was that the wheels would start to come off Fitzy's crazy plans anytime after six. Maybe earlier, but certainly not later than seven-thirty. He'd have his men in the air at six-thirty. Early, but not ridiculous enough for anyone to question. He could keep them out for as long as possible.

That would give Fitzy an extra hour of a small chance . . .

✧ ✧ ✧

The only one who waited well was Henry M'Batha. The others had all given up waiting for more fireworks and trickled off to bed, or back to their stations. But Henry refused to believe that it was all over. His relief didn't come in until seven. And then Henry would find reasons to stay a while longer. . . .

Chapter 40:
Maybe not.

Romantic places are made thus by the people in them. This was not the windswept gritstone edge above the stark and wild Yorkshire moors of her dreams. But the towering stacks of Maggot-grub cells through which they wandered hand-in-hand made a magical, beautiful place too, thought Ginny. Even the relentless munching noises from the racks had an almost musical charm.

Chip had explored the area. Off on the far side were any number of little open Magh' adobe cells. It took them some time to get there, because they kept stopping to work on this kissing bit. At the last stop Chip had nearly decided that this was a good enough place anyway . . .

Ginny looked at Chip. "This looks like the cell I was walled up in."

"Would you like to go somewhere else?" His hands were caressing her breasts, and his fingers were gently coming in to touch her nipples through her blouse, arousing her to the point where she wasn't thinking logically any more. Well, other than about how to get the material out of the way.

"Not if I'm here with you," she said, breathlessly, unfastening his shirt buttons, her fingers clumsy with haste.

And then, from the other side of the wall, someone said something. Both of them stopped, their hands in very compromising positions.

The voice from the other side of the wall spoke again.

Ginny's heart rose, despite wishing desperately that the interruption hadn't happened for another few, precious few, minutes. It wasn't a bat or a rat voice. It certainly wasn't Fluff's. Who else was there except the Professor? Well . . . it could be someone else, she supposed. "Er. Who's there?"

"Tell him to piss off," Chip whispered in her ear, through clenched teeth.

The reply they got could easily have been an excerpt from the Kama Sutra. Well, an alien version thereof, because whatever language that was, it wasn't human. And human voices didn't hit those sorts of notes. It could have been nearly anything because she didn't understand a word of it. She tried some Korozhet. She'd been amazed at how easy that had been to learn.

There was a silence. Then, in appallingly accented but clear Korozhet, the voice informed her that the Korozhet would get absolutely nothing out of it.

"We are not Korozhet," Ginny said hastily. That was a shocking idea, to be denied at all costs.

The appallingly accented Korozhet speaker asked, "Well, what are you then? Are you Magh'?"

"I understood two words. Korozhet and Magh'," said Chip. "What is it saying?"

"Um. It asked whether we were Magh'," Ginny translated.

"I'd like to know what the hell it is, even if it has the shittiest sense of timing in the entire universe." Chip's tone of voice was pure irritation.

She looked into his eyes, her mouth easing into that tiny almost anxious smile, revealing those slightly skew teeth. Hell, to make her smile he'd forgive anything. Chip sighed. "I suppose it is a Crotchet. Ask if it can get you out of here."

"Not without you." Her long fingers crumpled his shirt. She spouted a string of alien. It talked back. "It says it is a prisoner too. Live larvae food like us. Its ship was tracking the Magh' slowship routes to offer alliance to whoever the Magh' were attacking this time."

Ginny was glad to have the language mystery cleared up. "So that is why you speak Korozhet. They are our allies. They also came to give us warning. We owe them our lives."

There a long silence. Then whatever was on the other side of the wall replied. "Yes. The Korozhet warned us too. They had some very useful war materials for sale. Very convenient. Very expensive."

"What's it say?" demanded Chip. She translated.

"I'll say!" Chip sounded as if he might almost forgive the alien for being there. Almost. "Ask it whether they got slowshields from them. I'm really suspicious about those, after Doc's comments. I'll bet they sold them soft-cyber stuff and not an FTL drive."

Ginny shook her head violently. "I'm sure you're

wrong! You just don't like the Korozhet! But I'll ask. I'm certain you're wrong!"

She asked.

The alien made a noise like steel pan being caressed with a castanet. "Apologies. That is just ticklish . . . I mean . . . funny. Yes, they sold us kinetic movement shields and tried to sell us 'enhancement' cybernetics. Of course we would not buy such a crazy thing. No sentient is going to put alien-built logic-circuits in its head. And no, of course they didn't sell us an FTL drive!"

"So. What did he say?" demanded Chip.

Somewhat reluctantly, she told him.

"You can say that again. Well, at least we're not crazy enough to put soft-cybers into human heads. Ask it whether they managed to beat the Maggots."

Miserably, Ginny asked.

"Once we discovered that the Korozhet were passing all our military information to the Magh', it wasn't that hard," replied the alien voice.

"That's a lie!" shouted Ginny furiously, as soon as she finished translating. "The Korozhet saved our colony! The Magh' would have taken us by surprise and wiped us all out."

The creature on the other side of the wall sounded heated too. "The Korozhet farm wars. The Magh' are their animals."

"You LIE! You LIE!!!"

"We Jampad do not lie."

She turned instinctively to Chip. He held her gently and stroked her head. "What's wrong, Ginny?"

"It says . . . It says." She found the words impossible to get out. "It says it is a Jampad. They killed my parents." She turned on the wall and pounded it with her fists. "You murdered my parents you . . . monster. I *hate* you. Come out here and I'll kill you."

The creature on the other side of the wall appeared equally upset, if volume was any way to judge Jampad emotion.

"My ship—and my people only had the one FTL ship built—was destroyed! I saw how the Korozhet destroyed helpless lifepod after lifepod. My clan-kin are dead. My pod was damaged by their fire as I entered the atmosphere. I had no directional controls. I made a forced landing on the top of the Magh' force field. Then, when it opened, I fell through. I made the gesture of submission to the Magh'. I was brought here, for larvae food. I would hope that what you say is true. I would be delighted if my clan-kin had killed your silly kind. It would mean someone else survived. But they are all dead. Do you hear me. *Dead*. Who told you that the Jampad had killed your kin? Who? The stinking Korozhet told you. They *lie*. About everything!"

Virginia was now sobbing, her face pressed into Chip's shoulder. "There, Ginny. Don't talk to it any more," he said gently. Chip thumped on the wall with his fist. "You in there! I don't understand what you're saying, but I'll come in and beat your fucking brains out if you don't shut up and leave her alone."

He started guiding her away. "Come on, Ginny. Let's go somewhere else."

The creature on the other side of the wall didn't understand his words, despite Chip's faithful obedience to the First Law of Translation. *Shout*. It kept babbling something.

Ginny sniffed determinedly. "No, Chip. I've got to tell it how wrong it is about the Korozhet." She turned and faced the wall again. "You. Jampad. There are a few things you should know. Firstly, we're not prisoners like you. We are trapped in this brood-chamber, but we're not walled up and we got here by fighting our way in. We killed many Magh'. And we did that with a brave Korozhet at our side. He was also a prisoner." And she briefly told it the story of how they had got there.

There was a long silence. Then it asked. "Where is this Korozhet now?"

"It got separated from us. At the last. Just before we were trapped in here," she said.

"Ah. So. How many did it kill with its killing spines and its gas spines?" asked the alien.

She was spared having to answer that one, by the sound of falling masonry.

The alien continued. "It sounds as if the Magh' have broken in. Well. Should you not be able to escape immediately, I suggest the gesture of submission. At home there are stories of several prisoners who managed to escape. Magh' are stupid. Live to fight another day."

"How do we do that?" she asked, curious despite her anger.

The alien jangled. "Do you have anterior limbs? If so lie, down on your backs. Do you have backs?"

"Yes."

"Then lie down on them and cross your anterior limbs above your head. Magh' are creatures of instinct. The lower castes are not really intelligent at all. The different nests communicate with gestures. Our xenobiologists think that is the gesture whereby one nest would accede to another in a territorial struggle. But beware of the Korozhet!"

Chip shook Virginia gently. "Ginny, the Maggots have busted in somewhere else. No explosions." He hugged her fiercely. "Sorry, kid. We're gonna die. Can we spare the talking and have a last kiss?"

She hugged him fiercely. "No, Chip, we must lie down."

Despite the situation, he grinned. "Haven't we left it a bit late for that now?"

She blushed. "Unfortunately. But no, that's not what I mean. The alien says if we lie down on our backs and cross our arms above our heads, that's the gesture of surrender."

Chip snorted. "Ha. I'll be dipped in shit first! I'll go out fighting."

She held him. "Please. The alien is right. We'll just get killed. If we pretend to surrender . . . we just might escape. It says its kind have, in the past. Please. For me."

"It's not honorable," he said stubbornly.

"Stop being so Batty!" She caressed his chest. "Think what . . . Doc would say."

He sighed. "All right, Ginny. We'll try it your way." He pulled the four-pound hammer from his belt. Pushed it into the ventilation hole which led into the alien's cell. "They'll probably search us, and take everything away from us. Tell him to break out if he can."

"My mate," she said in Korozhet, and she said it with pride, if not perfect truth, "gives you this tool to break out with."

The alien jangled. She figured the noise must be the equivalent of a sigh. "Thank you. Good luck, alien," it replied.

She smiled at Chip. "It said 'good luck.' Lie down next to me, please. I can hear them coming."

"I should get invitations like that every day from beautiful girls." He lay down next to her, and then burrowed a hand into his pocket. He produced Melene's chocolate. "Can I offer you some candy? I'm afraid that's probably as near as we'll get to the rest of it," he said tenderly.

She tried to swallow away the lump in her throat.

"How about if we shared it," she finally managed to croak.

It was very old chocolate. It had melted and reset a good few times. It had traveled a long way in a rat's pack. But still . . . it could have tasted of soap and it wouldn't have mattered. It was still the finest chocolate they were ever likely to eat.

A Magh' paused at the doorway. It looked at them and then went on, hastily. And then the one next came.

"It worked!" said Chip in tones of amazement. "They didn't just kill us."

Chapter 41:
A walk in the park.

Major Fitzhugh had underestimated the determination of General Cartup-Kreutzler. The general had wasted precious time trying to find the telephone, at last finding the downstairs instrument which didn't work. . . . In the process of finding it, there had been this big vase. . . . The general knew he was going to have to go on the offensive with his wife for breaking that. But it was her own fault for putting it there.

The general realized he had underestimated his wife's paranoia about their little country place being burgled. Theft was an increasing problem on Harmony And Reason, because of unruly Vats. The general was among those calling for harsher penalties. His wife Maria's contribution to the war on crime had been to spare no expense making their houses as thief-proof as possible. It hadn't stopped a burglary three weeks before. Among the things taken had been all the clothing in the house. So, Maria had reinforced her precautions with the finest building materials available. . . .

The general rubbed his shoulder. He thought it might be broken. The front door still seemed remarkably intact.

"Are you all right, Stallion?" enquired Daisy from the darkness.

The general bit back an angry retort. He didn't have any trousers. A dark blue towel was the best he could do. His tunic top was soaked with whiskey, and his shoulder was damned sore. "Yes," he said in a grumpy voice that indicated the opposite. "And I'm going to crucify Fitzhugh. I'll try a chair."

"I'll get you one, Kreutzy-pie," she said sympathetically.

Minutes later he stood with the smashed remains of the chair, in front of a still obdurate door. A horrible thought trickled through his mind as he felt the velvety remains. "Where did you get this chair?" he choked.

"From the dining room. Do you want another one?"

In darkness of the hall, the general felt his face go white. Maria was going to *kill* him. He dropped the remains of the priceless Queen Anne chair as if it was burning hot. It was a matched set of three now. . . .

A marble statue of Cupid finally proved harder than the door. The lock, however, was of excellent quality. The general had to smash panels out of the door itself to get out. Then he had to get Daisy through in her tight skirt and high heels. Attempting to suck splinters out of his hand, he went down to his staff car. At least the guards wouldn't be able to see that he didn't have any trousers on while he was driving.

When he saw the open hood, he nearly returned to the house in despair. But he was determined. "Come on. We'll have to walk. And I'm going to skin Fitzhugh alive!"

"But Kreutzy, we can't walk. . . ."

"We've only got to walk to the gate. I'll get a car sent," he snapped.

"But you haven't any trousers!" she wailed.

He gritted his teeth. "I'll put that onto Major Fitzhugh's account, too. Come on. It's only about half a mile."

In his car, the general had never noticed the gentle gradient in the long curve of the driveway. It had been twenty years since he'd last walked half a mile. And his highly polished shoes were less than two days old.

Daisy was in a similar state. "My heels are killing me," she whined. "Isn't there a shorter way?"

He snapped his fingers. "You're right! We'll cut across the parkland. That'll be half the distance. It's all grass. I can walk barefoot."

At first it seemed like a brilliant strategy. Then the weather betrayed him. Cruelly. The moon disappeared behind a bank of clouds. The satellite center could have told him that there was a front on its way. In fact, they *had* told him, but the general had paid no attention. It hadn't concerned Fitz, either, because it wasn't heading towards the war zone.

The general discovered that a genteel stroll through the moonlit park had a become a nightmare obstacle course from hell. It was wall-to-wall tripping roots and snagging bushes, and he only had one free hand with a pair of shoes in it, as Daisy insisted on clutching the other hand. She was terrified of getting lost alone. So they were both lost together, instead.

He stubbed his bare toes on a rock and stumbled forward.

"AAARGH!"

He slithered wildly down the steep, microjet-irrigated bank of artistically textured "wild" violets and hanging maidenhair ferns. Daisy was of course dragged willy-nilly headlong down the bank with him.

The fat koi-carp in the pool probably wished they were piranhas a few seconds later, when the general's nether end landed in their tranquil beauty spot. A second later a shrieking Daisy arrived. A flailing handful of violets knocked his cap flying. Then she landed facefirst in the water.

Daisy was soaked to the skin. The general was better *and* worse off. He wasn't as wet. His top half was dry. Well, except for the whisky-wet area. His dark-blue towel was somewhere in the dark water. He felt around in the mud and the hairy lily roots. A forgiving koi nuzzled his hand. He shrieked and hastily gave up looking for the towel or one of his shoes.

The moon appeared. Daisy stood up, dripping. "This is all your fault!" she shouted hysterically. "My skirt is ruined, my makeup is ruined, and my stockings are *ruined*!" Sobbing, she hit him in the eye. Which was perhaps uncharitable, since the general had paid for all of the ruined things in the first place.

In the guard post the corporal lit a weed. "Spanking parties these generals have," he said dryly.

"Yeah. No wonder the major warned us."

It didn't get better. The moon hid itself again in embarrassment at the acrimonious scene below. Then there had been the riot of climbing roses . . .

When the general found the fence, it had been a relief. The landscapers had carefully hidden it in the shrubbery. On the other side was open space and easy walking. All they had to do was to follow the fence. The general was a broken man. All that kept him going was the delightful thought of hanging, drawing, quartering—and immersing in cold oil, which he would slowly bring to the boil—one Major Conrad Fitzhugh.

Of course, walking along the outside of the fence meant that he approached his own gate from the outside.

"Impersonating an officer. Drunk. Disorderly. Public indecency. Failing to produce identity card. Attempted assault of the arresting officer." The MP prodded the unfortunate general in the stomach with his nightstick. "Are they going to throw the book at you, sunshine!"

"What about me?" shivered Daisy. The evening was cold and she had quite a distracting case of shrivel-nipple.

"If you're lucky I won't run you in for soliciting. Get lost."

"But how am I going to get home?" she whined.

"Stick around, sweetie. We'll sort you out," said the corporal. "We're due for *relief* in a few minutes."

His mate said "For a fee, of course."

The corporal grinned. "Nothing a girl like you can't spare."

It was six in the morning before the general's wife came along to bail him out . . . and she was going to go straight out to the estate. . . .

Chapter 42:
When head and heart do war.

The Maggots, who came in a seemingly endless stream past the open cell where Ginny and Chip lay, were all of a closely related kind. They all had hooked feet which enabled them to run up and down the brood-racks with terrific speed. Many had long injection-like mouthparts, or odd little plate-shaped palps. They weren't warriors, or even particularly dangerous looking. It was very apparent that their main interest was the brood and that as long as Chip and Ginny lay there and didn't interfere . . .

But orders apparently came down from on high, which overrode the pressing instinctive need to see to the grubs. Chip and Ginny were prodded to their feet by hard but fairly harmless palps, and herded along. They were pushed down the newly-chewed passage.

The wall through which the diggers had burst, Chip noticed, looked just the same as all the other walls. It was obviously a hidden hard plug the Magh' had in the tower wall. In one place there was a crack in the tunnel through which fine sand was still seeping. It should have been obvious, thought Chip. *Of course* they would have a way in for just such an emergency as the tunnel to the brood-heart being dropped.

At the head of the passage waited a troop of seventy scorps. Obviously, ordinary Maggots didn't go into the brood chamber.

Chip thought that they'd die right there. But the scorps parted to allow them to walk forward into the middle of the warriors. Then they found themselves forced to walk up. And up. Past Maggots clearing blast damage with Maggotlike efficiency. Then they stopped. By the time Chip and Ginny realized that they'd stopped because the scorps needed to reoxygenate, another troop had arrived.

Chip's legs wished they'd been given a chance to reoxygenate too. He'd not realized there could be anything worse than abseiling *down* this lot . . . until he had been forced to walk back up it. He didn't have the breath to talk. A glance showed him that Ginny was in an even worse state. Limping. Panting.

The Maggots kept them separated. He couldn't even get close to her to give her an arm. A quivering sting menaced him when he tried.

And then they came to the level with the bridge to the tower. Here they had to wait, and could at last catch their breath. Another party was coming across the newly rebuilt narrow tracery of spars.

"Professor!" Ginny shrieked in delight.

The Korozhet, bold as brass, and a lot more red and prickly, spined along calmly between an escort of Maggots.

Chip noticed that while the Magh' pressed close to Ginny and himself, they kept their distance from that damn Crotchet.

"My dear Virginia!" exclaimed the Korozhet. "I am so relieved to see you safe and well. I was just on my way to try to rescue you! I have negotiated your release into my custody. You will be safe, Virginia, safe!"

Her mind was at war, fighting a terrible internal battle. She'd been so glad to see him. Relieved and happy. And then, unbidden, had come the questions. Her mind, or something in her mind, said that the questions were wrong, impossible. Yet they kept recurring, recurring.

But if the Professor could get them out of here . . .

"Can you get Chip and me free, Professor?" she asked.

"Yes, Virginia. I have used my status as a fellow exoskeletonite to convince the Magh' that we are just civilians caught up in the tide of war. Innocent bystanders. That you were lead astray by evil companions."

She shouldn't have laughed . . . but after what they'd done, at his urging! "So Chip and I can go?" she said incredulously. "But you were . . ."

The Korozhet clacked its spines. "Alas, the other human is a combatant. A prisoner of war. He will have to remain. I have begged for clemency for him, of course. The Magh' have assured me he will be kept prisoner under the most gentle of conditions, given the best of slops . . ."

"Ah, bullshit, Pricklepuss," sneered Chip.

It might still have gone differently if the Professor hadn't been advancing and Magh' hadn't stood aside. That had allowed Chip to move next her. To put a gentle hand on her shoulder. And to allow her to loop an arm around his waist.

"Virginia, cease clinging to the human and come with me!" ordered the Korozhet. "It is a troublemaker. A lower life-form, one of those Vat-bred creatures."

She looked at the red, spiny alien. She couldn't bring herself to say "No." But she shook her head and clung more tightly to Chip.

The Expediter had had a long and trying time of it since these stupid, irritating humans had "rescued" it from its bath. And, of all the annoyances, *that* human soldier had been the worst. And *now* he had made one of the Overphyle's implanted slaves resist! The Expediter was suffering from a lack of gamete discharge. She knew this made her extremely short tempered. . . .

There was only one cure for rebellious slaves, and that was killing them. But the resources attached to the Virginia slave were just too valuable to dispose of lightly. As sole "heir"—such an odd notion!—to the humans' largest chunk of wealth, the creature could be very valuable to the Expediter. As long as the wretched thing was under proper control . . .

The Expediter struggled with rage. It had been pleasant to deal with that rat who had dared to overcome the soft-cyber conditioning. She had also vented some of her rage on the bat, who had chosen to come into the tunnel at the wrong time. But she was still angry. Furious, in fact.

These Earth-creatures were poor slaves. They used their natural sophistry to disobey. Well, commands issued in English they could still twist and misinterpret. It was a language fraught with imprecision. But the Expediter could order in Korozhet. That was the default language and allowed no chance for disobedience. Her ocelli focused on the scruffy little

Vat-soldier. This one had done worse than any of them. He'd laughed at the Overphyle! He had dared to use derogatory terms!

"You know," said Chip, "the difference between you and a car full of sh . . . officers, is that the car has the little pricks on the inside."

The human soldier should never have made that comment. The Expediter was sensitive about her spine-length. She finally lost her temper completely.

Chip had survived an inordinate time in the trenches, fighting warrior-Magh'. They were fast. Really fast. The main reason he was still alive was that he was one of those lucky individuals with naturally fast reactions. The Expediter had only killed rich, middle-aged humans before. This was different. Chip saw the spines come up. He grabbed Ginny and dived across the back of the nearest scorp.

The hissing harpoon darts went home . . . into the scorp.

The Expediter was too late to stop the first toxin pulse. And it saw Chip reach for his belt. Fools! The Magh' hadn't even disarmed them! Magh' regarded bodies as weapons, and had yet to truly come to terms with the alien propensity for sharp-edged or heavy artificial tools of destruction. If the Vat creature still had his four-pound hammer, the heavy tool would smash right through her calcareous test. At a time like this, it was best to cut and run. She could grow new harpoons.

In a cloud of gas, the Expediter severed her harpoons and legged it away on fast-flexing spines.

The hiss . . .

"Hold your breath!" shouted Chip. He hoped the

gas might affect their guards, but it didn't seem to, or, perhaps, they were holding their breath too.

Chip and Ginny were thrust forward again.

Eventually, they just had to breathe. The air simply tasted of Maggot-pong, but Chip found himself feeling a bit odd, and slightly light headed. Ginny kept swaying into him. Not that he really minded that, of course. Actually, after a few seconds, the whole incident seemed like a good joke. The two of them started giggling. Chip even found himself chuckling about the fact that the stinking Crotchet could run at least as fast as a man and could climb perfectly well.

It was a good bridge to cross slightly stoned, even if that wasn't quite the safest way it could be done. There were no sides and the two of them could barely walk abreast. And the scorps weren't even following. So the two them stopped midway for a bit of lip-and-tongue gymnastics. They got rather distracted. Quite distracted, actually. Eventually a scorp had to come and prod them on. They crossed the rest of the way hugging each other, occasionally swaying into the outstretched chelicerae.

Chapter 43:
Third thoughts.

Getting them up the shaft was slow, and awkward. The oppressive warm darkness was overfull of depressed rats and bats. Bronstein was getting to the stage where if she heard another sigh, she was going to bite whoever did it. Given the way things were going, it would be Eamon or Nym.

She sighed. Then realized what she'd just done.

Oh, well. Fair was fair. She bit herself. "Yow!"

"Hwhat is going on now?" said O'Niel, in a "hope-I-can-bite-somebody" tone.

"Nothing," she said grumpily. Then reconsidered it. "Oh bejasus, O'Niel. There is a decent bit of ledge here. The rats and that galago can stop here. You and I can go for a fly up the shaft and see whether it actually does lead out or not."

O'Niel plainly liked the idea, even if it involved

flying. "If it doesn't, we can go back, indade."

"Go to it," grunted Nym from the ledge. "I'll bring the rest up. 'Tis a ridiculous idea to keep climbing, if we just have to come down again. And methinks you should take Eamon. He keeps sighing like a leaky gasbag."

The bats fluttered upwards. And upwards. The shaft curved slightly so that they could not sonar too far ahead but, at length, Bronstein detected what she both longed for and dreaded. Space. And then there was a circle of light.

They flew out into the first rays of early morning sunlight. Daylight was never a bat's favorite. Still, being out of the Maggot mounds felt . . . free. Looking back, and carefully substituting the word "Crotchet" for another word which must not even be thought, Bronstein could see that it had all been rank insanity. All driven by that Crotchet wanting to get back to its true allies. Treacherous, foul alien. She would hate it forever and ever.

She thought about their journey through the tunnels. Scenes came unbidden and clear. Madness! But, ah! What a glorious madness it had been. And they might even have succeeded, despite the traitor. They'd come so close to the group-mind before the Crotchet had misled them. It had taken them down instead of up.

It hit her like the morning sunlight. Warm, beautiful and wonderfully liberating. "Let us go down, fellow bats. Let us go down and finish what we came to do, to be sure!"

Eamon blinked at her "Bring them up here, you mean. 'Tis daylight. It will . . ."

Bronstein shook her head. "No! Eamon, it goes against my grain to admit this, but you are a better bat with explosives than I. Could we be bringing down that roof above the place where we saw the . . . Crotchet?"

Eamon's face shifted from gloom to a savage crinkled grin. "Michaela Bronstein, it goes against *my* grain, but you are a better thinker than I. Yes, indade, it'd take most of what we still have, but if we blew away those trusses . . . I am sure that the ceiling would fall, anyway. The whole roof it could be. And at the very least we'll avenge them!"

O'Niel looked somber. "We will have to explain it to the rats."

Bronstein bit her lip. Eamon too was silenced. The big bat looked shrunken. He looked like a bat carrying all the weight of the world on tired wings. Then he straightened his shoulders and spread his wings in Harmony And Reason's bright sunlight. "Indade. And you may put the blame on me, where it rightly belongs. But I'll not let my pride stand before our vengeance." He stepped backwards and fell into the shaft.

O'Niel chuckled. "Pistol has the right of it. When he does that, he looks like he's most terrible constipated. Come. Let's get to it, then."

Bronstein dropped into the shaft, and nearly hit the swearing Eamon on his way back up.

The rats and the galago perched uncomfortably on the ledge. Bronstein addressed them even as she fluttered down. "There is a way out. It is morning out there."

"Methinks, not for Chip and Ginny," said Fal lugubriously. "He was just like a rat, that human. Aye, and he *was*."

"Down to the tail," said Bronstein tartly. "Now listen. We could go back and die beside them."

"Whoreson. Back through that tunnel where I nearly stuck fast like a cork? Ah, well, what must be done, must be done." Fal didn't sound too dejected by the idea.

"Which will serve no purpose, and is what they have begged us not to do," said Bronstein sternly.

"Sometimes a rat has to make up his own mind. I just wish I hadn't squeezed through that tunnel first, just to squeeze back," said Nym. "At least Fal could just suck his gut in . . ."

"*Or* we can go ahead and do exactly what the Korozhet wanted us to do." Bronstein knew that was dirty pool. But she was playing to win. "When we came out earlier we found our way to above the brood-Magh'. The thinkers. We could go and bring the roof down on them. That would avenge Chip and Ginny. And if they really are the group-mind . . . it could even save our human comrades."

"Whoreson Achitophel!" said Pistol explosively. "Well, come on then. What are you bats waiting for? Move out, move out! We don't need this rope. We can chimney up this shaft."

"No, Pistol. We have to put this to the vote. It will leave us without explosives for our flight," said Bronstein.

"I' faith," Fal grunted. "Next you'll be wanting a sacred bullet, Bronstein."

Sarcasm, as always, passed right over Bronstein's head. "No, a show of hands will do."

"If I show you my hands, I shall fall off this ledge," said Doll. "Besides I can't see anything. I agree with Pistol."

There was a chorus of yesses. Even the galago nervously agreed. With a goal before them, the rats suddenly showed that they could manage the shaft. They just hadn't been ready to try before.

Doc, of course, put his finger on the crucial question. "It occurs to me that you could have told us this before."

Eamon cleared his throat. "I am to blame."

"Usually, but that's because you guzzle so much sauerkraut," said Pistol, from higher up the shaft.

But even Pistol's deflationary cracks weren't going to deprive Eamon of the joys of a histrionic confession.

Eventually, even the galago told him to shut up. Risking damage to life and limb was better than listening to any more bat soul-searching.

A second scorp had followed the first over the narrow bridge. In his mild dose of Korozhet chemically induced hysteria, Chip thought the scorps moved even more tentatively than the humans. The group walked forward into the heart of the scorpiary.

The mushroom hothouse had been brightly colored. This place was just plain garish. It was startling enough to send Chip into the giggles again. And that was enough to set Ginny off also. The two humans came into the presence of the group-mind laughing until the tears ran down their faces. After all, there is nothing quite like laughing in the face of death. Of course, it would have been a good idea to look behind them while they did this.

In the ceiling the sound of their laughter stopped work. Now thc entire crew was peering anxiously down.

"Whoreson!" said Pistol admiringly. "They must be stand-up fall-down drunk."

Melene looked at the way the two clung to each other. She smiled.

And then, behind the laughing two came the shock of the rats' lives and the horror of the bats: the Korozhet.

"Whoreson! we have to get down there," said at least three rats, led by Fal.

The little galago agreed. "Indeed, *señor* rat! But . . . how do we get past the grid?"

"What grid?" asked Fal. "Come on, we need to open this hole a bit more."

The galago looked startled. "The light grid? You cannot see it?" Fluff squinted down into the chamber. "I believe humans could not see it either. She is too far into the ultraviolet for humans to see, and obviously also for the bats. Look, the projector, there she is."

He pointed to a device on the far side of the room. "*Señor* Shaw, he had one too. A special Korozhet device, very expensive, for the detecting of flying objects. This looks very similar."

Bronstein closed her eyes briefly. "And what happens once they are detected?"

"Ah! She is hooked up to the device of the rapid firing of the projectiles. See." The galago pointed. "That thing she is standing over there. It is locking on to the object and firing."

"Slowshields? Would they help?" asked Melene.

"No," said Doc. "We'd just fall. And keep falling until the shooting stopped."

Below them somebody said something in Korozhet. But it wasn't the Korozhet. It was several of the Maggots speaking together. Still, they all understood. "Where are the tailed and the winged ones?" the group-mind was demanding.

Chip didn't understand the Maggot. That didn't stop him from replying, of course. "Same to you, O High Hemorrhoid. Why do you play with yourself in public?"

✧ ✧ ✧

Ginny, of course, did understand. "We won't tell you."

The creatures globbered.

"Is it talking Crotchet too?" demanded Chip. "What did I tell you, Ginny? What do the fat uglies say? Tell them we'd give them indigestion."

"They want to know where the rats and bats are. I said we wouldn't tell them." She squeezed his hand.

Chip assumed his best expression of innocence and humility. It certainly would never have fooled Henri-Pierre, but then the Maggot group-mind was less perceptive than the sarcastic little Frenchman. "Tell him it is just too bad that they were all killed when the tunnel collapsed."

She did.

Once again the Magh' spoke in their weird chorus. "That explains why the eggs and larvae were spared. The Korozhet had told us they were vicious, insatiable grub-eaters. The larvae tenders could not believe the grubs were untouched. Of course some will be born stunted and have to be killed."

"What do the bug-uglies say?" Chip wanted to know.

She told him.

He snorted. "Ask them if they always believe what the Korozhet say."

It wasn't a direct questioning of the Korozhet. She could ask.

"Yes," the group mind answered. "The Korozhet always tell us things. How did you find your way through the maze-tunnels of the Magh'mmm? This is the first attack to get near to our precious selves. We must prevent it ever happening again."

Without being asked, Ginny translated.

Chip grinned. "Tell them the Korozhet guided us here. That they sell us arms and advise us."

Ginny felt as if she was walking into a morass. Her head kept saying "this may damage your friends." But it was true, so she could say it. It was difficult until she prefaced it with "My mate says . . ."

"*Lies!*" The Korozhet spiked forward. "Deception, Magh'mmm! I have told you I was a prisoner and a hostage in their unprovoked attack."

The Korozhet pointed spines at them. "The soft squashy life-forms are pathological liars. We would never sell arms to such a species. Never. We have been your reliable providers for thousands of cycles. Always we provided the group-minds with the finest ships, the best shields. Have we ever failed the Magh? Bah. The one with the long head-filaments claims 'her mate says.' But I ask *her* now: Could we Korozhet ever do anything so evil?"

Now Ginny felt as if her head might explode. What she'd said was true. It *was*. It was! It was! It was! She *knew* that it was true. Undoubtedly and incontrovertibly true. And now she knew also, beyond all reasonable doubt, that the soft-cyber implant was influencing her thoughts. Obviously the Korozhet who designed the things had built in a pro-Korozhet programming.

Cold sweat beaded her forehead. She couldn't say it.

"Well?" prompted the Korozhet. "We Korozhet do not sell arms to other species. Tell the Magh'mmm you lied."

Chip squeezed her hand. "What's Pricklepuss saying?"

Ginny forced her vocal chords to do what part of her brain said they should not. Her voice came out in a squeak. But it was a loud determined squeak. "*I do not lie.*"

The ball of prickles raised a spine . . . and lowered it again.

Chip squeezed her. "What's happening, dearest?"

She looked at him, with victory in her eyes. "You were right about that—alien. It's just tried to claim they never sold arms to humans."

The Korozhet might have been out of gas and harpoon darts, but it wasn't out of wind. "This species is incapable of the truth, Magh'mmm!"

"Translate," said Chip quietly.

She did.

"Ask the Maggots if they haven't got another alien they can ask," he said in a whisper.

She did. The Magh'mmm seemed to like that idea.

The Korozhet did not.

Pistol had to be restrained from cheering when Chip called the Maggots hemorrhoids. But when the conversation switched to Korozhet, Bronstein backed off. She knew in her bones that this might be where she had to kill one of their rat-comrades because of the treacherous soft-cybers. She wasn't sure how well the rat psyche would deal with what she was certain would come.

It was a good thing that she was ready. She had to stop three of the rats—from clapping and whistling.

Doc could not restrain himself. "I told you all so!" he hissed. "I told you the Korozhet betrayed us."

Fal sounded positively choked. "Methinks our Ginny is as near to a rat as you'll find in human form. I'd liefer have put ratsbane in my mouth than try to say that!"

Eamon showed teeth. "She's far better than a rat!"

"Begorra!" O'Niel spat, "Be forgetting the silly arguments then. We need to get down there and help."

Nym looked at the gap. "If we made it bigger we

could abseil down. The rope is a bit short, but not much. . . ."

"That detection grid. Could the rats avoid it, Don Fluffy?" asked Bronstein.

The big-eyed galago shook his head violently. "No. The beams they move. It would not be at all of a possibility."

"Can't we just do it?" said Melene. "Some of us will make it."

"No. The first one to go will get shot at. That'll activate his slowshield and sever the rope. It is too far to fall," said Nym.

There was a long silence. "We'll have to drop the roof," said Eamon.

"No," said the galago quietly. "I will do it. For my Virginia I will do it. I can see the projector beams. I can climb down and avoid them. I alone am the one who can see them. I too am the only one who can climb upside down along the roof and the wall. Give for me a device of the explosive and I will destroy the projector." The little creature shivered.

Chapter 44:
Fluff at the Bridge.

" 'Tis a valiant Fluff! You're a hero!" said Doll, in a voice that suggested that receiving the hero's rewards didn't have to wait until after the deed.

The little creature shivered again. "No. I am just a scared galago. I . . . I admit. Not very brave, I am. You are all big tough soldiers. . . . Me . . . I am a rich lady's toy."

Doc patted the galago's shoulder. "The true nature of courage is to know fear, and overcome it."

"I think it overcomes me!"

"Here," said Pistol, "have a stoup of Dutch courage."

The galago took Pistol's bottle with shaking hands, and took a deep chug. He shuddered. "Now I must go and pee on my hands and feet, even if 'Ginia says it is a habit of the most vile. You can please make the hole bigger for me?"

Doll was distinctly puzzled. "Pee on his hands and feet?"

"Urine washing," said Doc. "It increases the adhesiveness. The hyraxes and some lesser primates practice it."

"Art sure he's not just kinky? I wouldn't have thought you'd have to practice it . . . much." Melene was definitely doubtful on this one.

Pistol chuckled. "Methinks his aim is lousy. Let's nibble that hole bigger. Fal's got to get through, never mind the galago."

The galago looked doubtfully again at the trigger bar. Then at the tiny bat-mine. "*Señorita* Bronstein, I am not very mechanical."

Eamon grunted impatiently. "Let me be explaining to this numbskull, Michaela."

"Good luck." said Bronstein dryly, going off to take down some of the mines they'd rigged on the stanchions. That galago was definitely overdue to get bitten. Damn those rats for giving it strong drink first. She'd swear it was swaying on those glistening black feet. Mind you, at least it had stopped shivering. That was a plus.

"See, you twist this arming button. Click it to 'remote.' Then you move off. As soon as you're more than thirty yards away, you depress both triggers. Simultaneously." The trigger bar was designed for bat-feet. The twin trigger at either end of the bar was a logical safety device. Eamon could work one in his sleep. It was difficult for him to grasp that any semisentient could not easily take one apart and reassemble it.

"Just show me one more time," said Fluff.

"Look. I'll arm it." Eamon was exasperated by now. "You're not supposed to move it once it is armed, but we have to take some risks. Then all you've got to do is press the triggers. Any fool can do that."

"I think so," said the galago doubtfully.

And then, because things were getting heated down there . . . he was off. With just a mouthful more brandy for the road.

Galagos are possibly one of the most acrobatic small primates around. Being nocturnal, however, they don't normally have an audience.

Fluff finally had the audience he'd so often craved for his magnificent, elegant gymnastic skills. However he kept finding that somehow he wasn't climbing with panache. It was odd. He *felt* like a superstar. He just wasn't focusing too well.

The rats and bats watched in horror as the galago swung wildly across the roof, flinging itself with remarkable drunken inaccuracy at small knobbles of Magh' adobe . . . and somehow sticking.

"It doth piss glue," said Nym. "There is no other . . ."

Everybody gasped.

Fluff's lurching progress had nearly come unstuck. A piece of adobe decided to stick to his hand instead of the curving roof.

Somehow, by giving the law of gravity a complete raspberry, the galago caught hold of something else with the other hand.

Then it was hanging there, with a piece of loose Magh' adobe in one hand and a minuscule handhold in the other.

"I shall have to throw it to you," whispered the galago.

It was surprising the Magh'mmm didn't hear the sound of gritting teeth in the ceiling. But the

Magh'mmm was in debate with the Korozhet. "If it is indeed as you say, then we must redouble our efforts. This species must be pushed to extinction."

The galago weighed up the throw. Then, tossed the chunk of adobe. Eamon dropped through the hole, snatched, and was back inside the ceiling before you could say "bogtrotter."

Fortune favored them. Neither the appalling throw nor the dart into the room had been detected.

The galago continued his progress. Lower. Lower. And lower down the wall. The projector was in full view of any life-form with eyes in the hall below. It sat on a platform just above human head-height.

The roof crew watched, hardly daring to breathe. And then when the galago was mere feet from the platform . . .

The Magh'mmm spoke: "But we do not see the need to keep these aliens alive any longer. You asked us to keep all the specimens in good condition. But we have sufficient humans for larval conditioning. Since you say they are incapable of telling the truth, they will not give us the information we have asked for. Once we have confirmed it with the Jampad prisoner, these are of no further . . ."

Chapter 45:
"Thar she blows!"

The grub-tenders had finished their frantic tending of their instinctively most precious charges. Now they began cleaning. The inputs to the group-mind from myriad Magh' in a scorpiary were just too numerous to have each individual directed specifically and individually all the time. Much of what the individual Magh' did was simply instinctive, within the broad parameters of the group-mind orders. The stack closest to the old entryway had an untidy wire to the old doorway. There was considerable alien junk lying there. There was also a mess of sticky diesel and fertilizer and a rat-trap and a bangstick-cartridge trigger.

The grub-tender pulled the wire.

6:28 a.m.

Henry M'Batha's vigil finally had its reward. In

another ten minutes the sun's heat would have masked the infrared explosion signature coming from the brood-chamber. He was dialing before the heat had dissipated.

"Van Klomp." The voice was very tense.

"Major! Another explosion! Right from the middle, sir! Right from the MIDDLE!"

There was silence. Then a big exhalation boomed down the line. "Boykie. That's the best news I've had for hours. We'll get airborne, just in case. I've given you the contact frequencies. Stay on it. You got me? Stay on it! And call that corporal of Major Fitzhugh's."

But there was no reply from Corporal Simms. Someone just clicked the beeper off. And the office wasn't answering either.

"We're looking for Major Conrad Fitzhugh," said the lieutenant to Corporal Simms. His voice had that *I am going to get answers or you are going to get hurt* quality to it. Behind him, the squad of MPs hefted their billy clubs.

Simms reached into his pocket and clicked the insistent beeper off. "The major hasn't been in this morning," he said truthfully. "But there is an envelope here, addressed to the military police."

The MP lieutenant tore it open. Johnny didn't get to see the letter. But he did see the rat-dropping Ariel had contributed.

Fitz's bangstick rested against the force field. An assegai balanced against a twinkle in the air.

This far from the brood-chamber, it was little more than a dull thump. However, it was plain that the Magh'mmm had felt a great deal more. "Aliens!

You said the grub-devourers were dead! You lied to us. You lied!" The hundred or so Magh'mmm chorused.

"I *said* they lied all the time," snapped the Korozhet.

"Kill them," commanded the group-mind.

"No. No!" shouted the Korozhet. "Spare the one with long head-filaments—she is valuable to me."

The Magh'mmm were past listening. "No. Kill—"

The galago shrieked in his ear-piercing fashion and jumped for the projector platform, trying to pull the mine from his waistcoat pocket as he leaped. He succeeded, but then he had the mine in his hands, and nothing to grab the platform with. He hit the projector with a *whuff* of breath that even the rats and bats heard. The mine skittered out of his hands and lay half-on and half-off the platform.

The galago stood up, taking the mine trigger bar from the other pocket . . . and slipped. He caught the edge of the platform and clung there by one hand, the trigger bar in the other.

"*AIEEE!*" His bellow carried a volume which nearly deafened the sensitive-eared rats and bats above. "*I die gloriously!*"

He pressed the trigger on the bar. Nothing happened. Except . . . one of the scorps who had been guarding Chip and Ginny advanced on him.

The galago shook the trigger bar furiously. "She is not *working*!"

"BOTH triggers—you idiot!" shouted the bats.

The galago tried and nearly fell in its fumbling haste. "I cannot!" he shrieked.

The Magh' scorp claw snapped at the tiny creature. Fluff squeaked in terror and flung the trigger bar at the scorp as he leaped in a twenty-five foot bound to Ginny's shoulder.

The scorp caught the trigger bar with contemptuous ease in one outstretched claw. The bar was taken neatly lengthways, held by the ends. The scorp displayed its strength. The claw closed slowly to crush and splinter the bar.

If only it hadn't depressed the triggers when it did that.

"GO!" shouted Bronstein, before the debris had even fallen.

The three-foot-high squat ball of blue fluff which called itself a "Jampad" had chosen a hell of a time to arrive. It wasted no time getting into the spirit of things, though. Those tentacles wielded a mean four-pound hammer.

Bronstein and Eamon missed the Jampad by inches as it took out its guard. They left the fray to O'Niel, the rats, and Chip and Ginny. Eamon took the bridge, and a slash through his wing membrane, in the process of sending a stream of frantic Maggot reinforcements hurtling into the pit. Bronstein dragged him back hastily through the entry where she'd put her mines, as the big bat couldn't fly.

Chip had dealt with the other scorp guard. The explosion which had blown away the beam projector had also shredded the first one. Ginny waded in to combat with a piece of reinforcing rod. The Magh' body-tenders, poodle-sized and with tiny little claws, flung themselves into an attack they were never designed for. Now Ginny, with her blunt weapon and more enthusiasm than skill, was the quicker Magh' killer than master craftsman Chip.

The rats had come hurtling down the two abseil ropes. While they'd been rappelling down, the bats had flung Molotovs at the Magh'mmm. In the burning chaos, only sixty or so Magh'mmm and a few of their tiny body-tenders remained alive.

And the Korozhet. The body-tenders had died like flies trying to help the burning Magh'mmm. They simply weren't big enough to make any headway against Chip and Ginny and their rat and bat allies.

O'Niel, a broken bottle in foot, shouted from on high. "Well, me foine boyos! We outnumber them one to five! Let's slaughter the salpeens, begorra!"

The rats found nothing wrong with O'Niel's mathematics. The pure ones, the Magh' caste of castes, the group-mind which ruled with an absolute and total power over several million of their own kind . . . were pitifully soft. And as they were repositories for all the genomes of the variants of Magh', they were of no warrior type. They did have stingers and claws, just as they had digging palps—but small and ineffectual ones. To boot, they were bloated virtually to the point of immobility. It was like kindergarten children against battle-hardened warriors. The Magh'mmm were plainly terrified, and had no idea how to fight.

But then, there was the Korozhet. The Korozhet and her equalizer. *If a laser beam intersects a slowshield there will be a cataclysmic thermonuclear reaction*, the Korozhet had told the Military Procurement Council. That, of course, had been another lie. Maybe the council should have checked it, but the colony didn't have many portable lasers anyway, and did not have the technology to make them.

The Korozhet's slaves built FTL for them. They were also capable of making laser pistols.

The Expediter slid her testa-plate aside and drew out the laser pistol. First she would kill that faulty slave. Virginia was a danger to the Overphyle. Firstly, she was a rebel slave who had somehow completely overcome the mental conditioning of the soft-cyber. And, secondly, she was a person of potential influence and financial power in her society. The others were mere cogs. Lowly soldiers. The human military commanders had shown a remarkable stupidity in not learning from their front-line troops. The rest of these were of lesser importance. The Expediter did not just decide to kill her first from mere malice. The hated Jampad would get the next shot. At all costs it must be silenced. She raised the pistol with careful spines.

The others were moving in on the Magh'mmm, intent on the slaughter, when Chip caught sight of the Korozhet spining forward. Whatever that device of rods and odd metal was, it said *gun* to Chip. He dived at Ginny, knocking her down and sending Fluff flying, somersaulting butt over teakettle. The bolt seared through Chip's shoulder.

"Help!" shrieked Ginny.

The rats and bats turned to aid her . . .

And could not.

The Expediter spined forward, focusing spine-tip ocelli on the prey. She was quite safe. The human soldier was down. The others all had soft-cyber implants. The soft-cyber slaves could not possibly override the most basic programming logic in their implants: *You will not attack a Korozhet.*

The Expediter took careful aim at Virginia.

And a tiny bellowing creature leapt at the gun.

"GALAGO DE LA MANCHA!"

Fluff could not attack the Korozhet. Not even though he wanted to, to the absolute core of his small being. Not even if it was going to kill Virginia. But the gun was a different matter. And arboreal primates are strong. Those tiny almost human hands have a very, very powerful grip.

The Expediter threshed and struggled in real fear, trying to pull the gun free. *How could the slave? How could it!* The laser pistol fired in a continuous stream of light . . . far above its target. Striking, without provocation, the wall. A wall laced with thick cables.

The fourth of July on Old Earth had never produced such fireworks. Fragments of Magh' adobe shrapnel splattered around the chamber. Everyone, even the surviving Magh'mmm, dived for cover.

Everyone but the Korozhet. She had always feared Chip's four-pound hammer. She should have made sure he still had it. The Jampad had no Korozhet conditioning either. The Jampad flung the hammer with such force that it shattered the Korozhet's testa explosively. Fragments of hard shell, red spines, and sticky greenish ichor puddled onto the floor.

Chapter 46:
Tan-tarah-tarah!

"Um." The communication officer looked very nervous at having to face Fitz. "Sir. I just received a strange radio message in from HQ, sir. Um. They're ordering your immediate arrest. Sir."

Fitz took a deep breath. Well. It had been inevitable.

Then his bangstick . . . fell over.

A laser beam had just cut a vital cable some twenty-seven miles away.

"It's a GO! GO! GO!" Fitz shouted, picking up the bangstick on the run.

The mousy lieutenant was carried along with the storming tide of three thousand men and seven thousand rats. The bats overhead didn't push.

When the initial unresisted charge was deep into Magh' territory, Fitz smiled at the panting lieutenant. "When this is over, you can find me and arrest me."

"If the stupid bastard is still alive," said Ariel.

The lieutenant started to say something, but Fitz had already turned away and was yelling orders.

Henry M'Batha had never hit anyone in his life before. He studied his split knuckles. That hand was damn sore. And the radio operator was squalling for security. It felt like he might have dislocated something.

He shook his head. There was no time for worrying about pain now. That's why he'd pulled that stupid officious by-the-rule-book son-of-a-bitch radio operator out of his chair and flattened his face. He had to raise the paratroop major *now*. The Magh' force field always reflected light on certain frequencies.

Right now it wasn't.

He could work radio comms as well as that idiot in the corner.

"Major."

"Yah, boykie?

"The force field is *down*, Major!"

Van Klomp nearly deafened him. "YES!" Then he said, "Try and get hold of Fitz. Tell him we're on our way. And keep me posted on any new developments. We should jump in about half an hour."

"Uh. Major. I think I may be just about to get hauled away by security. The radio op didn't want to let me call you. Things . . . got a bit physical."

Van Klomp gave a volcanic amused snort. "Let me talk to him, boykie."

The radio operator could hardly not have heard. Van Klomp made radio redundant. "The major wants to talk to you," repeated Henry.

"You're for it, M'Batha," snarled the radio-op, holding his nose gingerly. "They'll confiscate your share for this."

But he took the headset. Van Klomp boomed at him. "What's the name, Sonny?"

"Operator Chirik."

"Well, Shirk, you know who I am." It was not a voice you made a mistake about. Everybody in the colony knew the larger-than-life Van Klomp. "Henry is just doing his job. You make trouble for him and *I'll* come and pay you a visit."

"He hit me!" protested Chirik.

"Yah. The boykie was ordered to call the moment he had the news. You stopped him. If it had been me . . . I'd have killed you, *boeta*. Over and out." And the booming voice was gone.

The radio-op sat feeling his nose. Finally he said, in a more reasonable tone of voice, "What the hell is going on?"

M'Batha eyed him speculatively. "Sorry about the nose. I think I've dislocated my thumb, if it is any comfort to you. Listen, is that cousin of yours still with the newspaper? How would you like to give her the biggest story of her life?"

The radio-op grunted. "That's *not* what I'd like to give her, but . . ."

"Well, maybe you'll get lucky after this story," offered Henry.

The radio-op gave a smile. "Tell. But let me pull that thumb of yours first."

Chapter 47:
All is lost.

Chip's slowshield would have killed her if he hadn't somehow managed to roll clear, trying to reach the Korozhet.

Instead Ginny had been hit by a piece of falling Magh' adobe, just as she'd tried to stand up. He too was showered with fragments which, of course, just hit his shield.

But Ginny swayed and crumpled. Her glasses, caught by a shard of Magh' adobe, flew off her head. And Chip, helpless in his hardened slowshield, had to watch her fall. He saw another piece of adobe—twice the size of her head—miss her and smash her glasses to glass-dust.

The moment he could move, he dived across to her, oblivious to the agony from his own shoulder. He tried to lift her. His arm failed him, and his hand was wet with blood.

"DOC!" he screamed. But Doc was deep in the butchery of the Magh'mmm. The pure ones did not defile themselves with slowshields. The pseudo-chitin of their carapaces was soft. The shrapnel from the laser disaster had reduced their number still further. And not for countless millennia had Magh'mmm had to fight for themselves. It was pure carnage. Rat and bat heaven.

Chip was left with poor Ginny's bleeding head on his lap. He didn't dare to try pressure to stop the bleeding. Her skull might be fractured. Oh God, how it bled!

He was supremely unaware of the tears streaming down his face. Then her eyes opened. "Lie still. Lie still, love. Don't try to move." His voice cracked.

Ginny just remembered something hitting her head. The hammer-blow and the pain. Opening her eyes was involuntary. Chip, above her, was merely a blur. But his voice was recognizable . . . he'd called her his love. Her head was chaos and confusion. She closed her eyes again. Pain. Pain—and worse.

A terrible, terrifying woolliness enveloped her. Her mind was cotton, hay . . . and rags, rags of memory. Precious, precious memories. She opened her eyes. The blurring, if anything, was worse. She strained to focus. His face swam briefly into view. Dirty, covered in dark stubble, and tear tracked. Homely as hell. She loved him so much she thought her heart would burst. He blurred away again, into pain . . .

She tried desperately to think, and slipped away into a feathery limbo that she strained furiously against.

This time wakefulness was just as blurred and confused. Well, maybe a fraction less so. Because now she knew what was wrong. A tentative hand went up and touched her head . . . and confirmed her worst nightmare.

The warm wetness seeped from her left upper temple, just inside her hairline.

She'd touched the scar so often. The tiny cut that had given her back her life . . . Where they'd inserted her soft-cyber chip.

"Don't touch it, Ginny. You might make it worse." Chip's voice was overflowing with care.

She started to cry.

"Don't cry, my love. Don't cry. It'll be all right."

"It's *not* all right!" she said, shaking her head in anguish.

"Lie still, Ginny. Please. It'll be fine. I promise."

"No, it won't! You don't understand! I'm going to be stupid, stupid, stupid," she blurted out desperately.

"You'll be fine," insisted Chip. "You're three times as bright as me. Take more than a little knock on the head to spoil that."

"Yes, I will. I will! It hit me on my implant. My soft-cyber. Oh God, I didn't want to tell you about my implant. I'm going all stupid again. I can't think! You'll hate me now," she cried hysterically. "You hate implants!"

Everything blurred once more. His voice came from far off, and didn't make any kind of sense.

When the fuzziness receded again, she'd decided what to say. "Chip. I love you. I'll always love you. I'll always love you even after I go back to being a brain-damaged little girl again. I'm just so scared I won't remember you. I might end up just a cabbage. Please, kiss me again while I can still think. Oh God, I want to remember you. You won't love me any more now. I'm only a mechanical doll and now I won't even be that."

✧ ✧ ✧

Chip found speaking virtually impossible. His "Ginny" came out as a croak. But he did manage to kiss her. As gently as he might a flower.

"Kiss me hard!" she insisted. "Please. Nobody ever kissed me until you did."

He tried to oblige. "Ginny. No matter what, I'll love you forever."

"Kiss me again, Chip," she said faintly. "When I'm stupid you must go away. I don't want you to see me like that."

"No way am I leaving you, kid. No matter what." He bent and kissed her again.

"Yet lecherous as a monkey and the whores called him mandrake," said Fal. "Too busy to even lend us a hand, eh, Chip?"

"Get me Doc—quick!" The terrible urgency in Chip's voice had fat Fal leaving at a belly-wobbling run, and bellowing for the medic.

Chapter 48:
Or maybe not.

Doc came at a dogtrot. Well, a rat-trot. And he was carrying his pack, which he'd found. He took one look at Chip's pale face and said: "And which one is the patient, Fal?"

Chip was in no mood for funnies.

"She got hit on head by one of those fragments. Right on her soft-cyber implant. Help her, Doc! Please! She's bleeding something terrible."

The rat looked at Chip very strangely. Very strangely indeed. But, for a miracle, he didn't actually say anything. He just began examining Ginny's head, gently and carefully. He reached into his pack and produced a scalpel. Chip's eyes widened in horror. "Please, God . . ."

"I thought you were an agnostic," said the rat-medic. "Relax. I just need to remove some hair."

"You're . . . you're not going to operate?"

Doc snuffled with what might have been laughter. "Chip, I'm a field medic and a rat. What do think I'm going to do? Open brain surgery? I'd get you to do it except your hands are shaking too much."

The rat shaved the patch. "Get Bronstein for me," he said.

"I'm here. Above you," Bronstein replied.

"How is your infrasound examination of bones?" Doc asked. "In theory you should be able to do it."

Bronstein looked doubtful. "To be sure, if I have wet contact . . ."

"You can 'trink her bludd,'" said Doc dryly.

Bronstein put her ugly crumpled leaf nose against Ginny's bloody head.

The bat pulled it away. "This is giving me a headache."

"No holes?" asked the rat.

"Not even a crack, that I can find." Bronstein wiped her nose with a wing. Then sneezed.

The medic nodded thoughtfully. "Very well. Open your eyes, Ginny."

She did. "Everything is all blurry, Doc."

"That's because you've lost your glasses." The rat's tone was bone dry.

"Oh. I . . . I didn't realize." She felt her head vaguely.

Chip pulled her hand away gently and kissed her. "Your face is just as beautiful without them."

"Get your big head out of the way. I need to check pupil dilation." Doc pushed him aside.

"Well?" asked Chip anxiously.

"Well, *what*? Hold this pad on the wound, Ginny. I don't think it is even going to need stitching. That bandana of yours saved you a bit."

"Well, is she going to be all right?" demanded

Chip, on the verge of grabbing Doc and shaking him . . . like a terrier shakes rats.

"Medically, there appears to be no obvious fracture. I suppose we can't rule out the chance of a hairline crack. She may have had a slight concussion but she's got nice even pupil dilation." Doc continued packing away his tools.

"But why all the *blood*?" Chip demanded.

"Head wounds bleed, Chip," replied Doc evenly. "Even minor ones like this."

Chip swallowed. In a small voice he said, "But what about her soft-cyber chip. Is that all right? Is there anything we can do for it?

Doc shook his head and looked quizzically at Chip. "So you are now entirely in favor of soft-cyber chips? So! A new record for thesis becoming antithesis!"

Chip took Doc gently by the throat.

"He's just giving you a hard time, Chip," said Bronstein. "They showed us in basic training. Soft-cybers are tough. You can drive a ten ton truck over one. Now, let him examine your shoulder and then he can come and sew Eamon's wing up."

"Besides," chuckled Doc, "they are embedded between the parietal lobes. You'd have to turn the brain to jelly first."

Chip had a neat bandage on his shoulder. The Jampad was speaking to the others in Korozhet. Fal was making a fire for a Magh'mmm barbecue. Chip put his uninjured arm around Ginny. "Dearest, you and I have to have a deep, serious talk."

"Only talk?" she said provocatively, from under her lashes. She giggled. *As good as a rat-girl's repartee!*

Chip blushed. "Well . . . all right. Soon." He hooked a thumb at the Jampad. "What's he saying?"

"He says he wants to go home," she translated.

"Tell him we'll get him a new ship," said Chip savagely. "From the Crotchets."

Then Chip turned to Bronstein. "And you, Bronstein? Why do you look like you just found out you chose your honeymoon for that time of month?"

Bronstein tried to smile. "Because we bats take a long view. We've won. Humans *can* win. We've just proved it. And without the war there will be no more cyber-uplifted bats. Especially now that we have found out that the soft-cyber implants contain a fatal flaw. We cannot breed on our own, and without cybernetics . . . we are dumb. It doesn't worry the rats much, but we bats have always dreamed of *freedom*."

Ginny stopped talking to the Jampad. She turned to face Bronstein. "No. This is *not* the end of the road for that dream, Bronstein. Not while there is breath in *my* body."

Bronstein shrugged. "To be sure, that's nice of you, Ginny. But what can one human do? *You* understand, because of your own implant. But who else ever will?"

Chip stuck his hand up. "I do. And so will a lot of Vat soldiers who fought alongside you bats." He grinned. "So let's start a revolution. The Rat, Bat and Vat Liberation Movement. I'll be the chef. Work out new recipes for Shareholder supreme." He squeezed Ginny's shoulder. She smiled at him.

Fluff's eyes brightened. He pounded his chest. "Viva! Will there be gorilla warfare, *señor*? I always wanted to be a gorilla!"

Fal wandered up, trying to unscrew a bottle. "Doth beg the *real* vital question. Will there be strong drink?" He handed the bottle to Chip. "Do what humans do best," he commanded imperiously.

While Chip obediently opened the bottle, Ginny smiled at Bronstein. "Michaela, I think the Crotchet wanted me—and killed my parents—because I am heir to thirty-four percent of the shares in the HAR colony. Things *are* going to change. It may not be easy, but we *will* overcome."

"Why didn't you tell me, Ginny?"

"Because I was scared you'd despise me. Think I was just a doll. A wind-up Cathy Earnshaw. I'm *not*. I'm me."

Chip smiled and hugged her, one armed. "Cathy Earnshaw from *Wuthering Heights*? That wet-lettuce! Hah! You, Ginny, are worth fifty of her. You're the most fantastically wonderful person in my whole world. And . . ."

"And . . . ?" she asked, shyly, wanting him to continue.

"And I think we should go and find a quiet corner. I want to take all your clothes off and make passionate love to you." His hands were doing most distracting things.

She kissed him. "You're an absolute genius."

Chapter 49:
Finale.

The MPs pushed into the deserted trenches with no small amount of trepidation. They'd had to leave their vehicle more than a mile away. This place was as frightening as hell. . . .

For starters, why was it deserted? Were they going to meet Magh'?

For a second, dealing with drunken Vat-troops on leave in the city was one thing. Here in the front lines, they had a private suspicion that Magh' might be safer to meet than front-line soldiers. Still, they had their orders.

The sound of voices was a welcome one. It was a party of medics with stretchers.

"Halt!" said the Military Police captain.

"Fuck off, redcap. Get out of the way."

"That's an order, soldier!" snapped another MP.

"I'm a medic, asshole. With an injured soldier in my care. Go and look at your military law. Now get out of my way before I toss you out of the mine corridor."

It was something of a shock to the MPs. "Look, we just need to ask you if you know where we can find a Major Conrad Fitzhugh," said the captain, in a more reasonable tone of voice, walking next to the stretcher bearer.

One of the stretcher bearers halted. "Hear that, guys? The redcaps want to find Major Fitz." There was a ripple of laughter.

The medic gestured with his head. "He's back there. I guess about ten, fifteen klicks away. Where there is real fighting, you know. Not just poking a nightstick into a drunk's guts."

The captain bared his teeth at the disrespect. "How do we get there? We have a warrant . . ."

The orderly started walking again. He spoke quietly. "Turn around, MP. Quickly. And keep walking, until you get to your little truck. And then piss off. You go in there saying you've got a warrant for Major Fitz and you're not going to come back. Not even on a stretcher."

"If I don't get to you first," said a second orderly, darkly.

"We should let 'em go and talk to Ariel," said the man on the stretcher, waving a tourniquetted stump at the horrified MP.

Even the rest of the wounded laughed like hell.

General Cartup-Kreutzler was an angry, frustrated, underslept man. No matter how he tried he was not going to manage to hush this up. That stiff-backed major had said that the general could do his damnedest. Far from taking action against his guards, the major was going to reward them. It was their duty to arrest anyone who wasn't in possession of an ID card, even if they were an unrecognized drunk and disorderly general.

And on top of that the general knew his wife would be incandescent. Besides the Queen Anne chair . . . he and Daisy hadn't cleared up. He wasn't looking forward to going home. *Her* family had the money.

Then General Blutin barged into his office without even a knock. Cartup-Kreutzler's supposed superior was normally cowed in his presence. At power games in the channels of influence, Cartup-Kreutzler had a substantial edge.

But not now. General Blutin slapped the newspaper down onto the desk. "Just what is the *MEANING* of this, Kreutzler? You're supposed to keep me informed! I've just made a complete fool of myself denying this to three newspapers. And here it is, complete with *photographs*!"

The banner headline read **FIRST VICTORY!** above a high-res satellite pic showing a column of dust and several obvious explosions, against the background of spiral scorpiary walls. Cartup-Kreutzler read on. The subheading was *"Big push succeeds thanks to Commandos!"*

Then his eyes hit on the first three words of the article and blurred . . .

Major Conrad Fitzhugh . . .

His head hurt.

. . . leading the attack . . . hero . . .

General Blutin leaned over his desk, spraying him with spittle. "I want a full explanation. *All* the details. On my desk within half an hour. Do you hear me? How dare you do this without even notifying me? How *dare* you?"

The worm had finally turned. "Can I keep the newspaper?" Cartup-Kreutzler asked timidly.

"No! Get your own." The general stormed out past Daisy's empty desk.

General Cartup-Kreutzler sat silent. Captain Hargreaves would get back in a few minutes. He reached for the crystal whiskey decanter. It was rather low. He poured himself a good three fingers with a shaking hand, and knocked it back. Then he paused, the nearly empty glass still at his lips.

He sniffed.

Rat-urine has a characteristic odor.

Well, you could call it fighting. Some of the Magh' they encountered were warrior-types. But stupid, stupid, stupid! They'd only fight if you came too close.

The paratroopers had landed unopposed on the central dome. They'd regrouped and blown their way through into the scorpiary. There, on the upper tier of circles around the tower, they'd started hitting Magh' of all types. The Magh' were wandering around, aimlessly. Van Klomp soon figured out that all the paratroopers had to do was stay out of their way. The question was—where were the paratroopers going, exactly? There were plenty of signs that *someone* had been giving the Magh' hell. But where were they?

Then they heard the singing. A piece had been knocked out of the central tower's upper wall. And the sound of voices uplifted in joyous song could be heard . . .

"*Shaid me Jolly tinker we'll have another round! Oh indeed she did! Yas indeed she did . . .*"

It wasn't tuneful.

It wasn't Magh', either.

"Let's see if we can get a rope across there, Corporal."

All that practice with grappling hooks and assault

courses finally paid off. They got three ropes to hook up. And they swung across, and then hand over hand, up and over.

Van Klomp, of course, was in the lead. The huge chamber was smoky and dim. A fire burned on the far side. He dropped a rope down and rappelled in. And then stopped, bangstick in hand. He was ready for anything . . .

No. He wasn't. Not for this. With difficulty, he wrenched his eyes from the naked breasts of the girl sitting up on the makeshift bed in the corner. Not very big breasts, but beautifully formed. He did eventually manage to shift his gaze higher. He dropped his bangstick. Virginia Shaw's face, even without the glasses, was fairly unmistakable. But the pictures hadn't been adorned by an indecently large, happy smile.

"Who is it, Chip?" she asked, blinking at them.

A stocky, scarred, spiky-haired, unshaven, and very tough-looking little man sat up. He had a bandaged shoulder, but otherwise seemed as naked as the woman next to him. "It's some kind of Orificer, Ginny. A major. Parachute brigade, I think. I thought all they did was formation jumps at parades. And if he doesn't stop staring at your tits, I'm going to escalope his private parts."

Van Klomp was a good judge of men. His balls were at real risk. He hastily tried to concentrate on faces.

Virginia Shaw put an arm around her man and kissed him. Then she turned to blink at Van Klomp again, who had been joined by almost the whole squad. She smiled sweetly. "Why don't you come back later, Major? Much later."

For the first time in his life, Van Klomp, the loudest man on Harmony And Reason, was utterly silenced. He watched as she pulled the stocky dark-haired soldier down onto the bed again, and threw one long, slim leg over him.

The paratrooper corporal at Van Klomp's side turned hastily towards the fire, brandishing his bangstick. There was something blue, hairy and totally alien standing there. And—

A one-eyed rat, a slightly plump bat, and a tiny, big-eyed, delicate little creature staggered their way around bloated Maggot bodies toward them. Arm-in-arm. Or arm on wing, anyway. The rat held out a bottle.

The unsuspecting Van Klomp took it, and took a swig. While he was still gasping, the small fluffy-toy cute creature, swaying a little, gestured at the large, hairy-armed, two-hundred-ten-pound Godzilla-in-human-form corporal next to him.

"How much, *señor*," asked the soup-mug sized creature, "for your sister?"

THE END

APPENDIX

***Slowshields*:** A Korozhet device implanted subcutaneously, just above the breastbone of a mammal user. The device remains inactive, except for maintaining an ovoid spherical perimeter field—just outside of the reach of the user—for which it draws energy from the body heat of the user. If an object moving at greater than 22.8 mph impinges on the perimeter field, the slowshield device strips all the kinetic energy from this object. Effectively, the projectile will simply fall. The energy absorbed cannot be contained by the slowshield device. The device wastes the energy by projecting a hardshield (a force field). The time the hardshield is active for depends on the amount of kinetic energy absorbed. The slowshield device has a particle-size acceptor program. Should two slowshields intersect, a twin focus develops, making a larger perimeter than both combatants.

The shield is ineffective against laser or gas. However, the Magh' are not immediately affected by gas, as they stop active "breathing" (and use stored oxygen) while in combat. Contact of a perimeter field with a force field results in enormous energy influx into the slowshield device. Should this be a full-sized force field, the slowshield device is unable to cope. Attempts to take slowshield devices apart have ended catastrophically. X-ray and ultrasonic examination reveal little, except that the device is a complex one containing solid-state nano-circuitry within an artificial crystal matrix.

Weaponry: When small arms proved ineffectual against slowshielded Magh' and it appeared that hand-to-hand combat weapons were required, human troops were issued with three basic weapons:

1) The trench knife: a twelve-inch broad-bladed weapon with one serrated edge. Relatively ineffectual except for opening cans and breaking locks.

2) The ice pick: a good weapon against the Magh' pseudo-chitin—except that a swing was required to wield it effectively, which made it unreliable against slowshielded Magh' warriors.

3) The bangstick: the most effective weapon in the human ground troops' arsenal. A mixture between an assegai (broad-bladed short stabbing spear) and an anti-shark spear, the bangstick blade was hollowed out to allow a .410 shotgun cartridge full of birdshot to be set into the middle of it. The cartridge is triggered by a sharp blow on the base of the spear shaft, which knocks a pin into the percussion cap. The spear allows penetration; the birdshot then ricochets around the soft inside of the Magh' without breaking out of the pseudo-chitin.

Pole mines have been tried as well, but because

of slowshield interpenetration have proved a failure. The use of tanks was stated to be "disastrous" by the Korozhet advisors . . .

Both sides make extensive use of heavy artillery. The Magh' equipment is far superior to the human, both in rate and accuracy of fire.

Small AP mines are one of the basic tools of defense. They are painted to reflect infrared light. Human and rat troops can see this but Magh' do not. Human troops have infrared lenses. Bats act as chief mine distributors and also as the army's sappers. The mines are visible to the humans and rats but also make human advances slow and wary.

***Force fields*:** Only in the possession of the Magh'. Energy expensive, allow zero penetration, except for light. Certain wavelengths are reflected.

***FTL travel*:** Only the Korozhet and, in a far more primitive form, the Jampad have faster-than-light travel capability. The Magh' are restricted by their Korozhet overlords to sub-light travel in slowships.

***"Rats"*:** African elephant-shrews, basically—long-nosed insectivorous animals with much larger hind legs than forelimbs—but otherwise more or less rat-shaped (hence the name). Using *Rhychocynodon chrysopygus* as the basic blueprint, the genetic engineers spliced on some genes from *Elephantulus rufescens,* from ordinary shrews (noctural eyesight, speed and red-tipped toxic teeth) and a bit of bulk and dietary tolerance from rats. A "rat" is about the size of a small Siamese cat, but lighter boned. There is considerable sexual dimorphism. Females are smaller, weighing on average 1.7 kg. Males can weigh up to 2.3 kg. They are of relatively fecund origins but, because of the effects of gene mixing, sterile. Gestation would be short and reproduction frequent. They are fast growing and relatively short-lived (8-12 years).

"Bats": Genetically engineered from a very complex mixture of both Megachiroptera and Microchiroptera, built on a Pteropodid framework, modified to include the echolocation and detention and therefore the digestion of insectivorous bats. Bats are capable of very slow and very precise flight. Despite a wingspan of nearly 5 feet, the bats are not very heavy. Light-boned, they weigh in at between 800g to just under 1kg. Bats typically have long gestations and may practice sperm storage. Unlike the rats, they are fairly long-lived (30+ years).

Galago: In this case, *galago senagalensis*. A small primitive nocturnal African primate (similar to loris and lemurs), agile tree dweller, capable of prodigious leaps of up to forty feet. A galago's most salient features are the enormous eyes and delicate mobile ears. Their diet varies, but they are principally insectivorous, with fruit and acacia gum also being diet items. The galago, otherwise known as the "bush baby," has a harsh strident voice, totally out of proportion to the small size of the creatures. The fur is gray, soft and fluffy. They have long fluffy tails. The little hands have long slender fingers, but the thumb is not truly opposable. They are one of the species known to practice urine washing of the hands and feet, a practice thought to increase adhesiveness.

HAR: Harmony And Reason. The name given to the human slowship-colonized planet.

***Shareholder*:** Theoretically, what every citizen of the colony world of Harmony And Reason (HAR) is—or can become. In practice, only the crew of the slowship, those wealthy enough to come as corpsicles, and their children. The colony is in theory a "collective commonwealth" from which all the Shareholders receive dividends and access to various shared technical facilities. Control of the colony is maintained by a board elected on the basis of share-votes. Individuals, such as Virginia's parents, can hold many shares.

***Technology*:** On HAR, except for brought-from-Earth 21st century technology (mostly retained at the slowship), most technology is at the self-sustaining level—anywhere from 14th century to early 20th.

***"Vat"*:** Clone child bred from one of the frozen cell-fragments brought from Earth for a minimal fee. They may become Shareholders after repaying the costs incurred in growing them and raising them. In practice, this is extremely unlikely.

***Soft-cyber chip*:** A Korozhet-made neurological enhancement device implanted into the brain of the bearer. A lentil-sized piece of highly advanced nano-circuitry, it is nonmetallic and contains both cybernetic and software elements. The device secretes microfilaments into the brain to obtain raw data, whereafter it acts as an enhancement and logic coprocessor, enabling instant "uplift" of various nonsentient animals.

***Magh'*:** A superficially arthropod-like alien species characterized by extreme polymorphism. Certain differences from true Terran arthropods, such as an exoskeletal structure of a substance unlike chitin containing fullerene chains and considerable internal bracing, make creatures ranging from the size of toy breeds of dog to German Shepherds possible. Body shapes vary enormously, with six factorial possibilities. The Magh' are a voracious, invasive and habitat-destructive species living in immense magh' adobe scorpiaries—spiral mound structures centered on the breeders' nest (the brood-heart) and broodchambers. Each scorpiary of several million members is a single intelligence, sharing a group-mind with consciousness centered on the breeders, the Magh'mmm. The Magh'mmm practice group spawning with external fertilization and with a sextuploid-haploid DNA analogue.

Respiration is spiracular with a countercurrent flow of a fatbottomed decacupraglobin carrier. This allows for the accumulation of oxygenated blood during low activity, which can then be expended during high activity, allowing high burst speeds for a brief period. Magh' warriors have no stamina.

***Korozhet*:** An alien species, technologically advanced. Radially symmetrical, they look like spiny red beachballs. The spines are hollow and jointed. The Korozhet can exude suckerlike pedicellaria, ocelli (simple eyes) and other sensory organelles from the hollow spines. Like several mollusc species, the Korozhet are also capable of firing harpoonlike darts from two special hollow spines. These harpoons are hollow also, and act as hypodermic needles through which toxic enzymes can be delivered into the prey or enemy. Like starfish, Korozhet feed by stomach eversion into the body of their partially digested prey. Speech is by means of a gas-bladder. Gas is produced from digestive processes within the food remainder sucked back in with the stomach.

***Jampad*:** An alien species opposed to Korozhet and the Magh'. Jampad are short and stocky, bipedal, with four tentacular arms. Heavily furred, from a high g (1.3g) cold planet.